One Enchanted Evening

This Large Print Book carries the
Seal of Approval of N.A.V.H.

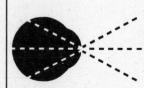

One Enchanted Evening

Lynn Kurland

THORNDIKE PRESS
A part of Gale, Cengage Learning

GALE
CENGAGE Learning™

Detroit • New York • San Francisco • New Haven, Conn • Waterville, Maine • London

GALE
CENGAGE Learning™

This is a work of fiction. Names, characters, places, and incidents either are the product of the author's imagination or are used fictitiously, and any resemblance to actual persons, living or dead, business establishments, events, or locales is entirely coincidental. The publisher does not have any control over and does not assume any responsibility for author or third-party websites or their content.

Thorndike Press® Large Print Romance.
The text of this Large Print edition is unabridged.
Other aspects of the book may vary from the original edition.
Set in 16 pt. Plantin.

LIBRARY OF CONGRESS CATALOGING-IN-PUBLICATION DATA

Kurland, Lynn.
One enchanted evening / by Lynn Kurland. — Large print ed.
p. cm. — (Thorndike Press large print romance)
Originally published: New York : Jove Books, 2010.
ISBN-13: 978-1-4104-3041-0
ISBN-10: 1-4104-3041-3
1. Knights and knighthood—Fiction. 2. Time travel—Fiction.
3. England—Fiction. 4. Large type books. I. Title.
PS3561.U645O64 2010
813'.54—dc22 2010021359

Published in 2010 by arrangement with The Berkley Publishing Group, a member of Penguin Group (USA) Inc.

Printed in the United States of America
1 2 3 4 5 6 7 14 13 12 11 10

One Enchanted Evening

Prologue

Artane Castle, England
Fall, 1229

Montgomery de Piaget believed in faeries.

He had good reason to. He had, over the past ten-and-seven years of his life, seen things of a most mysterious and faerylike nature that no lad with any sense at all could possibly have dismissed as a trick of light or the aftereffects of too much wine at supper.

Indeed, hadn't he as recently as the past spring seen his sister-in-law Jennifer spring up from the grass to bring her lovely and magical self to delight them all with her music and her beauty? Hadn't he been standing not fifty paces away from his current location when he'd seen his brother-in-law Jackson stride from the bejeweled courts below, as if he'd simply walked through a gate that no mortal eyes could see?

He had supposed that at some point in

the distant future he might be able to discount what he'd seen and perhaps learn to ignore the things about his siblings-in-law that puzzled him.

That day, he imagined, wouldn't be today.

He stood still, as still as if he'd been frozen there, on a spot near his father's keep, looking at something shimmering in the air in front of him.

The ground was nothing out of the ordinary. It was the last of the summer grasses, likely rather tasty to whatever animals were allowed to graze there, but in all other aspects quite unremarkable. If he'd walked over the spot another day, he wouldn't have marked it at all.

Today, however, things were different. Not only did the grass bear the sheen of something magical, the air was full of a strange and marvelous light that had nothing at all to do with the sun that had risen but an hour before. He would have suspected he was dreaming, but he had enough wit left to know he wasn't.

He knew one other thing as well.

He was looking at a faery.

There was no denying it. She had simply appeared, standing not twenty paces away from him, staring off into the distance as if she saw things he couldn't. Her clothing he dismissed immediately. It was very fine but unremarkable. What held his attention was the fairness of her visage and the marvelous cascade of dark curls that fell over her shoulders like a tumbling waterfall.

Well, that and her wings.

They were a gossamer bit of business that shimmered and fluttered as she breathed in and out. He knew he was gaping, but he couldn't manage anything else. He had never in his life seen anything so lovely, so wistful, so full of things he could not name but knew he was very interested in discovering. Aye, now, *there* was a gel worth snatching from the greedy clutches of the Faery Queen.

The air began to tremble, as if the gates to the netherworld had sensed his intention and were determined to thwart him before he could stop them. He started forward to take hold of the faery, but before he could touch her, he was jerked backward, almost off his feet. He spun around, curses halfway out of his mouth, to find his eldest brother standing there wearing an expression of the utmost gravity.

"Don't," Robin said quietly.

"Are you mad?" Montgomery demanded, trying to pull his arm free. "Let me go."

"Do not step on that patch of ground,

Montgomery."

He had every intention of doing just that, but he had other business to see to first. He stepped away from his brother and drew his sword, fully prepared to teach his brother not to meddle in affairs that were not his.

He was surprised enough to see Robin *not* do the same that he lowered the blade. Robin was never one to back away from a fight, especially one he could have fought whilst half asleep. That he merely stood there with his hands down by his sides and an expression of gravity on his face that bespoke truly dire things was remarkable enough that Montgomery resheathed his blade before he thought better of it.

"What are you talking about?" Montgomery asked.

Robin paused, considered, then dug his heels in and said nothing. Montgomery cursed his brother silently — no sense in provoking him unnecessarily — he then turned back around to get back to the business of capturing — er, rescuing, rather — the lass who had appeared in front of him as if from a dream.

Only to find her, and the magic that had accompanied her, gone.

Montgomery knew he shouldn't have been surprised, but he found himself gaping just the same. Unfortunately, all the protesting he could muster wasn't going to change the fact that the ground before him was now nothing more than what it should have been. The sparkling air that had hovered over it had dissipated. Of the beauty he'd seen, there was no sign.

Obviously, Faery had reclaimed her own.

He shivered in spite of himself.

"Montgomery, let us return home."

Montgomery took a moment to suppress the urge to run his brother through for interrupting what he was quite certain had been a singular opportunity to have a Faery for himself, unclenched his hands lest he be overly tempted to use them instead of his sword to teach his brother manners, then took a deep breath. Obviously, Robin knew more than he was letting on. The least he could do was divulge a few of those secrets. Montgomery turned around and looked at his brother.

"What lies there in that spot?"

"Nothing," Robin said with a shrug.

"Robin, I am no longer a child."

"I never said you were." He nodded toward the keep. "Let's be off. There are surely things enough inside to hold our interest."

"You're not answering my question."

"I'm not," Robin agreed seriously. "I have nothing at all to do with that spot of ground, so on its particulars I will remain prudently silent."

"Should I ask — ?"

"Cease," Robin interrupted sharply. He chewed on his words for a moment or two, then shook his head, as if he found the thought of uttering them unpalatable. He slung his arm around Montgomery's shoulders. "I am not the one to be asking, brother, and if you want my advice, you'll not look for others to pose your questions to. Bide your time and keep your mouth shut." He nodded knowingly. " 'Tis what a virtuous knight would do."

Montgomery started to protest, then reconsidered. The truth was, what he wanted more than anything was to be a virtuous knight, the sort of lad who would meet with the approval of not only his father but his four elder brothers. No matter the difficulty of the task set before him.

He supposed he might spend a moment or two now and again regretting that.

"Let's go train," Robin suggested. "That will occupy our morning quite well, don't you think?"

Montgomery nodded, for the second thing he wanted, after being considered the sort of honorable knight his father would admire, was to be the same sort of swordsman his eldest brothers were. If Robin was willing to indulge him now in the lists, he wasn't going to refuse.

"In fact," Robin added, "I think you might be worth my full attention and scrutiny for the next few months. Especially if you can keep your mouth shut about things I'm certain you didn't just see. What think you?"

Montgomery stifled the urge to drop to his knees and kiss Robin's dung-encrusted boots. Robin was notoriously choosey about the lads he trained, so to be thus singled out was indeed an honor worthy of a bit of discretion.

Though he couldn't help one final foray into things likely better left alone. That gel with the long, trailing mass of relentlessly curling dark hair and the wings . . . if he could just have even a fraction of an answer, simply to put his mind at rest about her. He took a deep breath, then looked at his brother.

"Was she a faery, do you think?"

Robin slapped the back of Montgomery's head sharply — no doubt in an attempt to dislodge good sense — then hesitated before he put his hands on Montgomery's shoulders. "I do not know what she was, or if you even saw what you think you saw," he said in a low voice, "but I can well imagine what happens to souls who consort with things not of this world."

"Like Jake and Jennifer —"

"I have no idea what you're talking about there," Robin said promptly. "What I do know is that faeries are for children, not for grown men."

"I know what I saw —"

"Then forget it quickly," Robin advised, "and instead think on what it would mean for you if it were noised about that you still believed in things better left to find home in children's tales." He slid Montgomery a sideways look. "Really, Montgomery. Faeries? At your age? Better that you concentrate on things that will keep you alive." He patted his sword. "Steel and cunning. We'll consider both at length over the next pair of months."

Montgomery nodded reluctantly, and then continued on for a handful of steps before the temptation to look over his shoulder became too great to ignore. He paused, then looked back at that particular spot in the grass that was now nothing out of the ordinary until he'd come to a decision. He hated to admit it, but Robin was right. He was ten-and-seven, well past the age of believing in things better left behind in childhood.

No matter what he'd just seen.

He stepped away from the sight, to give himself distance from it. It had no doubt been nothing more than sunlight on a bit of leftover morning mist, or too much rich food the night before and not enough time in the lists that morning. The possibilities were endless, but the truth was easily narrowed down to one simple thing: a true knight concentrated on steel and horses and honor. There was no room in his future for things of a more ethereal nature.

Surely.

"Montgomery?"

He turned back to the business at hand, nodded briskly, then followed his brother to the keep. Steel, horses, and honor. Those would be the stars he would guide his life by and thereby find himself comfortably joining the company of his father and brothers. That was, after all, what he wanted most.

He nodded to Robin, put on a determined expression, and left his childhood behind him as he should have done years earlier. It was done without a twinge of regret.

Truly.

Chapter 1

Seattle, Washington
Present Day

It wasn't often that a girl had the chance to get lost in a fairy tale.

Persephone Josephine Alexander wasn't one to find herself in those sorts of straits, but she was hardly in a position at present to do anything about it. She was captive in the darkened wings of a venerable Seattle theater, watching something undeniably magical unfold in front of her. The handsome prince, accompanied by a breathtaking set of strings, was vocally waxing rhapsodic about the charms of the appallingly lovely girl across the stage, while that girl was accompanying his waxing with her own musical commentary about his perfections. It wasn't long before the pair fell into each other's arms as if they'd been born for just that moment, their voices mingling in perfect harmony, soaring above the orchestra and leaving very few dry eyes in the audience.

Pippa was sure of that because she'd peeked out into that audience — after she'd dragged her sleeve across her own eyes, of course. Damned dust allergies kicking up at the most inopportune moments.

She got hold of herself, then turned back to her purely academic study of the love story going on in front of her. She had to admit, grudgingly, that it looked as real as anything she'd ever seen anywhere — or at least it did until the handsome prince stepped on the back of his soon-to-be princess's dress and tore it half off.

Pippa came back to earth abruptly at the two glares she found thrown her way as the prince and his lady attempted to dance as if nothing had happened. Fortunately there were no further mishaps before the couple managed to get themselves off stage for the last costume change.

"Lovely designs, Pippa," the princess said shortly as she ran off the stage. "Too bad you couldn't have sewn them better. I imagine Frank agrees."

"Pippa didn't design them," Frank whispered sharply, "and given what I've seen tonight, it was a mistake to let her sew them."

Pippa didn't bother to respond to that. She had indeed designed all the costumes, as well as having sewn most of them, but she was standing on the brink of a truly remarkable piece of good fortune, and she didn't want to jinx it by arguing the point with a successful show's director on closing night.

Though it was really tempting to take the pair of dressmaker's shears she had stuck in the back of her belt and cut off Frank's ponytail while he was otherwise engaged in sucking up to his leads and belittling the little people. Fortunately for his dignity, she found herself suddenly too busy repairing tears and replacing sequins to do any trimming.

By the time she had gotten all the costumes put away for someone lower than she on the food chain to worry about cleaning in the morning, she had given up the idea of revenge. Petty theater directors and grumpy actors were in her past. Her future was a sparkling green city in the not-so-distant distance and there was nothing standing between them but a no-nonsense flight to England. She got herself home through a damp and rather foggy Seattle night, then settled happily into her favorite pair of flannel pajamas before going in search of a decent post-production snack.

Half an hour later, she pulled her last cinnamon-sugar Pop-Tart from the toaster, then frowned at the smell. Something was burning, and it wasn't what she was holding in her hand. She leaned forward and sniffed her toaster. No, not there, either.

She followed her nose to her front door, then opened it and looked out into the hallway. Gaspard, her neighbor, flung open his door, shrieking curses in French as he jerked off his chef's hat, threw it on the floor, and stomped out the flames. He looked at her.

"Run, *chérie*."

It took her a moment to reconcile herself to the fact that flames were licking his doorframe, which meant he was obviously not just capable of dispensing advice on how to make a killer Bolognese sauce but could also run a mean escape operation. She watched the smoke begin to billow for a moment or two before she realized that she was about to become as crispy as the pastry she was holding in her hand.

She dashed back into her apartment, tossed her future into a suitcase, then bolted for the stairs.

Several hours later, she stood on a the edge

of tree-root-ravaged bit of sidewalk, pushed back the hair that was curling frantically around her face and dripping down the back of her now-soggy pajamas, and decided that there was only one explanation for the swirling events she'd been plunked down into.

Karma was out to get her.

She was a big believer in Karma. A girl couldn't grow up as the child of flower children and not have a healthy respect for that sort of thing — and for tie-dye as well, but those were probably memories better left for another time when she had peace for thinking and some mini chocolate muffins to ease the pain.

She rubbed the spot between her eyes that had almost ceased to pound, then looked around for somewhere to sit. Her sturdy, vintage suitcase was there next to her, looking imminently capable of standing up under the strain, so she sat and was grateful for the recent departure of fire engines and Dumpster delivery trucks. She rested her elbows on her knees, her chin on her fists, and gave herself over to the pondering of the twists and turns of her life.

She also kept a weather eye out for that rather large and clunky other shoe she was fairly sure was going to be dropped onto her head at any moment. One couldn't have the sort of spectacular good fortune she was about to wallow in without some sort of equal and opposite cosmic reaction. And to keep herself from breaking into the kind of jubilant rejoicing she was sure Karma took note of, she reviewed the path that had led her to her current enviable spot on a suitcase out in the rain.

It had begun, she supposed, when Susie Chapman's mother had given her a Barbie and a lunch sack full of fabric scraps for her seventh birthday. A world of possibilities had opened up for her, a realm that included plaids and paisleys, stripes and polka dots, all made from fabrics that weren't made from hemp and were probably anything but organic. Her parents would have rent their tie-dyed caftans if they'd seen any of it, but Pippa had avoided detection by keeping her contraband doll and those glorious mass-dyed fabrics hidden cunningly in a couple of Birkenstock boxes.

She had continued her illicit evening-gown-making activities even after she and her siblings had been dumped by her über-flaky parents on the doorstep of an aunt who had sprung, fully formed, from the pages of a Dickens novel. Pippa had in public sneered at romance, fairy tales, and designing clothes for dolls who savored both, but in the privacy of her little garret room she had sewn magical things from the best her lunch money could buy. She had gone on to major in art and costume design in college, then spent the ensuing four years slaving away over seams for others to wear in their own fairy tales acted out on stage.

And while designing for shows had been good practice, her burning and up-until-now secret desire had been to have her own line of clothing. In spite of her own avoidance of the like in her personal life, she dreamed of creating modern things with a hint of medieval romance and fairy-tale magic for others, things with little touches that only those looking for them would see. She wanted the women who wore her clothes to feel like the heroines of their own fairy tales, beautiful and beloved.

She paused. It was entirely possible she had some unresolved issues concerning romance, knights in shining armor, and her time at Aunt Edna's.

She made a mental note to consider therapy later — after she'd eluded Karma's steely eye and leaped at the chance she'd been recently offered to make her dreams come true.

Her sister Tess, who owned an honest-to-goodness English castle and made her living by hosting parties for all sorts of people with money and imagination, had shown some of Pippa's designs to one of her clients. The man had looked at the kids' costumes, then spontaneously uttered the magic words.

I say, your sister Pippa doesn't design for adults, does she? I'm looking for a new place to invest a bit of money.

Pippa had immediately begun fiendishly working on things to expand her collection, wondering all the while if there might be something bigger at work in her life than simply her wishing for it. She certainly didn't believe in magic, pixie dust, or any of the romantic drivel her older sister Peaches read on what seemed to be an alarmingly regular basis. She most certainly didn't believe in the fairy tales put on by any of the theaters she'd sewn for.

But in this, she couldn't deny that there was something, well, *unusual* at work.

"Pippa, what in the world happened?"

She looked up at that aforementioned over-romanced sister Peaches, who had suddenly materialized next to her on the sidewalk.

"Gaspard had his flambé get a little too friendly with his natural fibers, apparently," she said with a sigh. "What are you doing here so early?"

"It's not early. It's almost nine. And I'm here because I thought that since you were leaving tonight, you might need help packing."

Pippa supposed Peaches would have thought that. Her sister made a living by acting as a life coach, plucking people one by one out of a sea of bills, undeclared intentions, and old pizza boxes to send them off into a new life of organizational calm. Their parents were almost proud of her, though they would have preferred her credentials in feng shui be a bit more solid.

"It's all finished," Pippa said, patting her suitcase and hoping Peaches wouldn't want to check her work. "Costumes for the kids' party, my passport, and some granola. And my backup thumb drive with all the new designs I scanned for ease in display. I was sort of in a rush and left everything else behind."

Peaches glanced at the smoldering ruins of Pippa's building. "I imagine you were. And I suppose you can replace what you lost."

Pippa nodded, though she couldn't exactly agree. She'd spent years collecting one of a kind vintage fabrics and trims. In fact, she could have started her own store with what she had stacked on shelves in her apartment, or hidden cunningly under her bed and skirted end tables. There had been a few times — all right, there had been more than a few times — when she had simply sat there and stared for a few minutes — all right, it might have been for an hour or two at a shot — at the stacks and stacks of fabric she possessed, all full of possibilities, all waiting for her to take them and make them into something more than they had been before —

"I mean, it's not as if you don't have money in the bank," Peaches continued relentlessly, "or renter's insurance, or all your valuables tucked safely away in a safe-deposit box like I've been advising you to do for the past year."

"I don't have any valuables."

Peaches studied her in a way that made Pippa feel as if her sister really did know that she hid money in her mattress and family heirlooms in hot chocolate cans.

"But the insurance, Pippa," Peaches prodded. "You did take care of that, didn't you?"

"I have an appointment with the insurance guy," Pippa said, trying not to sound defensive. "At noon today, so yes, I did take care of that. And I did have savings, but I took it all and bought an embroidery machine last week. And a nicer serger. And a few bolts of velvet and silk." She paused. "Maybe a few sequins."

"How many sequins?"

Pippa waved her hand toward the wreckage she couldn't bring herself to look at any longer. "I think they would be the enormous swath of multihued sparkles you see up there where the second floor used to be."

"That's a lot of sequins." She took a deep, calming breath. "At least you have your scooter. It could be worse."

Pippa pointed over her shoulder to where the Dumpster had been dumped earlier that morning. A wheel and part of a fender stuck out from below the container.

Peaches looked, paused, then laughed a bit. "You've had quite a morning."

"Tell me about it."

"At least you have your trip to look forward to." Peaches nudged her over a bit to join her on her suitcase. "Tell me more about this guy who wants to look at your designs. He could be the reason for all this cosmic attention you're getting."

Pippa was happy to talk about something else besides the stench of incinerated fabric she could still smell lingering in the air. "I don't know anything about him except that he's nobility and he has really deep pockets."

"Nobility?"

"He's the son of an earl, I think, and runs in Tess's academic circles. And he has deep pockets."

"You already said that."

"His deep pockets are very attractive to my ultimate plan of fashion world domination."

Peaches laughed. "I'm glad to see you haven't lost your focus."

"Mr. Nobility might front me some dough for more sequins, and Karma is probably done with me," Pippa said with a shrug. She ignored the little niggling doubt at the back of her mind that said Karma was nowhere close to being finished with her. "You're taking me to the airport tonight, and I have enough money in the bank to buy more underwear. What else can go wrong?"

"You can open your big mouth, that's what can go wrong," Peaches said quickly. "Don't tempt Fate."

"Nah," Pippa said confidently, "I think the worst is over. After all, bad things come in threes and my quota is full."

"My little disorganized friend, *good* things come in threes. I don't think bad luck is constrained by the same rules."

"Ridiculous," Pippa scoffed, finding it in herself to rally a bit. She stood and wrapped an emergency blanket around herself because she was cold, not because she was unnerved. “You can go along with all that woo-woo business we were weaned on, but I’m not buying it.”

“Liar.”

Pippa shook her head sharply. “Look, Peach, Karma’s done her bit with me this week. In the past eight hours I have lost, in no particular order, my apartment, my life’s savings, my inventory of irreplaceable fabric and salvaged trims, my means of making a living, and my purple Vespa. I’m in the clear.”

Peaches only zipped her lips, locked them, and threw away the key.

Pippa put her shoulders back and stood tall. Her destiny was not controlled by some cosmic, unreasonable force. She was in charge. Hadn’t she just the night before looked life in its steely eye, clutched her Pop-Tart like a sword, and announced as much?

Approximately thirty seconds before she’d smelled the smoke, but surely the two were unrelated.

“Oh, no,” Peaches said, standing up so quickly, she knocked Pippa’s suitcase over. “Not this.”

“What?” Pippa asked, leaning over to right

her suitcase.

"I told you there was no limit," Peaches said pointedly. "Number Four's on its way. I'm not sticking around to see what Number Five's going to be."

Pippa looked over her shoulder, then found herself assailed by a sudden desire to collapse. Fortunately, her suitcase was still there, sturdy and dependable. She sat down heavily.

"This doesn't count."

"Keep telling yourself that, if it makes you feel better."

Pippa watched gloomily as the ultimate hippie-mobile came up the way. It was a tie-dyed Winnebago, powered by solar panels and used french-fry oil, with a faint cloud of cannabis hovering overhead and Grateful Dead stickers plastered all over the back.

"What are the parental units doing here?" she asked uneasily.

"Maybe they came to visit before you took off for yon blessed isle," Peaches offered. "Maybe they're going to insist they be the ones to take you to the airport, in style no less. You might manage to get them to stop by the mall, unless Mom has some hemp underwear hiding in a drawer you could have."

Pippa shuddered and stood up. "I'm not about to go looking in her drawers. I don't want to know what else is hiding there."

Peaches slung her arm around Pippa's shoulders. "How is it with parents like these we turned out to be so normal?"

"Don't ask," Pippa said darkly. That was the last thing she wanted to think about. She'd spent her entire life fighting against her parents' lifestyle, and that wasn't going to change anytime soon.

She paused. That wasn't exactly true. She had, at fourteen, been sprung for a couple of months from Aunt Edna's Gloomy Victorian Boardinghouse to go with her parents to England. She'd loved the place so much, she'd happily spent her time brewing herbal tea and creating Renaissance-inspired tofu delights to sell at all the reenactment gatherings they could find. One place she had fallen particularly in love with had been a castle on the northern coast. Artane, she thought its name might have been. She had been standing near that castle early one morning, when she could have sworn she'd seen —

Well, never mind what she'd thought she'd seen. She'd been fourteen at the time, an age particularly prone to vivid imagination. Gorgeous guys in chainmail just didn't pop up out of the mist, even in England. She'd been taking the whole reenactment thing too seriously, eaten too much refined sugar, and her mind had played tricks on her.

Never mind that she'd gone back to that exact spot every morning for the week they'd been there, hoping beyond hope to catch another glimpse —

She took a deep breath and rubbed her hands over her face. She was losing it. Maybe it was smoke inhalation, or the off-gassing of too many sequins. What she remembered most about that summer was that even though she'd done a very brisk business in medieval and Renaissance faire food, her parents had grown tired of her and dumped her with her aunt again so they could go back to doing their own thing. She had gone back to her usual habit of denying the existence of anything magical, wearing it even through college like a badge of honor.

And if she made cone-shaped headgear with sweeping netting cascading down behind them, or crowns of flowers with streamers placed just so, or low-waisted gowns with slight trains, it was strictly business. She had never indulged in any more romantic imaginings about the women who might have worn them and the medieval knights in shining armor who might have loved them. No sir. And she had *definitely* never indulged in any speculation about the more fantastical and magical items she made for fairies and their ilk. She was a steely-eyed, determined businesswoman sitting on a suitcase full of samples. The chance to impress an investor with her reasonably priced, impossibly charming line of little-girl fairy clothing and further impress him with an equal number of very subtle, medieval-inspired grown-up things had been an opportunity she hadn't dared turn down.

Maybe having her life burn to the ground in front of her had been a blessing in disguise. She had no choice but to go forward and put all her eggs in an English basket.

The Winnebago circled the block three times until it found a place to weigh anchor. It took a moment or two, but the door finally opened and belched out its occupants. Pippa pushed her hair back out of her face and braced herself for the onslaught.

First came her mother in a multicolored muumuu that set off her long, henna-dyed hair to perfection. She looked a little dazed, but since that was her usual condition,

Pippa didn't think anything of it. Her father came stumbling down the stairs next in acid-washed jeans and a ratty Grateful Dead T-shirt, and a dozen strands of Mardi Gras beads hung around his neck. The cowboy hat he was wearing was iffy, but it was probably made of hemp so she gave him a pass.

They both came to a screeching halt and stared at the ruins of Pippa's apartment. They couldn't seem to drag themselves away from the sight, but then again, they were probably being dazzled by the sequins.

Her mother held out a tin of something toward her husband. He fumbled inside it, pulled something out, and ate it, still gaping at the ruin in front of him.

"Those look like brownies," Pippa murmured.

"Just don't ask what's in them," Peaches muttered in return.

Pippa managed a smile. "You know, even though I don't have the warmest of feelings for them, I'm not sure I'd count them as karmic retribution."

"I don't think it was the parents you needed to look out for."

"Then who?"

Peaches pointed back toward the motor home.

Pippa looked at the doorway, then felt her

mouth fall open.

A foot had appeared in view, a foot wearing a shoe that had to have had at least a five-inch heel. A calf followed the foot, followed by more of a leg that went on forever. And then, as if the possessor of those incredible legs was eternally trapped in a Bob Fosse musical, the rest of the body appeared with a slinkiness that had left an endless trail of males in various stages of swoon for as long as Pippa could remember.

Cinderella Alexander, the bane of Pippa's existence.

Cindi glided over in her best beauty-queen walk, then stopped and looked at Pippa from a face so perfect, it made Pippa's teeth ache.

"I hear there's going to be a party."

Pippa retrieved her jaw from where it had fallen yet again to her chest. "What?" she asked, pretending to wiggle her ear to hopefully dislodge whatever it was that prevented her from hearing properly.

"In England. A party."

"Ah," Pippa began.

"And that fairies are involved."

Pippa looked at Peaches, who only lifted an eyebrow knowingly. No help there. Pippa turned back to Cindi.

"I don't know what you're talking about,"

she said, lying without a moment's hesitation or guilt. "Hadn't heard a thing."

"You'll need a queen. I've decided to come along and be that for you."

Pippa would have sat back down on her suitcase, but that would have drawn attention to it and perhaps led Cindi to become more acquainted with her wares than necessary. Pippa settled for not hitting Peaches when she began to pinch her arm, hard. The pain kept her from either swooning or bursting into tears — if she'd been the sort to do either, which she most definitely was not.

She was left with no choice but to admit the truth of it. She'd been cocky. She had stared Karma right in the face and dared her to do her worst. The platinum blonde bimbo unconsciously preening in front of her was proof enough that Karma did not like to be messed with.

Pippa knew she had every reason to hate her older sister. Cindi hadn't had to work her way up through her chosen employment as professional beauty queen; she'd pretty much started at the top. And once she'd realized Pippa could sew, she'd had her sewing at all hours, continually preparing for ball after ball where the prince always noticed Cindi, always proposed, and always went away dazzled and disappointed. Pippa never even got to meet the evening's left-overs. She was too busy slaving away over the next gala's gown, which of course had to be more elaborate than the last.

She could have lived with that if the indignities had ended there, but they hadn't. Every time Pippa thought she might have a meeting with someone useful, Cindi would somehow catch wind of it, then arrive in all her glory and walk off with all eyes on her, leaving Pippa to metaphorically slink along behind her, carrying her train.

She had gone to ridiculous lengths to ensure that this time Cindi would have no idea what was up. She'd sworn Tess to secrecy, made Peaches pinky swear she wouldn't tell, and threatened her other two sisters with grievous bodily harm if they breathed a word. She couldn't imagine how Cindi had found out.

Obviously, Karma had been busy.

"Where are your things?" Cindi asked imperiously.

Pippa eased in front of her suitcase protectively. "I have them packed away safely."

"Not that it matters," Cindi said with a dismissive wave of her hand. "I'm bringing my own designs."

Pippa blinked. "What?"

"Oh, didn't I tell you?" Cindi purred. "I've

been working on a line of fairy-tale fashions. I had lunch with David Jacoby last month and he mocked them up for me." She frowned, a perfectly elegant creasing of her equally elegant brow. "Did I forget to tell you?"

Pippa could only gape. Words were beyond her. The Jacoby studio was so far above where she'd ever hoped to even attempt a submission of her portfolio, she could hardly wrap what was left of her smoke-fogged brain around the thought.

"He shipped them to England for me last week. I imagine Tess has them now." Cindi reached out and patted Pippa on the cheek. "I just thought that since you'd been working so hard, I would take some of the pressure off you. You'll be bringing along your little costumes, though, won't you, darling?"

Pippa nodded.

"They're so sweet. I can hardly wait to dress up the girls and lead them around the castle." Cindi frowned suddenly, then looked slightly unsettled, if that was possible for a woman for whom everything in life clicked into place with a perfection that was truly appalling. "Oh, I'd forgotten about the castle. Tess said it was drenched in things I might not like." She looked at Pippa narrowly. "She mentioned drama."

Pippa didn't dare look at Peaches. The drama the castle was drenched in would increase exponentially when Cindi arrived, but there was no sense in saying as much.

"Do you know anything about that?" Cindi asked suspiciously.

"Oh, I don't think it's drama you have to worry about," Peaches said without hesitation. "Tess was probably trying to give you a subtle warning that what her castle is really drenched in is ghosts and rumors of mayhem in times past."

Cindi took a step backward, looking now definitely unsettled. "Ghosts?"

"And mayhem," Peaches repeated. "And other things that go bump in the night."

If there was one thing Cinderella Alexander couldn't stand, it was things that went bump in the night. The creaking wood in Aunt Edna's Victorian House of Warped and Hand-Scrubbed Boards had just about done her in. Pippa knew that because she had hopped up and down on the floorboards next to Cindi's door more often than necessary on her way to the bathroom in the middle of the night, just to hear her sister shriek.

She suspected Karma had definitely taken note of that.

Cindi took another step back, then turned

abruptly. "Dad looks like he's been sniffing too much of something. I'd better go rescue him."

Pippa watched her sister slink off, her perfect legs that went easily up to her ears carrying her away as if she'd been a black widow — perhaps a rather more nervous than usual black widow — reaching out to cover ground between her and supper in the most expedient way.

Peaches put her arm around Pippa's shoulders. "I tried to get rid of her for you, but I don't think she was terrified enough to cancel her trip."

"I appreciate the effort," Pippa said, trying to sound cheerful, "but don't worry. After all, how much trouble can she possibly cause?"

"I don't think you really want the answer to that," Peaches said with a half laugh, "so I won't give it. Let me go see if there's anything edible in the parents' fridge. You sit there and rest. I think you're going to need it."

Pippa agreed, so she sat and attempted a smile because she was, after all, going to England. Surely nothing else untoward was going to happen to her.

Then she realized what Cindi had said.

"Hey, Peaches," she said before her sister

got too far away. "What was Cindi talking about?"

Peaches turned around. "What do you mean?"

"I mean about the castle. Cindi said there was drama and you said there were ghosts." She laughed dismissively, because she wasn't at all unnerved by creaking floorboards or other things of a more paranormal nature. "I mean, really. You weren't serious, were you?"

Peaches smiled. "Well, Tess *did* say her castle has some strange things going on. She might have mentioned ghosts. And stuff."

Pippa felt her mouth fall open. "Get out."

"That's probably what Tess tells the ghosts all the time," Peaches said. "And there is a rumor about murder and mayhem, but I'm not sure if that applies to former inhabitants or if Tess knew ahead of time that Cindi was coming along for the ride."

"You're not funny," Pippa said darkly

Peaches laughed. "I imagine you'll know much more about it in the end than I will. You're not afraid of ghosts, are you?"

"I don't believe in ghosts."

"Famous last words."

"Peaches, you've been reading too many novels," Pippa said with a snort. "Let's just leave paranormal happenings safely tucked in your romances, where they belong. I'll stick with stuff that's firmly grounded in reality —"

"Like fairy-tale clothing geared to leaving women thinking they've stepped back in time hundreds of years?" Peaches interrupted dryly. "Yeah, you're a realist, all right. Come on, Miss Cynic. Maybe Mom went completely off the rails and bought sugary breakfast items for you."

Pippa couldn't imagine she would be so lucky, but she picked up her suitcase anyway and followed her sister over to the motor home with as much spring in her step as she could manage. Never mind that she had no apartment, no transportation, no underwear. She had a suitcase full of impossibly adorable fairy costumes, people across the deep blue sea who would appreciate them, and probably a sturdy castle guardroom she could lock Cindi in for the duration of their stay.

But ghosts? Ridiculous. Tess's castle was just a pile of old rocks that had acquired a few, well, *quirks* along the way: drafts, crumbling mortar, the odd bird nesting in an out-of-the-way spot. Nothing unusual, nothing spooky, nothing to worry about, just smooth sailing from now on. After all, she'd gotten all her rotten luck out of the way that morning. What else could possibly go wrong?

She decided it was probably better not to know.

She took one last look at the disaster behind her, then put her head down and marched off to find breakfast before she had to face the fact that she suspected her adventures in the unexpected had just begun.

Chapter 2

Sedgwick Castle, England
Present Day

'Twas no secret that Hugh McKinnon favored a well-turned seam.

He was actually quite proud of that, for he considered it proof that he had improved himself over the course of his unlife. When he'd had a mortal frame, he'd been mostly concerned with the turn of a nicely revealed bit of intestine or the arc of his blade as it dispatched without alacrity whomever was troubling his clan. It had been a violent life, and he had been a product of that. He had considered himself fortunate in that he'd lived out a full tally of years instead of succumbing to an early death thanks to the elegant curve of another's slice across his gut.

He wasn't quite sure when it had happened, but at some point during his undeath, he had begun to look at other things:

the weave of a particularly well-fashioned plaid; the drape of a woman's gown; the happy coupling of velvet and lace. His vague interest had eventually turned to enthusiasm, then passion. He had traveled far from home in search of things that he could imagine were soft and silky and luxurious to the touch.

That love of all things lovely had led him to locales he'd never in his life dreamed he might go. Across the Pond, to the Continent, into the bowels of theaters whose age and reputation had given him pause. Of course, the pause had been brief before he'd once again taken up his quest to breach their defenses and mount an assault on their prop chambers. It had been the overwhelming passion of his afterlife, his most pressing duty, his one and only goal —

He paused as he stood in the barbican gate. Perhaps his *one and only* goal was being less than honest. He had another work, of course, a *goodly* work that required delicacy and diplomacy and called on all the skills at reading men's hearts that he'd learned over the course of his years as head of the clan McKinnon. Perhaps there was no shame in admitting that he was first and foremost a matchmaker and that fondling fabric came second.

He was waging Cupid's war by himself for the moment because his companions were off laying the groundwork for another particularly troublesome case. Well, that and they had no inkling he'd taken up the cause of love on his own. But how could he have done otherwise? His compatriots weren't the ones with their ears pressed to the boards where rumors of costumial triumphs and matches unmade whispered along the well-trod wood.

He paused a bit longer. Very well, so he'd been eavesdropping in a swanky theater in Seattle and heard tell of a fabulously skilled seamstress who had created the garb for a rendition of a modern, lush version of *Cinderella* he'd quite thoroughly enjoyed for several nights in a row. Taking a wee peek back in her family tree had revealed that one of her ancestors had been the fifth cousin thrice removed of one of his cousins, which no doubt gave him the authority to see to her. She was surely ready for matrimony, and she sewed a marvelously turned seam. How could he not be the one to look for a proper mate for her?

All of which had led him to where he was at present: walking along the fixed bridge that led over what had originally been a moat but was now a pristine lake. The castle that rose up before him was stunning, despite its unfortunate flaw of being located not in the Highlands. He had popped in a time or two over the past fortnight to see the lay of the land, as it were, and prepare for the arrival of his vict — er, his *project,* whose sister owned the keep he was now walking into. That sister was in the business of dressing up and leading people in feasts where they pretended to live in the Middle Ages. She was missing several critical components such as disease, terrible food, and surgeons who thought less of sewing a man's flesh than they did repairing his boots, but he hadn't had the heart to tell her that. Yet.

His project — Pippy, he thought her name was — was set to arrive in a pair of days to put on a celebration for a wee gel who had a great love of faeries. Hugh had seen the lass and her parents a handful of days beforehand and approved of them all. And given what a lovely child she had been, he thought it wouldn't be inappropriate to have a look at the preparations to ensure they were as they should have been. After that was seen to, he would turn his mind to more important matters.

Namely, finding his Pippy a mate.

He walked into the courtyard, then made

his way to what the visitor's guide said had been the garrison's quarters in times past. Doors were, of course, no barrier to him as he simply walked through them, then continued on his way to a rather large chamber that the current owner affectionately called the "mother lode."

Hugh had to agree. Costumes of every kind hung in tempting rows from metal bars made just for that sort of thing. He knew this, for he had spent more than his share of time haunting and fondling costumes in other locales. Ah, what fond memories he had of La Scala. He supposed he'd spent ample time at the Met as well, but those Big Applers were sharp-eyed and quick-tongued — as well as being a little weak in the knees when they discovered his not-so-mortal status. The Italians were of sturdier stock, for they were generally wont to reach for a blade and attempt to do him in before they bellowed in fear and surprise. The French? Well, they tended to dismiss him with a bored look and merely return to their discussion of tulle.

But he digressed. He focused his attentions on what was before him, then made his way at a languid pace down the rows, admiring as he went —

"Are you allowed to be in here?"

He spun around in surprise, his sword halfway from its sheath, only to find 'twas the wee birthday gel standing twenty paces from him with her hands on her hips and a slightly disapproving look on her face.

He returned his sword to its place as unobtrusively as possible, then doffed his cap and made her a small bow.

"Just seeing as everything's in place," he said quickly.

She studied him for a moment or two. "Are you part of the castle?"

He shook his head. "Nay, missy. My home is far up in the Highlands. I'm here, er, for, um, for an . . . inspection," he said, hitting upon a useful word. "To see that all is well for your birthday celebration."

She walked up the row, stopped next to him, then turned to study the costumes. "These aren't the ones for my party. My costumes were made by Pippa, who lives in the States."

"Pippa," Hugh repeated. Aye, that was her name. He'd actually encountered her backstage more than once during the run of her last play, though he supposed she had thought him nothing more than a goodly gust of wind. He had no doubt blended in with the gusty discharges of the leading man and the director.

"Her things are ever so lovely," the gel continued, "and she's designed things especially for my party." She smiled. "I'm Hailey. Who are you?"

"The McKinnon," Hugh said without thinking. He paused. "You might call me Hugh, if you liked."

She regarded him without flinching. "The castle is haunted, you know."

Hugh choked. He hadn't intended to, but he didn't do well when he was caught off guard. "Is it indeed, lass?"

"My mum thought we should pick another castle, but my dad was keen on this one since Lord Stephen had said it was so lovely. I believe in ghosts. Don't you?"

Hugh was quite certain his face was nigh onto the color of his hair. "Weel, I suppose, er, perhaps —"

"Shall I tell you of the ghosts who belong to this castle? There's a seat over there."

Hugh could readily admit he wasn't particularly good with children. He hadn't known what to do with his own until they could hold swords — even the gels — but Mistress Hailey was a bright-eyed thing and she didn't seem to notice his discomfort. He followed her over to a prop trunk and agreed with her that 'twas a perfect place to take their ease and have a bit of a chat.

"*I* heard that a few of the ghosts who haunt this castle do so because they were involved in the ruining of a romance."

Hugh caught his breath. Ah, now here were tidings he could certainly put on the table and examine at length.

"You see," Hailey went on enthusiastically, "there was once a lord of this keep who captured a fairy. He brought her home and wanted very badly to make her his bride, even though the castle was fair falling down around his ears and surely wouldn't have been a very impressive place to live."

Hugh could see two problems with that right off. First, the faery in question would likely not be pleased at being snatched from her home — especially to live in a keep not up to her standards; and second, the English were not as well versed in things of a paranormalish nature as were the Scots. Had the creature landed at *his* hall, he would have merely ignored her otherworldly attributes and simply offered her supper without making a fuss. He imagined that when the poor wee thing had been brought back to Sedgwick, then every soul in the hall had likely wearied themselves sick making charms to ward off her powers instead of sitting her down by the fire and giving her something hot to drink.

The English. Truly, they were a hopeless lot.

"What befell the poor creature then?" Hugh asked, though he could readily imagine the trials she'd been subject to.

"*I* heard," Mistress Hailey said in a low voice, "that the faery went back to her land, to the lord's deep sorrow." She frowned. "I'm not exactly certain what happened then, for the lady in the gift shop claims he spent the rest of his days pacing outside his front gates, waiting for the faery to return, and the lad down at the petrol station in town said he suffered a more tragic end —"

"Hailey! Hailey, where are you?"

Hugh leapt to his feet, made Hailey a quick bow, then plopped his cap back atop his head and rushed over to hide behind an Elizabethan dress that was easily as wide as he was tall.

"Hailey, darling, there you are," said a slight woman wearing a very relieved expression. "I've been looking all over for you."

"I was talking to Hugh, Mummy. He's a Scottish laird."

Hugh thought it best not to introduce himself to Hailey's mother. She looked overwrought enough as it was.

"Of course, darling." She looked around as if she expected a dozen angry Highlanders to leap out at any moment, shouting clan slogans and brandishing Claymores. "Daddy's waiting for us in the tea shop, so let's go find him, hmmm?"

"All right, Mummy," Hailey said, jumping off the trunk. "I'd already told Lord Hugh most of the ghost story. You know, Mummy, he wasn't the only ghost I've seen today."

Hailey's mother shivered. Hugh shivered right along with her, then looked uneasily over his shoulder. He turned back to the pair to find Hailey looking at him.

"See, Mummy? He's right over there."

Hugh vanished before he found himself enjoying matronly shrieks of terror.

"It's the wind, Hailey."

"This is a bloody windy castle, Mummy."

"Hailey Marie Bleakley, where did you learn that language?"

"The last time we visited Hedingham Castle, Mummy. There were men in the lists, resting between bouts of training for their tournaments. That was what they said about the keep." She paused. "They were ghosts, Mummy."

Hailey's mother took a deep breath. "I fear I may need something a bit stronger than tea today."

Hugh listened to Hailey's voice fade as she continued to regale her mother with things she'd seen on their various outings to other historical landmarks. Hugh didn't doubt she'd seen what she'd seen.

He was living — or, rather, unliving — proof of that.

He walked back over to the trunk and sat down, stroking his chin thoughtfully. He supposed if the lord's end had been one of tragedy, perhaps Mistress Pippy should look elsewhere. Perhaps someone from her own time, lest she come to grief right along with that poor lad who had worn a trench in front of his gates, waiting for his love to return to him.

A breeze blew down the back of his neck, and he leapt up and whirled around in surprise.

There was nothing there.

He normally wasn't one to be spooked, but if there ever had been a time for it, the time was now. Too many bloody ghosts in the keep for his taste. He strode for the door, found himself momentarily preoccupied by a lovely watered-silk ball gown, then hurried off into less unnerving locales, happy to leave tales of unrequited love, ruined castles, and unseen ghosts behind.

He would worry about a romance for Pippy when he was safely ensconced in the tea shop, pretending to enjoy a fortifying cup of something hot.

One thing was certain: he wasn't going to see her sent back to a dilapidated castle where the inhabitants couldn't possibly appreciate her seams.

Chapter 3

Sedgwick Castle, England
Fall, 1241

Montgomery de Piaget stood on a small rise in the midst of vast swaths of forests and farmland, looked at the castle currently languishing in the midst of all that beauty, and wondered what in the hell he'd done to deserve the gift that beckoned to him with all the welcoming warmth of a warty-nosed, claw-fingered crone.

To call the keep before him a wreck was to grossly understate its unredeeming qualities. Adding to the insult was the fact that from his vantage point, he could see all those flaws without their having been able to hide behind some bit of solid wall or other.

Not that Sedgwick had very many of those.

"I can see why Father didn't want to come along," said a voice at his side. "Being the modest, reserved soul that he is, perhaps the thought of all the thanks that would come his way was simply too embarrassing to be endured."

Tittering ensued. Montgomery scowled at the sound. It was impossible to call the noises coming from the line of men standing with him anything else. He looked to his right just to see which one of his companions he would need to kill first. It was a welcome distraction from what lay before him.

They were, in order, his elder brothers Robin and Nicholas, his brother-in-law Jackson Kilchurn the Fourth, and then a younger generation of de Piaget males, Kendrick, James, and Jackson the Fifth. The lads weren't laughing. They were gaping at the castle in the distance as if they'd just looked into the jaws of Hell and discovered they were to be the next meal.

Montgomery understood.

The men were still struggling to keep their composure. Their eyes were watering madly and all three of them were stifling, with varying degrees of success, laughter behind their hands — damn them all to hell.

Montgomery firmly refused to dignify their amusement by acknowledging it, though he wasn't blind to the unnerving flaws of his future home. Though the great hall was of a decent size and the stables and the blacksmith's forge weren't without merit, the castle's men came and went out of a rickety garrison hall he wouldn't have used to house hounds. There was no chapel, and the walls surrounding the innards of the keep were poorly maintained and, from what he could tell, poorly manned. It looked as if someone had once considered putting a moat about the entire place but had hoped just digging it under the drawbridge would be enough to deter those with mischief on their minds.

The saints preserve him, 'twas a disaster.

"Uncle Montgomery?"

Montgomery looked to his left where his eldest nephew stood. Phillip was a sober lad and rarely spoke without having given his words great consideration.

"Aye, lad?" Montgomery asked, elbowing Robin on his other side as he did so.

"I fear there is much work lying before us."

Montgomery didn't want to agree, but he had to. He was no simpering gel, to be sure, but there was a part of him that couldn't help but admit that the sight before him was almost enough to make him want to sit down and rest. He suppressed the urge to shake his head in disbelief and instead turned to look at his nephew.

"Fortunately, Phillip, you are just the lad to help me take on this worthy task —"

"Are you daft?" Robin interrupted incredulously. "Do you actually think I'll leave my son to squire with you now that I've seen this rat-infested hole you intend to call home? Never. Come along, Phillip. We'll leave Montgomery to his, er . . ." He looked at Nicholas. "What shall we call it?"

Nicholas shrugged. "Words fail me."

Jake elbowed both of them out of the way. "He'll call it home soon enough. Besides, Robin, you don't know if it's rat infested."

"I have a sense about these things." Robin rubbed his hands together briskly. "Well, lads, we've delivered the boy to his roost. Let's make for Segrave. I'm sure Grandmère has something tasty on the fire."

"Father, Uncle Montgomery isn't a boy," Phillip said solemnly.

Montgomery looked at his eldest brother coolly but said nothing. Robin's favorite pastime, when not doting on his wife and children and decimating whatever garrison knights he could find to face him in the lists, was tormenting his younger brothers. Montgomery supposed he could be loitering on the far side of three score and Robin would still treat him as if he were a green lad of ten-and-two.

"Oh, I don't know about that," Robin said, stroking his chin thoughtfully, as if he actually gave serious thought to the matter. "He looks like a boy to me."

"He's taller than you are, Rob," Nicholas said, apparently struggling not to laugh. "I'd tread carefully."

"But he's weak in his limbs," Robin said, reaching for his sword belt and unbuckling it. He poked Montgomery in the arm with his sheathed sword, hard enough that Montgomery would have flinched if he'd been made of less stern stuff. "That comes, I understand, from too much time spent at court, delighting the ladies with his rapier wit and lovely eyes. It certainly doesn't do anything for the strength of arm or skill with a blade."

Nicholas laughed and walked away. Jake only lifted a shoulder in a half shrug and turned to follow him. Kendrick accepted his father's sword with wide eyes and a slackened jaw.

"I'll take your sword, Uncle," Phillip said, with only the slightest quaver in his voice. "You won't need it. Will you?"

"I wouldn't want to do any more damage to your sire than my fists will accomplish,"

Montgomery said, handing his sword to his would-be squire. He managed it in the heartbeat before that squire's father launched himself forward to prove his doubters wrong.

It had been, he decided as he landed flat on his back and lost his wind, too long since he had engaged his brother in a friendly contest of strength. Robin might have been rumored to have gone to fat, but he had certainly not gone to seed, and he was nothing if not wily. And strong. And full of insults that would have earned him a brisk slap to the back of his head had their grandmother been anywhere within earshot.

"Don't wear yourself out, Rob," Jake said dryly after an appropriate amount of time had passed. "You don't want to be too tired to enjoy a decent supper."

" 'Tis just a bit of light exerci —"

Montgomery slammed his forehead into Robin's mouth to shut him up. It earned him an instant increase in ill will from his sibling, as well as quite a bit of his brother's blood dripping onto his face. He finally shoved his brother off him, then staggered to his feet.

"Enough, damn you," Montgomery said, his chest heaving. "I've other things to do besides school you in manners."

Nicholas hauled Robin to his feet, then kept hold of his arm. "Aye, enough," he agreed with a half laugh. "He still has a castle to lay siege to."

Robin stood there, breathing more easily than he should have. He dragged his sleeve across his mouth, scowled at the blood left there, then looked at Nicholas. "I think his peasants have made off with great chunks of the foundation. As long as he doesn't mind slithering through one of the leftover holes, he'll be fine."

Montgomery brushed the leaves from his hair and declined to point out that he had been conserving his strength for the possibility of just such an assault. "A rematch, when my floor is clean."

"Let's just hope your floor is flat," Robin said with a snort, "and not sporting a dozen holes the size of your horse."

Montgomery hoped not as well, though he supposed that was more optimistic than perhaps he should have been. He allowed his brothers to gather up their sons and turned to face his own future.

Sedgwick, of all places.

What in the hell had he done to deserve *that?*

He could speculate on several things readily enough, though he knew he should put that speculation off until he'd gained his own supper table where he could think at his leisure.

Unfortunately, now that he was faced with the sight of his father's generosity, he couldn't keep himself from it. Sedgwick was, as Robin had rightly said, a rat-infested hole, but it had the potential to be a quite spectacular rat-infested hole. That his father had given it to him, the youngest of all, instead of to whom it rightly belong —

Robin slapped him — rather gently all things considered — on the back of the head, startling him.

"You think too much."

Montgomery shot his eldest brother a dark look. "How would you know?"

"Because I recognize the symptoms," Robin said, lifting an eyebrow. "My life now is nothing but easy movement from one moment of bliss to the next, but it wasn't always so."

Montgomery studied the castle for another moment or two, then looked at his brother. "Why do you think Father gave this to me?"

"Because you are the only one of us desperate enough to take it," Robin said solemnly. "Or stupid enough. I'm not sure which it is."

Nicholas laughed and pushed Robin out of the way so he could sling his arm around Montgomery's neck. "Ignore him. We'll discuss the vagaries of Fate and inheritances given by Rhys de Piaget after we've managed to get past your gate guards and see what's left of your keep. I have my own thoughts on the matter, as you might imagine."

Montgomery didn't doubt it, given that their father had gifted Nicholas a keep that had been missing most of its roof when Nicholas had taken possession of it. At least Sedgwick's roof looked to be intact.

With that cheery thought to keep him company, he put on his grimmest expression, then went to give his commands to the trio of guardsmen he'd brought with him.

And he ignored the fact that Robin had advised him to bring more. He would manage with the men who had served him freely, or not at all. It likely would have taken a king's ransom to convince anyone else to darken Sedgwick's unsteady gates. Unfortunately, given the condition of his new home, he suspected he was going to need most all of his gold to repair his foundations.

Besides, 'twas his own castle he faced.

Why would he need more lads than he had there already?

It took less time than he'd hoped to reach the keep and even less time to realize that he was indeed expected. The guardsmen leaning negligently over the barbican gate managed lethargic wigglings of their fingers as he rode under the walls. Montgomery ignored the insult partly because there was no sense in beginning his life there with a battle and partly because he was too distracted by the depth and quantity of horse droppings and other refuse layered over his inner courtyard to work up any anger. The layer of muck finally became too thick and his horse — not a beast in the slightest bit inclined to balking — balked in front of the great hall door.

It swung open with creaks that could have been heard leagues away and out tumbled a ragtag group of souls he honestly couldn't begin to identify. Garrison knights? Servants? Cousins? It was difficult to tell given that they were all equally filthy and unrelentingly bad mannered.

Montgomery glanced at his brothers. All three were wearing expressions befitting the battle-hardened warriors they were. Even the young lads were frowning severely, stealing looks now and again at their fathers to no doubt make sure they were getting it right. His own guardsmen were looking terribly unimpressed, as if they would require a tripling of the castle's occupants rushing at them to force them to even yawn.

Montgomery would have smiled if he'd had it in him, but he didn't, so he refrained.

He was grateful that Robin was keeping his bloody mouth shut, though he supposed he shouldn't have expected anything else now that the battle was upon them. His brother might have been impossibly arrogant and endlessly annoying, but he was the future lord of Artane and well aware of how to act that part. And whilst Sedgwick was, from all outward appearances, not much more than an open cesspit with a keep placed strategically nearby, Montgomery was lord of it and as such deserved respect.

It wasn't as if he hadn't earned a bit of it. He'd spent the last nine years with spurs on his heels either making his fortune in tourneys on the continent or building alliances at supper wherever court was being held. When he hadn't been at home being insulted by his brothers, he had been moving about in the world of Henry's nobles without misstep. That had brought him renown for his skill in battle and no small number of women wanting to see if he was capable of the same sort of exploits in the bedchamber. He supposed he had become just as famous for the number of offers he'd turned down.

He was perhaps too much a romantic in some ways and not nearly enough of one in others.

He looked back at the souls who peopled his new home and decided he would introduce himself, and then see if he couldn't encourage at least a few of them to brave an encounter with the water in the horse trough. He couldn't determine who came with his new home until he could determine what — and who — they were.

He anticipated that the day would drag on endlessly, and he wasn't disappointed.

An hour later he had counted a score-and-four surly garrison knights and a kitchen staff comprised of five maids, three scrawny lads under the age of eight, and a portly, unpleasant-looking cook who seemingly did more eating than cooking. The rest of his household included three obviously overworked serving gels, a clutch of randy serving lads, and a trio of sullen, disagreeable cousins who didn't bother to either stand or offer greeting when he approached. The only bright spot was his new steward, who was seemingly impervious to the unpleasant looks sent his way by not only those Sedgwick cousins but their mother as well.

He supposed he could understand his cousins' irritation. They had had the run of the keep for the whole of their lives whilst their father Denys had held Sedgwick in trust for Montgomery's father. When Denys had died and the keep returned to Rhys's possession, it had been well within Rhys's rights to do with it as he saw fit.

Montgomery still wasn't sure if it had been a very unpleasant joke on his father's part or something else, but he supposed the time for thinking on that was not now. He had a household to see to.

A long day? He suddenly realized it was going to be a very long life.

At sunset he climbed the stairs of one of the four guard towers and walked out onto the battlements. The two guards there glanced briefly his way, then went back to talking about the apparent bounty of ripe serving wenches in the village over the hill.

Montgomery leaned his hip against the wall — after making sure he wouldn't go through it and fall into the cesspit — and folded his arms over his chest. He watched the men steadily until they finally turned and looked at him.

"What d'ye want?" the first asked disdainfully.

That the other didn't catch his breath at the arrogance was telling enough. Montgomery didn't suppose it would serve him to kill off his entire garrison and start afresh, especially when some of the lads no doubt had families and he would be robbing wives and children of their husbands and fathers, but he also couldn't have any about him but men loyal to him and obedient to his commands.

He looked at the closest of the two men.

"I'll see you in the lists first thing," he said with absolutely no inflection in his voice. "Your friend will have his turn immediately thereafter."

"And if I says ye nay?" the first asked with a sneer.

Montgomery shrugged. "Try it and see."

The man put his shoulders back and spat at Montgomery's feet. "Then, na —"

Montgomery took hold of him before he could squeak, then heaved him up and over the wall. There was a splash, then silence. The second man looked at Montgomery with wide eyes.

" 'E can't swim."

"Can you?"

"Nay, milord," the second said quickly. "I beg ye, don't heave me over to follow 'im."

"Then go down to what seems to pass for the moat by more pedestrian means," Montgomery said calmly, "and fetch your mate. After you've cleaned him up a bit, I suggest you noise about the garrison that I'll see them all in the morning, one by one, until we've come to a right understanding about who is lord here."

The man nodded, bowed, then rushed toward the tower door. He stopped suddenly, then turned back.

"Who'll man the walls, then, my lord?"

"I'll see to this watch," Montgomery said, "then I'll have one of my own men take the rest of the night. And so it will continue until I've determined whom I can trust."

The man nodded uneasily, then walked swiftly away.

Montgomery watched him go, then turned to look over the countryside. The castle might have been an absolute wreck, but the surrounding countryside, dressed as it was in the first hints of its fall finery, was quite lovely. It was the same view he'd had from the bluff at dawn, but somehow, seeing it from the roof of his own keep lent it a more personal air. He wouldn't be at all displeased to look at it for the rest of his life. He loved the sea, true, and he'd lived on its edge quite happily for his youth, but he could easily be content with gentle hills, lush fields, and thick forests.

He put his hands on what was left of the wall, not because he needed to hold himself up, but because he didn't want anyone to possibly see their shaking. It was one thing to be the youngest son of the most powerful lord in the north of England and have the extent of his tasks be to arrive on time in the lists and show well. It was also one thing to take that sword skill and cut a swath through the continent where all he had to manage was vanquishing all challengers and being witty at supper. Even the task of inheriting a castle that was intact, with a useful garrison, a well-stocked larder, and all his enemies confined to the area outside the gates would have been one thing.

But this . . . this was something else entirely.

The creak of the door opening to his left had him turning with his sword half out of its sheath before he realized it was only Robin. He resheathed his sword with a sigh as his brother held up his hands in surrender and came to stand next to him without comment. Montgomery knew that couldn't possibly last, so he decided to have the sermon over with sooner rather than later.

"Well?" he asked, looking at his brother darkly.

Robin blinked. "Well, what?"

"I assume you came to bestow your vast wisdom upon my poor, hapless self. Please be quick about it."

"Surprisingly enough, I came to hear what *you* thought."

Montgomery let out his breath slowly. "Truly, there are no words."

"No one's tried to kill you yet," Robin offered, "unless you count what your cook delivered up for supper as an attempt to do just that." He shuddered delicately. "That was vile."

"You didn't have to stay. I thought you were headed for Grandmère's bounteous table."

Robin didn't answer. He merely stood there in silence for so long that Montgomery finally looked at him in irritation.

"What?"

Robin smiled faintly. "Montgomery, I worry about you. Why don't I go to Grandmère's and fetch you a few bottles of her finest? You can begin your return to being tolerable company with a glass of fine wine after dinner each night —"

Montgomery turned on him. "And just where will I put those bottles, Robin?" he asked shortly. "In my very fine cellar full of diligent servants? Or perhaps under the guard of my garrison who have gone to fat eating my winter stores? Or nay, perhaps rather I should ask our cousins who have welcomed me with open arms to watch over my goods? You tell me which, since you're so full of useful things to say."

Robin shook his head. "You used to be so lighthearted. Nay, you were never light-hearted, but you used to be pleasant. What happened?"

Montgomery hardly knew where to begin. Aye, perhaps he had been almost light-hearted now and again in the past, but that had been lost somewhere along the way. Perhaps it had begun with the keeping of many secrets. Added to that, he'd been weighed down by responsibility, by years of being prudent, of always being the one in charge, or never taking a single moment for his own happiness. He'd had his duty to his father, to his name, to his king, to his future bride and children whom he was actually fairly certain he would never have because he was too busy seeing to all the things no one else wanted to see to. But leisure? Nay, he would have none of that any time soon.

Robin studied him in silence. "I was provoking you before," he said seriously. "Forgive me. It might have been ill-advised."

Montgomery only looked at him steadily.

"Very well, I was an arse. I'm offering now to stay and do what you need. I will even go so far as to fight with my left if you need your garrison worked, so I don't reveal my true skill and terrify them beyond being useful to you."

Montgomery didn't want to smile, but he couldn't help himself. Robin's arrogance wasn't at all misplaced, and the truth was, Robin fighting with his left instead of his right was likely enough to terrify the garrison past reason just the same.

"And I will leave Phillip with you," Robin added.

Montgomery shook his head. "Too dangerous."

Robin waved dismissively. "The lad's cannier than he seems. He might be useful to you. Besides, fear over what I'll do to you if you lose my son will give you an added measure of courage and determination."

"No doubt."

"I'm not leaving you completely without the means to keep him safe. You have your personal lads, to be sure, and reinforcements have arrived as well. Well, if you can call him that."

"Indeed?" Montgomery asked in surprise. "Who has come?"

"Everard of Chevington," Robin said unenthusiastically. "Apparently his sire has decided that his elder brother Roland would be a better manager of his property, so he took the keep and the title away from Everard and gave it to Roland." Robin shook his head. "The perils of having a father who is mad, I daresay. He claims he has come to offer you his sword. *I* think he has come to eat through what remains of your larder and mock you for the holes in your foundation."

Montgomery shrugged. "He squired well enough for Father and he hasn't been an unloyal friend to me since then."

"That is a rousing endorsement."

"Robin, at the moment I'll take anyone who isn't coming at me with blade bared."

"I won't remind you that I advised you to bring more than your trio of lads," Robin said airily, "though I suppose the four of you could see to the cousins and the garrison easily enough." He pushed away from the wall, sending a bit of it down into the cesspit as a result. He peered over the edge, then looked at Montgomery. "I'd clean up that rot down there sooner rather than later. You'll never get a gel to come across that bridge if that's what she fears falling into."

"Attracting a bride is the last thing I'm worried about."

"I wouldn't wait overlong," Robin said, brushing stray bits of rock off his hands and turning toward the guardtower door. "I should think you'd like to marry before you reach two score."

"I've considered that."

"Perhaps you should consider some sort of otherworldly help." He looked back over his shoulder. "I'm fairly sure Denys's lady, Gunnild, is a witch. She might have some species of beautifying herbs for your visage, or perhaps a perfume to leave you smelling less like horse. Who knows? Perhaps Fate will send you a faery to appease your discriminating tastes."

Montgomery shot him a look. "I don't believe in faeries."

"Don't you?"

Montgomery gritted his teeth. "Are you helping?"

Robin only laughed and continued on his way.

Montgomery turned and stared gloomily over his new surroundings. Aye, magic was indeed what he might need, and a goodly amount thereof. There wasn't a woman of his acquaintance who would have set foot on that bridge, much less cross it to stomp through ankle-deep muck to get to the front door, never mind what she would find after she'd gained the hall itself.

He looked up into the heavens and watched as the first stars of the evening began to appear. He had done that often in his youth, standing on his father's battlements and watching the twilight fade to evening when the skies had been clear enough to do so. He supposed he could admit without too much shame that he had, now and again, dreamed of his future where he might be lord of a sturdy, useful castle filled with honorable men who looked up to him and fought alongside him when the time came. Perhaps he also could have been forgiven for filling that imaginary castle with beautiful tapestries, tuneful music, and a lovely gel who might enjoy both.

It had never occurred to him that his reality might be so completely different from what he'd hoped for.

He shook his head at his own foolishness. Sedgwick was not what he'd dreamed of, but he was damned fortunate to have anything to call his own. He would make it into something respectable and leave the dreaming to lads with more stars in their eyes than he had in his. He'd obviously eaten something that day that had ruined his good sense. The next thing he knew, he would begin revisiting his boyhood fascination with all things magic —

He froze. Then leaned carefully on the wall and looked down at the end of his drawbridge. Had that been a flash?

Surely not. 'Twas too late in the day for sunlight on steel and there was no one there with a torch that far away from the keep. It was almost as if something, well, otherworldly . . . He felt his mouth fall open. He'd seen that particular sort of shimmer before —

"Brother?"

Montgomery looked at Robin, who had paused by the guard tower. "What?" he asked hoarsely.

Robin looked down at the bridge, frowned deeply, then shook his head. "Nothing," he said slowly. "Nothing at all."

Montgomery shut his mouth with a snap. He was weary from a rather trying day and wasn't entirely sure he would survive the night with the foxes lying in wait for him below. He would consign anything he might or might not have seen to his imagination playing tricks with him, because the very last thing he wanted to encounter in his immediate future was anything that shimmered or sparkled or forced him to face anything that didn't carry a very long sword and need training. He dragged his hands through his hair, then turned and walked off his roof.

He found Ranulf, the captain of his trio of guardsmen, then asked him to walk what was left of the battlements. Sedgwick wasn't going to be attacked by anything more interesting than the stench from the moat, so he supposed there was little point in making certain the rest of his men were at their duties. That would come on the morrow when he began his remaking of the garrison.

At least there, the only magic he would need would come from his sword.

Chapter 4

Pippa wasn't one to panic unnecessarily, but she decided that if ever there had been a moment to indulge in it, it was the present moment.

"Can you just slow down?" she squeaked.

Her sister Tess shot her a look, then turned back to frowning fiercely at the road. "I'm only doing forty."

"Yes, but the road is tiny and you've already knocked off my side mirror on something buried in that hedge."

"It's a stone wall," Tess said, swinging out from behind a very large truck that was also going along at a ridiculous clip and flooring the gas to blow past him. "Probably eighteenth century, but that isn't my era, so don't quote me."

"No worries," Pippa said faintly. "You can do the carbon dating later based on the chunk that came through my window."

"I'm not the one who wanted the window down."

"I'm trying to keep Cindi from barfing in your backseat. She starts to dry heave in her sleep when the air isn't blowing into her face with the caress of a gale-force wind."

"You shouldn't have let her drink on the plane."

"*I* didn't let her drink on the plane," Pippa said, through gritted teeth. "I didn't have the chance to let her do anything on the flight because while I was too busy sitting in the back where the whole damned trip felt like a roller coaster, she was enjoying champagne in first class thanks to a wink and a smile delivered to some single, subsequently disappointed D-list actor."

Tess shot her a brief smile. "We could just dump her in a hedge, you know. She'd find her way back to the airport eventually."

"Don't tempt me," Pippa muttered. She gripped the armrest with renewed vigor and tried not to concentrate on the scenery racing past her at inhuman speeds. Fortunately she was distracted by the rattling going on in Tess's trunk. "What's that noise?"

"Box of spare side mirrors," Tess said mildly.

Pippa blinked, then laughed in spite of herself. "Do you lose lots of mirrors, or is this the deluxe tour just for me?"

"I lose one a week, whether I need to or not," Tess said with a smile. "That way I have business for the mechanic in the village we just drove through. Or, rather, I did until he sold his shop and retired to France. I haven't been in to see the new owner, but I'm sure screwing a mirror into the door won't be beyond his capabilities. We're all for that sort of stiff-upper-lip, make-it-do sort of thing here."

Pippa shot her a look. "Learn all that from Aunt Edna, did you?"

"I will admit, grudgingly, that she did instill a cracking good bit of character in us."

"How would you know? You escaped early!"

"And you got to come with Mom and Dad to England when you were fourteen."

"I had to wear fairy wings," Pippa returned. "Every day for two months. I was Persephone Alexander, Medieval Fairy. I still have scars from the straps."

"Cry me a river. You got to travel while I stayed home and pulled anything that looked like a weed from Aunt Edna's Victory Garden. I still have nightmares about morning glory wrapping itself around everything in sight."

Pippa smiled to herself, then watched the road for a bit longer. The tight walls were giving away to less claustrophobic hedges, but the road was still not as large as Pippa thought it should have been, given its reputation on the map as a fairly popular thoroughfare.

Tess turned off on another smaller road that led through yet more bits of forest. "We're getting close."

Pippa looked out her window and watched the scenery go by, feeling as if she were stepping back in time. They'd left civilization behind a village or two ago, and her sense of leaving modern life behind grew with every moment.

It was spooky.

"I'm sorry about the change in day for the party," Tess said. "The birthday girl had an unexpected invitation to go to Paris with her grandmother on Friday, so I couldn't say no — especially since all I had to do was convince the caterers to come a couple of days early." She looked at Pippa briefly. "I hope jet lag doesn't do you in."

"I'll be fine." Pippa yawned. "All I need is time to hide Cind's designs before Lord Moneybags sees them."

Tess looked at her mildly. "You mean the stuff she sent over last week that fell off the roof into the moat? It needed a good cleaning so I sent it out. Should be back in about a month."

Pippa closed her eyes briefly. "I shouldn't thank you."

"It was my pleasure, believe me. Now all you have to do is wow our lovely specimen of nobility with *your* stuff while I keep Cindi locked in the attic. It'll be great."

Pippa shifted in her seat to look at her sister. "Tell me about him. Again."

Tess smiled briefly. "He's Stephen de Piaget, son of Edward, the Earl of Artane."

"Artane?" Pippa echoed in surprise. "I know that castle."

"Everyone does," Tess said. "It's a spectacular place up the coast. I've been a couple of times, though only as a tourist. Why Stephen chose my castle to put on a birthday party for a friend's daughter when he could have used his father's place, I don't know, but I wasn't going to argue."

"Maybe he likes your castle better than his. Or he just likes you."

Tess shook her head. "He's not my type, in spite of his academic credentials. He's way too familiar with the mechanics of medieval geopolitics."

"Are you telling me he's packing a Claymore?"

"He's English, not Scottish, but no, it wouldn't surprise me if he had ventured over the border to add to his unwholesomely extensive collection of weaponry that I'm fairly sure by the look of him he uses. He doesn't seem to hang out at his father's castle much, so I'm wondering if he's harboring secrets he doesn't want the family to know — which I completely understand as I'm not into pointy metal things, my fascination with all things medieval aside."

"I can hardly believe he wants to see my designs."

Tess glanced at her. "He's already seen most of them, so you can believe it. And if you can stay awake, here comes another miracle." She pointed out the front windshield. "Look."

Pippa looked. And she felt her mouth fall open.

There, in front of her, was a medieval castle.

In fact, it was so steeped in its medievalness that she had to take a quick gander at her surroundings to make sure she was still in the twenty-first century. The countryside was of no use whatsoever in determining that. The forest was thick and lush and completely free of anything that might have passed for a Mini Mart. If she hadn't been riding in a car, she would have suspected she had stepped back in time hundreds of years.

Tess pulled into a car park that was nothing more than a few indentations in the grass, then stopped the car and turned it off. "Well?"

Pippa hardly knew where to begin. The castle was, in a word, spectacular. It sat smack in the middle of a small lake that was so still, she might have been looking at a stretch of polished glass. From where she sat, she could only see two towers on each corner, though she supposed there were two at the back corners as well. The crenelated towers and walls were in mint condition, the stone clean and sound. All it was missing was the sound of horses and perhaps a guardsman or two walking along those towers with the business ends of their swords shining in the sunlight.

She wanted to ask Tess to tell her again about the miraculous stroke of good fortune in winding up with the key to a castle she'd never expected to own, but maybe that could wait. She wasn't one to believe in magic, but in this, she couldn't deny that her sister's life belonged in a fairy tale. And now to see the castle in person . . . Well, it was one thing to imagine how it might be as she'd been slaving away over costumes made just for the upcoming party; it was another thing entirely to see the reality sitting there in front of her.

"I'd better write this in my diary," Tess said, sounding amused. "My little sister, speechless."

"I'm not sure speechless begins to describe my condition," Pippa managed. "I can't believe this is yours."

"Neither can I. I pinch myself every time I drive up the way." She pulled the keys out of the ignition and opened her door. "Let's go inside."

Pippa got out, then paused. "What about Cindi?"

"Maybe fairies will steal her."

Pippa smiled at Tess. "I knew there was a reason you were my favorite sister."

"Peaches is your favorite sister, but I know I'm always coming in a close second."

"Tess, you're twins. I love you both equally."

"That's because you can't tell us apart," Tess said airily. "You have to spread the love liberally on the off chance you're sucking up to the wrong one."

"And here I was going to tell you that after

today, you may have pulled ahead in the race."

Tess locked the car. "I deserve it, obviously. We'll come back to get Princess Pukesalot later. If she wakes up, she can crawl over to the tea shop for something strengthening." She linked arms with Pippa and tugged on her. "Let's go inside. I can't wait to hear what you think."

Pippa walked with her sister across the bridge that was indeed very stable and through a gate with three different sets of portcullis spikes hanging over it. She stopped in the courtyard and gaped. There was a garden in one corner, the stables and a smithy along one wall, then a little chapel tucked into the left-hand corner. Tess pointed to the big building dominating the other back corner.

"That's the great hall. We'll go upstairs and put your stuff down, then I'll let you rest for a bit before the madness starts."

Pippa trailed after her sister up the trio of stairs to the great hall, then had to stop on the topmost one. An enormous feeling of déjà vu swept over her — and she was intimately acquainted with all the ramifications of *that.* She immediately reclassified the sensation as a result of too much rich food at some point in the recent past, then carried on after Tess.

But she couldn't shake the feeling that somehow, at some point — no doubt still in a very vivid dream she couldn't remember — she had walked where she was walking.

Weird.

She followed Tess inside a great hall that was just as amazing as the initial view of the outer walls. Tapestries measured in feet, not inches, hung down along the stone walls, and enormous fireplaces flanked the room, set into the wall and sporting gigantic stone hearths carved with scenes of stags and boars. There were groupings of chairs in front of each hearth and a long table at the back of the hall, boasting heavy, high-backed seats. She fully expected to see servants dressed in authentic medieval peasant gear come spilling out of the kitchen, carrying trays of delicious edibles.

"What's the tofu quotient in your dinners?" Pippa managed.

"Nonexistent. We only use good English beef here, with quite extensive vegetarian selections for those so inclined."

Pippa looked at her sister, then laughed. "You sound like you know what you're doing."

"I would say that's only because it pays the bills, but the truth is, I love it," Tess admitted. "I don't think the reality of the Middle Ages would have been at all to my taste, but pretending for the evening while still having the conveniences of modern life upstairs is wonderful. And speaking of upstairs, I put you right next to Stephen, on the off chance that you encounter him in the middle of the night on your way to the kitchen to hunt for snacks."

"I imagine you just put me there to have something between him and Cindi."

Tess smiled. "Might have."

Pippa followed Tess up the stairs and down the passageway that was lit by lights in the shape of torches. The rock was smooth under her hands, as if countless fingers had been run along its surface over hundreds of years, and cold. She waited until Tess had opened a door, then found herself inside something that surely had looked in medieval times just as it did at present. There was a bed with a wooden canopy, hung with heavy drapes, and other less austere things that were obviously of a more recent vintage. Pippa walked in, feeling as if she were walking into a dream. She stopped in the middle of the room, then turned around slowly.

"It's spectacular," she managed. She felt her way down into a chair. "I can't believe this is yours."

Tess sat down on the edge of the bed. "I agree, but before we're both overwhelmed by the thought, why don't I let you get some rest, then we'll go have lunch in the tea shop?"

"I didn't see the tea shop," Pippa said, "but I'll admit I was a little distracted at the time."

"It's tucked away in the forest. I initially wondered about the location of it from a business perspective, but I've come to appreciate that keeping all signs of modern life out of a person's initial view of the castle is the best idea. I might as well make the experience as authentic as possible." She pushed herself to her feet and smiled. "I'll be back in an hour. I'm going to go pour coffee down Cindi and see if I can get her sober in time to flutter tonight."

Pippa was tempted to stop her sister and ask her a few pertinent questions about paranormal activities, but Tess escaped before she could. She watched the door shut, then went to look for some cold water to splash on her face. The last thing she wanted was to sleep through introductions to a man she was sure held the key to her future.

■ ■ ■ ■

A couple of hours later, she was yawning at herself in the bedroom's full-length mirror and wondering if she might have gone a little too far on the discreet scale. She could see the extra touches to her dress — the drape of her skirts, the shape of the bodice, the points of her sleeves — but she wasn't sure anyone else would. Subtle might not be what got her more than one date with Stephen de Piaget's deep pockets. Unfortunately, it was all she had at the moment, so she would just have to go with it and hope her scintillating personality made up the difference.

She made sure her backup stick was in her pocket, then adjusted her fairy wings and turned toward the door. No time like the present to get on with her future.

She opened the door and jumped a bit in spite of herself. A man was standing against the far wall under the light of a torch. He straightened immediately and made her a little bow.

"Miss Alexander? I'm Stephen de Piaget."

Yes, indeed he was. Pippa shook his hand because she had decent manners even while being dazzled by extraordinary good looks.

Tall, dark-haired, and yes, he obviously spent more time with a sword than poring over medieval manuscripts. The medieval-looking getup he was wearing only added to that impression.

"I wanted to meet the designer before the little girls made too much of a ruckus screaming over their lovely gowns," he said with a small smile.

"Happy to meet you," Pippa said, fighting the urge to fan herself. She had expected him to be attractive in a tweedy, professor-ish sort of way, not immensely distracting in a hunk-ish sort of way. Tess had a very annoying habit of leaving out pertinent details, a habit Pippa fully intended to chide for her at her earliest opportunity.

Stephen inclined his head down the hallway. "Perhaps we should go raid the kitchen for a bit of courage before the festivities begin."

She nodded, because that was all she could do. She followed him down to the great hall, concentrating on not rolling down the circular staircase. She would have gone along with him to the kitchens for the proposed snack and hoped it would cure what ailed her, but Stephen was pulled aside by his friend who was paying for the whole affair, and she found herself cornered by the mother. She realized she was more jet-lagged than she thought, because she didn't hear much of the conversation past *ghost* and *spooky*.

Unsurprising.

She grabbed a glass of something that looked like juice and got half of it down herself before she heard everyone fall silent. She didn't have to look behind her to know who was sucking all the oxygen out of the room. Tonight, though, she almost managed a smile. After all, she *had* made Cindi's dress.

"That is the most amazing gown," Stephen said faintly, coming to stand next to her. "I've never seen anything like it."

"Thank you," Pippa said modestly. If ever there were a time to take a little pride in all her hard work, this was it. "As I said before, it's a little more understated than what I usually . . . do . . ." She turned around slowly, looked at the apparition at the bottom of the stairs, then felt her mouth fall open.

Her sister was stunning, as usual, carrying herself as if she were indeed some sort of fairy-ish royalty deigning to grace mere humans with a glimpse of her glorious self. But it wasn't Cindi's frighteningly spectacular face, the fact that she looked almost coherent, or her enviable figure that left Pippa gasping. She could hardly believe her eyes, but there was no denying it.

Cindi was wearing a dress Pippa hadn't made.

It was white, with a fitted bodice and billowing skirts made of what Pippa could tell at fifty feet was an obscene amount of hideously expensive taffeta. Lace dripped from the sleeves and cascaded down from the waist, while tastefully marching up the bodice seams to curl lovingly around the neckline. There had to have been a small fortune in Swarovski crystals dripping from every reasonable location. Cindi sported a pair of fairy wings that were even wider than her dress. Pippa supposed that with the right gust of wind, she might have taken flight, damn her anyway.

Cindi's hair was swept up into a messy bun with tendrils curling artfully down her neck but not around her face — heaven forbid anything should compete with the absolute perfection of *that.* And atop it all, like a diamond-encrusted candle atop a fancy birthday cake, was a tiara that was almost blinding in its sparkliness.

Pippa thought she just might kill her sister this time.

"Well, I say," Stephen said weakly.

She could just imagine what he would say if he could manage to pick his jaw up from off the floor and use it for the purpose of speaking.

He looked at her in surprise. "Did you make that?"

"No," Pippa said shortly.

"I must admit, I thought not," he said, frowning thoughtfully. "It is lovely, to be sure, but I daresay your designs are a bit less . . . er, how shall we say it?"

"Gaudy?" Pippa suggested.

"Ah —"

And that was the last thing he managed before the beauty queen fluttered down in a flurry of skirts and tapped her chosen victim on the arm playfully with her wand that easily sported a thousand dollars' worth of crystals. Pippa was half tempted to follow Cindi around and gather up all the stones she lost. It might be a decent way to make a quick buck since it was obvious by the look on Stephen de Piaget's face that any conversation with him was going to be out of the question before the clock struck twelve and she turned back into a pumpkin.

She watched morosely as Cindi flirted with Stephen. In fact, she watched Cindi at it for so long that she began to have a grudging admiration of her sister's technique. Cindi was managing to keep Lord Stephen captivated and charm little girls at the same time with an ease that was truly remarkable.

Periodically, Cindi would excuse herself to Tess's office only to return with renewed energy for both her pursuits. Pippa followed her once, out of a morbid sense of curiosity, only to find her sister helping herself to something out of a little bear-shaped cookie tin she pulled from a pocket in her skirt. The tin looked suspiciously like what their mother had been clutching earlier in the week, a container that Peaches had been fairly sure contained brownies.

And they all knew what sort of things their mother baked into brownies.

"She's stoned."

Pippa looked at Tess who had materialized next to her, accompanied by a disapproving frown.

"Nah," Pippa said. "It's just jet lag."

"Are you kidding?" Tess said severely, gesturing to Cindi, who was again flitting off into the room with boundless amounts of energy. "She's giggling, for pity's sake."

"Maybe she took too many aspirin."

"What she's going to take is a very short trip into my moat if she doesn't get it together," Tess said furiously. "Damn her, she is *not* going to blow this for me. Stephen de Piaget is not someone I want to look like a flake in front of." She looked around very briefly, then took Pippa by the arm. "Let's go rifle through her things."

Pippa wasn't opposed to it. It might give her the chance to find and confiscate other sartorial goodies before Cindi could parade them in front of Mr. Deep Pockets.

She followed Tess up the stairs and down the hall — only to find herself squeaking in surprise at what she saw.

There was a red-haired, Claymore-bearing, bekilted Scotsman standing just outside Cindi's door, looking terribly guilty. Pippa grabbed the back of her sister's bodice and realized only after Tess complained that she had almost jerked her sister off her feet.

"What?" Tess asked, turning around to look at Pippa in annoyance.

Pippa pointed over Tess's shoulder. "Him."

Tess looked back down the hallway. "I don't see anything."

Pippa felt her mouth fall open. Now she didn't, either, though she was a hundred percent positive she'd seen someone standing there not ten seconds earlier, someone with knobby knees and dirks stuck down his socks.

"Jet lag," she managed. She was definitely losing something and she thought it just might be her mind. She turned around and looked at her sister. "I need a nap."

Tess took her arm. "Take one later. We've got investigations to carry out now."

Pippa let Tess pull her along down the hallway without complaint. It didn't take long to get into Cindi's room and even less time for Tess to unearth a bottle from a fluffy pile of tulle. Pippa sat down in a chair strewn with foundation garments.

"Advil?" she asked.

"Valium," Tess corrected. "It's Mom's stash."

"How do you know?"

"Because the bottle says *Mom's stash,*" Tess said. She sat down on top of an evening gown that had to have cost a small fortune — or been free from a designer. "Maybe we can assume she mistook the bottle for aspirin."

"Probably," Pippa agreed. "And she certainly can't help it that her drug-induced silliness is going to leave a dozen six-year-olds scarred for life from watching the fairy queen drape herself all over some dude dressed in a tunic and tights."

"I wish I could see the humor in it," Tess

said with a sigh, “but I’m having a hard time now. Well, at least the pills are gone and she’ll be back to herself tomorrow.” She tossed the bottle back into the middle of the pile of clothes and rubbed her hands over her face. “What else can go wrong?”

“Don’t ask,” Pippa warned. “Trust me, you don’t want Karma delivering the answer.”

Tess pushed herself to her feet. “Let’s go finish the party. I’m afraid we’re going to be earning every penny of our fee tonight.”

Pippa realized after only another half an hour that Tess had grossly understated the truth. No amount of money was worth the misery of covering for Cindi. The girls kept wanting to touch her, and all she wanted to do was touch Lord Stephen. Pippa took over when it was painfully clear that her sister had chucked her good sense over her shoulders along with her shoes that had somehow landed in the punch bowl.

By the time she had straightened her wings for the thirtieth time — that was definitely a design flaw to examine later — she was ready for the party to be over. She wasn’t sure how enchanting the evening had been for her, but the girls were completely starstruck by Cinderella the real fairy-tale queen and her handsome prince, the future

Earl of Artane.

For her, the evening had been less enchanting than exhausting. She had played games, directed the opening of presents, served cake, and handed out the special trinkets Tess had prepared for each of the guests. She was vastly relieved when Cindi clapped her hands together and gathered the girls close.

"Your mummies and daddies are outside waiting for you across the bridge," Cindi said brightly, slipping her arm through the crook of Lord Stephen's elbow. "Let's go find them, shall we? Now, where is — ?"

Pippa watched Stephen duck just before he would have been wing-whipped by the enormous appendages Pippa had definitely not had anything to do with. She admired his reflexes — if such a thing was possible while being disgusted with his apparently inability to resist Cindi's charms — until she realized Cindi was talking to her.

"What?" she asked, pulling herself back to the present.

"Hold my train," Cindi said. "You're my lady-in-waiting, remember?"

Pippa would have told her sister to kiss off, but there were ten pairs of six-year-old eyes watching her closely. No sense in not playing the part.

But after the party, Cindi was in big trouble.

She nodded deferentially and picked up the train of Cindi's gown. Perhaps she could have been forgiven for paying more attention to fondling crystals and lace than she did to where she was going. She ran into Cindi's back once and had a more-vigorous-than-necessary swat from Cindi's wand as her reward. She bit her tongue only because impressionable children shouldn't have to listen to her shout at her sister. She was released from her duties while Cindi made a valiant effort to deliver each little girl to her mother and father for safekeeping. Pippa didn't want to cut her sister any slack — it would really hamper her ability to do her in later — but she had no choice. When Cindi was on, she was really on.

With any luck, Pippa would get her *on* a plane sooner rather than later and get down to the business of getting her own business taken care of.

She stood at the end of the bridge and watched, then realized she wasn't watching alone. She looked up to find Stephen standing there. It was growing dark, but she could still see quite a bit of his expression, which seemed at the very least to be quite thoughtful.

"Your wings are a bit more discreet than hers," he offered.

"I'm not much for flashy, though I will admit I've been picking up things that fell off Cindi's dress all night." She patted her pocket protectively. "I could probably sell them and make a fortune."

He smiled. Pippa wondered at that moment why it was that Tess wasn't snapping him up. Maybe Tess could marry him, they could adopt her, and she could live out the rest of her life in Tess's fairy-tale castle, gathering inspiration from the surrounding walls.

"You must have interesting family reunions," he offered.

"We terrify my parents," she admitted. "We didn't turn out to be flower children, so we're all in some way a huge disappointment."

"I understand that," he said with a deprecating smile. "My father and younger brother tell me constantly that I was born in the wrong century due to my less-than-corporate interests. But I suppose you and I are consigned to the time period we have." He glanced at Tess. "I think your sister might have appreciated a different place in history, given her love for the politics and battles of the Middle Ages."

Pippa didn't want to blow it for Tess, so she kept her mouth shut about the sword thing. Unfortunately, as handsome as Stephen de Piaget was, if he played with swords, he wasn't the guy for Tess. Her sister needed a nobleman with buckets of money, a closet full of tweed jackets, and a pipe he smoked only in his library that he would build outside castle walls so Tess wouldn't have to smell the leftovers. He would probably need to drive a Volvo.

"I'm curious, however," he said, turning back to her, "what inspired you to create your designs. They have just the right touch of, well, whatever they have is just the right amount." He shrugged, looking quite uncomfortable. "I'd say magic, but I don't believe in magic."

"Neither do I."

And she didn't. Normally. At the moment, she was tempted to.

There was something about standing next to a drop-dead-gorgeous guy while in front of what was surely the most romantic-looking castle in all of England that inspired a bit of wishful thinking. Or just plain wishing. She wasn't sure which it was, but as she looked up into the fading twilight at the stars that sparkled in a particularly magical way, she couldn't help but do a little wishing for herself.

For a chivalrous sort of guy who would want to have a second date with her.

She shivered, and she was fairly certain that wasn't from the chilly fall evening. There was something in the air . . . something otherworldly. She looked over her shoulder to see if Cindi felt it too and was flipping out.

Nope, no freak out. Just Cindi walking toward her in a cloud of what could only be termed bippity-boppity-boo swirls, as if a fairy godmother had waved her wand and scattered sparkles all over her. Pippa looked up so quickly she pulled something, but there was no moon, no spotlight, no stray flashlight being shined out a window by some enterprising ghost Cindi had potentially made some sort of Faustian bargain with.

It was such a flabbergasting sight that Pippa could only stand there and gape. She didn't even flinch when Cindi spun around and she got a face full of wing. She absently picked a stray crystal off her tongue and pocketed it along with the handful of others she'd found in various states of abandonment over the past three hours.

Something was definitely up.

"I'm sorry," Stephen said politely. "I was

discussing clothing with your sister —"

"I know more about it than she does," Cindi said brightly.

"Well, I say —"

Pippa felt someone push her. She looked behind her but found nothing there.

Maybe Fate was trying to give her a little nudge in the right direction. She gathered her intestinal fortitude like a weapon and stepped between Cindi and Stephen only to have Cindi elbow her aside. She was torn between complaining to her sister and offering a few choice words to whomever was behind her, occasionally giving her a substantial push. Stephen seemed to be happy to get in on the game, for he moved around Cindi as if he would rather have been talking to the purveyor of less-flamboyant evening wear.

Not to be outdone, Cindi continued to put herself in his way. Pippa was to the point of giving her sister a big old tug, but her sister was stoned, as it happened, and Pippa couldn't bring herself to be that big a jerk.

But she also couldn't bring herself to be a doormat, so she stepped between her sister and Stephen only to hear Cindi squeak and fall into her. She in turn lost her balance with a squawk and went stumbling through a cloud of sparkles. She was too far off-kilter to save herself, leaving her with no doubt that she would soon find herself falling into Tess's moat without a hope of rescue.

She didn't suppose it was the best way to impress Stephen, but maybe Cindi would fall in with her and get a cold. She might then be required to stay in bed for a couple of days, giving *Pippa* a couple of days to ingratiate herself with a certain man with money to invest.

Or, even better, maybe she would fall into the moat, Stephen would pluck her from the water, then suffer an overwhelming case of chivalry and go out of his way to make all her dreams come true.

It could happen.

She closed her eyes, bracing for the shock of ice-cold moat water —

Hugh McKinnon stood on the edge of what he was quite certain was a time gate, with his hands outstretched, and thought he might have to rethink his plan to go at the matchmaking business alone.

He took off his cap and wrung it into a shapeless mass as he contemplated this new and undesirable turn of events. He had intended to push his Pippy into Lord Stephen's arms and thereby begin what he'd been certain would be the start of a beautiful relationship. Instead, the yellow-haired sister playing the Faery Queen had gotten in his way and he'd ended up pushing her, which had led her to pushing Pippy, which had led to his charge going off to places unknown and potentially dangerous.

He looked around him to see if anyone else had noticed his alarming faux pas.

That little gel, Hailey, was staring out from the back of her parents' motorcar. Nay, she wasn't staring, she was gaping at him as if it were all his fault. He wanted to tell her it was just a tactical error that could be rectified and would she please keep it to herself, but he didn't suppose he would have the chance. And given how many other ghosts she seemed to encounter on a regular basis, Hugh wasn't altogether certain she wouldn't rat him out to those he might rather have left in the dark.

He was no coward, but he knew when to retreat and regroup. He plopped his cap back atop his head and turned to march off into the gloom as if he had places to go. Which he did. And those places were very far away from anywhere anyone might have considered his usual haunts.

He would rethink, investigate, then solve, because he was all Pippy had, so he would rise to the occasion and do his best by her. After all, they were kin. If one looked far enough down the branches of the proverbial family tree. He had no other choice but to continue to take matters into his own hands and fix them.

Because if Ambrose MacLeod found out what he'd done, he would kill him.

Again.

Chapter 5

Montgomery didn't believe in magic.

He reminded himself of that with no small bit of enthusiasm. 'Twas true that he might have, in his youth, considered things of an inexplicable and magical nature, but he hadn't done so in at least a decade. If he encountered something he couldn't manage with his sword or explain away by normal means, he left it alone. Torchlight was something to give relief from darkness, moonlight was there to allow him to avoid riding his horse into a ditch, and air that shimmered was nothing more than sunlight on water, on blades, or on expensive jewels.

This, though, was another matter entirely.

He stood at the end of his drawbridge and stared at a spot in front of him where . . . well, the only way to describe the spot before him was that the air was bloody shimmering with some sort of — he had to take a bracing breath or two before he could finish the thought — otherworldly light. Worse still, in the midst of that shimmering he saw what he could only term a doorway opening where no doorway could possibly have found itself.

Damn it, anyway.

He blamed Gunnild. If she hadn't insisted on entertaining the entire countryside — at his expense, no less — he wouldn't have come outside to have a bit of relief from the entertainment he couldn't stand being provided for people he would rather not see again, and then he wouldn't have been faced with what he was facing.

Which was something, he was sure, that had nothing to do with magic.

Or at least he thought so until through that, er, *magical* doorway came stumbling a woman, slender, squawking, and sporting . . . wings.

He reached out and caught her by the arm before she went sprawling into his cesspit. He hoped, belatedly, that he hadn't ripped her arm free of its moorings. He started to say something to her, but apparently the gate hadn't finished with him. To his very great surprise, out stumbled a second woman, easily the most glorious creature he had ever clapped eyes on in the whole of his life — and he had seen quite a goodly number of very beautiful women. This one, however, outshone them all.

He thought he might have heard a splash, but he honestly couldn't have said. He was far too busy being overcome by the vision in front of him.

The woman, if that's what she was instead of some creature from a dream, was dressed in a white gown so exquisite, he could scarce look at it. Her hair was so pale a gold, 'twas almost white. Her face . . . Well, angels must have wept over a face such as hers for there was no flaw in it that he could see. Her skirts were voluminous, true, but he could see that her waist was slight and —

He shifted uncomfortably. She was well endowed, to be sure, in a way that made him slightly nervous, though he couldn't have said why. He averted his gaze, because his mother had taught him decent manners, and concentrated on anything but what he shouldn't have been looking at.

It was only then that he realized what it was past that perfection that stunned him so.

She had wings as well.

He wondered, with no small bit of desperation, if he'd lost his wits somewhere during the day. He drew his hand over his eyes to block out the vision before him and quickly reviewed the events of the day to see if he could divine the moment when that might have happened.

The day had been interminable, true, beginning well before dawn thanks to the shouts of the lady Gunnild that last-minute cleaning needed to begin. He might not have minded that so much if he hadn't been up half the night trying to settle on a figure that didn't seen unreasonable to use in fortifying the castle as a whole. He didn't care to spend all his gold on stone whilst leaving nothing to use for steel and new horseflesh, but he also couldn't fill his keep with men and horses and not have a way to protect them. 'Twas going to be damned expensive, but there was nothing to be done about it.

So, he'd risen well before he'd cared to, carried on with ingesting a disgusting breakfast — truly, he had to find a cook who could actually create things that tasted more like food and less like cesspit sludge — before he had retreated to the lists where he felt most comfortable.

The garrison was coming to heel, thanks in part to Everard of Chevington's willingness to take on the more amenable half of the lads and school them in swordplay whilst Montgomery took on the other half and schooled them in manners. Everard might have been a less-than-desirable companion when one wanted someone trustworthy to take a turn on watch, but he had been trained in swordplay by Rhys de Piaget and had learned his lessons well. Montgomery had been more than happy to use him to intimidate a few of the garrison lads.

The men he'd taken under his wing had been lacking not only in sword skill but in decent comportment. He didn't hold out hope that they would learn either in the near future, but he would either wear himself out — or them down — trying. It would have helped if his two male cousins could have been counted on to do aught but laze about the edge of the training field and comment loudly about the indignities they were suffering because of Montgomery's arrival. Montgomery had given them the day to spew their venom and hopefully empty their bellies of it. He had no intention of listening to the like on the morrow.

The only bright spot in the unrelenting gloom had been his steward, Fitzpiers, who had kept meticulous records and managed, obviously unbeknownst to Lord Denys, to lay by a bit of gold for a time of need. There was also a decent bit of income from rents and more arable land belonging to the keep than Montgomery had imagined. He had asked for the names of his people so he might become acquainted with them, a request his steward had agreed to with surprise, as if he couldn't imagine why Montgomery would want such a thing. Obviously, there was much work to be done in winning hearts and minds.

He had then emerged from his solar to face things he was far less comfortable with, namely Gunnild in the throes of her preparations. He had been very tempted, after an exceptionally tedious half hour of listening to her blather on about why she was better suited to managing the keep than he was, to simply tie her up and send her off to her son's hall, but he hadn't. It would take tact and a good deal of diplomatic maneuvering to resettle her without angering her beyond all reason. If her eldest son, Arnulf, required the same, so be it. He wasn't above convincing her that Wideton Hall was where she would want to pass the glorious autumn years of her life and convincing Arnulf that she would be a suitable adornment to that hall.

In truth, he had no choice. He knew he wasn't off the mark to imagine that if the opportunity presented itself, Gunnild would stab him in the back.

He had deigned to bathe before supper, then presented himself in the hall for inspection by the neighbors. Gunnild had ignored him, talked over him, and finally gone so far as to try to fight him for the lord's chair as they sat for supper. He had stared her down until she had relented, though she'd made him suffer for it for the rest of the evening by cutting off his conversation every chance she had. He had been polite and gracious, because his mother would have frowned at him if he'd been rude, but he had begun to seriously question his ability to carry on with those manners for any length of time.

In the end, he'd left the guests in the care of his cousin and departed for safer ground on the pretense of needing air. He had wandered out of the great hall, trudged through the muck still lingering in the courtyard, then walked under the comforting presence of not one but three portcullis gates with their silver spikes glinting above his head. He wasn't quite sure what they would protect given the deplorable state of his walls, but at least the gates would intimidate anyone who decided to assault him that way.

All of which had left him standing where he was, awash in an otherworldly glow, looking at a woman whose beauty — and wings

— left him uncomfortably speechless.

By the saints, was she a faery?

He could hardly believe he was seriously considering the like, but he realized quite suddenly that he was. He also realized with equal abruptness than he was no longer holding on to the first creature who had appeared from the netherworld. He looked to his right and saw her struggling to get out of the cesspit. He reached down and pulled her out, more gingerly than he was proud of. He considered how to aid her — perhaps from a distance — but before he could attempt it, something from the cesspit dropped from her hair into her mouth, which was opened in astonishment.

She began to retch.

He was tempted to join her.

Fortunately, he was distracted by the woman in front of him who turned herself about several times before her eyes rolled back in her head and she fell senseless into his outstretched arms. He struggled to manage not only her weight but the unusual burden of her wings, then found himself distracted by the other gel who had stopped retching long enough to start gasping. She looked at him, then looked at his castle.

And then she began to scream.

Montgomery reached out for her only to

have her jerk away before he could touch her. She turned and fled — right into what was left of an outer stone gate. The sound of her head against it was a sickening crunch. Montgomery watched helplessly as she stumbled backward, then twisted and fell against his outstretched arm. She closed her eyes and descended into senselessness, as well.

He was, for the second time that evening, speechless. He was holding two women, two insensible women, who had simply appeared out of nowhere. Sporting, of course, wings.

Just what in the hell was he supposed to do now?

He was tempted to speculate wildly on things he hadn't considered in years, but didn't dare until he had the peace for it. He couldn't stand there all night simply holding the two in his arms, but he knew with equal certainty that he would be a fool to take them inside the keep. His household would take one look at them and either flee in terror or attack him in a frenzy for bringing demons into their midst. He didn't suppose he dared hope his guardsmen had been too lazy to man the walls and would therefore have not seen things they couldn't easily explain. He looked up to make certain of that.

Only to find Everard of Chevington was standing not ten paces from him, watching him with absolutely no expression on his face.

"How long have you been standing there gawking?" Montgomery demanded, hoping bluster would take the man's mind off things he shouldn't be contemplating having seen.

"I heard a shriek and came to make sure no one had you backed up against the cesspit with his sword to your throat," Everard said slowly. "I had no idea you were overwhelming not one but two wenches with your considerable charms." He frowned. "What are those things attached to their backs?"

"Wings," Montgomery said without hesitation, then he launched into the best lie he could invent on short notice. "These gels are players. Pretending to be faeries."

"Players," Everard repeated skeptically. "Where are their companions? Their servants? Their guardsmen?"

"The lassies were on their way to enteratain the king," Montgomery continued, wishing he were a better liar. He sounded daft even to himself. "Their servants saw something that frightened them and they fled, taking all the gear along with them.

The women couldn't help a shriek or two whilst relating their sad tale."

Everard frowned. "That little one looks a little bedraggled. Did she have a swim in the cesspit?"

"An unfortunate one," Montgomery said. "She'll need aid, lest she catch her death from the ague. She'll need a bath at the very least."

"You can't mean to bring them inside," Everard said in disbelief.

"What else am I to do?" Montgomery asked shortly. "Leave them out here?"

"I would," Everard muttered.

Montgomery imagined Everard would, but he would make a different choice himself, though he supposed it wouldn't go well for him if he carried either of the women into his hall in their current condition. Questions would be raised, superstitions stoked into a raging fire, and he would be trying to protect the gels against his entire household with nothing more than his three guards, his squire, and possibly Everard — though with the way Everard was studying the white-garbed faery, he wasn't at all sure the man would be standing with him.

"You take the maid," Montgomery began.

"Are you daft?" Everard said, wrinkling his nose. "I'll take the lovely one, or none at all." He paused. "I'd like a closer look at her, truth be told."

"You'll have it later," Montgomery said, though he had no intention of allowing the like. "Help me now by putting your cloak over this fair-haired lass so I can carry her inside. But do it *carefully,*" he added. He didn't want to say as much, but he wasn't entirely certain that her wings, if that's what they were, wouldn't pain her if they were mishandled.

"I want something dear in return for this," Everard said, draping his cloak over the woman on Montgomery's left. "I want something *very* dear."

"Name it later," Montgomery said. He suddenly found himself very reluctant to hand over the dark-haired girl, but he knew he had no choice. He couldn't carry two of them at once. He would simply have to trust that Everard wouldn't do much damage to the dark-haired lass before he could return. He lifted the blonde up, then paused just the same. "That one's hardly responsible for her smell, you know."

Everard only scowled at him and kept the lass at arm's length.

Montgomery supposed he could ask for nothing else. He took a deep breath, then walked swiftly across the drawbridge and under the gates. He entered the hall to find the occupants too far into their cups to notice him, thankfully, and walked quickly to the stairs that led up to the upper passageway. The stairway was difficult to negotiate with a woman in his arms — especially considering her wings — but he managed it. He gained the upper passageway, hastened to his bedchamber, and found Phillip standing outside the doorway. Phillip was watching him with very wide eyes.

"Don't ask," Montgomery warned.

"I didn't intend to, my lord," Phillip said, swallowing convulsively. He opened the door, then stepped aside.

Montgomery strode across the chamber and laid the woman down on his bed. He supposed he should have done something to make her more comfortable, but he honestly had no idea what that something would have been. He didn't even dare pull Everard's cloak off her, lest he touch something he shouldn't — such as her wings — and offend her faerylike sensibilities. He could hardly believe he was entertaining the thought of her actually being such a creature with any seriousness at all, but perhaps there were truly things in the world that were beyond mortal ken —

He rubbed his hands over his face. By the saints, he wanted nothing to do with this. He had affairs of his own to see to, affairs that would require all his attention. He had no use for a pair of helpless lassies who were from . . . well, he had no idea where they were truly from, but he couldn't deny that something akin to magic had been involved with their arrival.

The saints preserve him from it.

"I've another one to fetch," he said, turning suddenly to Phillip. "Guard this one, please."

"Of course, my lord."

Montgomery left his bedchamber, avoided an encounter with a rather inebriated Gunnild of Sedgwick on his way through the hall, and escaped into the courtyard unscathed. He walked swiftly through the gates, fully prepared to again see that very odd shimmer at the end of the bridge, but he did not.

He also didn't see any sign of either Everard or that poor, fragrant faery.

He cursed himself succinctly, then turned and ran back along the bridge. There was no sign of either of the two in the cesspit, so perhaps Everard had found sense and brought the gel inside the keep. Montgomery could only hope the man hadn't dumped her in the well to have done with her.

He found her lying on the floor in front of the fire in the kitchens, apparently senseless and obviously the recipient of a recent bucket. Montgomery caught his cook's arm before he upended another bucket of water on her.

"Do not."

The cook looked no less disgusted than Everard had, but he at least refrained from commenting. Montgomery looked about him but saw no sign of his companion in the night's events. He supposed Everard had retreated happily to where he might strip off his clothes and have a wash. Montgomery wasn't entirely sure he wouldn't do the same thing before the night was through.

He lifted the maid up in his arms, giving up the thought of not touching her sodden clothing. He was filled with less disgust than pity, but he also had no desire to wear more of his cesspit's filth than necessary.

He was favored with lewd suggestions and other unpleasantness on his way through the great hall, but he ignored it and continued on his way. It was only as he reached his bedchamber that he realized he hadn't covered the gel's wings. The saints be praised the revelers below had been too far gone to realize that.

Or so he hoped.

"Another one?" Phillip squeaked.

"To my surprise," Montgomery said shortly. "I imagine I'll remain here in the passageway to guard these two since they aren't able to lock the door. I don't dare leave them to trouble they might not want."

"I understand, my lord."

Montgomery imagined Phillip did. Artane was not without its own share of odd happenings. He smiled briefly at his squire. "Find Sir Ranulf and send him to me, then bolt yourself into my solar so I'll know you're safe. We'll resume our duties in the morning."

Phillip nodded, wide-eyed, then turned and trotted off down the passageway. Montgomery watched him go, looked up and down the short passageway to make certain he hadn't been observed by anyone else, then let himself into his bedchamber and shut the door behind him with his foot.

Well, the first thing to do was to see to the most pressing issue and that was ridding the poor wench in his arms of her clothing. Montgomery wasn't completely untried in the matters of removing women's gowns, but he had to admit, as he laid her on the floor in front of his fire and looked at her garb, that what he saw gave him pause.

Her wings were crumpled and ripped in a place or two, and he wondered with no small bit of alarm if that pained her.

He rolled her over gently, then realized to his great surprise that her wings were simply fastened to her gown with small round bits of bone. He was tempted to linger over that discovery, but the stench of her clothing was truly difficult to bear. He would see to that first, then turn his mind to the other riddle. He was quite grateful that his cook had done her the favor of ridding her hair of most of the filth. Her gown, however, had not fared so well.

He left her wings alone and worked on the laces that held the back of her gown together. They were easily undone and in short order he had her gown removed. He steadfastly ignored the fact that her wings were fixed not to her skin but to the cloth and that she wore the most alarming undergarments he'd ever seen in his life.

He supposed 'twas fortunate for them all that he had a strong stomach for things of an otherworldly nature.

He studiously ignored looking at her lithe form, then lifted her into his arms and carried her to his bed. He laid her down, took off her slippers, then covered her quickly with an extra blanket to preserve what modesty she had remaining her. He then happily went about the more pedestrian business of washing her gown as best he could in the basin of water standing on a table beneath the window. He tossed the water out the window, hung her gown over a chair near the fire, then paced in front of that fire for far longer than he should have before he could even think about turning around to look at the two women in his bed.

He considered the very sensible thought that he should go downstairs, find a wall sturdy enough for his purposes, and bang his head against it repeatedly until good sense returned.

The alternative was to believe what his eyes told him.

He turned away and looked for someplace to sit. He rubbed his hands over his face, then wondered what in the hell he was going to do now. He didn't want to believe in the fables he'd given credence to in his youth. He was almost a score and eight, far too old to be beguiled by tales told by his mother to entertain small children.

He couldn't deny, however, that he had seen things earlier that evening that had been nothing less than magical. If he'd been a more gullible lad, he might have believed what all signs pointed to.

He had the Queen of Faery and her handmaid in his bed.

He rose and began to pace, only because he thought better when he was moving. If the women were faeries, then why had the maid's wings not been attached to her flesh? Was she merely a servant who had not earned any privileges, or were there rites of passage in her world that he knew nothing of? He had no idea, but he certainly wasn't going to examine the queen to see if the answer lay on her back.

He found himself longing for nothing more taxing than a morning spent in his solar, listening to his very capable steward scratching on his parchment, tallying up numbers that continued to march across the page thanks to that steward's diligence.

He stopped at the foot of his bed and looked down. The queen, if that's what she truly was, was still an angel of perfection. Her maid, if that's who she was, continued to be lovely in a way that he couldn't lay his finger on. She seemed almost familiar, if such a thing were possible. And he continued to be just as baffled as he had been not half an hour ago.

Where had these gels come from, if not Faery?

He took a deep breath, then walked around to the side of the bed and looked down at the maid. He leaned over to make certain she was still breathing, then reached out to touch the bump on her head.

She hit him so hard he staggered back. He realized only then that she was still unconscious and her arm had fallen off the bed. It had to have been a reflexive reaction to the pain. He picked up her hand, settled her again, then smoothed the hair back from her face. She was very lovely, true, but there was something about her —

He stepped back and shook his head sharply. It had been a very trying handful of days and he needed nothing so much as sleep. Unfortunately, he suspected that wasn't to be found that night. But before he took up his vigil in the passageway, he would go make certain Phillip was seen to and the hall as secured as it was going to be. He took one last look at the women in his bed, shook his head, then turned and left the chamber.

He ran bodily into Ranulf before he realized his captain was standing in the passageway, waiting for him.

"My apologies," Montgomery said with a weary smile. "It has been a very long day."

Ranulf waved aside his words. "Not to

worry, my lord. Our young lord Phillip told me you'd wanted to see me. Forgive me if I took the time to make one last check of the hall."

Montgomery was profoundly grateful for the lads nearest him who were consistently diligent beyond what he could reasonably ask of them. "And?"

"Most of the guests are snoring where they've fallen, Lord Phillip is safely ensconced in your solar, and the gates are secured." He paused. "Lord Everard seems to be looking for someone to tell questionable tidings to, but there are none sober enough to listen to him. I had no interest in them, if you'll forgive my saying so."

"He has a vivid imagination," Montgomery said slowly. "I'm not sure I would give credence to what he says, either."

Ranulf shrugged. "The world is full of inexplicable happenings, but there is no purpose in discussing them overmuch."

Given that Ranulf had squired for Montgomery's brother-in-law, Jackson, Montgomery supposed Ranulf had seen more than his share of inexplicable happenings and had acquired the good sense to leave them alone.

Would that he himself had had the same good sense.

"I've arranged for the watch, my lord," Ranulf continued, "and will take my turn when appropriate to see that all is well. Is there aught else you require?"

Montgomery shook his head. "You've done more than enough, Ranulf. Thank you."

Ranulf made him a bow, smiled briefly, then went off to see to his duties. Montgomery made himself at home against the opposite wall from his door. He was beginning to wonder if he hadn't so much stumbled into a dream as a nightmare. He had a hall full of drunken guardsmen, cousins, and neighbors. He had holes in his walls and rats in his cellar with no cat in sight. And now, if his own eyes were to be believed, two faeries in his bed. He was half tempted to ask Fate what else it was she planned to throw at him, but he decided he'd best not, as he was quite sure he didn't want to know.

Magic.

Despite how thoroughly he had shunned any mention of it for years, he'd known it would catch him up eventually.

He could only hope it wouldn't be the death of him.

Chapter 6

Pippa fought her way out of what was without a doubt the most unpleasant night's sleep of her life. She couldn't quite call it a nightmare because there had been no monsters in it besides her sister, but it could definitely be classified as a very bad dream. Obviously she'd indulged in too much British chocolate the night before. Tess had warned her it was powerful, but she'd ignored her sister, trusting in her own ability to ingest vast quantities of it and remain unaffected. Never again. If her head ever stopped killing her, she would swear off the stuff for good.

She lay still for quite some time, then opened her eyes.

And she rather wished she hadn't.

The light in the room wasn't all that great, but perhaps that was just as well. She couldn't understand why Tess would have kept one of the bedrooms in such a, well, *rustic* state, but what did she know? Maybe people paid good money to sleep under scratchy sheets and wake up to a canopy that looked as if it had been carved with a woodsman's axe. And what was that horrible smell —

She realized, with a start, that it was her.

She would have given that a bit more thought, but she was too distracted by the noise. She carefully turned her head and found her sister lying next to her so profoundly unconscious that Pippa might have thought she was dead if she hadn't been snoring like a trucker. Why she herself was in her underwear and her sister was still wearing her party clothes was something she probably didn't want to know. Maybe Tess had rescued her from the moat and decided taking off her dress was enough and been too exhausted after the fact to mess with Cindi. Maybe Cindi hadn't wanted to let go of that small fortune in crystals she was wearing and had kicked up a fuss, beating Tess with the wand she still held in one of her traitorous hands.

When she could see straight again, Pippa fully intended to check the scene of battle and collect more crystals. If she was feeling particularly feisty, she just might start cutting them off Cindi's dress while she was passed out. She could probably start her own bead store with the plunder.

She lay there for another minute or two until the smell — which was definitely coming from herself and not Cindi — became just too bad to endure any longer. She pushed herself gingerly to a sitting position. She was going to find a robe, then go get in the shower before she went immediately back to bed. Maybe Tess had a friendly family doctor who would come look at her head and give her something for the pain. She was a little surprised her sister hadn't done that already, but maybe things had gone too crazy to. She wouldn't have blamed Tess for wanting a little rest. In fact, that sounded like a very wise idea. Pippa lay back down, vowing to get back up when the stars stopped swimming around her head.

Once she could think straight again, the events of the night before came back to her in a rush. She had gone swimming in Tess's moat, which was definitely not as clean as advertised. She suddenly remembered with perfect clarity the events leading up to that, all of which were overlaid with a nagging annoyance directed toward her sister for once again hogging the spotlight. She remembered standing at the end of the bridge, talking to Stephen de Piaget and having Cindi repeatedly try to come between them. She wasn't entirely sure someone hadn't pushed her once or twice. She actually wasn't entirely sure that someone hadn't been Cindi herself doing that pushing, especially given that the final shove had landed Pippa in the moat.

No, that wasn't right. Stephen had grabbed her hand and kept her from falling into the moat, only he had let go. That had probably been thanks to the fact that Cindi had passed out conveniently close to his outstretched arms and he'd had no choice.

She had specific, unpleasant memories of resurfacing to discover the true contents of Tess's lake floating all around her and covering her from head to toe. Things were a little hazy from there. Someone — Stephen, probably — pulled her out, then she had stepped into a full-blown hallucination where Tess's castle had turned into a dilapidated wreck and Stephen de Piaget had ignored her in favor of her sister.

She frowned. That had been a pretty damned vivid hallucination. She had serious doubts that even British chocolate could produce that sort of delusion.

She remembered panicking, screaming her head off, then bolting right into a brick post that hadn't been there five minutes earlier.

She had bounced off it, turned, and been caught by someone she had been fairly sure had said *eewww.*

Though that could have been her.

She turned away from that memory because it made her queasy. The sooner she was clean, the happier she would be, but she didn't think she would enjoy her shower until she could stand up all the way through it. She reluctantly put off getting up for another moment or two, distracting herself with a few things she hadn't noticed before. The mattress she was lying on felt as if it were a collection of twigs, and she thought there might have been things chirping in her pillow. Her blanket was scratchy and not really up to the task of warding off a chill that was listing toward arctic, though she supposed she couldn't blame Tess for covering her up with something she could simply pitch when she was finished with it.

But none of that explained why she was still in her underwear.

She decided she would talk to Tess about that sooner rather than later, so she put her hand to her head and very carefully pushed herself back up into a sitting position. The floor was ice cold under her feet, but that was rather bracing in a useful way so she didn't complain. She kept her hand pressed against her head and staggered across the floor, using first the footpost of the bed, then various bits of furniture to get herself over to the hearth. She managed to nudge a couple of pieces of wood onto the burning coals left there from the night before, then hung on to the mantel until the fire caught and her dizziness receded a bit.

She found her dress hanging on the back of a chair, but it was sopping wet so she didn't bother to put it on. She did check the pockets for her thumb drive and collection of crystals. They were still there and would probably dry out in time, so there was no sense in taking them out to stash them somewhere else. She shuffled across the room and bumped her toes on a trunk sitting there underneath the window.

She sat on the trunk and looked around her — carefully, to spare herself any more spinning than necessary. The bedroom was much more rustic than she'd remembered any of Tess's bedrooms being, though she certainly hadn't had the chance to look through them all. For all she knew, she was in a place Tess had left in a more Middle Ages sort of state to remind her of the castle's beginnings. Pippa sighed, then knelt beside the trunk and felt inside it. She was somehow unsurprised to find a pair of tights and a tunic inside instead of a fluffy, monogrammed bathrobe.

She stripped off her disgusting underthings and put on what she'd found. The shirt was huge and the tights less baggy than she might have liked, but there was nothing to be done about that. She rolled the tights at her waist as if they'd been dance gear and decided the tunic would have to do as it was. After all, she was just getting decent to go to the bathroom, not to make a formal appearance. She tossed her underclothes in the chair, put her feet in her shoes, and trudged over to the door, keeping her hand to her forehead and trying to keep her non-breakfast down where it should have been residing.

She fumbled with the latch, then braced herself against the doorframe and opened the door. Stephen was leaning against the wall opposite her, dressed in his medieval gear. She couldn't see him as clearly as she would have liked thanks to both her squinting and the dimness of the torchlight, but maybe it was best they not have too close an encounter in her current state.

"Hey," she said, wincing and declining to wave. Her tights weren't cooperating, forcing her to keep one hand clutching them in place and the other over her eyes. The flicker of torchlight was particularly annoying, but she didn't suppose turning the lights off would improve matters because then she wouldn't be able to see anything at all. "I'm just going to run to the bathroom . . . to . . . um . . ."

She felt herself wind down like a music box that had seen better days, one note at a time with increasingly lengthy pauses between those notes.

Flickering torchlight?

Stephen de Piaget with hair that had suddenly grown a few inches and a sword that even in her feeble state she could see was lacking the bright, shiny newness that blanketed most things for sale at Renaissance faires?

Pippa wished quite desperately for some place to sit, but since she wasn't sure she would make it to a chair, she settled for leaning heavily against the doorframe and having a good long look at a man who wasn't Stephen, but couldn't have looked much more like him if he *had* been Stephen.

Then again, he somehow didn't look like Stephen at all. Stephen was tall and very nicely fashioned, of course, but this guy . . . well, she wished she'd been able to do something besides squint. She was certain she was missing quite a few details she might otherwise have enjoyed. All she could say with any certainty was that he had a face modeling agencies would have killed for and the homespun he was wearing did nothing to obscure broad shoulders, powerful arms, and a long, very muscular pair of legs —

"Good morning, *demoiselle.*"

She jerked her gaze back up from where it shouldn't have been and focused on his mouth, a rather beautiful mouth, as it happened. Then she frowned, even though it hurt her to do so. He was speaking French, but it was done with a sort of accent she most definitely wasn't familiar with, and she had had a different private French tutor each year during her incarceration at Aunt Edna's Victorian Institution of More Painful Learning so she would be able to function in all sorts of polite society.

She considered, then frowned a bit more. There were actually quite a few things that just didn't add up.

First, there was a guy standing ten feet from her with a sword belted around his hips and his foot propped up against the wall underneath him who looked as if he belonged on a medieval movie set not in her sister's castle. He was showing off his quite buff self thanks not to a handful of fake torches, but thanks to what looked to be the real deal —

She felt her mouth fall open as she realized something.

It was *him.*

It was the medieval knight she'd seen years ago in that full-blown, daytime hallucination she'd had near Artane. She could hardly believe it, but it was the absolute truth. She had no idea why he was standing not ten feet from her when he should have been safely tucked away in her childhood dreams, and that was something she supposed she didn't dare ask him yet. She tugged self-consciously on her shirt, wishing she'd had a decent push-up bra to give herself courage — Cindi swore by that sort of thing — and that she could see straight. Deciding that wouldn't really help with what she couldn't possibly be seeing, she did the only thing she could.

She stepped back and slammed the door shut.

She rested her head gingerly against the wood and waited until the new batch of stars stopped spinning. It took quite a while, which gave herself time to get a hold of her rampaging imagination. She felt fairly confident that she would open the door and see what should have been there, namely an empty hallway.

She took a deep breath, then made attempt number two.

Really, she never should have called the man gorgeous, because he wasn't. He was actually so handsome, it almost hurt her to look at him. His face was perfectly proportioned, his cheekbones chiseled, his eyes the most remarkable shade of something that wasn't brown but wasn't blue. She supposed she would have to get a closer look at him to tell. She imagined when she did, she might be privileged to have a closer look at his mouth, which was very nicely done as well.

But somehow, in spite of all that male beauty, there was something just a little bit rough around the edges of his features, something that kept him from being pretty. Maybe it was that little crook in his nose that said that at some point in his life, it had been broken. Or that little scar that ran just above one of his eyebrows. Or the grimness that seemed to be settled around him like a cloak.

One thing was for sure: that wasn't Stephen de Piaget.

And he was staring at her as if he'd seen a ghost.

She shut the door again, because she panicked. She looked for a lock, but there wasn't one, so she had no choice but to lean back against the wood where she could take stock of her situation and keep herself safe at the same time.

She wasn't sleepwalking, so chalking things up to waking nightmares was out. She wasn't on drugs — unless one counted a night spent breathing Cindi's brownie-laced breath as a contact high — so a drug-enduced stupor was out as well. That left the possibility of Tess's castle having been taken over by marauders, marauders who looked like hunks from her teenage fantasies.

Well, her choices were obviously limited to escape or a quicker escape. She pushed off the door and staggered over to the window. She managed to get the shutters open, then leaned over to see what lay beneath her. Granted, she hadn't really had time to check out the scenery yesterday, but she was fairly sure the bedrooms overlooked the moat. But there was no moat beneath her now.

She frowned. It wasn't possible that someone could have drained that lake while she slept. Was it?

She started to shut the shutters then looked at them with dismay. Those were certainly not the nice, tight-fitting reproductions she had seen before. And there was no glass in the window. She turned around slowly and looked at the room. Austere was one thing — goodness knows all of her siblings were acquainted with *that* virtue — but this was taking it to an entirely new and rather *medieval* level.

Obviously, there had been a disaster of some sort.

She couldn't help but wonder if that guy standing in the hall was responsible for it.

She felt a little lightheaded, as if she weren't firing on all four cylinders, because she was starting to wonder if the entire castle had been overrun by bad guys. That wasn't the sort of thing modern-day castle owners were prepared for. There was no one walking along the walls, ready to shout, "Drop the portcullis, Bob!" the moment he caught sight of a group of medieval-looking guys with mischief on their minds. Pippa half wondered if Tess even had a big key for that outer gate.

No, they were sitting ducks, and they had obviously sat too long.

She looked at Cindi and realized there would be no help there. Her sister was still sawing logs like a drunken lumberjack. Pippa walked unsteadily over to her, then leaned over to look at her. There were crumbs on her pillow. Pippa picked one up, then sniffed.

Brownie.

She could only imagine what was in it. She would have frisked her sister for other contraband substances, but she thought that perhaps it was better to let sleeping show-stealers lie. Cindi certainly wasn't going to be of any help should a crisis arise, though Pippa supposed the crisis had already arisen and its ringleader was standing out in the hallway looking every inch the appealing bad boy.

She considered jumping out the window and running to get help, but two things stopped her: one, the window was too small; and two, there was nothing beneath her but grass to break her fall.

She would have to go out the door.

It was her only choice. She couldn't remain where she was, she couldn't call for help on her nonexistent cell phone, and she saw no point in screaming given that Tess's castle was so far out in the sticks, a signal fire probably wouldn't have attracted any attention.

She would get out of the keep, then first try the gift shop. If that didn't work, she would take off through the woods and hope she got far enough away quickly enough to get help before she was caught by the hunk in the hall and whomever he'd hired to help him trash Tess's castle. Cindi was on her own. Hopefully she would wake up and screech too loudly for anyone to do any damage to her.

She took her courage and her tights in hand, then crept over to the door. She put her ear to the wood and listened carefully. She heard nothing, but that was no guarantee that the hallway was empty. She would just have to deal with what she found.

She jerked the door open and found that she was still not alone. Her captor, if that's what he could be called, didn't even flinch. He simply watched her, wide-eyed and silent. Pippa looked to her right and gasped. She pointed for good measure and gasped again. Apparently she'd done a fairly good job of faking because the man actually pushed off the wall and looked where she'd pointed.

She took off down the hallway in the opposite direction. She didn't immediately hear heavy footsteps following her, so maybe she would get farther than she'd dared hope. She ran to the end of the hallway and practically leaped down the circular stairs that had somehow lost their very useful rope handrail at some point during the night.

She was unsurprised. Mr. Universe upstairs and his band of merry marauders were thorough, she would give them that.

She burst out of the stairs and was halfway across the hall before she skidded — literally — to an unsteady halt. She wished she could have blamed the sight that greeted her on her headache or on her former hallucinatory state, but she felt quite unfortunately in full possession of most of her faculties.

Unfortunately, she couldn't say the same about the state of her sister's great hall.

The place was a disaster. The floor was strewn with hay — and not very nice smelling hay, as it happened. The lord's table was in the right place, but the chairs were rickety and the walls were devoid of those lovely tapestries she had admired. All right, she'd coveted them in a fairly dangerous way, but that was beside the point. The walls were bare, the furniture — what there was of it — wasn't even worth taking to the thrift store, and the fireplaces were belching smoke as if they'd never had a good chimney sweep take a look at their innards. The people in the hall were just as unkempt.

And they were all staring at her as if she'd just sprouted horns.

"Demoiselle," a voice behind her began

carefully.

She knew that voice and she was fairly sure she didn't want to hear anything else it might have to say. Besides, she was too busy trying not to hyperventilate to listen. She wasn't one to freak out, not really. She was unflappable in the face of actors with split seams and stuck zippers. She was a rock when faced with screeching beauty queens with hems that dragged or buttocks that didn't fit into skimpy swimsuits. She generally reclined on an island of serenity when the seas around her heaved and roiled with violent fabric-strewn storms.

But now she thought she just might lose it.

She hitched and hit the road again, barely escaping a hand that reached out for her. She had no idea what was going on, and she had even less desire to figure it out. She wanted out, and the sooner she got there, the better.

She ran through the crowd that had gathered near the door. They looked tempted to stop her, but suddenly they all backed away as if they'd been commanded to. Pippa looked over her shoulder and saw why.

The poster boy for *Medieval Monthly* had drawn his sword.

She might have muttered a very unladylike expletive. Or she might have squeaked. She couldn't have said which, and she didn't want to know. She shoved a teenage boy out of her way and bolted out of the door. She put her head down and slopped through what had to have been six inches of muck now slathered over her sister's courtyard. She lost her shoes on her trip to the gate, but didn't stop to try to liberate them. She just ran on, under the three portcullises and across a drawbridge that was quite a bit sturdier than what she would have expected it to be. She continued to run until she was almost to the forest, then felt herself slowing to a halt.

She came to a stop.

There in front of her where the gift shop should have been was . . . nothing. Just forest that was quite a bit farther back from the castle than she remembered it being the day before. And there, between her and that forest, was not a green, grassy place but a brown, muddy place half full of men going at each other with swords.

She was just sure she'd stumbled onto a movie set and that the movie was a very realistic, very ruthless something about the realities of life in the Middle Ages.

Only there didn't seem to be any lights, or

cameras, or trailers for the stars and tents for the caterers. There was definitely not a prop trailer or prop mistress hollering at people to keep themselves clean until they weren't supposed to be. No, none of those things seemed to be in the vicinity, nor was there a director screaming at her that she'd walked onto the set and ruined his shot.

Where in the *hell* was she and what had happened to her world?

She turned and looked at the castle behind her.

Her mouth fell open.

The ruin she had seen hinted at in the great hall and vaguely remembered from the night before was on full display in front of her. Walls were missing parts of themselves, the moat had disappeared, and there were holes in just about everything else. It was as if the whole place had been bombed while she slept. She didn't think she was particularly dense or particularly susceptible to an overactive imagination, her flights of fabric fancy aside, but she was beginning suspect she just wasn't in Kansas anymore.

And if that wasn't bad enough, she also wasn't wearing any underwear.

She felt something begin at the base of her spine. It wasn't quite a tingling and it wasn't a warmth, but it was somehow both.

She watched the Stephen de Piaget non-look-alike walking toward her, an expression of concern on his face. His sword was sheathed, which she thought boded well.

He said something to her, but she couldn't hear him for the sudden rushing sound in her ears that sounded a great deal like wind. The stars swirled around her head, then even they faded as blackness descended.

She surrendered without a protest.

Chapter 7

It wasn't every day that a man lost his wits whilst being able to watch them vanish into the ether.

Montgomery stood in the middle of his great hall and contemplated that. He wasn't one to indulge in idle thoughts, but he couldn't deny that he was beginning to fear for his sanity. There was something going on in his keep that defied all rational thought. That he was taking any of it seriously — or allowing himself any improbable speculations about the homes of his uninvited guests above — said much about the condition of his mind.

He had no time for the distraction, but in truth he had absolutely no idea how in the hell he was going to get the two lassies in his bed back to where they'd come from. He had an enormous and quite useless amount of faery lore stored in his memory, but he wasn't sure he dared begin to think about it seriously — or try to put any of it to use.

He didn't like to dither, though when faced with a delicate and unfamiliar situation possibly requiring a decent amount of diplomacy, he wasn't above holding back for a bit to see how events were going to proceed before he inserted himself into them.

His household obviously didn't share his patience. His cousins were whispering amongst themselves, his servants were pretending to go about their chores whilst not doing anything at all, and his garrison knights were standing in little clusters as if they awaited something terrible they couldn't name. The hall was full of a heaviness that came from superstitious souls who feared what the future might bring.

He supposed they had cause.

He listened to the faint sound of otherworldly laughter float down the stairs at the back of his hall and realized one of his charges was awake. It wasn't an overly large hall, as it happened, so the laughter sounded a bit louder than it might have otherwise. He looked over his shoulder at his garrison knights, who were now standing as an uneasy group near the door, apparently unsure if they should come farther inside for something to eat or depart with all due haste back to the lists where things went on that they understood. Montgomery nodded at Ranulf and his two companions, who firmly and without brooking argument ushered the men to the long tables placed by each hearth.

The servants were not so easily convinced. They had now all come into the hall and were gaping at the stairwell opening as if they expected a demon to come bursting forth from it at any moment. Montgomery wished he had, at some point in the past, asked his mother for an idea or two on how to manage servants, but 'twas too late now. He would just herd them back to their places with his sword if he had to.

His cousins were taking up their accustomed amount of space at the lord's table. Gunnild had gone so far as to look to her left with a deeply suspicious expression but she had not vacated her chair. Her children seemed less interested in that than they did what might be coming from the kitchens. Well, save Martin, who looked at Montgomery and winked. Montgomery had to admit that he liked Martin, though he supposed he shouldn't trust the man any farther than he could throw him. The others only glared at him as if he were responsible for all their ills. He shrugged and looked away.

His steward Fitzpiers had come to stand at the door of his solar, and he looked particularly unperturbed. Montgomery sent him a fond thought. His father's steward was also an excellent man, one Montgomery had never truly appreciated for the size and complexity of his task. Artane was a small city in comparison to Sedgwick, yet his father and his father's steward managed it with ease.

Montgomery had much ahead of him, he could tell.

Before he could truly give that the thought it deserved, a vision burst into the hall with a magnificence that made him catch his breath. Her wings fluttered, her wand waved, her crown was askew, but somehow that didn't detract in the slightest from her regal carriage or her beauty.

The Queen of Faery had arrived.

Montgomery didn't want to believe that of her, but what else was he to think? He had never in his life seen anyone like her. And had he not realized the day before that her maid was the same gel he'd seen standing in the midst of that odd spot of ground near his father's hall? He'd been convinced in his youth that she was a faery, though he'd put that thought behind him along with other trappings of childhood.

Now, he wasn't convinced he hadn't made a mistake there, though he wasn't sure how clinging to the memory of that vision would have helped him. It wasn't doing a damned thing for him now save giving him a pounding pain behind his eyes.

He drew his hand over those eyes briefly, shook his head to clear it, then looked at his household. His garrison knights were gaping as if they'd just seen an apparition. Some were standing, some were half standing, and some looked as if they might soon become senseless. The kitchen staff looked no less affected, nor did the rest of his servants, though some of them had begun to cross themselves furiously. The cousins had deigned to put their feet on the floor, but Montgomery thought that might be the extent of their reaction. Gunnild had stood up, as if she sensed there might be trouble coming her way.

Montgomery watched the Faery Queen make her way about the great hall, twirling, sparkling, singing as if she were still in her own realm and they her loyal and adoring subjects. Montgomery couldn't look away from her. The woman was graceful, as if every move was a dance created especially for those who watched her, and benevolent, as if the smiles she bestowed were destined for none other than those she favored with them. She spun in the middle of the hall and sparkles flew from her wand, floating through the air and landing with a tinkling sound that reminded him of rain on the roof of his father's stables at home.

She floated over to the cluster of servants and kitchen staff and trilled at them.

Montgomery watched with resignation as the majority of them shrieked, then bolted past the queen, across the hall, and out the front door. Perhaps *majority* was the wrong word to use. *All* of them bolted save a lone gel, who stood there with a long knife in her hand and a scowl on her face.

Montgomery glanced at his garrison. His own men were leaning negligently against a wall near the doors, but he knew them too well to believe them uninterested. They were just too well-mannered to give any indication of their thoughts. Sedgwick's garrison seemed divided between those who were annoyed at the cloud of dust left by the departing kitchen staff and those who now seemed less terrified by the white-garbed woman than intrigued by her. He wasn't sure that was an improvement over his servants, but he wasn't going to argue at present.

He nodded to his own men, then walked across the hall to stand next to the remaining kitchen lass. He reached her as the queen fluttered away.

"I don't imagine you'll need your blade," he said quietly. He looked at the Faery Queen, who was now dancing in the middle of the great hall to music apparently only she could hear. "I think she's fairly harmless."

The girl stuck it back into her belt. "I've seven older brothers. It'd take more than a silly twit to frighten *me* away from me post."

Montgomery considered for a moment or two, then looked at her. "Can you cook?"

"Of course," the girl said, though she looked as if the very thought of it terrified her to the core.

"Then the kitchen is yours. Unless I can bring back the others."

"Begging your pardon, my lord, but I think you would be better off without them."

Montgomery couldn't help but agree. Even if he managed to find his servants, he imagined he wouldn't find them willing to work. He wasn't about to beat them into compliance, nor would he manage to convince them to do their jobs well if he did, so perhaps 'twas best he forgo a search for them until he'd dealt with the woman now singing bawdy French songs before the lord's table.

Montgomery looked at the girl standing next to him, trembling. "We'll find aid elsewhere then. What is your name, lass?"

"Joan, my lord."

"Thank you for your aid, Joan."

She looked at him as if she wasn't sure he if were kind or mad. He wondered, wearily, if he might be a little of both. Joan bobbed a curtsey, then turned and bolted back to the kitchen. Montgomery turned again to look to the hall. The men were still there, obviously too accustomed to some sort of food every day to feel like trying to search for it elsewhere. Either that or they knew that in their case, he would hunt each of them down and compel them to return. Perhaps they thought there was little sense in expending the energy to flee. His lads were still in their places. Montgomery would see them fed first. They couldn't guard his back if they were faint from hunger.

But first to see to the woman who had already half emptied his hall. He looked at the high table to find his cousins where they'd been before, looking irritated, calculating, and utterly bored depending on the soul in question. The Faery Queen didn't seem to find their participation in her dance to be necessary, which likely only irritated them the more.

Montgomery realized with a start that the queen's handmaid, that beautiful, ethereal gel he hadn't thought about in years, was standing at the bottom of the stairs, looking equal parts exhausted and apprehensive. Everard had appeared next to her, regarding her with equal amounts of suspicion and interest.

That bothered him, for some reason.

Everard was, however, a former member of his father's household, and Montgomery was waiting to see which way the wind blew, so he allowed the events to proceed for a bit longer. That gave him the opportunity to watch them as they did so — the events and the handmaid both. He studied her as she stood pressed back against the wall, looking numb to the goings-on. Perhaps she'd seem them before. He wondered how she had come to be in her mistress's service, and how she felt being so far from her world. He wondered if she could return.

He turned to study the woman in white. She was obviously not of this world, obviously quite used to the privilege of royalty, doubtless used to those around her immediately and without question seeing to her every need. She was no doubt rich far beyond even his rather high standards for the like, and he wasn't precisely certain she didn't possess magical powers. How else had she walked through a gate from her world to . . .

He felt his thoughts grind to an ungainly halt.

How else had she walked through a *gate* from her world to his?

His thoughts took him in a new and rather alarming direction. It was a rather well-kept secret that there were a few souls in his family who weren't — how was he to say it? — exactly from the current day, as daft as that sounded. His sister-in-law Jennifer, for instance, had seemingly sprung up from the grass, yet Montgomery had spent enough of his youth with his brother Nicholas to realize that Nicholas's wife was not a faery, but rather from a time not their own.

The Future, as it happened.

It couldn't be that the Faery Queen was . . . it couldn't be that she came from . . .

He rubbed his hands over his face and wished he'd had more sleep. Any sleep, actually. He'd spent all night either sitting or standing in front of his bedchamber door. He'd had no other choice. Only one brief trip to the garderobe had resulted in his two male cousins trying to sneak into his bedchamber. His vigil had kept the women safe, but it had apparently resulted in the complete ruination of his wits. The women were nothing more than he'd said they were: players who had wandered away from their company and become lost. Anything else was too fanciful, too improbable, too far out of his normal sphere of existence to be believed.

He clung to that thought desperately as he watched the queen flit around the back of the table and come to a stop next to his chair. She looked Gunnild over, as if she considered her potential prowess in battle.

"Move," she slurred, in French. The word was accented strangely, but perfectly intelligible.

Gunnild obviously understood her, for she bristled. "I will not."

The Faery Queen didn't wait for another response, she merely wrestled the chair away and sat herself down in it, catching both Gunnild and Boydin with her wings. War would have ensued, Montgomery was certain, if he hadn't rushed forward and stopped it before it could bloom and flower.

"Our guest will of course have the place of honor," he said with a pointed look at Gunnild.

Gunnild stepped aside, though Montgomery didn't doubt he would pay for that concession at some point in the near future. Montgomery ignored his cousin's look of fury, then saw the queen seated.

She yawned hugely, then shook her head. A few of her sparkles fell and some of her hair came lose from its coiffure. "I'm hungry."

"I'll fetch you something," Montgomery said politely.

The queen looked at him, then looked at him a bit longer. Apparently she saw something she liked very much because she wielded her wand with great deliberation on Boydin until he got up out of his chair and retreated with a curse to safer ground. The queen patted the seat.

"Come sit."

Montgomery suspected he knew how it felt for a man to be bewitched. She was just so lovely, so flawlessly beautiful, so achingly perfect that he supposed a man could do nothing but watch her draw breath —

"Persephone!" she bellowed. "Food!"

Montgomery blinked and the spell was broken.

The queen's handmaid looked as if she would have liked nothing better than to have bolted — that, or have silenced her mistress as quickly as possible. Unfortunately, she appeared to be unable to decide what she should do. She winced every time her queen shouted at her, but she seemed unwilling to move past Everard, who was looking at her with a now less-than-friendly eye.

Montgomery walked across the great hall and stopped next to her. She regarded him warily as well; not even his most unassuming and unintimidating expression seemed to ease her. He elbowed Everard out of the way, then put himself in front of her so she wasn't favored with a full view of what was left of his household. Unfortunately, that left him with a full view of her.

She looked impossibly tired. Indeed, he suspected that the dual trials of the bump on her head and her lady's demands had been very wearing on her.

"I daresay your mistress requires supper," he said carefully. "Unfortunately, my servants seem to have decamped for more promising larders. I'm not sure if your duties include preparing your lady's food, but I wonder if you might manage it today."

She looked at the queen for a moment or two, then up at him. "Kitchen?" she echoed faintly.

"Aye. Shall I show you the way?"

She nodded slowly. "Thank you."

"You're welcome. Persephone, is it?"

"Yes."

He made her a little bow. "I'm Montgomery de Piaget. Of Sedgwick," he added, because he supposed he should, though it felt strange on his tongue. Sedgwick was not a place he'd enjoyed visiting in his youth — indeed he could remember only a pair of occasions when he'd been forced to do so with his father and brothers — and there were still times he could hardly believe the keep was now his. He could only hope at some point that he could make it a hall that inspired something besides headshaking and sneers.

He looked at Persephone to find her gaping at him.

"De Piaget?" she said, putting her hand to her head and wincing. "Montgomery?"

"Persephone, *now!*" the queen bellowed.

Montgomery wasn't about to insert himself between Persephone and her lady, but he could readily see she was in no condition to be doing aught but going somewhere quiet and having a lie-down. He looked at Everard.

"Would you fetch our displaced noblewoman there a bit of wine?" he asked, nodding toward the woman sitting in his chair looking particularly out of sorts. "I'll find her food quickly, before her complaints increase."

"Is she a noblewoman now?" Everard asked with a deep frown. "I thought she was a player."

Montgomery sighed to himself. Yet more lies that he would rather have avoided. But desperate circumstances called for desperate measures. He took a deep breath.

"I thought so, too, at first, but now I understand she is one of Henry's acquaintances." He cast about for something else plausible. "From Italy," he added. "Her clothing is part of her, ah, charm."

"A pity her charm doesn't extend to quietly voicing her demands," Everard said with a wince. "Perhaps you'd best send her little maid here to the kitchens quickly, so we might have a little peace."

"My thoughts exactly," Montgomery agreed. "So please, offer her wine, if you will, until we can see to food for her." He didn't wait for Everard to comply; he simply took Persephone's hand and drew it through the crook of his elbow without thinking, as he might have done with his mother or his sisters. Her hands were icy cold. He looked down quickly into her face to find her visage very pale.

Who knew the horrors she was experiencing? She was obviously from a lovely and more cultured world, so how must his world seem to her?

And how daft must he be to be thinking anything of the sort? Faery? He had obviously gone too long without sleep.

But the very noisy woman sitting in his chair, queen of the netherworld or no, had obviously gone too long without food. The faster that was seen to, the sooner he would have peace for thinking.

He walked Persephone through the passageway to the kitchens. Joan had styled herself a benevolent monarch and was directing none other than Phillip of Artane to do the fetching of water and lifting of heavy things for her. Phillip looked at him and smiled briefly.

"I thought I might be of use."

"You are too good for me," Montgomery said with a sigh.

"So says my father," Phillip said with another smile. "I think, however, my lord, that we won't be able to feed the garrison with just us two here." He paused and set his water down to come closer. "Forgive me for speaking freely, but I wouldn't trust our cousins near the cooking fire."

"Neither would I, Phillip. We'll manage until I find other souls suited for the task. There might be a lad or two in the garrison happy to leave the lists for a bit."

Phillip nodded, then shoved a stool closer to the fire with his foot. He looked at Persephone and made her a small bow.

"Perhaps you would care to sit?" he asked gallantly.

Persephone felt her way down onto that stool, then looked around her as if she'd never in her lifetime seen a kitchen before. Montgomery considered that for a moment or two. Perhaps she was accustomed to loftier surroundings. Or perhaps surroundings that didn't look as if they'd just recently suffered a lengthy and quite injurious siege. She said nothing, but her shoulders slumped slightly.

Joan apparently thought she'd acquired help, for she walked over and began to give Persephone numerous instructions that showed she had either cooked for her mother at home or paid close attention to how things carried on inside a keep. Persephone only stared up at her as if she couldn't understand a bloody thing she was saying. Montgomery frowned. Perhaps she wouldn't have any cause to know the peasant's English, but still . . .

He would obviously have to stay nearby and translate. In fact, he supposed he might do well at the moment to simply stay nearby and help. Persephone looked as if the simple act of sitting upright was taxing enough. He squatted down next to her to be more easily heard over Joan's commanding of Phillip, then realized that he had made a grave tactical error.

Persephone's queen might have been perfection embodied, but that queen was somehow not nearly as lovely as was Persephone herself, wearing his spare tunic and hose. She was lovely, and grave, and very, very lost. He reached up before he thought better of it and tucked a strand of her wildly curling hair behind her ear. She startled, as if she'd been a deer, then took a deep breath and visibly forced herself to remain calm.

"I will see to supper for both you and your queen," he said quietly, pulling his hand away. "What will please her, do you think? Bread and cheese, perhaps? Stew, if it can be found in that pot yonder?"

Persephone blinked. "Queen?"

"The Queen of Faery," he said. "Your mistress."

"Oh," she said, drawing the word out a rather long time, as if she'd just begun to understand something she hadn't before.

"Persephone!"

That voice carried better than it should have. Persephone sighed, then rose.

"Thank you," she said, apparently not having heard his offer. "I'll help her." She looked around her, then shuffled about the kitchen to see what it contained.

Montgomery supposed that looking would be the extent of what she would manage given that she was having to hold his tights up with one hand and keep the other pressed against her head. She hitched, rearranged, then took a bucket and walked toward the back door to no doubt go fetch water.

"I hate my life."

He supposed he understood the sentiment. There had been times during his life when the difficulties had been such that he might have expressed something akin to —

He blinked.

Had she just said what he'd thought she'd said? In the same English that Jennifer, Abigail, and Jake spoke to each other — which, as it happened, Robin, Anne, Nicholas, Amanda, and Miles could converse in with equal ease? The same English tongue he had learned vast amounts of thanks to copious and unknightly amounts of eavesdropping?

The same English his siblings-in-law had brought with them . . .

"My lord?"

"Not enough sleep," Montgomery said promptly, shutting his mouth with a snap. He left Joan standing there with a long wooden spoon in one hand and a knife in the other, then walked out of the kitchens to follow Persephone.

He caught up with her as she was standing at the well, peering into its depths as if she intended to call forth the water with words alone. He pulled up the bucket, filled hers, then dropped it back into the water. Then he looked at her. In the light of day, he realized he had been overtaken by a bout of stupidity. There was an easy answer to all the questions he had about her and that woman inside pretending to be the Faery Queen, he just hadn't wanted to look at it.

Because if he admitted what he knew about times not his own, he would have to face things he would rather not, things that ate at him still, things to do with more than just his siblings-in-law —

He took a deep breath. Nay, it could not be. The queen was a well-dressed noblewoman pretending to be a queen and Persephone was . . . well, he wasn't sure what she was, but she was surely just a wench. A beautiful wench, but a simple wench after all. Not a woman from the Future, nor from Faery, nor from other places he couldn't convince himself existed. What he needed was sleep. It would clear his ears and his head.

But first things first. He carried water back into the kitchens, discussed with Joan what had already been planned for supper, then paused next to Persephone.

"I will take the bread to your . . . your queen," he finished, because he couldn't bring himself to acknowledge any of his other ridiculous thoughts.

The Future?

Impossible.

"That is kind of you." Persephone's accent hadn't improved, but her words were intelligible enough.

A bit like Jake's had been, and Jennifer's as well when they'd first arrived from . . . well, wherever they'd come from.

" 'Tis actually self-preservation," he said without thinking. He managed a brief smile. "My servants have fled at the sight of her. I don't want her terrifying the garrison as well." Though he imagined she would do less terrifying than she would bewitching, he declined to say as much.

Persephone looked very, very pale. He

thought there might have been tears beginning in her eyes, but those could just as easily have been from the onions Joan was cutting. He suppressed the urge to pat her on the back and flee, as Robin would have done. Instead, he nodded his head briskly and fled, because he imagined he would do less damage to her that way.

He had things to do, and those things didn't include wasting time with wenches who weren't where they were supposed to be. He would see the woman masquerading as the Faery Queen fed, hope Joan fed Persephone, then he would get himself the hell out to the lists where there were swords and curses and other things he could understand. Perhaps he would stay there for the rest of the day. Perhaps he would have torches brought and stay there far into the night until he'd rid himself of any more fanciful imaginings about faeries and the Future and things that didn't belong in his nice, orderly, responsible world.

He paused and wrestled with himself for a moment or two. He gave in, only because he allowed himself to, and looked back over his shoulder. Persephone was standing at Joan's worktable, looking off into the distance as if she could see things he couldn't. Her profile was hauntingly familiar, and now he understood why. She had obviously been standing in the middle of a time gate and he'd somehow seen her from his side of it. That she was now in his hall, in his care, within his reach meant nothing but that he was responsible for finding a way to get her home.

Because he was the only one for leagues who would know how.

Chapter 8

Pippa didn't think she was one to overreact, but she was fast coming to a conclusion that was about to make her do so.

Her sister was delusional.

It wasn't just the little *let me show you how well I internalized that method acting class I took in New York from Someone Famous* or the less erudite but equally annoying *let me show you that this tiara I have on my head comes with an attitude so fetch me some carrots and hummus.* It was a full-blown *I'm the Faery Queen so deal with it,* only Cindi had taken it to a level that made Pippa wonder if her sister had had one too many crowns pinching her poor head and they had finally cut off blood flow to important reality centers of her brain. For all she knew, all the parts of her body Cindi had injected and scraped and lifted had finally rebelled and pushed her over the edge.

"Serving girl," Cindi said, sitting in a

hard, uncomfortable chair that had been made less uncomfortable by the addition of a pillow, "fetch me something to drink."

Well, one thing could be said for Cindi, and that was her French was excellent. Maybe the utter craziness she was wallowing in had tapped into previously untapped reservoirs of language aptitude. Either that or the thrill of sitting at the lord's table the day before and having the entire cast of castle characters staring at her as if she'd really been the bloody Fairy Queen belched out from the land of fairies to astonish and delight them had finally shorted out her Botox-drenched brain and given her abilities far beyond the norm.

Maybe it had simply been the deliciousness of being waited on hand and foot. Pippa had supposed she didn't have much choice but to humor her sister so she didn't break into some sort of Broadway tune or throw some sort of tantrum in modern English that would have changed admiration to anger. A vision of villagers with pitchforks was right there for examination, but Pippa pushed it aside because it wasn't helpful.

The question of where they might have been or why she was sharing so fully in her sister's hallucinations was one she hadn't been able to answer. It had been all she could do the day before to keep her sister fed, keep herself from throwing up from the pain of the bump she still had on her own head, and finally get them both to bed in accommodations that were substantially less comfortable than any KOA campground she'd frequented in her youth. She'd hoped for a better day — or a return to reality — when she'd awoken.

No such luck, but she wasn't ready to toss in the towel yet. Her headache had receded a bit, her determination had increased, and she was ready to ditch her sister and do some investigating. The last was an especially attractive alternative to sitting locked in a chilly castle room with a beauty queen who had become far too empowered by her crown.

She poured her sister a glass of wine that Cindi downed with abandon, dribbling a bit down her chin. It went down her cleavage, but Pippa wasn't about to dive after it there with a Kleenex — not that any were to be found in their mutual delusionary state. Cindi didn't seem to mind, so Pippa moved on. She gathered up a few more crystals from the floor out of habit, stashed them in the little pile she'd made inside one corner of the trunk, then took stock of her day.

First on her list was figuring out where the hell she was.

Second was figuring out how she was going to get out of wherever the hell she was.

She looked at her sister, but Cindi was staring into the fire as if it held answers she couldn't get anywhere else. "Cindi?"

Cindi looked at her. "I will rest now. Leave me."

"No problem," Pippa muttered under her breath. She made her escape before she got to indulge in any more servitude. She heard the door lock behind her, so she supposed she could go on her little explore without undue anxiety about the safety of her clueless sibling.

She hitched up her tights, then remembered they weren't hers. She suspected that they — plus the cloak someone had delivered to her door the night before — belonged to Montgomery de Piaget. She had deduced from Joan's rustic English that she and Cindi were sleeping in his chamber. The fact that he was a de Piaget and looked as much like Stephen de Piaget as he did was enough to make what was left of her puzzler sore. He didn't look like a thug, his rather serious and grim expressions aside, but he also didn't look like a reenactment fanatic who was hiding his rather ordinary Marks and Spencer shirts in his very medieval-looking trunk.

That was just the beginning of what bothered her. Why did the castle — which she was certain was Sedgwick — look nothing like it should? Where was Tess and running water? Why was there nothing in the kitchen that would have made a quick snack except a few carrots? She could have gone on all day with the things that alarmed her, but she decided to just deal with the most troubling, which was why the castle looked as if it had been overrun by a medieval French reenactment troupe with a few members who'd escaped from Cambridge's department of Anglo-Saxon literature. It was almost as if she'd stepped back in time —

She put the brakes on that thought before she finished it. She knew all about those impossible time-travel romances Peaches read. She'd even read the start of one in which a poor girl had fallen asleep on a park bench and woken up in medieval Scotland, only to find herself tossed into the castle dungeon while the laird tried to talk himself into burning her as a witch. That was entertaining when read in an overstuffed chair with a cup of hot chocolate nearby, but not so diverting when considered after two days in backwoods England without a single sighting of toilet paper.

It was time to have a few answers.

She pulled Montgomery de Piaget's cloak around her and started down the passageway. She'd already begun day three without the appropriate twenty-first-century hygienic items — in an inside biffy that looked a great deal like the garderobe Tess had showed off with pride and a great amount of descriptive detail — and poached a bit of what Cindi had found too far beneath her to eat. She would have preferred to have had some sort of weapon, but maybe she could nab a kitchen knife later.

The hallway was empty, but the stairwell wasn't. She'd made it only partway down the stairs before she ran into one of the men who'd been sitting at the lord's table the night before. She suspected he was related to the other man sitting with him and perhaps to the woman who'd just about stabbed Cindi with her glares. He had been, she could readily admit, the most unpleasant looking of the lot.

"You and I should speak privately," he said with an ugly smile.

"We should," she agreed, feinted to her left, then dashed past him to the right. She kept on trotting right through the great hall, ignoring her would-be friend's family and continuing on outside before anyone could stop her.

She concentrated on her usual slog through the courtyard mire, managing to keep her shoes on her feet this time. She paused by the barbican gate, then looked over her shoulder.

The place looked worse in the daylight. The courtyard was full of shells of buildings that had been perfectly restored in her sister's castle. She knew she should have turned away, but she couldn't. It simply wasn't possible that within hours, the castle should have gone from perfectly glorious to perfectly horrible, but she couldn't deny what she was seeing. It was truly as if the clock had been turned back.

And not in a good way.

She turned away and walked through the gatehouse. It was just as functional as it had been three days earlier, with the portcullis spikes hanging down through three separate gates. Where things took yet another turn for the worse was the bridge. Her sister's bridge was a solid, well-built thing with no propensity to rising and falling depending on the mood of the guards in the tower. Pippa hurried over it and had to jump off the end thanks to a couple of jokers who laughed as she did so.

Karma was going to give them something nasty for lunch, she was just sure of it.

She walked over to where the gift shop should have been and sat down. She did so even though the shop with its quaint table and chairs was gone and all that was left for her to sit on was a fallen log. At least she had a good view of the reenactment practice going on in the field in front of her.

Men were training with swords. She thought she might have recognized a few of them from the night before, particularly the blond man named Everard. The rest of the guys were a guess, but she felt fairly confident in identifying their leader. He was tall, exceptionally handsome, and definitely knew how to use a sword.

Montgomery de Piaget, apparently.

She would have gaped, but she was tired of gaping. She was just plain tired of everything — and cold, and rather frightened, truth be told, so she just sat there with her knees pressed together to keep them from trembling and her chin resting on her fists. She watched the madness in front of her with a detachment that should have worried her, but somehow she just didn't have the energy for that, either.

That detachment helped her ignore the fact that there was something about the whole scene that just didn't belong in the twenty-first century.

Take, for instance, Montgomery de Piaget. He didn't look like he was simply practicing for a mock fight, but what did she know? She was a costume designer from a sleepy little town on the West Coast where people recycled their theater programs and it rained a lot. She knew actors with collapsible swords and the occasional crazy method guy who carried his weapon around with him at all times to stay in character. Not even those rare birds ever looked as serious about their training as Montgomery did. Either he was somehow the real deal or he was planning on putting on one helluva show. He wasn't flashy, or loud, or obnoxious; he was just in charge. She might have liked that about him if she hadn't been so uninterested in the whole thing.

The morning passed. She was sure the three men who seemed to always be closest to Montgomery would give up, or give in, or beg for mercy, like the man named Everard had. To her surprise, they seemed as driven as their leader was, as if their primary task was to whip the rest of the guys into shape. The other, less skilled men weren't as driven, but still they worked as if their paychecks depended on how well they did their jobs.

Their paychecks, or maybe their lives.

She didn't want to believe it, but she couldn't help but think that somehow, beyond all reason, she had become trapped in a paranormal romance novel where she — as the heroine's servant, of course — had been sent back in time to watch the gorgeous, if slightly gloomy, hero fall in love with the gorgeous, if slightly batty and undeniably buxom, heroine named Cindi. The only thing that kept her from believing that fully was that not even Karma would have been so cruel as to relegate her to watching her sister get the guy. Again.

It certainly wasn't as if she wanted any of the guys stomping around in the dirt in front of her, no sir. If this was some other century than her own and this was the way guys passed their time, that meant the bad guys had swords as well and were likely spending their time running around not saving maidens in distress, but creating them.

Sort of like the guy who had just grabbed her from behind and jerked her to her feet.

She shrieked before she could stop herself, then, blessing Peaches for having dragged her to more than one self-defense class, she put into action the training she'd never been sure she would have the guts to use. She bit the hand that was covering her mouth, then elbowed her captor as hard as she could in the stomach.

"Duck!"

She dropped to her knees partly because her attacker had let her go and her knees buckled, but mostly because Montgomery de Piaget had a knife in his hand and looked like he meant business with it. There was a thud, then the man who had attacked her fell over her, rolled over the log she'd been sitting on, and landed on his back in front of her. She stood up and stared down at him in surprise. She realized she was screaming only after Montgomery took her by both arms and shook her.

"Cease," he said loudly. "You're safe."

She shut her mouth, but that didn't help at all with her teeth chattering. There was a man lying at her feet with a dagger shaft poking out of his chest and Montgomery didn't look like that bothered him. He patted her, as if by so doing he could calm any and all hysterics, then reached down to jerk his knife free of the man's flesh. He cleaned his blade on the man's tunic, then looked over his shoulder at one of his men.

"Rid us of this refuse," he said simply.

Pippa turned away and threw up. It was becoming a very bad habit, that getting so worked up over things. She felt a hand on her back and shrieked again in spite of herself. She realized almost immediately to whom it belonged, though that wasn't terribly useful in ending her shivering. She dragged her sleeve across her mouth, then found herself turned around. Montgomery dabbed at her cheeks with the hem of his sleeve, then patted her again.

"You should go back inside."

Pippa was desperately tempted to have that nervous breakdown Montgomery de Piaget was trying to stave off, but instead settled for a shuddering breath. "He could have been a nice man."

"Nice men do not assault women."

"Maybe he wanted my seat."

Montgomery pursed his lips. "Then he should have asked. As he didn't, he paid the price. Now, lady, I think you would be served to perhaps seek out the fire in the great hall."

Not when the hall wasn't her sister's, with running water, a roaring fire, and lack of rough-looking actors. Pippa took a deep breath, a steadier one this time around. "I'd rather stay, if you don't mind. I think I need fresh air."

He hesitated, then shrugged. "As you will." He stepped back over the log, called to someone to come look after her, then went back to his work.

She sat, she shivered, and she realized she hadn't thanked him for the rescue. She would, when she thought she could get two words out without some new sort of hysterical display. She looked away from the extreme sports going on in front of her and stared at her sister's castle, which was looking not nearly as pristine and magnificent as it should have looked. It was definitely her sister's castle, but then again, it wasn't.

It was as if the castle — and she herself — had been pulled out of her time and plunked down in another reality entirely, one full of people who didn't have any reason to think what they were doing — namely hacking at each other with very sharp swords — was weird. But that sort of thing was something that belonged in a book; it wasn't the sort of thing that happened in real life.

Was it?

She wished she could stop questioning it, but just saying the words was soothing in a way she wouldn't have expected. It wasn't possible. Reality was reality, and space-time-continuum stuff didn't just intrude on it. Or at least didn't in her life.

Then again, it was hard to argue with what was right there in front of her. Cindi might have been delusional, but she was most definitely in full possession of all her faculties. She was sitting on a rough, uncomfortable log, and she was wearing a tunic and tights made of something that had been spun on an old-fashioned loom. The cloak, which was surprisingly warm, had also been made by hand, though the quality of it was very nice. The ring of steel was audible and the sound of men cursing in a version of French she wasn't entirely familiar with didn't seem to be a figment of her imagination. They certainly seemed to be pretty sure they were just going about their daily business.

But how was it possible that she could have been sent to another reality . . . or another time?

She considered all the sparkles she'd seen around her and Cindi, but that could have been the glitter Tess had been throwing over the girls to give them a good send-off. She hadn't really felt anything unusual that night besides an intense desire to push her sister into the lake so she could actually have a conversation with a very nice man. Had there been a stray star she had inadvertently wished on, or a fairy godmother hiding in the bushes she hadn't noticed?

She froze.

She *had* wished. She had wished for a guy who would want a second date and something — Karma, probably — had taken note. Maybe it was that other shoe she'd been waiting for. Maybe that blast of good fortune in having Stephen de Piaget actually like what she was doing was so amazing that she was being thrust back into hell to pay for it ahead of time. Maybe she would pay the price, then get a one-way ticket back to where she was supposed to be, life would become amazing, and her current straits would all be nothing more than a bad dream.

Assuming she could get herself out of them to enjoy that amazing life in the future.

She honestly had no idea how she was going to do that, but she supposed the first thing to do was figure out where she was — or perhaps *when* she was. She couldn't get to an ending point if she didn't have a starting point.

She just hoped her ending point wasn't anywhere near a stake surrounded by a robust pile of kindling.

She took another look at the men in front of her, trying to decide who might best help her without helping her to her doom. Montgomery looked less unkempt than the rest of that rough-looking group, but he more than made up for that by the aura of toughness he exuded. She didn't suppose he would go all medieval on her, but there was no sense in tempting Fate.

She knew where that led.

She searched for a likelier suspect, then realized that there was someone she had overlooked. There was a teenager standing about ten feet away from her, watching her surreptitiously. He might be young enough to still intimidate, though he was wearing a sword as well. Maybe he didn't know how to use it very well yet. She scooted over on her log, then looked at him. When he didn't move, she patted the seat next to her and nodded in a casual way.

He looked momentarily taken aback, then he seemed to consider. He looked at Montgomery, who had glanced over his shoulder, possibly to make sure there were no more murderers hanging around the edge of his training field. When Montgomery nodded slightly and turned back to his exercises, the teenager took a deep breath and sidled over a step or two at a time. It took him a few minutes to get close enough for speech to be possible. Pippa wasn't sure how good her as-yet-to-be-determined-vintage French was, but she thought she could make herself understood. She smiled her most unassuming smile.

"I'm Pippa," she said. "Who are you?"

He frowned. "My lord uncle said your name was Persephone."

"Pippa is my short name. Montgomery is your uncle?"

"Aye." He paused, then smiled very slightly. "I am Phillip. My father is Robin, my uncle's eldest brother. He will be the lord of Artane when my grandfather passes."

Well, that sounded like the usual sort of English nobility structure that might have been found in the twenty-first century. There was no reason to assume Phillip or his family was of a Victorian vintage, or Tudor, or . . . or an earlier time. It didn't mean that at all.

She thought about that for a bit until she realized what was starting to bother her: Phillip kept looking behind her. Surreptitiously, of course, but he was still doing it. She looked behind her as well, but saw nothing unusual.

"What is it?" she asked.

Phillip shifted uncomfortably. "You had wings before, my lady. I don't see them today."

She blinked. "Wings?"

He nodded earnestly. "I think my lord uncle thinks you come from Faery. I know I do," he added, not entirely under his breath.

She would have laughed, but Phillip was obviously quite serious. She supposed that it was understandable, from Montgomery's point of view. After all, both she and Cindi had shown up with wings on. Montgomery wouldn't know that they hadn't been attached unless he'd —

Her thoughts ground to a halt. Unless he'd been the one to pull her dress off her, in which case he'd seen far more than he should have. She supposed the time for blushing furiously was long past, but she did it anyway just on principle.

"Lady, are you unwell?"

"It's warm out," Pippa said, fanning herself. She looked at Phillip, grasping for a good distraction. "Do you believe in fairies?"

"My father and I don't believe in paranormal oddities." He paused, then shrugged. "I will admit there are strange happenings in the north, however, for which I can conceive no reasonable explanation."

"Paranormal oddities?" she echoed.

He flashed her an utterly charming smile. "None that I would admit to having seen." He paused and seemed to chew on his words before he was ready to spit them out. "I must say, my lady, that your mistress could hardly be mistaken for anything but a queen. I don't have much experience with royalty, but I have seen the king. She carries that same air about her."

"The king," Pippa said, as if she expected Phillip to fill in the blank for her. "And that would be king . . ."

"Henry," he supplied, looking at her as if she'd lost her mind.

"Of course," she said quickly, pretending to smack her forehead. "Bump on the head, you know. Lost my recent memories. Henry, the son of . . ."

"John Lackland," Phillip said, looking slightly relieved. "Do you remember him?"

"It's coming back to me," she said. She looked up at him. "Have you met the king?"

"Aye, when in the company of my father, though it was a dodgy business indeed. My father complained quite loudly about the king's habit of spending the people's money on such lavish buildings." He shrugged. "At least we have a bit more power since the barons forced John's hand, though I'm not sure Henry will hold to the bargain."

"You know a lot about politics," she said with frank admiration.

He smiled, a little sheepishly. "My father

is very outspoken and has the sword skill to defend his views. I'm mostly just repeating what he says —" He looked toward the castle and stiffened. "Someone comes."

That someone turned out to be Joan, who had apparently come for her.

"The queen calls for you."

Pippa decided it was in her best interest to answer that call. She accepted Phillip's very gallant aid to get to her feet, thanked him for the pleasant conversation, and walked back to the castle with Joan as if she were doing nothing more interesting than taking a little Saturday afternoon stroll to the Mini Mart for a bag of peanut butter cups and a cup of slushy, cherry-flavored courage. She wasn't going to lose it, especially not in front of witnesses. So she was living with people who thought they were hanging out in the middle of the thirteenth century where there was no plumbing to speak of, no running water, no lovely Aga stove in the kitchen to provide a place to set a cheery tea kettle. No problem. It was a collective hallucination.

And when she could breathe again, she would look for a way to get them all out of it.

But the first thing she was going to do was stop sleeping in the same bed with her sister. No more of that drug-laden breath for her.

Because a collective hallucination made a lot more sense than thinking she had walked through a shower of sparkles and landed herself back in the Middle Ages in the care of a man who patted her to keep her calm, killed guys who tried to abduct her, and loaned her his clothes.

She needed to get home, and fast.

Chapter 9

Montgomery listened to the comforting scratching of his steward's quill across parchment. It made him feel secure to listen to the business of the keep running so smoothly. A pity that was the only thing in his life running smoothly.

"Uncle?"

Montgomery looked up. Phillip was standing in front of the fire, no doubt warming his backside. Montgomery would have smiled if he'd had it in him, for he had done the same thing on many an afternoon, in more than one hall. "Aye, lad?"

"Did you know the Faery Queen's name is Cinderella?"

Montgomery didn't want to admit he did, for that would lead to questions about where he'd heard Persephone calling her that — in less-than-dulcet tones, truth be told — and he wasn't about to admit he'd been sleeping in the passageway outside his bedchamber. Then again, he supposed Phillip knew that already. He supposed the entire keep knew that by now. It wasn't as if he could do anything else, not with Boydin roaming the halls at all hours and Everard leering at both guests whenever possible. But he didn't need to dwell on those two gels and neither did Phillip. He frowned at his squire, then went back to his business.

"And Mistress Pippa," Phillip whispered. "She seems unfamiliar with the politics of the current day, if you don't mind my saying so."

Montgomery didn't want to hear it. Bad enough that he now knew not only Persephone's full name but a pet name for her. Worse still that he knew when she entered the chamber and when she left it. He had no desire to hear anything about what she might and might not know about the current day.

For obvious reasons.

He shot Phillip a look, the same sort of look Robin was wont to use when he didn't particularly care to continue a certain conversation. He most certainly didn't want to carry on that conversation where his steward could hear it.

Besides, it wasn't unusual for a body not to be familiar with the politics of the day.

His family enjoyed a rousing discussion about the foibles of the king and his court, but there were others he knew who would rather have faced an army of irritated Scots than discuss the like.

Phillip fell silent. Montgomery went back to his study of what was before him and tried to recapture the happy feelings he had at looking at what stood to be a decent fall's harvest if Gunnild didn't raze the larder with what he'd discovered were her endless plans for feasts involving large numbers of important guests.

"Uncle?"

Montgomery sighed before he could stop himself, then looked up. "Aye, Phillip?"

Phillip seemed to be chewing mightily on his words. Montgomery could only imagine why. In fact, he could imagine quite a few things, but given that they were things he didn't care to examine too closely, he knew he would be better off to ignore them as long as possible.

He didn't imagine that happy bit of avoidance would last very long.

"But Mistress Pippa," Phillip said in a loud whisper. "Her wings . . . well, her wings aren't always on her. Have you noticed?"

"Nay, I had not," Montgomery lied

shortly. He had most certainly noticed that, as well as several other things including her very lovely blue eyes, the fairness of her face, and her glorious dark hair that fell down her back in a cascade of curls — especially since that she had managed to wash it the day before and it was now free of cesspit leavings.

But more particularly, he'd noticed her hands, long-fingered and delicate. He realized that even after so short an acquaintance, he could tell her mood by her hands. They were most relaxed when working in the kitchen. They tended to clench when she was talking to her, er, queen.

Unfortunately, they seemed to be clenched during those very brief moments when she'd talked to him, as well.

Then again, it wasn't as if he'd exercised any of his copious number of knightly virtues on her. For the most part, he had avoided speaking to her — though he supposed he had made up for that by the amount of looking at her he'd done. He had treated her with a stiff formality that would have appalled his grandmother and shocked his mother.

Though, who could blame him? If he had speech with her, or considered the strangeness of her accent, or gave thought to the fact that no rational man could, after a certain point in his life, have given credence to the myth of faeries, or ghosts, or travelers from a time not his own —

Nay, 'twas best he ignore her completely.

"Queen Cinderella abuses her mightily."

Even Fitzpiers looked up at that. Montgomery laughed, though it sounded a bit forced to his ears.

"Queen Cinderella? Phillip, you have been listening to too many tales spun by your grandmother."

"The lady Gwennelyn doesn't consider them idle fancies," Phillip pointed out.

"My mother, whom I love dearly, has a very tender heart and a great love of small children with large ears," Montgomery said, shooting Phillip a look of warning he couldn't have missed. "But her tales are meant for children, Phillip, not grown men. They *are* nothing more than idle fancies."

Phillip lowered his eyes immediately and looked appropriately miserable. Montgomery sighed. One of his greatest failings, something Robin pointed out to him as often as possible, was that he had inherited more than his fair share of his mother's tender heart. He waited until his steward had gone back to his labors before he rose and went to stand next to his squire.

He could readily admit that he had loved Phillip from the very moment he'd first clapped eyes on him not half an hour from his mother's womb and wailing like a banshee. He had spent untold hours playing with the lad, laughing at his antics, and — it had to be admitted — recounting innumerable tales from his own store of idle fancies for the boy's amusement. If Phillip believed in things he couldn't see, Montgomery knew most of the blame for that could be laid at his feet.

"Let's go see if anything's on the fire in the kitchen," he said quietly, ruffling his squire's hair. "We'll save your Mistress Pippa from the terrible demands of her queen, if we can."

Phillip shot him a grateful smile, but sobered immediately. "As you will, my lord."

Montgomery paused. "Discretion, Phillip, is a knightly virtue that you should strive to develop. I promise it will serve you in good stead the whole of your life."

Phillip looked at him from clear, innocent gray eyes. "Has it served you, my lord uncle?"

"In more situations than you might expect, my lad." He started toward the door. "Let's be away."

Phillip was silent only until he had shut

the door behind him. Montgomery had expected nothing less and braced himself for a new onslaught of questions he wasn't particularly going to want to answer.

"Is Cinderella the Queen of Faery, Uncle?" he asked very quietly.

Montgomery looked about him, but saw no one. He dragged his hand through his hair, then sighed deeply. "What do you think, lad?"

"I have never seen a gown so fine," Phillip said reverently, "nor a lady wearing wings, though she seems to have taken them off and left them in your chamber. She drops little bits of stardust from her wand, though, and from her gown. Mistress Pippa is continually going along behind her, gathering those things up. I was thinking that perhaps those were bits of faery magic and that if the queen lost them all, she wouldn't be able to return home." He shifted uncomfortably. " 'Tis possible that I think too much."

"A fault we share, my lad," Montgomery conceded.

"Should we not then help Mistress Cinderella return home to her realm?" Phillip asked. "Is that not something our knightly duty demands?"

Montgomery nodded, because he could

say nothing else. Aye, he had a duty to help Persephone and her mistress — whoever she might be in truth — return home. The real question was, where was that home?

Or, rather, when?

He walked with Phillip across the great hall over to the passageway that led to the kitchens. He imagined Persephone would be there, only because it was nearing noon and Cinderella would have wanted something to eat. He had come to realize over the past several days of her habitation in his keep that while she might not have eaten very much at a sitting, she ate often and she was generally displeased with what her servant brought her.

'Twas little wonder Persephone clenched her hands so often.

He paused at the entrance to the kitchen, because he could go no farther. He leaned against the entrance and simply watched something that wouldn't have made an impression on him at any other time, but now was easily one of the most peaceful, lovely sights he'd seen in months.

Persephone and Joan were standing across the worktable from each other, chopping vegetables. Joan was talking nonstop, which now that she was free of Cook's ready spoon seemed to be her habit. Persephone — nay,

Pippa he would call her for that seemed to suit her at the moment — Pippa was listening, smiling just a bit. For some reason, seeing her standing there in his kitchen caught him so tightly around the heart, he winced. He almost started forward toward her, just as he'd attempted to do over ten years earlier.

She looked at him in surprise, and that broke the spell. Montgomery stepped backward so quickly, he knocked Phillip over. He turned to give his squire a hand up only to see Fitzpiers trotting down the passageway toward him.

"You have a guest, my lord," the steward said with a smile. "Or, rather, a gift."

"A gift?" Montgomery asked, happy to latch on to any sort of distraction that had nothing to do with who he'd recently been gaping at.

"From your brother-in-law, the lord of Raventhorpe. He sends it with his most sincere compliments."

"I'll follow immediately," Montgomery said without hesitation.

And he did. He didn't even turn about to nod to Pippa. He simply caught his squire by the arm and strode after his steward toward something he hoped wouldn't be as disturbing as what he'd just left.

"Phillip," he said as they walked swiftly back to the hall.

"Aye, my lord?"

He started to tell his nephew that indulging in fanciful imaginings in one's youth led to complete madness in one's majority, but he decided that such a declaration would only lead to more questions he couldn't answer.

Or questions that he didn't want to answer, rather.

"Nothing," Montgomery said. "Nothing at all."

"As you say, my lord," Phillip said uneasily.

Montgomery declined any further comment on the matter and merely walked into his great hall and across it without hesitation. Standing just inside the hall door was a man he recognized, a man he would have kissed heartily on both cheeks if he had dared. He embraced him just the same, slapped him on the back a time or two, then pulled away.

"Petter," he said gratefully.

Petter of Jedburgh, a master stonemason who had over the years become nothing less than part of the family, laughed. "My lord Sedgwick, I can see you have need of my services, if you don't mind my saying so."

"How many men did you bring with you?"

"Half a dozen."

Montgomery couldn't help but smile. "What am I going to owe various brothers and sundry for stealing your services for a time? And you, for being willing to travel so far?"

"My exorbitant fee, which judging by the condition of your walls, you'll pay without hesitation," Petter said with a smile. "As for what you'll owe your brothers, I can't answer that, but they were well aware of your need." He shrugged. "In truth, I'll simply be happy for someone with whom I can natter on in the native tongue."

Montgomery had learned Gaelic during a miserable year of squiring for a certain Lord Pevensy, then perfected it with Petter over the course of watching the man repair his brother Nicholas's roof and his brother-in-law Jackson's entire hall.

"I'll gladly oblige you," Montgomery said. "When can you start?"

"After I've had something to eat," Petter said, "if you don't mind. I'll get my men settled and start looking for stone. I can't imagine what was here before has gone far."

"I doubt it has," Montgomery agreed.

Petter studied him assessingly for a moment or two. "I heard in the village that you have the Faery Queen in your bed."

Montgomery spluttered in spite of himself. *"What?"*

"The Faery Queen," Petter repeated. "In your bed."

"Ridiculous," Montgomery said promptly. "She was in my hall, not my bed." And that was true. Now and then.

Petter began to grin. "I also heard that all your servants fled."

"How long were you with your ear to the local ale keg?" Montgomery asked sourly.

"Long enough," Petter laughed. "I brought you a trio of kitchen lads, courtesy of your grandmother, the lovely lady Joanna of Segrave. Will that help?"

Montgomery closed his eyes briefly. "The only way in which you could improve my life at present is to have brought me a decent garrison, but I daren't hope for that."

"My lads can wield a sword in a tight spot, but they're not men-at-arms."

"I don't know that tight spots aren't in our future," Montgomery said seriously, "but I'll pray they don't come until I have loyal men of my own. Let me see you fed and settled, then you can examine my ruins and see what's possible."

"And you'll introduce me to your guest?"

"I value your friendship too much to want

to," Montgomery said with a snort, "but if you insist, I'll attempt it. You can chat her up whilst I'm rifling through my coffers to see if I can afford you."

Petter glanced at the walls, then whistled in a particularly expensive-sounding way.

Montgomery didn't want to think about the cost. His gold wouldn't do him any good if it had been stolen by thieves who'd crawled through holes in his walls, so 'twas best he see to his defenses first of all. He walked with Petter back to the kitchens, grateful beyond measure for brothers who saw his need and filled it without his having to ask. Truly he had been blessed to have such a family.

He wondered what sort of family Pippa had.

He watched Petter introduce Segrave's lads to Joan and instruct them to follow her every order with exactness or they would answer to him. They seemed properly intimidated in a good-natured sort of way, and Joan looked very pleased at the possibility of aid. Petter then turned to look at the entrance to the kitchens. His mouth fell open, which led Montgomery to believe someone interesting was there. There was no screeching involved, so it couldn't have been Cinderella. He was unsurprised to hear Pippa's voice from directly behind him.

"Excuse me, my lord."

Montgomery stepped out of her way to find her carrying a wooden tray piled high with useful things. He lifted an eyebrow. "Not suitable?"

She only sighed.

He picked up a spoon and tasted what looked to be eggs hesitantly, on the off chance Cinderella had it aright. He was somewhat surprised to find they were delicious. He looked at Pippa.

"May I finish?"

She shoved the tray into his hands. "Help yourself."

He set the tray down on the table, pulled up a stool, and ate what had been a perfectly delightful supper. The bread was hard as a brick, but he'd eaten worse, so he made do. He also shot Petter a warning look when the man introduced himself to Pippa with an overabundance of charm. Petter only laughed and tucked into supper happily with his lads. Joan was currently instructing her newly acquired crew to do the things she had been doing on her own for the past two days.

Or, rather, with Pippa's help, no doubt. Montgomery had assumed she had been upstairs, waiting on Cinderella, but given how quickly Cinderella had rejected her supper, he suspected Pippa had spent more time below than he'd realized, trying to find something Cinderella would eat.

He was half tempted to take over that task for her and let her rest, but that would have meant going upstairs and having to look at beauty he found unnatural in its perfection. He wasn't above admiring a handsome woman. Indeed, he had admired more than his fair share. But Cinderella . . . well, she was something else entirely. He could admit it freely.

She terrified him.

Pippa was looking over the selection of vegetables and fruits available. Given that the kitchen was in the throes of its usual chaos, he took that opportunity to casually walk over and stand next to Pippa. She was remarkably tall, based on his experience, and slender, based on what he was accustomed to. She was still wearing his clothes, which he supposed he would have to remedy sooner rather than later, though he couldn't deny that there was something quite charming about seeing her in a tunic that was too large and knowing it was his —

He rubbed his face with one hand. He most certainly couldn't have her, he wasn't at all sure he wanted her, and even if either of those things had been remedied, he wasn't at all sure she would want anything of a serious and romantic nature with him.

Besides, he knew nothing of her. She could have been full of vile humors and unreasonable expectations. She might have been jealous, conniving, endlessly unhappy with what he was able to provide for her.

She held up a knife.

He nodded to himself. Already she was showing her foul humors. For all he knew, she would take that knife and plunge it into his chest. Well, she might have, if there hadn't been a carrot skewered onto the end of it.

"Tasty," she remarked.

He reached out and gingerly took it, not taking his eyes off her. He tasted, because she had offered it to him. "Aye."

She continued to chop. He didn't want to watch her, but he couldn't help himself. He had a score of questions he wanted to ask her, beginning and ending with who she was, where she came from, and when she was born, but he supposed it wasn't the proper time or place to be asking those sorts of questions.

So, because he could think of nothing else to do, he drew a knife from his boot and took a few carrots to chop for himself. It was, he had to admit, a rather satisfying work. It wasn't the first time he'd done the like. He had certainly fed himself more than once, but he had never styled himself as a kitchen lad to impress a woman as he was doing presently.

Daft. He was daft, and Robin would have made himself ill laughing over it.

"Do you have siblings?" he asked, because he had to know something about her.

"Sisters," she said, not looking up. "Five of them."

"What are their names?"

"Moonbeam, Cinderella, Peaches, Tess, me, and then Valerie."

The names weren't the sort he was accustomed to, but then again, he wasn't from . . . well, he wasn't from where she was from.

"Interesting names," he managed.

"Interesting sisters."

He reached for a turnip, then paused. "Cinderella?"

She looked up at him. "Aye."

He considered for a moment or two, then lifted his knife and pointed upstairs with it.

She nodded.

"But she is a queen," he said carefully.

"Or so she seems."

Montgomery lifted an eyebrow, but said

nothing. Very well, so he'd known that Cinderella couldn't possibly be the Faery Queen. He'd suspected the very moment he'd clapped eyes on the pair of them that there was more to them than sparkles and faery dust. That particular tingle in the air had been suspiciously familiar, but what had he known of it in truth? Pippa was like something from a dream . . .

"Why don't you go sit," he said suddenly. "I'll chop."

She looked up at him in surprise. "Why?"

"Because your . . . queen . . . is demanding."

"Only when I have to listen to her."

He managed a faint smile, then turned back to his chopping. He handed her a few things, then watched her arrange them onto another wooden trencher.

"I'll try this," she said.

"And I'll eat it when you come back."

She smiled, a more sincere one that time. "At least it'll be good for you. Thank you, my lord."

"Montgomery."

She only looked at him briefly, nodded, then took the trencher and left the kitchen.

Montgomery watched her go, then looked around the kitchen. His grandmother's lads were busy, Petter's men were eating, and

Joan was concentrating on her labors. Petter and Phillip, however, were watching him. Phillip quickly looked elsewhere, but Petter only lifted his eyebrows briefly before he smiled and turned back to his supper.

Montgomery scowled, because that made him feel comfortable. He had been polite, nothing more. He scowled at Petter again, then chopped himself a pair of carrots, shoved his knife in his boot, and left the kitchen. He didn't run; he merely walked quickly and with purpose. After all, he had things to do.

But while he was doing those things, he suspected he might have to take a moment or two for thought about how he was going to get Persephone and Cinderella back to their home in the Future.

He could scarce believe he was facing the same thing others in his family had, but perhaps there were more paranormal oddities in England than anyone in that family wanted to admit. He'd just never imagined such things would become a part of his life.

Along with, the saints pity him, a woman he couldn't have and couldn't stop thinking about.

Chapter 10

Pippa stood in the shadows in Montgomery de Piaget's bedroom and plotted. She wasn't a particularly good plotter, but she had the feeling she might just give Shakespeare a run for his money with what she was currently cooking up.

She had been thinking about it for most of the night, a process made easier by the fact that her sister's thunderous enjoyment of her own slumber had kept Pippa awake. The truth had been staring her in the face for the entire afternoon the day before, a truth she had been turning over and over in her head all night long.

She was currently living in medieval England.

It felt a little ridiculous to say it out loud, so she'd kept it to herself and just indulged in lots of thinking about it. And while she'd thought about it, she'd mulled over the inescapable conclusion that she couldn't remain in the past even if she'd wanted to — which she most certainly didn't. Cindi had hearts to break, and she had Manhattan fashion editors to woo. Time was a-wastin' and she couldn't waste any more of it.

She had come to the conclusion, as she'd stood at the window, swathed in Montgomery's cloak, that there had to be something unusual at the end of the bridge. She was certainly no expert, but she couldn't deny there had been some sort of portal that had led from her century to the one she was currently loitering in. All she had to do was get herself and her sister down there, walk back through the way she'd come, and bingo, she would be back at Tess's castle where she would first raid the fridge, then take a shower, then go straight to bed and sleep for days. She had even started to fantasize about a bed that didn't crunch when she rolled over in the night. It was pathetic, really.

"Servant," Cindi said, waving her hand languidly. "Fetch me something to eat."

Pippa counted to ten very slowly, then walked over to stand in front of her sister. She needed Cindi's cooperation, so there was no point in antagonizing her unnecessarily.

"My queen," she said, wondering not for the first time why *she* hadn't been named Cinderella and Cindi hadn't been given a more evil-stepsister-ish sort of name. Given that she was the one continually in servant mode, that would have been appropriate. "Queen Cinderella," she said, trying again, "I have tidings."

Cindi seemed to have problems focusing on her, but that could have been because her eyes were crossed. "Give them to me immediately."

"Your people have been calling for you, my queen," Pippa said, trying not to sound as desperate as she felt. If Cindi didn't go along with her plan, she was doomed.

Cindi frowned. "What people?"

"*Your* people, Your Majesty. The fairies that wait for you outside the gates. We must go home to them."

"Don't wanna," Cindi said with a formidable pout. "I like it here, because I am queen and it's good to be queen. Plus I like having a servant." Her pout turned into a dark frown. "You look more like a servant today and less like a boy. That's better."

Pippa had put on her marginally clean underclothes and dress only because she was convinced she would be taking them off again very soon within arm's reach of

Tess's trash can.

"I wish the bathroom here had a mirror, though," Cindi said, sounding slightly displeased.

And a flush toilet, a sink with running water, and a shower with an unlimited amount of hot water flowing through it, Pippa finished silently. She would have been happier with better bathroom facilities, too, but at least Cindi had gotten to just hang out upstairs and avoid the drudgery in the kitchen. She didn't have a lot of extra sympathy for her sister.

"I have made the sacrifice, though," Cindi said, reaching over her shoulder to pat herself on the back, "because I am the Fairy Queen and the queen must sacrifice for her people."

"That's right," Pippa agreed. "And since you are so giving, you of course realize that you have to make the sacrifice to go back across the drawbridge and go through the gate. If you don't, all the fairies will perish from the lack of your marvelous self to worship."

Cindi considered. "My people will die?"

"Absolutely."

She considered a bit longer. "And when we leave this medieval-ish wasteland of lousy food, I'll get to return to my court?"

"Definitely. The food will be great and you'll have people waiting on you hand and foot." And she would, never mind that they would be dressed in white and probably carrying a straightjacket. Cindi would have all kinds of attention. In fact, Pippa wasn't sure her sister wouldn't find fame and fortune by winding up in some sort of medical journal somewhere.

Cindi rose abruptly. "I'll come."

"Not yet. We have to wait for twilight. It's the magical hour of the day."

"I knew that," Cindi said, sitting down with a plop. "Fetch me a snack."

"What would you like?"

"Something salty."

"No problem. I'll go as soon as I've polished your wings."

She gathered up two sets of wings, made sure there was nothing left of their stay in Montgomery's bedroom, then dawdled a bit longer until her sister was snoring happily in her chair. It was odd that Cindi slept so much, but Pippa suspected she didn't really want the answer to why that was.

She went back to her vigil at the window and waited for the afternoon to wane.

She managed to get Cindi out of the castle with only a minimum of fuss during the changing of the guard. Montgomery was talking to someone she assumed was a stonemason and didn't seem to notice her. She left him to it, waved briefly to Phillip, then kept on going before Cindi changed her mind and kicked up a fuss. Even the gate guards seemed to somehow agree that she was on an important mission because they didn't mess with her or try to dump her into what served as a moat.

She thought Karma just might be on her side for a change.

She hustled Cindi across the bridge and waited for that magical hour of twilight. She didn't see anything special, but that wasn't discouraging. She would just give the portal no choice. She was ready to go home; Karma would just have to sit up and take note of it.

Dusk fell, twilight glimmered, but no door opened. She had to use harsh language on her sister a time or two to get her to stay where she was, but on the whole Cindi was remarkably cooperative.

And then Pippa saw a glimmer.

Of bare steel.

Before she realized whom that knife belonged to, Cindi had jerked away from her. She looked at Montgomery, batted her eyes — visible even in the semi-dark — then spun around and looked at Pippa with a serious lack of sisterly affection.

"I see what you're doing here."

"What?" Pippa asked, looking surreptitiously behind her sister for the damned gate that should have been there.

"You," she said in English, lifting her arm and pointing accusingly, "are trying to keep me away from this delicious studmuffin."

Pippa shook her head quickly. "I'm not," she said in French, hoping Montgomery wouldn't mistake her for a modern-English-speaking witch and toss her in the moat to see if she would float. "I'm trying to get you back to your people, my queen —"

Pippa watched events proceed as if in slow motion. Cindi caught her foot on something in front of her and tripped, which sent her stumbling forward, which sent Pippa stumbling backward into a place she hadn't wanted to go.

She resurfaced, choking and spitting out liquid she knew from experience wasn't all water.

Cindi seemed not to notice. "Come with me, my beautiful prince, and we'll dance."

"After I rescue your handmaid," Montgomery said firmly. "If you'll excuse me, er, Your Majesty, 'tis my knightly — er, my *princely* duty, of course, to see to that sort of thing."

"Oh, did something happen to my servant?"

Pippa wasn't sure what Montgomery's reaction to that had been and she wasn't sure she cared. She took hold of Montgomery's hand and was happy he was strong enough to pull her out of the muck and to her feet. He released her hand without hesitation, which she couldn't blame him for in the slightest. She could, however, blame her sister for immediately monopolizing the conversation, yet again.

"There are many who have competed for my hand," she announced, "but I've decided I like *you* best."

"Ah," Montgomery began.

"There will be a contest," Cindi announced. "Between you . . . and you!"

Pippa could have sworn Montgomery flinched.

"A *beauty* pageant," Cindi continued, taking Montgomery by the arm. "I'll plan it all. Come along, my prince, and I'll describe your duties."

Pippa imagined she would. She took a deep breath, regretted it, then trudged along behind them, squelching in her shoes and grossing herself out with her smell. She didn't throw up, but that was from sheer willpower alone.

Cindi looked back at her. "Don't you dare come anywhere near my bedroom. I want to be alone."

Pippa wanted her to be alone, so she was happy to comply. Maybe she would just pull up a patch of floor near the fire in the kitchen until she was the one covered in soot and cinders. It would inspire her to get back to real life as soon as possible. She had things to do, bestselling clothing lines to create, *Vogue* pages to grace. Playing a part in a fairy tale — especially a fairy tale in which she wasn't the one wearing the tiara — was just not for her any longer.

No, the sooner she got herself and her sister back to the future, the better. Her timing had just been off that evening. She was momentarily tempted to be completely devastated, but she staved off that urge. She knew things happened in their own good time. Obviously, that gate from Montgomery's century to hers had a mind — and a timetable — of its own. She would just wait it out.

She watched Cindi pause in front of the great hall and hold out her hand regally. Montgomery sighed, then offered her his arm and escorted her into the great hall. Pippa considered, then decided that perhaps a trip around the side of the hall to the kitchen would be better for everyone involved. She was tempted to take a dive into the horse trough, but that might have made the horses turn up their noses. She would just have to settle for some water from the well.

She made her way to the well, finding that everyone she met gave her a wide berth. She would have happily avoided herself, but she couldn't. She slopped her way over to the well and considered. One inadvertent trip into the sewer was one thing, two was another thing entirely. It was almost as if Cindi had tripped on purpose and, well, *pushed* her in.

To get rid of her.

She stood there for quite some time, considering the ramifications of that. She'd always thought Cindi was slightly ditzy, but she never would have credited her with maliciousness. But now? Now she could credit her sister with quite a few things, up to and including an intense bout of craziness. And the more she thought about it, the more she decided that the trips into Montgomery's moat — both of them — had been intentional.

It was an unpleasant conclusion to come to.

She started to reach for the crank to the well only to find a hand in her way. She jumped a little in surprise, then realized it was only Montgomery standing next to her.

Only Montgomery. She shook her head. She was looking at a man who was a lord's son and a lord in his own right, a *medieval* lord who was good at all sorts of things, beginning and ending with waving his sword around as if he knew what to do with it, and she was treating him like he was just another stagehand down at the theater.

She supposed that sword should have been her first clue that he was more than that. His sword, or his knives stuck down his boots. Or the way he was always referred to as *my lord* whenever anyone approached him. Or that she'd seen the tiniest of smiles the day before when he'd been standing next to her in the kitchen, chopping vegetables with a knife she was almost positive wasn't sterile. It had been for Cindi's lunch, though, so she hadn't cared.

"I'm having Joan prepare a bath for you."

She dragged herself back to the present. She would have pushed her hair out of her eyes, but she just couldn't bear to touch any part of herself.

"Thank you," she managed, "but I don't think I want to get in the tub with myself.

I'll just rinse off here."

"The well water is freezing," he said. "You'll catch your death."

"I'm willing to chance it."

He sighed. "I don't like it, but I can't say I don't agree with you." He pulled up a bucketful of water. "Hold your breath."

She did, but she gasped just the same. The water was bitterly cold, but she was so desperate to get most of the disgusting stuff off herself before she got into a tub with herself that she didn't care. The bucket had made a good start on her hair, but she suspected there might still be things down the front of her gown, so she pulled the wet fabric away from her skin as best she could.

"Again, please."

He obliged her, then dumped a third bucket over her head to finish getting the gunk out of her hair. She couldn't say that the soap she knew she had to look forward to would be much better than straight water, but when desperate in Rome . . .

"I'll clear the kitchen." He stepped back a pace. "Perhaps if you bathe by the fire, you won't be so chilled."

Pippa pushed her hair out of her eyes and looked at him by the light of a faint moon. "Thank you. That's very kind."

" 'Tis nothing," he said dismissively, then

his expression lightened just the smallest bit. " 'Tis unfortunate that you've become so acquainted with my poor excuse for a moat."

"Accidents happen."

"Hmmm," was all he said, though it wasn't a terribly convincing *hmmm.*

Pippa couldn't have agreed more. She followed him through the back door of the kitchen. A wooden tub that looked a bit like half a wine barrel sat near the roaring fire, already halfway full of water.

Montgomery shooed everyone from the kitchen, then looked at her briefly. "I'll stand guard."

"Thank you, my lord."

"Montgomery."

"Thanks to him, too."

He smiled faintly, then turned and walked up the passageway toward the great hall. Pippa looked at Joan, who was putting another bucket of water to heat over the fire.

"I appreciate this," she said. "I don't think I can stand myself much longer his way."

Joan looked at her briefly. "Don't let her push you again."

Or at least that's what Pippa thought she said. Anglo-Saxonish English wasn't exactly the Cockney stuff she'd been used to hearing on stage, nor was it the crisp vowels of the Shakespearean actors she'd listened to.

"I'm not sure she pushed me this time," Pippa said slowly. Or at least that's what she hoped she'd said. Her conversations with Joan had been pretty basic, but she'd had a lot of them. She could converse fairly decently about food.

Joan shot her a skeptical look, then gestured toward the tub. "The lord has brought you his clothes to use again."

"He's very kind," Pippa managed.

Joan shrugged. "A hard man, it appears, but fair enough. But I only know what I've heard of him from his cousins."

"Cousins?"

"The lords Boydin and Martin, the lady Ada, and their mother, the lady Gunnild. I imagine she wasn't happy to learn her sons wouldn't inherit what she'd thought they would after Lord Denys's death."

Pippa only nodded, first because she wasn't entirely sure she was translating that all correctly, and second because she wasn't sure she wanted to have anything to do with servants' gossip.

She shook her head. Servants' gossip. Who would have thought she would have cared anything about that? Or even been in a place where it mattered?

Life was, as she'd decided before, very weird.

She looked behind her, saw no one there, then decided there was no point in worrying about it. If the choice was between being seen in her altogether and having to endure her smell, she would chose the first without hesitation. She stripped, hunkered down in the tub and did the best she could. Disgust was a powerful motivator and she was very disgusted.

She was also very happy for the buckets of warm water Joan dumped over her head. She wasn't quite sure she'd gotten all the soap out of her hair, but she supposed that didn't matter because she was equally sure she was going to find a way to get back to where she came from before too long and she would use that really lovely lavender shampoo Tess kept in the guest bathrooms.

She washed out her dress and her underthings, then considered the last. She wasn't about to give up her knickers, but she supposed she could claim those were some sort of French invention if pressed. But being stuck in the past and possessing a bra with modern hooks . . . well, that might not go so well for her. She looked at the fire, then tossed her bra into the roaring middle of it. It didn't take long before the cloth was consumed. The hooks wouldn't melt, but hopefully no one would dig around in the ashes for them before she was long gone back to the future.

Pippa put on Montgomery's clothes again, feeling very grateful for them. It could have been a lot worse. She combed her hair with her fingers, then sopped up what she could of the moisture with the cloth she'd used on herself. By that time, she was fairly cold and beginning to wonder where she was going to sleep since Cindi had banned her from the bedroom. Maybe she would manage a night in the great hall without having more company than she cared for. She gathered up her clothes, thanked Joan for her aid, then turned and walked slowly up the passageway to the great hall.

She almost ran into Montgomery before she saw him there, leaning his shoulder against the arch with his back to her. She stepped to one side and looked up at him.

She really wished she didn't have to catch her breath every time she saw him. He was just too good-looking for her peace of mind. She was fairly tall herself, but he had to have been pushing three or four inches over six feet with broad shoulders and muscles she could see from where she stood. It was completely ridiculous, but he made her feel fragile. Too bad he never seemed very happy to see her.

Of course, it wasn't as if she wanted him to be happy to see her. She was apparently hundreds of years out of her time, living in a point in history that she most certainly didn't want to have any more to do with than necessary. The sooner she left the whole thing behind, and that included the man in front of her, the happier she would be.

"Persephone?"

She blinked at the use of her full name. "Yes, my lord?"

"Montgomery," he said.

"Yes, my lord Montgomery?"

He frowned, as if he wasn't quite sure what to make of her. She understood completely.

"Let us check on your . . . charge," he finished. He paused. "Then again, perhaps I should just send Phillip."

"You might want to, unless you want Cinderella remembering she thinks you're a prince."

He lifted one eyebrow briefly. "I'll send Phillip. Perhaps you would care to sit by the fire in my solar and dry your hair."

She suffered a small twinge of something, responsibility perhaps, but turned her back figuratively on that soon enough. Cindi wanted Montgomery's room all to herself. It was her fault if she didn't have her servant to stoke up her fire and fetch supper for her. Besides, it would be rude enough not to accept Montgomery's hospitality. No sense in not leaving him with a good impression of fairies.

"Thank you," she said, realizing he was still waiting for her answer. "That would be lovely."

He nodded toward his solar. "After you, my lady."

She refused to blush at the term. He was, she imagined, well within his right to call her whatever he wanted. She squelched her way out into the great hall in her clean but definitely not-dry shoes, waited while he talked to a man he called Ranulf, then continued on with him to his solar. Ranulf disappeared upstairs, so she supposed her sister would be safe enough. Given her newfound suspicions about her, she almost wasn't sure she cared.

Or she would have been sure of it if she hadn't suffered from a deplorable sense of responsibility. She supposed she could blame Peaches and Tess for that. She certainly hadn't learned it from Cindi.

"Will she be safe?" she asked quietly as

Montgomery opened the door.

He looked at her in surprise. "Why wouldn't she be?"

She hesitated, then decided to cast caution to the wind. "That man, Boydin. He isn't . . . nice."

The change in his expression was slightly unsettling. "Has he hurt you?"

"No," Pippa said quickly. "I just don't trust him."

He blew out his breath, then smiled very briefly at her. "I've no love for my cousins, but you needn't worry for your sister's safety. Ranulf will watch over her well. And you will be equally safe with me watching over you."

She imagined she would be. She would have thanked him, but she was suddenly too busy being overwhelmed by where he'd led her to. In Tess's day, the solar was the castle's office. Over there against the wall where a table sat was where Tess's desk was, a desk Pippa had tossed her portfolio on that fateful afternoon before she'd gone back upstairs to dress for the birthday party. Pippa tried not to wonder if her sister was sitting in the same room over seven hundred years in the future, wondering where she was.

"Persephone?"

She looked up at Montgomery. "Nothing."

He frowned thoughtfully, pulled up two chairs in front of the fire, then gestured for Pippa to take one. Pippa sat down gratefully, realizing only then that she'd been on her feet almost all day long. She wasn't unused to physical labor — sewing was harder on the back than it looked — but the past few days had been absolutely draining. Maybe time travel was harder on a person than she'd imagined it might be.

And Montgomery de Piaget was more distracting than any man had a right to be.

She watched him as he built up the fire, then continued to watch as he sat down and stared into that fire, apparently looking for answers to deep thoughts he couldn't seem to find in the cups of ale he had also poured for them both. She wondered where he got his soap because he looked remarkably fresh scrubbed, but perhaps there were tricks of the trade she hadn't learned yet.

She wondered quite a few things about him, actually, things she wasn't sure she dared ask him on the off chance he would think her completely bonkers and decide his solar fire just wasn't hot enough to get her out of his hair and maybe a bonfire in his courtyard would do the trick.

She realized he was watching her and she wondered how many of her thoughts had shown on her face. She smiled slightly.

"Just thinking."

"Shall I guess?"

She shook her head. "I'm not sure you would want to, but I'll tell you just the same. I was just wondering about you."

He shifted a bit, as if the topic made him uncomfortable. "I'm not a very interesting subject, but I'll answer your questions, if you'll answer mine." He tilted his head to look at her. "Is that not a fair bargain?"

"That depends on how far away from your hands your sword is."

He pointed to the sword propped up in the corner. "You're closer to it than I am."

"I don't think I could use it even if I had to."

"You might be surprised." He reached down and pulled both of his knives free of his boots. They were sheathed in worn leather and the handles were equally well loved. He held them out. "Will holding these make you feel safer?"

She wasn't sure it would, but she wasn't going to argue the point. She also wasn't about to discuss the fact that he seemed to be speaking slowly and carefully, as if he was afraid she might not understand him.

She couldn't imagine he had any inkling of where — or *when* — she was from. Maybe he thought she was a servant and not very bright. It wasn't flattering, but she couldn't blame him. Why would he think differently? She put his knives on her lap, then attempted a smile.

"You start," she said. "Where did you grow up?"

He looked at his hands for a moment or two, then up at her. "In the north. My father's keep is Artane. Do you know it?"

Pippa knew she wasn't good at masking her reactions. She had played innumerable forbidden card games with her sisters in Aunt Edna's attic and never won a single one. Moonbeam had always had the best poker face, followed by Tess and Peaches. She, however, had never been able to hide either her glee or her disappointment.

She didn't imagine she'd been able to hide her surprise at present.

"I've been near it," she managed, after she'd attempted to come up with a reasonable answer. "With my parents." She didn't dare say that she had seen Montgomery there, standing in the sunrise and looking like something out of a dream. "It's enormous," she added. "Very impressive."

He shrugged. "I didn't think anything of

it when I was a child. I was too busy learning swordplay and keeping myself from being killed by my older brothers."

She smiled. She could just imagine. "How many brothers do you have?"

"Four elder, and two elder sisters."

"You're the baby?"

"It defies belief, doesn't it?"

She laughed a little, then forced herself to sober when she realized she was on the verge of getting too comfortable with him. She wasn't in the market for a guy, and the guy in front of her wouldn't have been on her shopping list even if she had been.

Really.

"So," she said, grasping for something innocuous to say, "you grew up on the seashore in that magnificent castle and your father is very famous."

He only nodded slightly.

She cast caution to the wind. Maybe if she sounded disinterested enough, he wouldn't think anything of the question. "When were you born?" she asked casually.

"In the Year of Our Lord's Grace 1213."

She had almost expected the like, but it was shocking just the same. She didn't realize just how shocking until she found Montgomery was taking his knives back and rescuing her cup of ale. She was shaking so badly, she almost fell off her chair.

He moved her, chair and all, closer to the fire, then sat down on a stool and took her hands. "The cold has caught you up."

"I'm fine," Pippa said, her teeth chattering. His hands were callused, likely from all that swordplay he'd been working on since 1213. It defied belief, but there with the truth holding her hands, she couldn't believe anything else.

She had gone back in time almost eight hundred years and landed in a castle with her sister who thought she was the Queen of Faery and had decided the castle's ultra-studly lord would make a good consort for her.

Karma had a lousy sense of humor.

And that didn't begin to address her most pressing problem, which was how in the hell was she going to get home?

"Persephone."

She focused on him. He was still chafing her hands, as if he thought that might help. Or maybe he just thought he'd stand a better chance that way of catching her before she pitched forward into his fire.

"What?"

"You're pale as a ghost."

Ghosts. Right. Not only was Tess's castle haunted, it was a veritable hotbed of all kinds of paranormal activities. If she ever saw her sister again, she'd tell her to put up warning signs. It might ruin some bits of her business, but it would certainly save people an unexpected trip to a place where the swords were real and the garderobe fully functional.

She felt Montgomery's hand on her head and she looked at him in surprise.

"Your hair is still wet," he said quietly.

And it would dry in a mass of curls that would stick out vertically if she didn't put some gel on it. Oh, that was right. She couldn't. Because she was stuck in the Middle Ages.

"How old are you?" she croaked, because apparently she just couldn't keep her mouth shut.

"A score and seven. You?"

"A score and four," she said. No sense in not fitting right in with the times as far as speech patterns went. She wasn't about to tell him when she was born, though, and he didn't seem poised to ask.

Then again, that might have been because he was looking at her with no small bit of alarm. Maybe she looked as unsettled as she felt. It was one thing to imagine she was in the past; it was another thing entirely to *know.* If he was twenty-seven, that made the current year 1241.

Unbelievable.

"Phillip, lad, there you are. Fetch more wood, if you please. Let's make her a pallet here and cover her with what furs we can find."

Pippa looked up to see Phillip standing nearby, watching her with worried eyes. She hadn't noticed him until that moment, but perhaps that wasn't unexpected. She'd been pretty busy toying with the idea of losing it over the now-undeniable facts staring her in the face.

"Shall I stay with you, Uncle? I can sleep in the corner."

"Aye, lad. That's likely the safest place for you."

Pippa soon found herself being fussed over by a medieval lord and his squire, and couldn't bring herself to protest. The fire against her face was divine and she had never had a couple of blankets on the floor be so comfortable. She supposed Cindi was safe with Sir Ranulf standing guard. And she herself, for the first time in what had to have been a handful of days, would be warm.

She felt those days catch up with her fully. She managed to tilt her head back and look at Montgomery who was sitting at her head, resting his elbows on his knees and watching her silently.

"Thank you," she managed. "Very chivalrous."

He only watched her gravely. "One act a day, or so my father instructed me."

She had no idea how to ask him if that chivalry might extend to helping her figure out how to get home, or if she even dared ask. She was living in a place where she couldn't dial 911, but she could tap the lord of the keep on the shoulder and ask him to draw his sword in her defense. Her sister had lost her marbles, there wasn't a Mini Mart in sight, and she had no idea how she was going to get home again. It was enough to make her wish heartily for a paper bag so she could avoid a bit of well-deserved hyperventilating.

Montgomery leaned over and brushed a stray lock of hair back from her face.

"I don't think you should go swimming in my cesspit again," he said quietly.

"I'll try not to," she managed.

He sat back and stretched his feet out behind her head. "Sleep in peace, Persephone. I'll keep watch."

In a place hundreds of years out of her time. She took a deep breath. "You are a very kind man, Montgomery de Piaget."

"You are easy to be kind to, Pippa."

She felt a flash of envy sweep over her for the woman who would eventually find herself the beneficiary of that very quiet sort of chivalry. Of course, that woman couldn't be her, but she couldn't help but wish for the very briefest of moments that it could be. She wasn't looking up at any stars and there were no untoward sparkles in the area, so she felt fairly safe doing so.

She closed her eyes, then felt herself drifting off to sleep.

Safely.

Chapter 11

There was nothing worse than having to admit Robin was right.

Montgomery cursed under his breath at the thought. When that didn't make him feel any better, he cursed out loud, rather enthusiastically. Robin had told him, many years ago, that he really should learn to curb his curiosity because it was going to get him in trouble one day. That he should have listened irritated him. That Robin had been right galled him beyond words to express it. He frowned fiercely, but that didn't distract him from his damnable curiosity.

He wondered about Pippa.

He knew he shouldn't. She had no business being in his time, and he had no business looking at her twice. He had his hands full with a keep that needed to be restored, cousins that needed to be resettled, and a titled, trouble-free bride to acquire at some distant point in the future. The last thing he needed was a woman who kept falling into his cesspit thanks to her sister who was daft as a duck.

Watching over her the night before had been very hard on his heart.

His personal discomfort had been good for the swordplay of his men, however, given that he'd left Pippa sleeping peacefully under Phillip's watchful care at dawn so he could retreat to the lists and take out his frustrations on his garrison. That had taken up the bulk of the morning quite nicely, but not done much for his heart. He supposed the only thing that would do that would be watching Pippa go back through her gate and seeing it close behind her.

Something he didn't particularly care to think about, actually.

He cursed again as he walked across the bridge and into his courtyard, hoping for mud and swords and other things he didn't have an unhealthy curiosity about. Petter and his lads were making steady progress on the worst spots in the walls and a few of the garrison lads had been willing to work on the roof of the garrison hall. With any luck, he would have most of his basic defenses in place before he had snow to deal with along with marauding ruffians. He supposed mucking out his courtyard would have to wait until spring. That and ridding his great hall of its tendency to be so smokey he couldn't breathe.

At the moment, though, even smoking fires sounded better than the chill that had suddenly descended outside. He walked into the great hall to find something warm to drink, then suddenly wished he hadn't.

Cinderella was sitting in a chair next to the fire, alternately coughing from the smoke and shouting for Pippa to come serve her something to eat. Montgomery came to a lurching halt one step too late. He'd been spotted.

Cinderella stood up and fixed him with a look that rooted him to the spot. He wanted to run, but he found he couldn't. He had begun to suspect that Cinderella was a witch, not just a refugee from the Future. When he looked at her, he felt just a little bewildered. Her crown was listing so far to the right that it was almost over her ear and her gown had started to look a little bedraggled, but somehow that didn't detract at all from her perfection.

"Well, good afternoon," she purred. "Are you prepared to perform in my beauty pageant?"

"Ah," he began, suppressing the urge to

flee. He was a bloody bespurred knight with scores of battles, skirmishes, and tourneys behind him. Surely facing a simple woman wasn't beyond his skill.

It wasn't Cinderella that terrified him, truth be told, it was what she was suggesting. She had begun to mix into her French the same English Jennifer did, but even with all the words he knew, he had no idea what a beauty pageant entailed. He suspected that demonstrating his talents, something Cinderella had announced the night before he would be doing, would unfortunately include something performed on the lute. As for the rest, he hoped whatever questions she wanted him to answer in the Final Five would be painless.

The saints preserve him, he didn't think he could endure much more of the woman.

Cinderella raised her wand to tap him, but before he could wince at what he knew from experience was not a pleasant feeling, a hand caught it on the way toward him.

"Sit, my queen," Pippa said, taking Cinderella by the arm and tugging. "Your prince must go on his way to prepare himself for the entertainments he will provide."

Cinderella's perfect brow creased. "For whom?"

"Why for you, my queen," Pippa said. "Of course."

Montgomery watched her settle her sister, then he frowned thoughtfully. Why Pippa continued to humor her sister, he couldn't have said. Perhaps she feared Cinderella would say something she shouldn't, something that would draw even more attention to herself than she had already. His household thought her nothing more than a daft noblewoman from the continent — something he had gone out of his way to noise about — but even they were growing weary of her screeching. He wasn't sure he could listen to it much longer.

He also couldn't watch much longer as Pippa tried to keep Cinderella in check, do all the tasks she'd taken upon herself in his hall, and no doubt spend the rest of her time worrying about how she was going to return home. Even if he hadn't been entertaining feelings for her that were completely out of the question, he would have been concerned simply because she was a lovely, responsible woman bearing a burden that he could see was wearing on her. He supposed he could simply tell her what he knew and hope she would believe him, but he couldn't quite bring himself to do that yet. There was no sin in wishing that she might remain in his hall another pair of days, surely.

Was there?

He watched her distract Cinderella with a bowl of carrots, smile briefly at him, then start off toward the kitchens. He would have counted himself well rescued and hurried off to do more of his manly labors in the lists, but he caught sight of something that he didn't particularly care for.

Boydin and Martin slinking off along behind Pippa.

He glanced at Cinderella, but she seemed perfectly happy where she was, no doubt examining each carrot for flaws. That left him free to go see to Pippa, who most certainly wouldn't see danger where it might be lurking.

He stopped at the entrance to the kitchens and looked at Pippa who was standing next to the fire, leaning over to stir something Joan had hanging there. She tasted, then straightened with a spoon in her hands.

Boydin and Martin were easing toward her. Montgomery supposed he should have gone close enough to listen to what they were saying, but he didn't need to. He could see by the way they stood that they were not intending anything good. They began to crowd Pippa at the fire, leaving her no choice but to back up until she had no more room to do so.

He stepped up behind his cousins and cleared his throat. Boydin turned slowly, his hands on his sword. Martin was apparently assuming that a scowl alone was enough to intimidate.

"I think the gel needs room to breathe," Montgomery said calmly.

"And I think she'd like me a bit closer," Boydin said, with an unmistakable look of challenge in his eye.

Montgomery looked at Martin. "And what do you say?"

"I say 'tisn't your place to tell me what to do," Martin said, all trace of any friendliness gone from his features. "The whelp of Rhys de Piaget you might be, but you've no authority here."

Montgomery lifted one eyebrow. "I wonder which of you has the sword skill to accompany your very fierce words? I suspect neither."

One thing he could say about his cousins: they weren't choosey about the places they fought. He saw the thought to use Pippa as a shield cross Boydin's face, so he immediately plunged his second eldest Sedgwick cousin into oblivion by means of a fist under his jaw. He scarce had time to draw his sword before Martin's blade came down toward his head.

He never would have called it a fair fight. Martin had had the double misfortunes of being born at Sedgwick and having Denys of Sedgwick as his father. Denys had unfortunately possessed neither sword skill nor the talent of convincing another man to take his son on as squire. Martin was strong, Montgomery would give him that, but he was not skilled. Within a handful of strokes, Martin was swinging so wildly, Montgomery began to fear for what was left of his kitchen. He looked behind Martin at Pippa and Joan.

"Move," he suggested.

They moved. He pushed Martin back out the door and into the courtyard. Perhaps it wouldn't serve him overmuch to thoroughly humiliate his cousin, but he supposed there might not be a better way to instill respect in the fool — and whatever other fools might be watching.

He was slightly distracted by the sight of Cinderella fluttering into the courtyard and beginning to shriek out curses in English that singed his ears, but he found that less irritating than what he was used to from Robin in French, so he ignored her and concentrated on beating a bit of deference into his cousin.

Or at least he did until he realized that things on the far side of the courtyard had taken a turn for the worse.

He glanced Cinderella's way to find she was now shouting at Pippa, who had apparently come outside to attempt to convince her sister to be quiet. Montgomery shook his head. Pippa endured far more than he ever would have, had he been in her shoes.

Such as her sister's fist in her eye.

Montgomery dropped his sword in surprise. He almost earned a blade in his gut as a result, which he likely deserved. He dove for his sword, rolled up with it, then swept Martin's feet out from underneath him as his brother-in-law Jackson had taught him. He reached over, clunked Martin on the head, then watched as his cousin slipped blissfully into senselessness.

Montgomery resheathed his sword and ran over to where Pippa was backed up against the castle wall, trying to simply shield herself from the attack of a well-wielded wand. Montgomery pulled Cinderella away and started to reach for Pippa only to find himself with his arms full of a purported Faery Queen.

"My hero," she breathed.

Then she tried to kiss him.

He was so stunned, he almost didn't move in time. That she missed his mouth didn't seem to trouble her. She wrapped her arms around his neck and crawled up into his arms that he had no choice but to provide for her use.

"Let's discuss what you'll want to do to win me," she said loudly.

"Ah —"

"Concentrate on *me,*" she said sharply.

Montgomery didn't have a choice given that she had taken his face in her hands that were more like claws. He turned toward the hall, managing to catch a glimpse of Pippa as he did. She was bending down and collecting things from the dirt — no doubt the sparkles that had fallen from Cinderella's gown and wand. Montgomery winced as Cinderella's crown poked him in the eye.

"Me," she commanded.

He caught Phillip's eye. Phillip needed no further instruction, bless him for being his father's very canny son. He immediately walked over and stood in front of Pippa with his sword drawn. Montgomery would have preferred to be doing the like, but he couldn't until he had rid himself of his burden — something he would do at his earliest opportunity. He walked back into the hall with Cinderella.

"Perhaps," he said carefully, "my lady would like a rest."

"Are you resting with me?" she asked, tapping him playfully on the head with her wand.

By the saints, nay was almost out of his mouth before he could stop himself. He took a deep breath, then attempted a smile. "I wouldn't think to disturb your rest, my queen," he said, hoping the term would work as well for him as it did for Pippa. "You must rest, then remain upstairs and think on all the things I must needs do to win you."

She sighed gustily. "I'm hungry."

"I'll see to that, Your Majesty."

That seemed to satisfy her. He carried her through the hall and up the stairs, then set her back on her feet in front of his door. He avoided another kiss, then bowed and scraped his way back down the passageway.

"Lock the door," he called.

He waited at the top of the steps until he heard the bolt slide home, then he turned and ran bodily into Everard.

"You know," Everard said slowly, stroking his cheek with the knife he had drawn, "there are very strange portents surrounding that woman."

Montgomery realized suddenly that his

own guardsmen were standing behind Everard, far enough in the shadows that they weren't readily visible. Their expressions were inscrutable. Montgomery might have wondered at another time why his lads seemed to think he needed protection, but not at present. Everard of Chevington looked capable of just about anything at the moment. Montgomery looked at him coolly.

"I don't think I understand what you're saying."

"What I'm *saying,* my self-important friend, is that the wench inside your bedchamber is very strange, something that I suppose shouldn't come as a surprise given that your entire family has a murky reputat—"

Everard stopped speaking abruptly, his eyes rolled back in his head, and he fell to the floor with an ungraceful crash. Sir Ranulf stood directly behind where Everard had fallen. He resheathed his sword.

"Forgive me, my lord Montgomery," he said, inclining his head. "I must have tripped on a rough patch in the passageway." He motioned to his companions. "Help our good lord Everard to the garrison hall where he can be nursed back to consciousness with all due care."

Montgomery watched as a senseless Everard of Chevington was picked up and carried off to a much less comfortable place than he was accustomed to. Then again, he didn't suppose Everard had led a very comfortable life so far, so perhaps he would find his temporary accommodations nothing out of the ordinary. Montgomery turned back to his captain.

"I wonder why it is you felt the need to silence him so quickly?"

"Because, my lord," Ranulf said, "he has a loose tongue and I had heard enough. He has been sojourning about the countryside in the afternoons, chatting up with that loose tongue the local peasantry who are either your missing servants or others with a ready ear for gossip. I thought it best that he cease with those activities." He shrugged. "If I could somehow help him see the wisdom in that, my honor demanded that I must."

"Indeed."

"Indeed," Ranulf agreed. "I've no ear for gossip, nor do I believe what I hear noised about by —" He paused, then smiled briefly. "By those with perhaps a grudge held too long. I find nothing murky about your family at all."

"Not even Amanda's husband, Jackson?" Montgomery asked mildly.

Ranulf didn't hesitate, which was to his credit. "My lord Raventhorpe plucked me out of a life of thievery and worse," Ranulf said quietly, "for which I will be eternally grateful to him. When the opportunity presented itself to serve you, my lord, I leapt at it without hesitation. As did Alfred and Roland. No small bit of gossip will fracture the oaths we made to you."

Montgomery dragged his hand through his hair, then smiled at his captain. "Thank you."

"My pleasure. Shall I guard your guest here so you can be about other things?"

"Aye," Montgomery said, "if you would. Until I can sort those other things to my satisfaction."

"Willingly, my lord. What shall we do with Lord Everard?"

Montgomery sighed deeply. "I cannot imprison him for speaking against me, though I can certainly withdraw my hospitality."

"You would be more than justified in that." Ranulf clasped his hands behind his back. "The lads will alert me when he wakes. Shall I then have him put outside the gates?"

"For all the good it will do us, aye," Montgomery agreed. "Thank you again, Ranulf.

I'll come relieve you after I've seen to Mistress Persephone."

"As you will, my lord."

Montgomery nodded, then left his captain to his work. He loped down the stairs to the great hall, did them all the favor of rendering Boydin unconscious for the second time that day, then walked out of the great hall and around the corner.

Phillip was currently examining the eye Pippa had been struck in. Montgomery thanked his squire, then took charge of the investigation himself. It was already red, though the eye itself seemed to have escaped damage.

"Phillip, lad," he said quietly, "run fetch me a rag soaked in cold water."

"Aye, my lord."

Pippa leaned back against the wall and said nothing as he took her face in his hands again and lifted it up where he could look more closely at her eye.

"I fear 'twill be blackened by morning," he said quietly.

"It's nothing."

He ran his finger gently over the bone above and below her eye. Nothing was broken that he could tell, but she would indeed bear the mark of it. He released her, then turned to lean back against the wall next to her. "Why do you let her treat you thus?"

She sighed. "No reason that would sound reasonable, my lord."

"Montgomery."

"My lord —"

"Nay," he interrupted. " 'Tis just Montgomery."

"Your servants don't call you that."

"And you aren't my servant, are you? And you're not hers, so do not let her strike you again." He paused. He wasn't in the habit of taking women to task, but he imagined he wouldn't be above locking Cinderella in a chamber if she couldn't control her fists. "I don't like it."

She looked up at him, a faint smile on her lips. "Very chivalrous, my lord. And trust me, I've thought more than once about punching her back."

"Then why don't you?"

"Because I like the moral high ground."

He almost laughed. He shook his head, then took the cloth Phillip handed him. He folded it carefully, put it over Pippa's eye, then took her hand and put it over the cloth. "Hold that there and come rest in my solar. You'll be safe there."

"You will be, too."

He took her by the arm. "Should I worry

about Cinderella coming after me next?"

"Your cousins, rather. I don't think you made any friends today, but I appreciate the rescue. Again."

He only nodded, then walked with her back to the hall. He made Pippa comfortable in front of his fire before he sent Phillip off for something to eat. He rested his hand on the back of his chair and looked down at her. Her eye was beginning to swell shut, but she made no complaint. He wouldn't have been nearly so pleasant in her shoes. Then again, perhaps she was simply trying to keep her sister from blurting out dangerous things. That he could understand from his own brushes with men who hadn't been afeared to call a man a warlock. Who knew what tales the servants had already spread? If Pippa were watched for because of those tales and somehow carried off . . .

Nay, the very of idea of that was unthinkable. The truth was suddenly very plain to him. He should be far more concerned about keeping Pippa *within* arm's length instead of pushing her away.

There. That sounded reasonable enough.

Indeed, as he studied her sitting there so grave and lovely in front of his fire, her dark hair curling over her shoulders and her arms wrapped around her knees, he decided that it was nothing short of his chivalric duty to care for her. He could surely do that and continue to look on her as nothing more than a sister. His honor would be satisfied, his fears allayed, and his mother made proud. He imagined she would have liked Pippa very much. A pity they would never meet.

He was surprised at how much the thought bothered him.

He was suddenly quite grateful for the arrival of Phillip bearing a bottle of wine and a sack full of things Montgomery hoped they might eat without undue hardship. He relieved his squire of his burdens, then pushed aside thoughts of things that could never be. The worthy task before him was to make certain Pippa was as comfortable as possible. He could spend an afternoon or two with someone he was fond of in a sisterly, very platonic way. No harm would come of it and indeed, some good might instead arise from it. Perhaps Cinderella would learn not to abuse her younger sister so terribly. Pippa might pass a bit of time in a place where she didn't have to worry about appeasing her sister.

Nay, no harm would come of it.

Not to his keep, not to his heart.

He was sure of it.

Chapter 12

Pippa dragged her sleeve across her forehead, then winced as the fabric touched her eye. It had been two days since Cindi had punched her and left her with the most impressive shiner she'd ever seen reflected in the blade of a medieval lord's sword.

Those past two days hadn't been without their bonuses. She'd spent the afternoons in the solar, discussing politics with Phillip and surreptitiously stealing looks at Phillip's uncle. Montgomery had joined in the conversations on occasion, but he seemed mostly content to simply listen while frowning over the sheets and sheets of numbers his steward Fitzpiers produced like an ink-jet printer in overdrive.

Unfortunately, those lovely afternoons had been balanced out nicely by mornings and evenings spent watching Cindi's increasingly speedy descent into madness. Pippa had thought her sister was nuts before, but she'd been proven wrong. Cindi had lost it somewhere along the same way where she'd gained the ultimate assurance that she was indeed queen of the castle.

All of which had led Pippa to wonder if there wasn't something more going on than her sister still suffering from jet lag and buying into her own magnificence. Surely Cindi had to have realized at some point that she wasn't living in the same vintage castle Tess was. That she hadn't made Pippa suspect she was indulging in some sort of contraband substance hidden upstairs. Unfortunately, Pippa hadn't been able to find it. The only time she'd managed to get into Montgomery's bedroom had been to serve Cindi breakfast and dinner, which hadn't given her much chance to investigate.

Today, things were different. Cindi had decided to take a walk and had ordered Montgomery, Phillip, and as many of the garrison knights as would come to accompany her. Pippa had watched them go, then decided the time was ripe for a little snooping.

Once she'd gotten in the door and jammed a torch into a handy sconce, she wasted no time in rifling through her sister's things. She found the bear-shaped tin her mother had been clutching in Seattle under the bed.

There were exactly three crumbs left from brownies Pippa was sure hadn't had their ingredients limited to what was in a Betty Crocker mix. She shoved the tin back where she'd found it, then continued her search.

She didn't have to look far. Under Cindi's pillow was a Ziploc bag with ten pills.

Valium.

Pippa held the pills in her hand and felt slightly sick to her stomach. It would of course be easier to let her sister just keep on keeping on, but there was the possibility that her sister would overdose. Then again, medieval England probably wasn't the best place to detox. Pippa stood there and wished fervidly that she hadn't stuck her nose where it shouldn't have gone. She wouldn't have been responsible that way, at least.

She realized, with an unpleasant start, that she had wished that more than once about more than one thing.

She looked at the small pills in her hand and decided that if she were wishing, she might as well do a thorough job of it and wish that she hadn't agreed to come to England in the first place, that she hadn't walked into Tess's castle, and that she hadn't met a man who, while he had spent a great deal of time treating her as he might have a sister, had indeed been the very embodiment of chivalry.

That was undoubtedly the worst part of her whole adventure. How in the world was she ever going to find that sort of guy in the twenty-first century? She was used to dating theater types who invariably asked her out, then tried to get her to pay for the date. Montgomery had been the polar opposite. Not only had he fed her and housed her, he had gone out of his way to make sure she was comfortable and safe —

A male throat cleared itself from the doorway. Pippa turned to see Montgomery himself standing there. She wondered how long he'd been there and how much of her wrestle with herself he'd seen.

He made no outward note of it; he merely walked into the bedroom, then sat down on the bed and looked up at her. Pippa had to close her eyes, just briefly, to get a hold of herself. She was sure she didn't feel anything for him past a lukewarm sort of interest she might have entertained for someone she'd met in passing at the theater. Yes, that was it. Nothing special. Nothing important or earth-shattering.

"Pippa."

She had to look at him then, because it would have been impolite not to. He looked slightly worried, but that was just because he was that sort of man. A lovely, chivalrous, polite sort of man who didn't have it in him to kick puppies or small children, despite how ferociously he fought in the lists.

Or how thoroughly he defended her against his cousins.

"You should sit," he said.

"I'm fine," she managed.

He moved over a bit and patted the place next to him. "Sit, woman, and tell me what ails you before I must pry the tidings from you with my sword."

"You wouldn't," she said with as much of a smile as she could muster. "Would you?"

"I don't suppose it would fit in with the list of knightly virtues my father endeavored to teach me," he said, "so perhaps not. I reserve the right, however, to wear you down with endless queries until you give in and allow me to aid you as I can."

She had to blink fairly rapidly a time or two. She realized, with another bout of clarity that she didn't enjoy at all, that despite her independence, she had relied on others for a great deal of things. She'd always known that if things really went south for her, she could crash on Peaches's couch for an extended period of time. Aunt Edna, bless her crotchety soul, would have let her have her old room back, though the price would have been high indeed. She'd been successful in her work for various theaters because at least at the beginning she'd mostly been making someone else's designs and hadn't needed to take responsibility for anything past a good seam. Even when she'd begun designing things herself, she'd known a steady paycheck was waiting for her at the end of every couple of weeks. Branching out on her own hadn't required anything beyond dreams that had yet to materialize.

But that had been easy stuff. Taking responsibility for someone else's life? That was another thing entirely.

She suspected that Montgomery took responsibility for the lives of others without thinking about it. He was responsible for his nephew Phillip, his cousins, his garrison, and all the people who would come running inside his gates expecting him to protect them if France decided to overrun England any time in the near future.

She looked at him once again, then sat down next to him. She had to take several deep breaths before she thought she could even begin to broach the subject at hand.

"I think," she began, feeling her heart beating uncomfortably all the way up in her throat, "that before I can tell you about this, I need to tell you about something else."

He waited. She waited, too, because she wasn't sure she wanted to tell him anything. For all she knew, he would think she was completely crazy and toss her in his dungeon — if he had a dungeon, which she wasn't sure he did. The cesspit might make a good substitute, but that was an even less appealing destination.

"It must be dire," he murmured.

She sighed. "You have no idea."

He simply waited, silent and grave. Pippa clasped her hands around Cindi's pills and looked at her knuckles, which were almost white with the strain. She couldn't believe she was actually considering telling him the truth. It sounded too fantastical even for her, and she had indulged in all kinds of unbelievable imaginings when she'd been young. She didn't imagine he was going to say anything until she did, so she supposed she would have to go first.

It would have been so much easier to concentrate if he hadn't been so perfectly handsome. She realized, now that she had a bit of afternoon light to help her out, that his eyes were gray. That had nothing at all to do with her current straits, but it was interesting to note. She suppressed the urge to reach up and brush hair out of his eyes, then clutched her hands together more securely and took a deep breath.

"I'm not sure you'll believe any of this," she began slowly.

"I have a strong stomach."

She imagined he did, but she wasn't sure that would extend to ramblings about time traveling and prescription drugs. Then again, Phillip had said Montgomery had in his youth believed in fairies, so maybe he had more imagination than she was giving him credit for. The question was, how did she begin a story that he would likely laugh at?

Well, laughing was better than drawing his sword, so she would press on and hope for the best.

"Where's your sword?" she asked, just to be on the safe side.

He stood up, unbuckled his sword belt, then handed the sheathed blade to her.

It was heavier than she'd figured it would be, especially since she only had one hand to hold it with. She propped it up against the bed on her left side where it might be slightly harder for him to reach.

"My knives, too?" he asked, sitting back down.

She smiled in spite of herself. "I'm counting on your being too lazy to bend down and reach them."

"Well, I am naturally lazy," he drawled, "so you're probably safe."

She almost laughed at his dry tone. He was just more charming than any man had a right to be. She just hoped he wouldn't lose that charm during the next ten minutes.

"I'm not sure where to start," she admitted.

"Why don't you start with what you're clutching in your hand? It seems to trouble you."

She took a deep breath, then opened her hand. Ten pills lay there, looking extremely innocent.

"Pebbles?"

"Pills," she corrected. "Drugs." She had more trouble than she'd expected looking for the right word in French. "Things that make you act in ways you wouldn't normally. As if you'd had too much strong drink, only these are a dozen times more powerful."

He looked at them, but he didn't touch them. "Your sister's?"

"Yes."

"Where did she get them, do you think?"

"Probably out of my mother's underwear drawer," she said with a snort. She shook her head. "My parents are . . . interesting. Anyway, that's beside the point." She glanced at him. "It's the next part that's going to sound absolutely crazy."

"I don't think you're daft, Persephone."

She smiled in spite of herself. She had never liked her name until he'd said it. It was as if he thought it pretty.

She knew she should stop taking so many deep breaths. She was going to start hyperventilating soon. But maybe just a few more, to really give herself a chance to get through what she had to.

"Here's the thing," she said, getting up because she couldn't sit still any longer. She walked over and set the pills down on a little table near the window. "Several days ago — I think it's probably been more than a week, but I haven't done a very good job of keeping up with the days." She took another deep breath. "Anyway, I was helping out at a party for a little girl's birthday, a party that my sister was throwing at her castle."

"Your sister owns a castle?" Montgomery asked in surprise.

Pippa turned around and leaned back against the wall. The stone was bone-chillingly cold, but she didn't think anything of it. "Yes. One day an old man walked up to her, invited her to come see his castle, then gave her the key to it and disappeared." She had to pause again. "Her castle looks at lot like your castle." Well, it wasn't missing so many critical things, like walls and indoor plumbing, but perhaps he didn't need to know that. "Cinderella was pretending to be the Fairy Queen."

"And you her loyal servant?"

She nodded. "My first mistake. We walked out of the castle and across the bridge, only something strange happened." She paused. "I'm not sure how to say this without sounding completely crazy, but it was as if I walked off my sister's bridge and . . . well, onto your land."

He only continued to watch her steadily. His hands weren't twitching toward his sword, which she took to be a very good sign. He only lifted one eyebrow, but said nothing.

"This is the part that's *really* crazy," she said, trying to laugh a little. It would have worked, too, if it hadn't sounded so little like a laugh. "My sister's castle is —" She had to take another deep breath. She supposed she had one more to spare before she completely lost it. "Well, it's your castle. Only it's in a different year. A different century, really."

He tilted his head. "How does it look?"

"How does what look?"
"The castle?"
She frowned. "Do you believe me?"
"Depends on how the castle looks."
She had to force herself not to gape. "I just told you something that should make your head spin and you're worried about how your castle looks?" she demanded incredulously.
"I'm curious by nature."
"Curious and lazy?" she said shortly.
He turned slightly and leaned back against the footpost of the bed. " 'Tis a potent combination, isn't it?"
"You're impossible."
He smiled. "My worst fault." He drew his foot up onto the bed and wrapped his hands around his knee. "Satisfy my curiosity and tell me how my castle looks in your century."
"Well, it looks perfect, that's how it looks." She could hardly believe he was taking it all so well. "It's one of the most beautiful castles left in England. People come from all over the world to look at it and imagine what it was like to live in the Middle Ages."
"The Middle Ages?"
"Those middle years after William came conquering from France and before Henry the Eighth and then Elizabeth launched that whole era of wide dresses and even wider

ruffs around their necks. After the Renaissance comes the Regency period with those empire waists that were so comfortable, then that whole stretch where Victoria was queen and corsets were all the rage, then the Industrial Revolution where London got really smoggy. I won't go into the slew of wars and uprisings and all sorts of geopolitical messes that came afterward." She paused. "But that's when your castle finds itself with my sister holding the key. In the twenty-first century."

He only looked at her steadily. "I see."

She wasn't sure he did, but she wasn't going to give him any more details than he absolutely had to have. "I'm really not sure how it happened, but somehow I walked from my time back to your time. I need to get home, but I'm not sure how. I've gone back and looked at the bridge a few times, but nothing feels like it did that night." She began to pace again, because she was too restless to stand still. "Worse still, now I know about these pills Cindi's taking. If I take them away, she might completely lose her mind, but if I put them back where I found them, she might take too many and die." She stopped and looked at him. "I don't know what to do. I'm not asking for advice, because this is my responsibility, but

I'm a little out of my depth."

He looked down at his hands clasped together for several very long moments, then looked up at her. "Can you ride?"

"What?" she asked, nonplussed.

"Can you ride?" he asked again. "A horse, I mean."

"I've been on a horse," she conceded uneasily. "Briefly."

He glanced at the window behind her. "The day is relatively young. I'll teach you to ride, more than briefly."

"Did you hear anything I just said?" she asked in surprise.

"Aye."

"And so in answer, you're going to give me a horseback-riding lesson?"

He stood and reached for his sword. "When my father has deep thoughts to think, he walks along the roof of his keep. My eldest brother runs about the lists, then he runs through his garrison. I ride." He shot her a look. "It clears my head."

"Oh," she said quietly. "I see."

"Why don't you leave your sister a pair of those little beasts where you found them and put the others in your pocket. We'll think about a plan after we return."

She didn't move. "I'm not asking you to solve this for me."

"I know," he said easily, "but you needed a listening ear before and now you need a clear head. Let's go ride so we'll both have one."

"My head won't be clear if I fall off a horse and land on it."

He smiled, the first genuinely amused smile she'd ever seen on his face.

Heaven help her, the man had a dimple.

"Concentrate on staying on, then —"

"What are you doing here?" a voice screeched suddenly.

Pippa ducked behind Montgomery. She was extraordinarily grateful when Montgomery distracted Cindi long enough for her to put two pills back where she'd found the rest of them. She hid behind the bed curtain, changed her clothes, then shoved her dress under the bed where she could retrieve it later. She ducked past Cindi and was faintly surprised not to have her sister notice her.

"My prince, you should get your servants better fitting clothes," Cindi advised. "That boy there looks ridiculous."

"I will see to it posthaste," Montgomery said deferentially. "You, my lady, should rest. It has been a taxing day so far."

"I want the bathing suit competition tonight," Cindi said with an enormous yawn. "Better find a two-piece. Those get better marks from the judges. I should know."

"I imagine you do, my lady." He managed to shut the door before Cindi could reach for him. "Bolt the door, Your Majesty."

Pippa heard the bolt slide home, then found her hand taken by a man who was obviously not going to waste any time in hightailing it away from danger.

"Run," he suggested.

She did. She ran with him all the way out to the stables that were now being seen to by a stable master who had been sent, along with a handful of horses, as a gift from his brother Miles. Montgomery and one of the stable lads saddled two horses before she could come up with a good excuse why she couldn't do what he wanted her to. Before she knew it, she was looking at the horse Montgomery had chosen for her. She looked at the stirrup, then at Montgomery.

"I don't suppose you have any suggestions on how I'm supposed to get my foot up there."

He cupped his hands. "Put your knee in my hands and I'll give you a leg up."

Up and over, she was sure, but apparently she was more graceful than she'd suspected. Either that, or Montgomery was a better horseman than she'd given him credit for being. Her mount moved around a lot more than she remembered from one disastrous and very brief ride at a Renaissance faire in her youth, but Montgomery seemed to think nothing of it.

"Hold the reins thus," he said, demonstrating, "and try not to squeeze with your knees. Steud will think you wish him to go faster, else."

Well, she certainly didn't want to give the beast any ideas. She frowned. "What's his name again?"

"Steud." He paused. " 'Tis a Gaelic word."

"What does it mean?"

He smiled, and that appalling dimple peeked out at her again. "Horse."

She laughed in spite of herself. "Very original."

"Lazy, curious, and unoriginal. I'm revealing all my finer characteristics today." He looked up at her. "I suppose that leaves me with no choice but to investigate yours this afternoon as we ride."

"I'll save you the trouble. I'm terrified, terrified, and really terrified," she said, trying not to clutch both her reins and her saddle. She hazarded a glance at him. "You're going to scrape me off the ground when pony boy here leaves me behind, right?"

"Will it ease your terror if I say aye?" he asked politely.

"You know, you're not funny."

He smiled again, a tiny little smile that was so utterly charming, she couldn't help but smile in return.

"You might hold on to the saddle if that makes you feel more secure, but we won't do anything but walk today."

"Dull for you," she managed.

"Somehow I'll manage to stay awake." He put his hand over hers. "Don't pull on the reins. Steud will stop if you just sit back and breathe out."

"If I sit back, I'll fall off."

"There is a back on your saddle, my lady," he said, "so you needn't worry about that. Just follow me until we are free of the gates. Then we'll ride together." He shot her a look. "I promise to catch you if you fall."

She didn't imagine he would manage that, but she wasn't going to argue with him. She held the reins as lightly as she could manage in one hand and clutched the front of the saddle with the other. Steud seemed to sense there was something very wrong with his rider and bless him if he didn't follow along behind Montgomery as docilely as a sleepy, exhausted lamb.

It was, she had to admit, a very lovely afternoon. Montgomery didn't say much past commenting on the superior qualities of her horse and the beauty of the fall colors. She confined herself to the subjects of his health and the weather and might have thought she'd fallen into a Jane Austen novel if it hadn't been for that quite useful sword her companion was packing and the fact that she could generally see not too far away a castle that was firmly rooted in the Middle Ages.

Well, that and she realized after only ten minutes that they were most definitely not out riding alone.

She looked at Montgomery, feeling startled. "Who are those men behind us?"

"Our guard."

She swallowed uncomfortably. "Do we need a guard?"

He considered his words for a moment or two. "Were I out riding by myself, I might possibly go alone, but I am not alone and I have given my word to keep you safe."

She fanned herself with her reins before she thought better of it, which seemed to send some sort of signal to Steud that she was much improved and ready for a flat-out gallop.

Actually, it probably wasn't really anything more than a lazy trot, but it almost left her on the ground. Montgomery stopped her horse before she landed on her head, then looked at her with a smile.

"First lesson: don't flap your reins."

"I'll remember that."

"Second lesson: don't panic."

"I wasn't panicking. I was getting ready to abandon ship."

He smiled, a deep smile that was so utterly adorable, she almost fell off her horse in self-defense. She didn't flap with her reins, but she did fan with her hand.

"Hot out, isn't it?" she asked.

He looked up at the cloudy sky, then back at her. "I think it threatens rain." He looked at her. "Is that daunting?"

It was half out of her mouth that she was a Seattle girl and his light English drizzle was not intimidating in the least, but she stopped herself in time and simply shook her head. Then she decided there was no reason in not being honest about part of what she was thinking. "I'd rather stay out here for a bit longer," she admitted. "Even if it means taking my life in my hands to ride this demon horse."

"Then we'll make another circle around the castle," he said.

"Is that what we've been doing? Going around in circles?"

"I thought if you fell off, I could at least carry you back home without too much trouble."

"Careful, my lord. Your chivalry is showing."

"Montgomery. My name is Montgomery."

She laughed a little, because she couldn't help herself. It was ridiculous and foolhardy and could only lead to a serious crack in her heart, but she couldn't not, just for the day, pretend that there was no good reason not to enjoy a lovely day with a very lovely man and a horse that hadn't killed her yet.

Life was good.

Even in medieval England.

The afternoon had waned completely before she rode with Montgomery into the courtyard. She followed him over to the stables, then found herself very grateful when Steud stopped moving. Montgomery dismounted easily, then walked over to hold up his arms for her.

She let him help her down, feeling rather more breathless than she should have. She backed up, before she lost the remains of her good sense. He only nodded toward the hall, seemingly unaffected by the day's events, then walked with her through the ever-present layer of muck without comment.

He stopped just outside the hall door. "How often does she take those little pills?" he asked quietly.

"Maybe every four hours."

"What is your decision regarding them?"

Pippa took yet another in the series of deep breaths. She wasn't happy to be responsible for her sister's life, but she obviously had no choice. "I think I should keep letting her have them, though maybe not so often." She paused. "I can't guarantee what she'll do if they wear off."

"We'll confine her to her chamber, if need be," he said grimly. "I've seen drunkards suffer from a lack of drink."

"This will be much worse."

He looked at her seriously. "I want you within sight at all times. Do not leave if I'm not with you."

She nodded weakly.

"We'll discuss other things pertaining to your future in my solar later." He paused before he spoke again. "I imagine you will want to return home as quickly as you're able."

"Of course," she agreed. "Thank you."

He cocked his head to one side. "Thank

you, who?"

She smiled. "Thank you, Montgomery."

"You're welcome, Persephone."

She walked into the hall first, because he held the door open for her, then walked alongside him because he'd taken her by the elbow and didn't seem inclined to let her go. It was, as she'd noted several times earlier, completely ridiculous to even feel the slightest bit affected, especially since she wanted to return home as quickly as possible.

But still, she couldn't quite keep herself from imagining things she knew she shouldn't have. She was in a castle — albeit a very dilapidated castle — she was keeping company with a very chivalrous — albeit noble — guy, and her sister probably wouldn't stay awake all evening so she might actually be able to enjoy the fairy tale for another night.

She would figure out in the morning just what she was going to do to get back to real life.

She was, surprisingly enough, not particularly looking forward to it.

Chapter 13

There were places a man might be willing to go and things a man might be eager to accomplish for the cause of chivalry and knightly virtues, but Montgomery decided that stooping to singing in front of his garrison was not one of them. That had never been a written rule at Artane, but he was certain his father would have agreed with him, as would Robin. Nicholas had a stronger stomach than the rest, but even he might have balked at the things Montgomery had been asked to do since dawn.

He had no idea what a *bathing suit competition* was, but it seemed to involve parading about in something close to his altogether, so he hadn't bothered to dignify that request with a response. He had no mind to blather on about the benefits of *world peace,* either, especially given the always dodgy relationship between England and most of the rest of the known world. That had left him facing a very stern-looking Faery Queen, who had demanded, whilst shoving her crown back atop her hair that was now hanging about her shoulders in straggling locks, that he produce a talent, such as dancing, or singing, or performing on an instrument.

He would rather have put his own eyes out with hot pokers than dance before his men, even though he would have admitted, if pressed, that he had in the past not embarrassed himself at court when called upon to caper about to music. His trio of lads had generally been in the garrison hall during such humiliations, which had been a relief. He supposed he could sing without causing others to wince and play the lute without sending hounds to howling in agony, but to do any of it because Cinderella required it?

Never.

He'd been tempted to immediately and quite loudly express his refusal the night before, but he'd caught sight of Pippa's rapidly darkening eye. She had looked at him without any expression at all on her face. It hadn't been a look of pleading; it had been, well, just a look. Perhaps the most unsettling thing about that look was that he'd understood it without having to have it explained to him. She was trying to keep her sister's ship on an even keel and a bit of aid in accomplishing that would have been useful.

So, he had accepted the blow to his pride and agreed the night before to sing for Cinderella the next day — in his solar. He had put off the unpleasant exercise until the afternoon in hopes that one ballad might be enough to put her to sleep, leaving him free to see to other, more pleasant tasks, such as pretending to read what Fitzpiers handed him whilst listening to Pippa and Phillip discuss the foibles of the king. If he managed to put Cinderella in a deep sleep, he also might manage to spirit Pippa away for an afternoon ride.

All of which left him where he was, finished with his morning's duty in the lists and deigning to humor Cinderella so he might have what he truly wanted.

Cinderella swept into his solar as if she had truly been a queen, waited for Phillip to arrange a chair for her, then sat. She pushed her crown back up from where it had fallen forward over her eyes, then took a moment to focus on him before she waved her wand imperiously.

"Begin," she commanded.

Montgomery glanced at Pippa, who was sitting on a little stool near Fitzpiers with her arms wrapped around her knees. He lifted his eyebrows briefly and had a faint smile in return. There was obviously no more opportunity to stall, so he sat down in a chair, took the lute his grandmother insisted he bring with him in hand, and dredged up a ballad or two.

He supposed he wasn't mortally embarrassed, for the knowledge of the more refined arts could surely be counted among the knightly virtues, but he couldn't help but be vastly relieved when midway through his third song, he heard the welcome sound of snores. He immediately — and gratefully — stopped his song.

"Oh, don't," Pippa protested immediately, then clapped her hand over her mouth as Cinderella sat up and looked around blearily.

She frowned, then leaned her head back against the hard wood of the chair and drifted immediately back into slumber. Pippa waited for a moment or two before she spoke again.

"Don't stop," she said quietly. "It was lovely."

He pursed his lips. "Do you enjoy seeing me so discomfited?"

She smiled. "As entertaining as that is, I was actually just enjoying your music."

He supposed she wasn't teasing him, so he started his song over again, but quietly. There was no sense in waking sleeping royalty before he had to. Once he'd finished with that, he simply played for a bit, snatches of things he'd heard on his travels and other things he'd taken a fancy to at court.

"You're very good, you know."

He shrugged. "My brother John is — was — much better, but he is gone so 'tis left to me to carry on the tradition, I suppose." He set his lute aside and rose silently. "How long will she sleep?"

"Hopefully all afternoon."

He walked over to her and pulled her up to her feet. "Let's ride."

She looked up at him. "Do you need to think?"

"Aye," he said seriously. *And have you to myself* would have been the next thing out of his mouth if he hadn't had such self-control. He looked at his squire. "Play something if she begins to stir. She won't know 'tis you if you sit behind her."

"Phillip plays as well?" Pippa asked as they left the solar.

"My grandmother, who has attained a truly alarming age, requires it of all her grandchildren and their children. I think she was sorely vexed when my father took her daughter to live so far in the north, and this is her way of making certain we aren't a pack of savage hounds." He walked across the hall with her and out toward the stables. "I apologize. I didn't ask you if you cared to ride."

"I still can't walk from yesterday," she said with an uncomfortable half laugh, "but I'll go along if you like." She paused. "I'm ready to be free of the walls for a bit."

He nodded, then silently saddled her horse for her. He likely should have put her up on a docile mare the day before, but the truth was he'd wanted her on something speedy should trouble arrive. He had very vivid if brief memories of killing a man who'd tried to make off with her soon after her arrival in his time. That lad had been nothing more than a fool obviously quite desperate for a way to extort a bit of money for Pippa's safe return. But another man with more skill, or more desperation . . . Montgomery shook his head. There were so many dangers in his world that she was unprepared for.

Not that it mattered, in truth. She wouldn't remain with him forever, so his dangers would not forever be hers. He wasn't sure why the gate hadn't worked for her that night Cinderella had pushed her into the moat, though he supposed he bore some of the blame for that given that he'd startled Pippa before she'd been able to make a proper go of things.

He hadn't been able to do anything else. He'd been following them, then noticed something that bespoke too clearly of someone else lurking outside who perhaps shouldn't have been. He hadn't had the chance to investigate, though he hoped he didn't come to regret that at some point. For all he knew, it had been Everard, looking for something else to add to his already overlarge store of murky tales about the de Piaget family.

He shook aside his unproductive thoughts, but remained silent until they were away from the keep. He finally turned to look at Pippa. "We should discuss your plans for returning home. I fear your sister's wits will not last much longer."

She studied him for a moment or two in silence. "Then you believe me?"

"I have no reason not to."

"I was afraid you would think I was a witch and burn me at the stake," she said with a weary smile.

"No burnings here," Montgomery said lightly, though he supposed that might not have been the case in another keep. He attempted a smile. "You will want to return soon, no doubt."

"Of course," she said firmly.

Montgomery would have liked to have believed she sounded less sure of that than she had earlier, but he had, over the past se'nnight, found himself entertaining many more romantic notions than usual. It had obviously had a detrimental effect on not only his common sense, but his hearing.

"I'm just not sure what to do," she continued quietly. "I don't think that spot on your bridge works anymore — and it's not as if I have a map of other portals through time." She laughed, but there was no humor in it. "I imagine I don't dare run around and ask a bunch of other people if they've seen refugees from the Future."

He cleared his throat. "Nay, I don't think I would, were I you."

She studied him for so long, he thought about squirming — if he'd been one prone to squirming, which he most definitely was not. He just hoped his thoughts didn't show on his face.

Aye, he knew where other portals were.

He would likely be damned for not being terribly fond of the thought of taking her to one.

"You haven't seen anyone else like me come through your front gates, have you?"

"Never," he said honestly. And he hadn't. He had never seen any woman from the Future come through his front gates.

He studiously avoided mentioning what he had seen come through his *father's* front gates.

The thought occurred to him suddenly that perhaps Pippa's and Cinderella's ability to travel through time wasn't necessarily limited to the gate in front of his hall that he'd never suspected might be there. Indeed, hadn't he seen Pippa standing in the midst of that gate near Artane ten years earlier? He was tempted to ask her if she'd seen him as well, but that might make it sound as if he knew more about paranormal happenings than he should have.

Nay, 'twas best he not tell her that he did indeed know where there were a few more spots in the grass she might try. For all he knew, she was required to go back to her time through the gate she'd come to his, so perhaps she would just have to stay with him until her gate was willing to take her back. That might take days, or it might take weeks.

The thought wasn't nearly as displeasing as it likely should have been.

Or it wasn't until he realized that it wasn't just Pippa he would have in his hall; it would be her sister as well.

"Let's try trotting," he said suddenly.

She blinked. "What?"

"If you ever needed to travel, you would want to know how to trot," he said, knowing he sounded every bit as daft as he suspected he sounded. "It seems prudent."

"Um," she began hesitantly.

"I'll fetch rope from the lads for a lunge line."

"If you're sure."

If it meant he could spent half an hour with her riding circles around him, then aye, he was sure. He collected rope from one of his lads, turned his horse over to Phillip, then walked over to where Steud stood waiting. The horse looked at Montgomery, sighed as only a horse could sigh, and prepared to be the means of schooling a green rider. Montgomery smiled, promised the beast an extra measure of oats, then fixed the rope to Pippa's saddle. She looked at it in alarm, then turned that same look on Montgomery.

"What are you doing?"

"Taking control."

"Why do I suspect that's how you're most comfortable?"

"You might be surprised," he said dryly. "I am by far the most tractable of my brothers."

"Unless you're practicing with your sword."

"Well, I do have a reputation to maintain," he agreed. "But I have been known to be deferential to whomever of the gentler sex might be within earshot."

"So, you'll let me get down right now because I'm nervous."

He met her eyes. "Nay."

"And if I told you I was terrified beyond reason and couldn't face the thought of being on a horse another moment?"

He put his hand on her foot. It was a far less personal touch than he was interested in, so he supposed there was no harm in it. He looked up at her.

"I would tell you that I had perfect confidence in your ability to do difficult things, then ask you to trust me."

"That's a lousy answer."

He smiled. "Trust me, Pippa. I won't let anything happen to you."

She took a deep breath. "Are you always so kind to unexpected guests?"

"I usually run them through with my sword. I made an exception for you."

Pippa laughed uneasily. "All right, I'll trust

you. I want it noted, however, that Lord Tractable is suddenly nowhere to be found."

"He has disappeared in favor of Master Sensible," Montgomery said. "The truth is, I will be more successful at keeping you safe if you can ride. Unless you'd rather me drag you off your horse and pull you behind me as we ride furiously away from the first sign of danger."

"I'll trot."

"I thought you might."

He showed her how to hold the reins properly, tried without much success to ignore how truly lovely she was when viewed by pale sunshine and not the glaring light of her sister's unsettling perfection, then backed away and clicked at Steud. He taught her the most rudimentary of skills, then simply watched her as she practiced.

In time, he realized she'd stopped only because he heard her say his name. He looked at her, feeling as if he'd just woken.

"Aye?"

"How am I doing?"

"Brilliantly."

"You weren't paying attention."

The truth was, he wasn't paying attention to her riding, but he'd been most definitely paying attention to her.

"I think you need a nap," she added.

"Do you think your sister has vacated my solar yet?" he asked, not daring to hope that might be the case so he could retire there with Pippa and ply her with another ballad or two.

To what purpose he couldn't have said and didn't care to answer. She was in his care for the foreseeable future and 'twas only chivalrous to make certain she was content.

Surely.

"We could go see if she's gone upstairs," Pippa said. "If you like."

He did. He coiled the rope as he walked toward her, then unfastened the end of it. He put his hand briefly on her knee, then stepped back. "You did well."

"You're a good teacher."

He didn't particularly want to be that for her, he realized, but he couldn't offer her anything else even if she were interested in it. He nodded, accepting the compliment, then returned the rope to his guardsman, mounted his own horse, and turned with Pippa back to the keep.

He rode into the courtyard to find something of a standoff there before the great hall. Gunnild was flanked by her children, the garrison was huddled in a clump, and a new contingent of souls was standing in the courtyard, the leader of which was looking about himself with an assessing gaze that bespoke serious business indeed.

Montgomery dismounted and shot Phillip a look. Phillip moved his mount closer to Pippa and put his hand on his sword. Montgomery walked over to the man standing in the middle of his courtyard and clasped his hands behind his back.

"Good e'en to you, sir," Montgomery said politely. "May I be of service?"

The man looked him over, then made him a low bow adorned with a handful of flourishes. "You are, quite obviously, Lord Montgomery."

"I am," Montgomery agreed.

"I am," the man said, putting his hand over his heart, "François."

Montgomery felt his ears perk up. "Are you, indeed?"

"I am, indeed. I am a gift from your brother Nicholas, who keeps an excellent cellar and an enviable larder." He lifted an eyebrow in a doubtful arch. "I don't suppose I can hope for the same here."

"You cannot," Montgomery said, with genuine regret, "but dare I hope that won't stop you from creating things to delight and astonish?"

François looked at him calculatingly.

"Your brother promised me you would appreciate my efforts."

"My brother is always right."

"Then I will repair to the kitchens and see what is available." He looked with distaste at the occupants of the great hall. "I will not be cooking for the garrison, will I?"

Montgomery didn't imagine that was a question, and more important, he suspected he would do well to respond correctly.

"Nay, just for me and my guests."

François clapped his hands together and a trio of imminently helpful-looking helpers leapt immediately to his side.

"We will investigate," François announced. "Then we will forage. Fortunately, I brought my own supplies."

"That was fortunate," Montgomery agreed, feeling rather more relieved than he likely should have for the possibility of something edible on his table. He hoped he looked appropriately grateful as he watched François venture off to points unknown and no doubt unsuitable. He let out his breath slowly, then went to help Pippa down from her horse.

"Who's that?" she asked.

"A culinary gift from my second-eldest brother, Nicholas," he said. "He has a keep in France."

"And exquisite taste in truffles," came floating back on the breeze left by François's attendants.

Pippa smiled. "You look relieved."

"I am," he said, "and so are you — as in relieved from any duties you've taken on in the kitchen. You'll retire to my solar and rest from your afternoon's labors."

"Lord Tractable, back in the saddle."

He smiled. "Very well. You may briefly see to your sister, but you will no longer be serving her or helping in the kitchen."

"But —"

"I am not accustomed to being gainsaid."

Her mouth fell open. "You bully."

He leaned closer so he could whisper in her ear. It put him much too close to her for his peace of mind, but he had already spent an afternoon doing things that were ill-advised, looking where he wasn't allowed, wanting things he couldn't have. Whispering in her ear didn't seem any worse than those things.

She might have shivered.

He knew he had.

"Humor me and let me care for you properly."

"I can take care of myself," she said faintly.

"Allow me."

"I can't."

"Aye, you can. And you will."

She looked up at him. "Because you're not accustomed to being gainsaid?"

"Exactly."

"Well," she said slowly, "maybe just this once."

He was about to tell her she wouldn't regret it, but he wasn't sure they wouldn't *both* regret it.

He handed Pippa's reins to a stable lad, then offered her his arm. It seemed perfectly natural, as if he'd been doing it for years. He tilted his head toward the hall and she nodded and walked with him. He knew the peace couldn't last, but he fully intended to enjoy it whilst it did.

He walked into the great hall with Pippa only to find it in a complete uproar, with Joan and her kitchens lads and lasses running about as if the king himself were set to arrive. That couldn't have been caused by François's arrival, which meant something else was afoot. Montgomery stopped one of his lesser guardsmen who had been pressed into kitchen service.

"What is it?"

"There is going to be a wedding, my lord," the man said breathlessly. "The queen has said so."

"Who is the bridegroom?" Montgomery

asked in surprise.

The man looked at Montgomery as if he'd lost his wits. Montgomery felt something slide down his spine. It wasn't the healthy bit of anxiousness he briefly felt at the beginning of a battle or the slight unease he occasionally enjoyed at the sight of a very formidable opponent.

This was something that made him want to turn and bolt.

"Well," he managed, "speak up, man. Who is the bridegroom?"

"Why, my lord, 'tis you."

Chapter 14

Pippa looked down at herself and felt as if she'd been in a dream for days, a dream that had been full of things she hadn't expected, a dream that had ended the same way it had begun: with her walking out of her bedroom to go downstairs to a party where her sister would be, as usual, the center of attention.

Only the torches on her current walls weren't fake, and Montgomery de Piaget hadn't said a word when he'd been informed he was going to be getting married to the Fairy Queen.

Pippa had checked under Cindi's pillow and found only five pills left, which meant her sister was coming to the end of her good-times road, though she was probably still firmly entrenched in the land of delusion. She could only hope Cindi didn't pop out of her daydreams, break into some modern song, and then expect everyone to sing the chorus with her.

She walked down the stairs to the great hall, slipping by cousins who snarled at her, and the lady Gunnild, who looked at her as if she would have liked nothing better than to take the knife she wore openly in her belt and stow it in Pippa's back. She ran for the kitchens before Cindi could notice her and before she had time to see if Montgomery was looking forward to or dreading his wedding feast.

She paused at the passageway leading to the kitchens and looked back over her shoulder. Cindi was standing in the middle of the great hall, looking upward at the ceiling that was in need of a patch here and there, and spinning around and around with her arms stretched out. Her hair was hanging in filthy strands around her face and down her back, her dress was very much worse for the wear, and her crown kept falling off her head.

It was tempting to say that served her right, but Pippa couldn't. She couldn't even bring herself to continue on to the kitchen. It certainly wasn't anything she particularly wanted to do, but she found herself turning and walking back out into the great hall. She caught her sister by the arm, then made her an elegant curtsey worthy of the finest of Shakespearean actors.

"My queen," Pippa said deferentially.

Cindi scowled at her. "What do you want?"

Words she hadn't intended came out of her mouth. "I came to prepare you for the wedding feast, Your Majesty." She reached up and touched Cindi's crown. "A beauty queen must always look her best."

Cindi's own mantra must have penetrated her fogged brain because she nodded slowly. Pippa looked for a likely spot, but there really wasn't anywhere private besides Montgomery's solar. She supposed that would have to do. She took Cindi by the arm and walked her across the hall. She knocked and smiled at Fitzpiers when he opened the door.

"Don't you ever stop working?" she asked.

"I'm making up for years of something approaching neglect," he said with an answering smile. "Lord Montgomery inspires that sort of labor, doesn't he?"

Lord Montgomery inspired a great many things, but she supposed she shouldn't list them. She nodded, because that was the safest thing to do.

"Are you looking for a bit of quiet?" he asked.

"If you wouldn't mind."

He shut the door for her, then went back to his work. Pippa sat Cindi down in a chair in front of the fire, fetched a cup of wine for her sister, then started from the bottom and worked her way up.

By the time she was finished trying to resurrect Cindi's appearance, she was fetching wine for herself as well. It was a good thing she'd had so much practice in getting Cindi ready for pageants when Cindi's assistant had flaked out yet again or she might have been less sure of her results. She had done the best she could with what she had. She certainly hadn't had the time to sew on all the crystals she was keeping in her pockets, but she doubted Cindi would miss them. At least Cindi had kept herself in Montgomery's room most of the time so her contact with the local soil had been kept to a minimum.

Pippa stood back and admired her work. Cindi looked up.

"Well?"

"Stunning."

"Of course," Cindi said, but she didn't sound as majestic as she usually did.

Pippa didn't want to push her. She was nervous enough about the dwindling supply of drugs in her sister's possession. She was definitely not one to advocate mind-altering substances — she had seen what they had done to her parents — but she also didn't want her sister have a full-blown freak-out in the middle of dinner.

After dinner, maybe, when Montgomery would be taking her upstairs and making her his wife. Cindi could lose it completely then. Maybe Montgomery would put his foot down then. She couldn't help but wonder why he hadn't before. After he'd received the news of his impending nuptials, he'd simply deposited her in his solar, then retreated to the lists. She'd almost wished she'd known how to use a sword. She would have gone with him.

She hadn't seen him at all that morning, though she suspected by the looks of the men straggling back into the hall that he'd continued his workouts.

She wasn't sure she wanted to speculate why.

She sighed deeply. The fairy tale had turned into a nightmare and she was still the one covered in soot. There was a comforting familiarity about that, though, so she didn't fight it. Especially since she had other things to do besides be a part of any fairy tale. Manhattan called and she fully intended to answer. Her sort-of-woven plans to get back home were getting a little threadbare, but she hadn't given up. Sooner or later Cindi would find herself back in reality — married or not — and then they would have to make a decision.

And Pippa's would be to get the hell out of Dodge.

"I'm certain lunch is ready," Cindi said, lifting her chin. "Pave the way, serving girl."

Pippa opened the door, but that was as far as she got before Cindi shoved her aside and swept into the great hall, looking for all the world as if she really had been the Queen of Fairy come to gaze upon her loyal subjects. Pippa could almost wrap her mind around the thought of a man, namely Montgomery, being willing to marry her sister. She was nothing short of stunning.

She left Cindi to twirling again in the middle of the hall, rather tidier than she had been an hour before, and walked off to check on the goings-on in the kitchen. There were two sets of cooks at the fire — difficult even on a good day and made all the more difficult by the temperament of François. Joan had done her best to stay out of his way since last night, but that was difficult when she was cooking for fifty and he was cooking for less than ten.

She backed into Montgomery before she realized he was behind her. She turned in time to have him catch her by the arms to steady her. He looked down at her gravely.

"How do you fare, lady?"

"Better than you, I imagine," she said brightly. She knew she sounded less bright than brittle, but since she had no reason for it, she pressed on. "Bridegroom jitters and all."

"Hmmm," was all he said.

"Cindi's waiting for you in the great hall," Pippa continued, because if she'd stopped talking, she might have allowed herself to realize just how much her life sucked.

Wasn't it enough that she was semi-stuck, hundreds of years out of her time, without a serger? Or electricity to run that serger? Or even some decent bolts of fabric and a needle and thread? Now she had to be perky and cheerful when her sister was poised to marry a guy she had started to like?

And what wasn't there to like about him? He was bossy, true, and irritatingly medieval in his attitudes, but he had a lovely smile, a dimple, and a deliciously dry sense of humor. He wasn't an actor. He hadn't asked her to check her pockets for cash so he could fill up the feed end of his horse.

Of course, the fact that he was living several centuries in the past was a big Karma-engineered relationship obstacle, but since she was making a list, there was no sense in not being positive.

"Persephone."

She closed her eyes briefly. If he would just stop saying her name that way, she might stand a chance of being truly objective about him. She looked up at him and attempted another bright smile.

"Aye, my lord?"

He started to speak, hesitated, then shut his mouth and shook his head. He put his hand on her shoulder exactly as she'd seen him do a dozen times to his squire, then he nodded to her and walked away.

Well, obviously he wasn't too broken up by the thought of only getting to call her *sister* for the rest of his life.

She clapped her hand to her forehead on the off chance it would dislodge some last vestige of common sense. There was no reason to consider any of it seriously. Cindi couldn't marry Montgomery de Piaget because he was eight hundred years older than she was and he lived in a time without plastic surgeons and photo shoots. Her sister would be satisfied with her life for about seven seconds after she'd come down off her high and realized what she'd gotten herself into. Even if she'd managed to reconcile herself to camping for the rest of her life, she never would have been able to appreciate Montgomery's finer chivalric qualities.

Pippa put her shoulders back. Obviously, she was going to need to take matters into her own hands. She didn't want to be the one to be the impediment to a happily ever after, but obviously she was going to need to. All she had to do was wait for the right time during the ceremony, then come up with some sort of reasonable-sounding objection.

She was going to check her sister for sharp objects first, though given Cindi's powerful right hook, maybe she should just check for room to duck.

François was fussing over something that actually smelled heavenly. She didn't want to ask what sorts of unhealthy fats were loitering in it. She tasted when a taste was offered, then heaped well-deserved praise. François accepted the accolades with a modest smile and handed her something sweet.

She almost envied Montgomery his dinner table and expanding waistline.

She made herself scarce until lunch was served, then hovered at the back of the hall by the kitchen passageway not because she wasn't hungry but because she almost couldn't bring herself to watch what was going on. It was like a train wreck, just too horrible to look away from. Montgomery was sitting next to Cindi, looking gorgeous and charming and more wonderful than he had any right to. Cindi was flirting madly with him, but Pippa knew her sister was seeing only a gorgeous face, not the man who was kind to his squire, ruthless with his men, and generous enough to teach a greenhorn how to trot so she would be safe in a time that wasn't at all safe for a city girl with only twenty-first-century skills.

What a waste.

As was attempting to enjoy a wooden bowl full of things that one of François's assistants brought her. She couldn't taste it, so she merely held on to it and felt quite thoroughly ill.

Toasting began as dinner wound down. Gunnild rose and reminded everyone she was the lady of the hall and was happy to see her cousin so happily settled. Boydin followed, telling a ribald tale or two about Montgomery that couldn't possibly be true given that the stories were completely out of character for the man she knew. Montgomery shifted uncomfortably, as if he were considering getting up to offer a few corrections. Pippa was ready to offer a few thoughts of her own, but before she could, Gunnild had shoved a frail, sickly looking man Pippa could only assume was a priest to his feet.

"The time for the ceremony has come," he wheezed. "Unless there are impediments to the marriage." He looked at Gunnild. "The banns have not been read —"

"Never mind that," Gunnild said shortly.

"We have no chapel —"

"We don't need one," Gunnild snarled. "Be about your work, old man."

The man had another drink, spilling most of it down the front of his tunic, then he apparently took his courage in hand. "We'll carry on, unless anyone has a reason to protest —"

"I do," Pippa said loudly.

She realized only as the company was divided between looking at her and looking at Montgomery that she hadn't been the only one to voice that sentiment. The priest looked first at her, then at Montgomery.

"Aye, my lord?" he said weakly. "Is there aught . . ."

Montgomery stood up, looking rather grim. " 'Tis a pleasure to enjoy such a fine meal," he said slowly, "and such fine company. I fear, however, that I am unable to wed this exceedingly lovely queen sitting here."

Pippa stuck one finger in her ear because that's all she had free. She looked at Cindi to find her beginning to frown. That wasn't a surprise. Cindi was never dumped; she always did the dumping. Pippa could hardly believe dumping was going to be a part of the afternoon's festivities. Gunnild looked equally displeased. Maybe she had hoped to get rid of Montgomery by marrying him off to a fairy.

Stranger things had happened.

"You see," Montgomery went on, looking supremely uncomfortable, "there is indeed an impediment to, um, to this noble venture into, ah, matrimony."

"What impediment?" Boydin drawled. "Are you already wed in secret?"

Montgomery shot him a look that should have shut him up, but apparently Boydin had had a little too much to drink. He only continued to speculate just why it was that Montgomery couldn't marry the lovely and very available Queen of Faery. Montgomery glared at his cousin once more, then took a deep breath and turned back to the company.

"I would like to ask Mistress Cinderella to forgive me for not being forthcoming. I was too dazzled by her absolute perfection to remember a, um, prior commitment."

Cindi preened.

Pippa couldn't stop from gaping.

"I am . . . betrothed," Montgomery said, spitting the words out as quickly as possible. "Have been for . . . for quite some time."

Pippa heard a noise. She only realized it was her dinner landing on the stone at her feet because a kitchen helper began to clean it up.

She wasn't sure if she should be relieved Montgomery wasn't about to be stupid enough to marry her sister or angry he'd been so nice to her when he was engaged to someone else. She was definitely overcome with some sort of emotion. Maybe it was heartburn.

She turned around and walked back to the kitchen, because she couldn't stand to be a witness any longer to what was going on in the great hall. She didn't care what Montgomery did, of course, because he wasn't for her and she wasn't for him. Obviously, she wasn't for him if he was already committed to someone else. She put her shoulders back and continued on. She had been distracted there briefly, but she was back to herself. And now that Cindi had just been given a bracing dose of reality — not that she would recognize it as such, or even remember it in a week — maybe she would give up the idea of . . .

Pippa slowed to a stop as something occurred to her.

What if the reason she hadn't been able to get herself home had been because her sister had wanted to stay right where she was? It was, after all, very good to be queen. Maybe all she and Cindi had to do was stand on the end of the bridge, hold hands, and be in full possession of their wits as they clicked their heels together and wished themselves home. If it had worked for Dorothy, surely it would work for them.

She continued on her way out to the stable, not for any other reason than she thought she might need a bit of air. The place had definitely improved since she'd first seen it. It probably helped to have a professional horseman in charge of things. She greeted the stable master, asked permission to go visit Steud, then did just that. The horse seemed to be pleased to see her, but that might have been because she'd poached a carrot on her way out of the kitchen. She fed it to him in stages, then simply stood there and stroked his nose.

She was also happy to list for him his very

fine characteristics, such as the ability to keep her on his back under what she definitely considered duress. She was surprised by how happy she was to stand there and do nothing more than converse with a horse. No wonder Montgomery rode when he had deep thoughts to digest. It certainly took her mind off other things.

Such as the fact that Montgomery was standing at the entrance to the stables, watching her.

She didn't jump because she'd known for the past five minutes that he was there. She supposed she could have stood in any room with her eyes closed and known the moment he walked in. Engaged man that he was.

She was really in trouble.

She took a deep breath, then turned her head to look at him. "My lord?"

He walked over to stand next to her, then reached out to stroke Steud's nose. He had a wicker for his trouble and smiled in return. Pippa waited for him to say something, but he was apparently not in the mood to divulge secrets she supposed he really hadn't needed to before. After all, it wasn't as if she'd worn her heart on her sleeve, or blurted out that she thought she might have a crush on him, or gazed at him longingly from across the room.

Well, that last part she suspected she'd done at least twice, but he probably hadn't noticed.

The bottom line was, he didn't owe her anything. He had already done far more for her than he'd needed to. She leaned her forearms against the stall door and looked at him. He was very grave, even more than he was usually. She supposed the day hadn't been easy for him. His lengthy retreats to the lists were likely indication enough of that. She reached out and tucked his hair behind his ear before she thought better of it. He was perfectly still, but his breath caught.

Maybe he had a headache. She was fairly sure it couldn't be because he was affected by her.

"How are you?" she asked quietly.

He lifted an eyebrow briefly. "I'm not sure how to put it without offending you."

"I don't offend easily."

He looked at her then. "I am vastly relieved not to be wedding your sister. Especially since I didn't ask for her hand."

"I really don't think she's your sort of gal," she said, suppressing the urge to ask him just what sort of gal he liked. Obviously the sort of medieval miss he was going to marry.

She attempted a smile. "I probably should go back and get her upstairs before she causes a scene."

"Joan has done the honors." He looked at her quickly. "Stay, if you would."

If he was going to ask that nicely, she wasn't going to say no.

He chewed on his words for a moment or two, then reached back over the stall to pet Steud again. "Your sister doesn't look well."

"She'll run out of pills tomorrow."

He nodded, then remained silent for several minutes before he spoke again. "Perhaps it would be safer for us all if you and I were to spirit her out of the keep," he said slowly. He shot her a quick look. "My cousins are a suspicious lot, you know, and already have reason enough to want me dead. No sense in giving them any more."

"And the Faery Queen having a fit in your great hall wouldn't help?"

"I don't think it would. My grandmother's keep is a bit to the north. Or we could go farther still and speak to my brother. He would never admit as much, but I suspect he can lay claim to knowledge of a few —" He took a deep breath. "A few paranormal oddities."

"Phillip says his father doesn't believe in them."

"My brother Robin has no imagination, something I'll readily admit. But I was speaking of my second-eldest brother, Nicholas."

"He's more open-minded, then?"

"A bit." He looked at her seriously. "I would wait your gate out here and brave your sister's unruliness, but I fear that my cousins won't stop at spewing their venom my way. They'll look for other targets soon enough."

It took her a moment to figure out what he was saying. She looked at him in astonishment. "You mean me?"

"I fear so. They want to kill me, of course, but I have given them cause just by drawing breath. You, however, have done nothing to them."

"Oh, I don't know," Pippa said faintly. "I called Boydin an ass a time or two."

He smiled. "I'm sure it wasn't undeserved. Still, I think you would be safer if we left for a bit. Besides, we might find aid in unexpected places."

"What about your betrothed?" Pippa asked, because she apparently just couldn't leave well enough alone. "Won't she expect to see you soon?"

He shifted uncomfortably. "She, ah, understands my present straits."

"Patient girl."

"The most patient," he agreed.

Pippa thought it was probably unhealthy to loathe someone she'd never met before, but if ever she'd had reason, this was it. She watched him turn back to stroking a soft horsey nose and took the opportunity to try to get a hold of herself.

She should have developed more self-control during her incarceration at Aunt Edna's. Her aunt had told her it would come in handy, but had she listened? Of course not. She'd been too busy plotting how to get a scholarship and get out of the house early so she wouldn't *have* to have self-control.

"What do you do?" he asked suddenly. "In the Future?"

She was surprised by the question, though she supposed she shouldn't have been. She smiled up at him. "I design clothes. I usually do them for plays, but I want to design them just for women who want to feel beautiful."

"Did you make Cinderella's gown?"

She shook her head. "I made her something else, but she didn't wear it. She was trying to impress . . ." She paused. "Well, she was trying to impress the son of an earl who was supposed to be overwhelmed by what I had designed, not what Cindi was wearing."

"Do you have lords in your day?" he asked, looking at her in surprise.

"We do. And sons of earls that need to be impressed by ball gowns."

Montgomery smiled. "Did this son who was no doubt more enamored of your gowns than your sister's have a name?"

"Stephen." She couldn't help herself from adding what she probably shouldn't have. "Stephen de Piaget. His father is Edward, the current earl of Artane."

Montgomery's knees buckled. Pippa caught him and staggered as he threw his arms around her. Then she realized that he was far less unsteady that he pretended to be.

"Faker."

He smiled and hugged her very briefly before he stepped away. "I'm not sure what that means exactly, but I can guess." He leaned heavily against the stall door. "Are you in earnest about the other?"

She nodded. "He couldn't look much more like you if you'd been related. Which I suppose you are."

"No wonder Robin shuns all things he can't best with a sword," he said with a shiver. "I'm beginning to see the wisdom of it." He put his arm around her shoulders. "Come back to the hall, my lady, and we'll ask François to see us prepared for at least some of our journey."

She didn't want to enjoy that feeling of his arm around her, but she did, just a bit. It was a particularly platonic, brotherly sort of arm around the shoulders, but she supposed she couldn't — and shouldn't — ask for more.

She stopped him just outside the kitchen. "Thank you," she said quietly. She attempted a smile, but she wasn't sure she'd been all that successful. "For helping me, that is. I know you have other things to be doing."

"It is not only my duty," he said just as quietly, "but my pleasure to aid you how I can. If there is aught else —"

"There is."

He tilted his head slightly. "What would that be?"

"Sing another song for me tonight?"

"Now, woman, you go too far."

She smiled and turned away. "You'll survive."

"I doubt that," he muttered under his breath, but he caught up with her and tucked her hand into the crook of his arm. "One song."

"Three."

"None, then," he grumbled.

"I believe I'll have four."

He scowled at her again, then pursed his lips as if he strove not to smile. He said nothing else, so she supposed he wouldn't refuse her request. She also supposed she wasn't a complete idiot to enjoy his company for one more night.

She might actually get home in the next few days. She was vastly relieved and very excited to get back to her real life. It had been an interesting foray into times and places not her own, but that interlude was coming to an end and she couldn't have been happier about it.

And she supposed if she continued to repeat that, she might actually believe it.

Eventually.

Chapter 15

Montgomery had never once, during the course of his score-and-seven years, come close to even considering entertaining the thought of taking his sword and clouting a woman on top of the head with it. That he was seriously contemplating the potentially fatal blow it would deal to his knightly reputation said much about the past handful of days.

Cinderella had run out of pills three days earlier.

Gone was the woman who, whilst daft, had at least been somewhat manageable. The woman who had taken her place was so full of ill humors, Montgomery wondered if they would manage to keep her from killing them all.

They had been traveling for four days in a haphazard fashion that made him uncomfortable, but he had been severely limited by the fact that Cinderella could not ride. If he'd been a different sort of man, he might have just strapped her to the back of a horse and carried on, but he was who he was, so he had provided her with the comfort of a small, decrepit wagon he'd been forced to purchase from a shrewd and subsequently very content farmer. He supposed it wouldn't have mattered if he'd had one of the king's luxurious carriages, Cinderella wouldn't have been happy.

He had intended to stop at Segrave to provide Pippa with a bit of a rest, but Cinderella had become so unpleasant he hadn't dared do aught but continue on toward Wyckham and hope to seek out Nicholas's advice. He wondered, generally accompanied by a sigh, how it was that Pippa not only endured her sister, but had compassion on her. He wouldn't have managed the same in her place, of that he was absolutely certain.

He looked at the compassionate woman in question. She was riding alongside him in his clothes, attempting to look like a lad. He studied her surreptitiously, wondering if the look of worry she wasn't able to conceal was limited to her sister's behavior, or if she was concerned that she might not manage to return to her time.

He didn't dare hope that she might not

want to return to that time.

He looked up at the sky, almost dreading the waning of the afternoon. One more day behind him, which meant one more day closer to sending Pippa back to her time. He had no doubt he would manage it. If nothing else, he supposed he could send them home through that gate near Artane. The irony of that was almost more than he could stand —

"My lord?"

Montgomery turned to look at his squire, frowning as he did so. There was a note in the lad's voice he didn't particularly care for. "Aye, lad?"

"I haven't noticed Sir Ranulf returning recently. I think surely an hour has passed since —"

"Damnation," Montgomery said, because that was the least of the things he could have said. Nay, his captain hadn't returned to deliver scouting tidings in at least a pair of hours, and he should have noticed sooner. He would have, if he hadn't spent all his time worrying that Cinderella would lure every ruffian in England away from their comfortable fires to see who the banshee was shrieking out curses. "Hell," he added, because that seemed fitting, given it was where he had likely plunged his entire company.

"Actually," a voice drawled from behind him, "I would say you were leaving Hell and moving on to more interesting parts of our blessed isle, but perhaps I'm not the most unbiased one to ask."

Montgomery looked at Pippa, who had turned in her saddle to look behind her. All the color had drained from her face. He would have reassured her that all was well, but he supposed he shouldn't until he'd assured himself that such was the case. He had no doubt he wouldn't be free of what had caught him up without some sort of penalty to be paid. He looked at Phillip.

"Guard her."

"Of course, my lord uncle."

Montgomery turned his horse to face a sight he was sure he wouldn't enjoy and a bit of censure he would most certainly deserve.

Nicholas de Piaget, lord of Wyckham, Count of Beauvois, and possessor of copious amounts of sword skill learned at his peerless father's knee, sat twenty paces from him, surrounded by a small army of guardsmen. Montgomery knew they were only a fraction of the lads Nicholas laid claim to, but that was because his brother wouldn't have left his family unprotected by anything less than a mighty force.

Montgomery realized just how far he was from having a garrison he would have trusted to protect anyone he might have loved.

The only bright spot in the gloom was realizing he'd traveled farther that day than he'd hoped. Judging by the landscape, Wyckham was but another half day's ride ahead. He supposed it might be premature to hope he would enjoy something edible at his brother's supper table before Nicholas killed him.

Nicholas only lifted an eyebrow in challenge.

Montgomery suppressed the urge to roll his eyes. "Am I to fight you for my freedom," he asked briskly, "or will you simply take a ransom for it?"

"As it happens," Nicholas said thoughtfully, leaning on the pommel of his saddle, "I've had ample time to think on just that given that I've been following you for at least an hour." He nodded to his captain. "William, if you would be so good as to keep watch over my lord Sedgwick's company whilst we speak of our business in private?"

To his credit, Nicholas's captain didn't give in to so much as a ghost of a smile. He merely nodded solemnly, then nodded to the men surrounding his lord. Montgomery sighed, then backed his horse up until he was where he could look at Pippa.

"All is well."

"Who *is* that?" she asked faintly.

"My second-eldest brother, Nicholas."

"He of the useful imagination?"

"Aye," Montgomery agreed darkly. "An imagination I'm quite certain he'll use exhaustively in divising ways to humiliate me for daydreaming whilst I should have been watching over our company. He's likely holding Ranulf for ransom. We can be relieved, I suppose, that 'tis Nicholas here and not Robin, else I couldn't afford to free us."

"I must agree," Phillip ventured. "My sire would have demanded either acceptable swordplay or all your gold. Perhaps both, plus a shining of his boots." He looked at Pippa. "My father is —"

"Impossible," Montgomery finished for him. "Impossible and irritating and a whole host of other things I'll list for you later." He paused and looked at Cinderella who had taken a good look at Nicholas and his guardsmen and begun to scream. He looked back at Pippa. "Can you silence her?"

"Absolutely."

"Do you require aid?"

She smiled briefly, then shook her head. "Go chat with your brother. I'll be fine."

She dismounted before he could help her, then walked over to speak urgently to her sister. Phillip jumped off his horse and trotted off after her when it looked as if Cinderella might be fancying another go at Pippa's eye. Montgomery turned away with a curse, dismounted, then walked over to look up at his brother.

"I am in haste," he said. "Be about your criticism of my care of these two gels without delay so I might see to what I must."

Nicholas dismounted with a grunt. "I'm not about to give you a lecture on your knightly duties. I believe I gave you one or two during your youth and that fulfilled my obligation completely."

Montgomery dragged his hand through his hair. "I'm distracted."

"By the woman in the wagon or the woman riding next to you, pretending to be a lad?"

"Both, for different reasons."

Nicholas looked at Cinderella. "Brother, you must talk sense into that one. The noises she makes —"

"What am I to do?" Montgomery asked

shortly. "Gag her?"

"After having listened to her for the past hour, I would say aye. You would be doing her and the one I suppose by the look of her is her sister a favor. I have lads enough with me, but not for an extended battle if we're set upon fiercely."

Montgomery hesitated. "I don't care for this treatment of even a daft wench."

"Shall I do it for you?"

"Would you?" Montgomery asked wearily.

Nicholas only smiled. "Of course not. You've been able to fight your own battles for years now, Montgomery." He fished about in his saddlebag for a moment or two, then came up with a strip of cloth. " 'Tis clean, though I don't suppose it will taste very nice just the same."

Montgomery suspected the taste of her gag was the last thing Cinderella was going to notice. He had a moment's hesitation about what he planned to do, then set that aside when Cinderella crawled out of the wagon and started toward Pippa. He leapt forward and caught her by the arms before she could touch her younger sister. He looked at Pippa.

"Gag her," he said quietly.

Pippa didn't hesitate. She also didn't manage to accomplish the task before Cinderella had sunk her teeth into his wrist. Montgomery wouldn't have let her go if she hadn't elbowed him so hard in the belly that he doubled over with a gasp. He missed catching her before she threw herself at Pippa, her claws unsheathed, but he supposed his aid had been unnecessary.

Pippa had caught her sister under the chin with her fist.

Cinderella slid gracefully to the ground like a fine, long length of silk, smacked her lips a time or two, then began to drool. Montgomery looked at Pippa, openmouthed.

"Well," he managed.

"I had to," she said defensively.

He held up his hands. "I wasn't condemning you. Just admiring your technique. Perhaps you'd care to supplant Ranulf as captain of my guard."

She rubbed the knuckles of her right hand gingerly. "I'm not sure you'd want me. I think I might burst into tears soon."

She looked as if she were ready to do just that. He took her hand on the pretext of examining it when what he wanted to do was take her hands and use them to pull her into his arms. When he felt her trembling, he cast caution to the wind and did just that. He put his arms around her and held her whilst she shook.

"You spared us unwanted company," he said quietly. "Something had to be done."

"I've never hit anyone before."

He looked over her head to find his brother standing there, watching with a small smile on his face. Nicholas shook his head wryly, then turned to have his lads see to securing their unhappy traveling companion. Montgomery left him to it and concentrated instead on the woman in his arms.

For not nearly as long as he would have liked, as it happened.

She took a deep breath, then pulled away. "Right. So, what now?"

"Food," Nicholas said, turning away from the wagon where Cinderella had been made as comfortable as possible, "then a continuation of our separate journeys." He held out his hand for Pippa's, then favored her with a courtly bow. "Nicholas de Piaget, at your service."

Pippa smiled. "I can see where Montgomery learned his chivalry."

"I will admit," Nicholas admitted modestly, "that I taught him most all of what he knows. About chivalry, dancing, singing, the playing of the lute —"

"Enough," Montgomery said, rolling his eyes. "Don't encourage the braggart, Pippa, else he'll go on all day about the mighty virtues he managed to instill in me." He looked at Nicholas. "We would appreciate a meal, but before that, I must speak with you."

Nicholas winked at Pippa. "He's trying to squeak out of a hefty ransom. I'm not entirely sure why he was so distracted —"

"The premonition that I would have to listen to you babble on for the whole of the afternoon," Montgomery said shortly. He nodded to Phillip. "Keep your hand on your sword, Phillip, and please tell Ranulf I will apologize to him for sending him into a trap after I'm finished here." He looked at Pippa. "Phillip will watch over you until I return."

Pippa nodded, then walked with Phillip over to a fallen log away from the main road. Montgomery watched them go, then turned to his brother.

"Well?"

Nicholas only smiled. "Interesting company you keep."

Montgomery grunted, then rubbed his hands. It had been a very long journey with an end in sight he didn't particularly care to reach. He sighed, then looked at his brother. "When they first arrived on my threshold, I thought, if you can believe this, that they were the Faery Queen and her servant."

Nicholas laughed, then he stopped abruptly. "You can't be serious. Well," he amended, "I know you fully believed such things in your youth —"

"With good reason, I might add, given the mysterious circumstances surrounding a trio of my siblings' spouses," Montgomery said pointedly.

"I don't have any idea what you're talking about," Nicholas said promptly.

Montgomery shot him a look he hoped fully revealed his disgust.

Nicholas shifted uncomfortably, then laughed, also uncomfortably. "I don't know what you want from me."

"I want a look at a particular map you reportedly keep hidden in your strongest trunk," Montgomery said. "John found it, if you're interested."

Nicholas shut his mouth that had fallen open. "He didn't."

"He did."

"Did you look at it with him?"

"I didn't, but Kendrick did."

Nicholas's mouth fell back open. "Why, that little wretch. And damn that John for no doubt leading the way to things he shouldn't have been toying with."

"A terrible habit of his," Montgomery said in a tone he hoped said he didn't care to discuss the subject any further. "And to clear up the other for you, of course I knew Pippa and her sister weren't from Faery. The only thing I don't know is how to get them back to where they do belong."

"And why would you think I would have any . . . er . . ." He paused, then sighed. "Very well, you needn't look at me that way any longer." He nodded toward his left. "We'll speak of it further in private."

Montgomery was happy to oblige him. He walked with his brother for a few minutes, then waited whilst Nicholas looked about him, then frowned.

"I'm not admitting to having seen anything . . . unusual."

"Nick, I am no longer a child," Montgomery said with what he thought an admirable amount of patience. "In fact, not only am I no longer a child, I am responsible for the care of two women who are, by their own admission, hundreds of years out of their time. If you cannot be frank with me now, when will you be?"

"I knew this day would come," Nicholas said with a sigh.

"Consider me practice for your wee ones. You can't imagine you won't be answering their questions at some point in the future."

"The saints preserve me," Nicholas said

faintly. He took a deep breath. "Very well, I will be frank — and brief. There are, from what I understand, gates scattered over the whole of Scotland and much of England. Jennifer has a cousin — a distant cousin, of course — who was in a former lifetime a Scottish laird. He wed himself a gel from the Future, traveled to the Future himself, then began an investigation of all things paranormal."

"Robin would loathe him."

Nicholas smiled. "I daresay he would. This cousin, as it happens, is a very keen maker of maps. He made one for Jennifer as part of her dowry, one that contains all the gates in England and as much of Scotland as he thought we might be able to reach. So, aye, I can aid you in getting your lady and her sister back to their proper time."

"She isn't my lady."

Nicholas only lifted an eyebrow. "If you say that often enough, you might begin to believe it."

Montgomery dragged his hand through his hair. "I told her I was betrothed to another."

"You fool," Nicholas said, with a shocked laugh. "What were you thinking?"

"To escape a marriage to her sister, who is under the impression that she truly is the

Faery Queen, which I believe I mentioned before, and who had determined I would make an excellent bridegroom."

"Well, you *are* an attractive lad."

Montgomery scowled at his brother. "I had to have some excuse to say the wench nay. Pippa and Cinderella have their lives back in their time, and I have holes in my walls and cousins who want me dead."

"Have you considered that perhaps Pippa might be interested in your very skilled chef, your rapier wit, and deliciously pretty eyes?" Nicholas countered. "How could she resist all that?"

"Easily, I assure you," Montgomery said. "Now, if you would be so good as to direct me to one of these gates you know about, I would be most grateful."

Nicholas studied him for a moment or two. "Very well," he said quietly. "Make for the crook of those hills you see there to the west. If it were springtime, you might find an odd ring of flowers there in the grass. Now, I imagine you'll only see a circle of things gone to seed." He paused, then smirked. "I suppose *you* might call it a faery ring."

"Amusing."

Nicholas only smiled. "If I were Robin, I would enjoy the irony more, but I can't for

I see this is a parting that will be — how shall we say it?"

"Inevitable," Montgomery said. "And unfortunately quite necessary."

Nicholas put his hand briefly on Montgomery's shoulder. "I'm sorry for it, brother, truly. Why don't you come to Wyckham when you've seen your charges safely delivered to their time? Jenner and the lads will be happy to see you."

Montgomery nodded, more grateful for the invitation than he wanted to admit. Aye, he would go to Wyckham once he was finished with his business.

It would be a distraction to spend a day or two with family so he might think on something besides what he would have just recently lost.

Three hours and the return to consciousness of Cinderella later, he found what his brother had told him to seek. He wasn't quite sure how he was to go about sending Pippa and her sister home with his guardsmen and his squire as four gaping witnesses to the fact, so he sent his lads back the way they'd come to wait for him. The excuse of the sisters' kin being too cautious to want to encounter men-at-arms had seemed a decent lie, though he wasn't any happier about that one than he was any of the others he'd told in the past fortnight.

He waited until he was alone with Pippa and Cinderella, then drew his knife and cut first the gag from Cinderella's mouth, then the cloth Nicholas's lads had apparently used to bind her wrists and ankles together.

Cinderella sat up and looked around her, dazed. "Where are we?"

"Going home," Pippa said shortly. "Behave while I go change —"

"No need," Montgomery said quickly. He suspected it would sound daft if he told her the thought of her having something of his in the Future was comforting, so he pressed on without hesitation. "Your gown is in the wagon. Just carry it along with you."

Pippa looked at him gravely, then nodded and walked over to the wagon to fetch her clothes. She shook the gown out, then slipped her hands into the pockets one by one.

The blood drained from her face. He would have stepped forward to aid her, but she was searching the wagon so frantically, he didn't dare get in her way. He glanced at Cinderella in time to see her watching her sister with a rather lucid expression on her face, all things considered. It wasn't a very pleasant expression, which made him wonder what mischief she was combining. He kept Cinderella in his sights on the off chance she decided to bolt suddenly, then walked over to stand next to Pippa as she leaned back against the wagon.

"What is it?" he asked quietly.

"I had something in the pocket of my dress," she said faintly.

Montgomery looked again at Cinderella to find her smirking, as if she'd done something she found vastly amusing. Pippa pushed away from the wagon and strode over to her.

"What did you do with it?" she demanded.

Cinderella flipped her hair back over her shoulder. "I'm just sure I don't know what you're talking about."

Montgomery listened to them converse — in Future English, no less — in tones that became less dulcet with every exchange.

"Cindi, where's my flash drive!"

"You hid my pills," Cinderella snapped, "so I hid your little backup stick."

"I didn't hide your pills," Pippa said through gritted teeth, "you swallowed them all. Now, where did you put my drive?"

"Maybe you'd better go back and look for it in the castle."

Pippa froze. "Did you leave it there?"

"I guess you'll just have to go check and

see, won't you?"

Montgomery watched Pippa turn and walk away. Cinderella strolled past him to sit on the end of the wagon as if she had nothing more pressing to do than be at her leisure. He left her where she was, smiling triumphantly, and hastened to catch up with Pippa.

"Wait," he said, reaching out to take her by the arm.

She stopped, then turned to face him. "You know," she said flatly, "I've always thought my sister was just not too bright, that she couldn't help overshadowing me in everything. Now, I think she's been doing it on purpose all these years."

Montgomery wouldn't doubt it. "What has she done now?"

"She took something I can't leave behind here."

"Something from the Future?"

"Yes."

He very briefly entertained the thought of seeing if she cared to return to Sedgwick with him to seek out that thing, but quickly dismissed it. The journey was long and she was no doubt eager to go back to her world. "Tell me what it is and I will destroy it, Persephone," he said quietly. "You needn't worry."

She laughed a little, but it was a laugh of desperation. "The problem is, my life's work is on this thing. It's very small, but it has pictures inside it of all my designs." She paused. "It's the only one I have."

"Then you must have it," he said, vowing to ask Nicholas later how it was that Pippa could have sheaves of drawings on something that could fit into a saddlebag. "We'll turn for home immediately."

She took a deep breath, then shook her head. "I couldn't ask you to go to all that trouble."

"Well," he said slowly, as if he pondered the enormous inconvenience it would cause him instead of furiously calculating how many more days it would mean he could have her company, "I do have things to do. Walls to patch, François's delicacies to sample — that sort of thing. It might take a bit before I could bring you north again. Assuming this gate works as it should."

She blinked rapidly a time or two. "I couldn't ask it."

"If the roles were reversed and you could help me save my life's work, wouldn't you?"

She nodded silently.

"Then allow me the same privilege."

"It won't bother your fiancée?"

"Wha — Oh, her," he said. He knew at

that moment why he'd never lied. It was a complicated business, what with all the tales he needed to keep straight. He would see Pippa home, eventually, then he would return to his habit of never telling anything but the absolute truth. It was less painful to his poor head that way.

He wasn't quite sure why he just didn't blurt out the truth of it right there, but he couldn't bring himself to. It might be the only thing keeping him from yanking Pippa into his arms, professing undying love he couldn't possibly feel for her after such a short time, and begging her to stay in his time and allow him to spend the rest of his days being as dazzled by her as Nicholas was by Jennifer.

"What about Cindi?"

He pulled himself back to the matter at hand reluctantly. "I suppose we should take her with us," he said, though he didn't imagine he could think of many things he would rather *not* have done.

"Or we could send her on by herself."

He considered. "Would she be safe?"

"No less safe than if I went with her."

That was all he needed to hear. He put his arm around Pippa's shoulders and led her back to where her sister was singing rather loudly to herself and stroking her ragged locks. Once she saw Pippa, she felt her chin gingerly, then checked all her teeth.

"You hit me," she said, her perfect brow beginning to furrow.

"You deserved it," Pippa said shortly. "We'll discuss it later. We're going home now."

"Good." Cinderella straightened her crown and glared at Pippa. "I do *not* like to camp."

"I know," Pippa said, taking her sister by the arm, "which is why I'm going to make it so you don't have to any longer."

"What are you doing?" she demanded, trying to jerk away. "Tossing me in the moat? Oh, wait, that's what I did to you." She wrinkled her nose. "You still smell like it."

Montgomery didn't think anything of the sort, but he supposed now was not the time to make that clear. He also didn't think now was the time to alert Pippa to the fact that he could understand her native tongue. He put that aside as a revelation to make if and when he ever admitted to the nonexistence of his betrothed, took Cinderella's other arm, then looked over her head at Pippa.

"Up ahead," he said quietly. "In that ring in the grass."

"You're trying to get rid of me," Cinderella said incredulously. She looked from him to Pippa, then back. "One of you is jealous of me, but I'm not sure which one."

Montgomery could have corrected her about that as well, but he didn't bother. He was suddenly too busy pulling Cinderella away from her sister with a bit more enthusiasm than he probably should have used and subsequently giving her an equally enthusiastic bit of urging — accompanied by a fervent prayer she would land in the right time — right into the middle of the faery ring.

She took two steps inside it.

And then she disappeared without fanfare.

He gasped. Or perhaps that might have been Pippa. He wasn't certain whose expression of astonishment had been louder. Even with all the tales he had fully believed in his youth and all the speculating he had done about things of a paranormal nature, he had never actually been a *participant* in those things. To be one now was profoundly unnerving.

He reached out and pulled Pippa close to him. "She's gone," he breathed.

"It's spooky."

"Aye," he agreed.

Pippa shivered. "I know I should feel bad about sending her off, but she's probably safer wherever she is. If she'd stayed here any longer, I would have killed her."

Montgomery managed a smile. "Truly you have the patience of a saint."

"Moral high ground," she said with a faint smile. She paused, then pulled away and turned to face him. "I really could just follow her now —"

"Nay," he said, likely with more enthusiasm than he should have. "Nay, you'll come back to Sedgwick and find your flash drive. I'll bring you back here afterward."

She looked up at him for a moment or two in silence. "You know," she said finally, "I think that might be the nicest thing anyone's ever done for me."

He shifted uncomfortably, mostly because he wasn't one to accept praise for something he hadn't done. And he most certainly hadn't offered to keep Pippa in his time for any altruistic reasons.

The saints pity him for it.

He clasped his hands behind his back before he did something foolish with them, such as use them to pull her into his arms. "Perhaps we should spend a day or two at Wyckham," he suggested. "In the event that perhaps she wanders back into my time and needs aid."

"Will your brother mind?"

"He would only be irritated if we traveled

so close to his hall and didn't make an appearance at his supper table."

She glanced at the patch of grass there beyond the wagon. "Did he know about this gate?"

Montgomery shifted — truly it was becoming an alarming habit. " 'Tis on his land," he said carefully, "and he's very particular about knowing what passes on his land. I imagine he listened to rumor. Fortunate for us that he did, isn't it?"

"Very," she agreed.

He wondered if she was wondering things she shouldn't have been, but since she had reason, he couldn't fault her for it. He quite happily left that unassuming patch of grass behind him, then offered Pippa his arm before he walked with her back to where his lads were waiting. He made up what he hoped was a believable tale about relatives fetching bedraggled queens and wagons being left for someone less fortunate, then distracted his men with thoughts of Nicholas's kitchens. He helped Pippa mount Steud, then looked up at her as he handed her the reins.

"Thank you for learning to ride."

"Thank you for taking the time to teach me," she said with a smile. "Master Sensible was very wise."

Montgomery smiled, then went to swing up onto his own horse. He wasn't sure he would have called himself wise — he was, after all, encouraging a woman he most assuredly couldn't have to remain with him long past when she should have gone back home — but perhaps he could take a day or two and forget that his life was full of duty and responsibility and a castle fair to falling down.

Would that it could have been full of Persephone Alexander.

CHAPTER 16

Pippa woke to sun streaming in the window. For a split second, she wondered if she'd dreamed the past two weeks, but no, that was definitely a carved canopy above her head. It was too handmade-looking to be the right-out-of-the-shrink-wrap sort of thing found in Tess's castle, but somehow too intricate to be a mass-produced reproduction.

It was the real thing, which meant she was still hanging around in 1241.

The upside was, she was in a castle that had looked the night before to be capable of withstanding the whole of the English army. It had probably been midnight before their company had ridden through the gates, and she had listened to the comforting sound of the portcullis slamming home behind her. Stable lads had taken their horses and servants had come to see them settled. Pippa hadn't remembered much past the impression of a spectacular castle, a warm piece of bread, and a rapid trip to a bed so soft, she'd wondered if she'd died and gone to heaven.

If she'd still had a crappy futon mattress to return to in the future, she wouldn't have ever complained about it again.

She supposed it would be rude to just hang out in bed all day, so she forced herself to get up, wash, then put on a dress apparently left for her. It was made of such lovely fabric she couldn't help but linger and fondle just a bit. She continued to study the weave as she left her room and walked down the passageway. It wasn't linen, she didn't think, nor was it cotton —

Pippa paused at the sound of humming. She watched who she could only assume was Jennifer, the lady of Wyckham, walking down the hallway in front of her toward the stairs. Jennifer blew her hair out of her eyes, adjusted the baby she was carrying, then held down her hand for what looked to be a two-year-old boy.

"*Allons-y,* Thomas," she said. "Let's find you some supper."

And then the humming, which Pippa realized was coming from Jennifer herself began again. It was something she half recognized, but she couldn't lay her finger on the name of the tune. She frowned. Had she been in the Middle Ages too long? Admittedly, it had been a little unnerving not to be able to immediately identify the composition of the cloth she was wearing, but surely that was no indication of the arrival of a complete mental breakdown. She briefly ran through the collection of things her parents had hummed for her — which included but hadn't been limited to Grateful Dead tunes and Beatles standards — but came up empty-handed. Maybe she would try again after she'd had something to eat.

She followed Jennifer — which seemed to be an odd name for a medieval woman to have, but what did she know of the time period? — down the circular stairs, then paused at the edge of the great hall.

It was no wonder Montgomery sighed a lot when he looked at his hall.

There was an arch that spanned the hall from one side to the other, with an enormous fireplace set in one wall and a dozen gorgeous tapestries lining the rest of the stone. There was even a second-floor gallery with light coming in from windows set back too far for her to see. The entire effect was one of elegance and refinement.

It was spectacular.

She lingered there in the shadows for a

moment or two and wondered about Montgomery and his family. His brother was obviously rich as Croesus with the castle to prove it. She wasn't sure why Montgomery had gotten stuck with Sedgwick, but maybe there was more to medieval inheritances than she knew. He seemed to have the money to pay his stone masons to fix his walls, which she supposed he would need to have done if he ever managed to kick his cousins out. No sense in having a way for them to come back inside and kill him.

She shook her head over the thought. She had obviously been in the Middle Ages too long. Murder and mayhem were starting to seem like standard —

Murder and mayhem. She frowned. Hadn't Peaches said something about Tess's castle having more than its share of that going for it?

She shook her head. That surely had nothing to do with Montgomery. He would drop her off at the time gate, go pick up his future bride, and his life would go on without incident.

And without her.

She shook aside her unproductive thoughts and wondered if she might possibly get something decent to eat. She looked for Montgomery, didn't see him, then decided the best thing to do was follow Jennifer to the kitchens — assuming that's where she'd gone.

She stopped at the edge of the kitchen as she had the edge of the hall to have a look at the lay of the land. The kitchen actually looked a lot like Tess's with happy staff, ample workspace, and what apparently passed for a medieval rack with pots hanging on it. The lady of the hall was in mid-discussion of something with her cook when she apparently realized she wasn't alone. She turned to Pippa, then smiled.

"Persephone," she said, walking over with her boys in her arms. "Welcome to Wyckham. I apologize for not greeting you last night."

Pippa thought a little curtsey couldn't go wrong, so she offered it and had a laugh in return.

"Take a baby instead of bowing," Jennifer said, handing over a boy who had pale blond hair and enormous blue eyes. "Let's go find something to eat. Montgomery and Nicholas ate hours ago and are now out in the lists, though that probably doesn't surprise you."

Pippa shook her head, then enjoyed the happy distraction of a little lad who regarded her with serious eyes, as if he saw things in her he really shouldn't have been able to. She followed Jennifer out to the great hall, surrendered the baby to his mother, then sat down to what was definitely the best meal she'd had so far on her involuntary vacation. She wasn't sure what passed for polite small talk in medieval England, but she supposed she couldn't go wrong with confining her remarks to the weather and the lady of Wyckham's health, which she did.

Half an hour later, Jennifer held a very sleepy baby in her arms and a fractious toddler by the hand.

"I think the lads have had enough," she said easily, "so if you'll excuse me, I'll get them upstairs." She smiled. "I don't think you'll have any trouble finding the lists, if that's where you'd like to go. The garden is also lovely, but perhaps a bit chilly today."

"Thank you, my lady," Pippa said, getting up and pulling out Jennifer's chair for her. She had another laugh in return, then stood back and watched the lady of the hall lure her older son up the stairs.

Howls soon ensued when the lad apparently realized just what sort of activity his afternoon was going to include. Pippa smiled to herself, then left the great hall and walked out into an unseasonably comfortable fall afternoon. She followed the sounds of swords and soon found herself on the edge of what apparently served as Lord Nicholas's training field.

She was quite happy to find a bench there, ready to accept her swooning self.

All right, so she had no business looking where she couldn't have, but since she was stuck in the Middle Ages for at least another few days without really much to do she supposed she had to keep herself occupied somehow. And if that keeping included appreciating a medieval knight in all his glory, how could she be faulted for it?

She was accustomed to dating — generally just once — academics. She'd dated PhDs, MSes, BSes, and even the occasional dean. They had been, without exception, acquaintances of Peaches's, and they had, without exception, never asked her for a second date. She had occasionally wondered if she unnerved them by staring a bit too long at the weave of their shirts. Now, she suspected she'd just never had the good fortune to run into a real man.

One like the man on his knees in the lists, fighting off the ferocious advances of a seven-year-old wielding an obviously well-used wooden sword.

Pippa couldn't help but smile. Montgomery's sword was made of wood as well and looked to have been designed for his opponent's stature. The contest didn't go on for much longer, though she supposed by the groan Montgomery made when he got up off his knees that he had been at it for quite a bit already. He made his vanquisher — Nicholas's son, by the look of him — a very low bow, then handed over his sword. The boy threw his arms around Montgomery and hugged him tightly, then collected his brother, who had been training with his father, and walked over with a swagger to a bench set against a far wall. Montgomery said something to Nicholas that made him laugh, then glanced her way.

"Wait, 'tis my turn," Nicholas said loudly as Montgomery walked away.

"In a moment," Montgomery threw back over his shoulder. He strode over to her, then stopped and made her the same sort of formal bow he'd made his nephew. "Good morning, Persephone," he said, with a smile. "Sleep well?"

"Frighteningly well," she admitted. "It was luxurious."

"Nicholas must have put on the good featherbed for you. Usually he trots out the one stuffed with twigs, lest his guests feel too comfortable."

She couldn't blame his brother. Between the bed and the lunch, she was tempted to hang around as well. She nodded toward the boys. "Training the future generation?"

"Aye, my nephew James," Montgomery agreed. "I fear he will soon outpace me and I will be digging deep for skill I don't often use."

"Yes, I'd be worried about that," she said dryly.

He started to say something, then hesitated. "I was going to train with my brother, but if you —"

"Would like to watch?" she interrupted. "I'd love to."

He hesitated, then shrugged. "If you don't mind, I think I will, though I'll beg him not to humiliate me. I won't be long."

She honestly didn't care how long he took. She soon found herself wrapped in a very luxurious blanket thoughtfully sent out by the lady Jennifer, she was enjoying a sunny day, and she had a gorgeous man to ogle while he was too busy working to notice. What wasn't to like about that?

So she spent a good part of the afternoon lusting after the young lord of Sedgwick. He was, she could say with all objectivity, the most handsome specimen she had ever had the good fortune to lust after. He was built like his brother, fought like his brother, and apparently talked medieval trash as well as his brother. They were mirrors of each other, but one fair-haired and one dark, and obviously quite good friends. She supposed that made sense given that Nicholas had sent Montgomery a cook and Montgomery hadn't taken offense at the gift. Their banter reminded her sharply of the way she and Peaches —

The thought of that caught her so tightly around the heart, she found it difficult all of a sudden to breathe. She wasn't sure why — she was going to get back home eventually — but for some reason just the thought of never seeing her sister again was enough to leave her blinking hard to avoid tears.

She wrapped the blanket up around her face not because she wanted to hide her expression but because she was getting cold. She shivered for good measure at the chill breath of air that had blown down her neck.

That was just as well, because it restored her sanity. What was she thinking to even look at Montgomery de Piaget as anything but potential material for extensive fantasizing later when she was safely back in the future, sitting in a new apartment full of fabric and notions and the patterns for her own designs strewn from one end of a very long worktable to the other?

Yes, she could hardly wait to get back to the twenty-first century. In fact, she was so ecstatic about the thought of it that she couldn't keep from making lists about all the things she just couldn't wait to see again. She started with Cheetos and moved through the four food groups of cheese-and-butter-slathered grains, sauce-covered vegetables, pizza, and finally chocolate. Once she'd examined the food to her satisfaction, she turned to the wonders of modern plumbing, modern sanitary items, and modern indoor climate control.

After that, she examined what was most important: complete fashion world domination. First she would take New York by storm, then Paris, then Milan. Her shows would be standing-room only for those who had booked years in advance; her innovations would be the talk of every design school of note; her clothes would be plastered all over billboards and buses and fashion magazines. Maybe she would even allow the occasional photo shoot for Cindi. No sense in not being generous since she could be.

She was slightly less enthusiastic about the other pieces of her life she would be trying to salvage and put back together. She envisioned doing time on Peaches's couch where she would be lovingly beaten over the head with lectures on the virtue of getting her affairs in order and getting to know a good insurance agent.

No, she could ignore that part. Once she found her flash drive, she would have her designs in one place and the wherewithal to come up with others in the person of Stephen de Piaget, who no doubt still had his checkbook at the ready. Really, what wasn't to like about any of that?

Well, there was the fact that she would be leaving in the past a man who obviously loved little children, had the patience of Job, and made her feel fragile and protected.

Then again, he probably made his fiancée feel fragile and protected, too, so maybe she was missing something that was just part of a fairy tale she wouldn't star in.

Typical.

And a part of her past. She was finished with being supporting cast. She would, when she got back to her proper place in time, wrench that bloody crown off Cindi's head and plop it down on her own. She had somewhere along the way — probably when Montgomery de Piaget had taken the time out of avoiding being killed by his cousins to teach her the completely unnecessary skill of riding a horse — discovered her inner diva. She was finished with letting her sister run roughshod over her. She might not even let Peaches get too far with her I-told-you-to-get-renter's-insurance lecture. She was going to create her own fairy tale, complete with clothes to go with it, and she was going to attract the kind of guy who would deeply admire her diva-like qualities, then go off to do manly things like eat pork rinds and watch football, leaving her free to design other things to use as props in the happily ever after she was living that starred hers truly.

She studiously avoided thinking about the fact that she was almost living that medieval fairy tale she was so hell-bent on designing.

Not that that fairy tale would have come true, even if she'd been willing or able to stay in the past. Not only was Montgomery very inconveniently engaged to a woman he never talked about, he was medieval nobility and she wasn't, which made him about as available as a quick trip to the Mini Mart located on the far side of the moon.

She looked up to find him standing five feet in front of her, watching her with a grave smile playing around the corners of his very beautiful mouth.

"What?" she said defensively.

"You were looking fierce."

"I was thinking diva thoughts." She lifted an eyebrow. "A diva is sort of like a queen. She's the star of her own play and everyone there has to bow to her wishes."

He smiled a bit more. "You?"

"Don't you think I have it in me?" she asked archly.

He considered for a bit. "I think you might be a benevolent diva," he conceded. "Perhaps."

"Is your fiancée a diva?" she asked.

He looked faintly startled. "Good heavens, nay. She is, um, quite submissive. To a fault. Never gainsays anyone. The perfect wife, I'm sure."

"I should think you'd want someone with a bit more spunk," she said tartly

He shook is head. "I like quiet women without opinions. Plain, unattractive, and quiet."

"You said quiet twice."

"That is, obviously, how much I value quiet."

She didn't think quiet would wear very well with him, but perhaps she was wrong. She accepted his hand and stood, then didn't protest when he clasped his hands behind his back. He was engaged, after all.

"My brother will provide music tonight,"

he said slowly. "Would you care to dance?"

"With you?" she asked in surprise.

He gave her what obviously passed for his best diva imitation. "Do you think me incapable of it?"

She laughed before she thought better of it. "I wasn't worried about you, buster — I mean, *my lord.* I was worried about me."

"I'll teach you the steps."

And that was exactly what she was worried about. He would spend the evening being nice to her, quite potentially touching her hand and looking at her with those very lovely gray eyes of his, and she would be in big trouble.

But if he wanted to dance with her, who was she to refuse? She could dance with him, spend a couple more days camping with him to get back to his castle, then back to the fairy ring, then she could get home and forget about him.

Then she might just take a tent and hang out on Tess's front lawn for a while. She had a good imagination; she could pretend she heard the ring of swords, or the clucking of chickens, or the endless bellows from François for quiet so he could create his masterpieces properly. Just the memories of those things would be inspiration enough for an entirely new line of clothing that would bring Manhattan to its knees.

Montgomery offered her his arm. She took it because it was like having a big brother, yes, that was it. A big, rough, football-playing, hockey-loving, ready-with-his-fists kind of brother who would have surely picked up the slack her father had left hanging.

And that had been a lot of slack.

She rubbed her eyes suddenly. She needed sleep, chocolate, and jeans. She was really starting to lose it. She cast about for something useful to talk about.

"Will your fiancée mind if we dance?"

He shook his head slowly. "She's a good gel."

Pippa didn't think his fiancée was a good girl, she thought she was the luckiest girl in the thirteenth century. And as long as she could imagine that lucky girl as a total hag, complete with warts and an irascible, if not tractable, set of personality flaws, she would probably manage to get through the rest of her diva-saturated life.

Probably.

Montgomery put his arm back around her shoulders suddenly. "I think perhaps you sat in the shade too long this morning. You're chilled."

She wasn't, but wasn't going to say as

much. She took another in her endless series of deep breaths, then supposed if she was going to have her heart be broken, she might as well do a proper job of it.

So she didn't protest when when Montgomery saw her settled in front of the fire in the great hall, then made sure she had something to drink before he ran upstairs and did the fastest changeroo she'd ever been witness to. Within ten minutes he was sitting next to her again, laughing at something his brother said and accepting onto his lap Thomas, the two-year-old reluctant napper, who seemed to find his uncle very much to his liking.

Pippa couldn't help but envy the woman who would someday be a part of that lovely, traditional family circle — even though it found itself in medieval England.

She didn't want to think about how much she suddenly wished that woman could have been her.

Montgomery reached over to tuck a stray strand of hair behind her ear, interrupting her unsettling thoughts. "Are you still going to dance with me tonight?" he asked with a small smile.

"If you want," she managed.

"I want."

Heaven help her, she was in trouble.

Chapter 17

Half a se'nnight later, Montgomery paused on the edge of the clearing next to Sedgwick, looked at the wreck that lay before him, and sighed. Perhaps he would do well not to go to Wyckham very often. It provided too sharp a contrast between what he had and what he wanted to have, though at the moment, he would have been happy with walls that were intact and a garrison he could trust to protect him.

He shifted in his saddle, more weary than he should have been. It wasn't that the journey had been unpleasant, for it hadn't been. Pippa had been grateful for whatever he'd been able to do for her, she made delightful conversation, and she wasn't opposed to sleeping out under the stars when no obliging structure could be found to house them for a night. The weather had been cooperative, their meals edible thanks to gifts from Nicholas, and the journey noteworthy in its lack of ruffians encountered.

It wasn't that he was weary in body; he was weary in his heart. Robin would have mocked him endlessly for such an admission, but there it was. Worse still, he had no one to blame for it but himself. He had been the one to make his situation worse by spending an evening with Pippa in his brother's great hall, teaching her how to dance. Of course he'd needed to look at her constantly, just to make certain she was learning the steps properly, and he'd needed to touch her just as often to make certain she understood when in the dance that was called for. And when he'd thought she might like a rest, he'd sat with her before the fire, watching the way the light fell on her dark hair and flickered over her fair features. He had tried not to be too obvious about his scrutiny, but even so Nicholas had looked at him knowingly a time or two.

With good reason, unfortunately.

He looked again at his castle and found in the sight a bracing dose of reality. His home wouldn't withstand the most feeble assault from ancient ruffians with creaking knees and rusty swords, and his cousins wanted him nowhere near the place. No medieval woman with any sense would have accepted an invitation to dine with him. How was he to ask a woman from the Future to give up what he was certain was a world of marvels to come live in his hovel?

He wasn't Nicholas with a luxurious keep on the shore in France where he could retreat whilst his English home was being repaired, nor was he Robin, who had a spectacular, impenetrable fortress in which to shield those he loved. Even Miles had taken his hall and made it a place of beauty and security for his beloved wife and wee ones. He himself had only one place to lay his head and it might as well have been on a battlefield for all the protection it offered.

He looked at the woman he couldn't have and shouldn't want sitting next to him on a horse she had ridden quite well over the past se'nnight and attempted a smile.

"Here we are," he said.

She only nodded. "I'll go search."

He hesitated. "I would rather you wait until I've seen what disasters have occurred during our absence. It galls me to say as much, but I'm not convinced you're safe in the keep without my looking after you."

"Of course," she said, looking slightly surprised. "Thank you."

She was certainly welcome, but he couldn't bring himself to say it. Perhaps she wouldn't find her little box for quite some time and she would learn to appreciate not only his castle but he himself.

A man could dream.

He could also have his chest pierced by an arrow if he wasn't watching where he was going. He breathed still only because the man standing atop the gate was a poor shot. Montgomery pulled his knife free of his boot, fully intending to fling it, only to realize it was Boydin standing there.

"Oh," Boydin called with affected horror, "is that you, Monty lad?"

Montgomery clamped down on the almost overwhelming desire to drop to the ground, then chase down his cousin and kill him. He looked up at Boydin without smiling.

"Aye," he said evenly, " 'tis I. Perhaps if your eyes fail you thus, you should leave the guarding of the gate to someone more able."

Boydin only smirked and walked away. Montgomery replaced his knife, then urged his stallion forward and kept control of his temper only barely as he dismounted in front of the stables. He handed his reins off to a stable lad, then went to help Pippa down from her horse. He set her on the ground with great care, then looked at her. She was studying him as if she'd never seen him before.

"What?" he asked warily.

"You have amazing control over your temper."

He shrugged, a little uncomfortably. "I do not like to act hastily, never mind that Boydin seems more than willing to do so if it means seeing me dead." He attempted a smile. "I think I may live to regret not having thrown them out the front gates the first day."

"You're very kind."

" 'Tis my gravest fault."

"No, I think that would be your dimple," she said solemnly.

He laughed briefly, in spite of himself. "My mother considers that my greatest asset."

"Your mother is a very wise woman, then," Pippa said. She took her gown from her saddlebag, then paused. "Where to now?"

"With me to my solar," he said seriously.

"I might like a trip to the garderobe first. I think I can manage that without help."

He supposed so, but he wasn't particularly happy about watching her walk away, so he didn't. He would be doing that soon enough in truth. There was no sense in doing it more often ahead of time than he had to.

He caught sight of Petter and his lads, hard at work on different holes in his walls.

Progress, such as it was, was being made. For all he knew, his keep might be battle-worthy before winter. At least he would have the pleasure of François's delights to savor in front of the hearth in his solar.

A pity he would be enjoying the meals alone.

He waved away one of the stable lads and set to tending his and Pippa's horses himself. It wouldn't be a long distraction, but it would be welcome one.

A pair of hours later, he had reassessed the condition of his home. The kitchen had undergone a pleasant transformation in his absence. Apparently, François had unbent far enough to give Joan a lesson or two in how to improve her stews, to the great delight of the men who were partakers of her efforts. Fitzpiers had delivered a report of a robust late harvest, which would keep not only their people fed but the table supplied well into the winter. Montgomery had been pleasantly surprised to find Everard had departed for points unknown and not returned. Unfortunately, that had been balanced out nicely by the reports he'd heard from Joan of how his cousins had eaten copious amounts of food and discussed in very loud voices each and every rumor that had surfaced that Montgomery had been entertaining the Faery Queen and was likely either a faery or a warlock himself.

'Twas unsurprising, to say the least.

He had released Pippa from his scrutiny half an hour earlier, simply because she looked restless and he was certain his cousins were too occupied with supper to bother her. He supposed the sooner she found her little stick, the happier she would be, though he couldn't say the same for himself.

He also couldn't say he wanted to help her look for it, lest they find it too quickly, but good manners demanded that he at least offer his services. He left his solar and wandered up the stairs and down the passageway, considering the rumors Everard had started and wondering absently when the entire countryside would rise up against him. He supposed he wasn't the first man to be accused of ridiculous things —

The sound of a chair falling abruptly against a wooden floor startled him into a run. He skidded to a halt at his bedchamber door, then threw himself forward and jerked Boydin away from Pippa. She dragged her sleeve across her mouth, her eyes flashing.

"Hold him for me so I can kill him."

"You might hurt yourself," Montgomery said, spinning his cousin around to face him. "Allow me the honor of seeing to that menial task for you, my lady."

"You fey changling," Boydin spat. "You haven't the courage —"

The rest of Boydin's comment was lost in the sound of his neck snapping back. Or that could have been his nose breaking. Montgomery wasn't sure which it had been and he honestly didn't care. He looked up to find Ranulf standing in his doorway with Phillip hovering behind him.

"Be so good as to take him to his mother," Montgomery said calmly. "I think he requires further instruction in manners before I send him off to the afterlife."

"I didn't get to hit him yet," Pippa said from behind him.

Montgomery exchanged a brief smile with Ranulf, then waited until his captain had hoisted Boydin over his shoulder and carried him away before he turned to Pippa. She was clutching the neck of his tunic together and looked very, very angry. He didn't dare touch her in her current state, so he decided comfort would have to come from words alone.

"I have made a decision," he announced.

She glared at him. He didn't take it

personally, for he imagined it was her way to keep from showing weakness. He had retreated into silence in his youth and into the lists during the years of his manhood. Now, he simply kept a tally of insults worthy of repayment and bided his time. But he imagined that for Pippa, anger was what served her best.

"I have decided," he continued, "that you will not leave my side. Day, night, all hours in between, where I am, you will be. Is that understood?"

"I'll think about it," she said, her teeth chattering.

Montgomery studied her in silence for a bit. "Did he hurt you?" he asked finally, much more calmly than he felt.

She shook her head sharply. "I elbowed him in the throat, so I suppose you can say I hurt him." She paused. "I don't think he liked that."

"You are quite the diva."

"Damned skippy."

He would have smiled, but he didn't think she would appreciate it. Instead, he pulled her into his arms, then rubbed her back briskly before he stepped away. "Have you found your little stick?"

She shook her head. "I've only looked in this room, but I suppose that doesn't mean anything. It could be anywhere, couldn't it?"

Montgomery didn't want to express any opinion yet, for her sake. Cinderella had been downstairs to supper, in his solar, and up in his bedchamber. She could have lost it anywhere, or put it any number of places out of spite — in the garderobe, for instance. He wasn't sure he had the stomach to drain the cesspit and look for something no larger than his thumb.

He walked around Pippa to fish in his trunk for another tunic. He shut the lid, turned to look at her, then hesitated. "Pippa, are you —"

"Don't," she said sharply, lifting her chin. "Don't ask. I'm fine. And he'll be very sorry if he comes near me again." She took the tunic from him and clutched it to her. "I can't guarantee what I'll do."

He vowed there would never come a time again when Boydin was close enough to even look at her askance. He reached for Pippa's hand and led her from his bedchamber. He couldn't bring himself to let her go even as they descended the stairs and walked out into the great hall.

Gunnild stalked over to him, obviously intending to chastise him for his treatment of Boydin, but Montgomery held up his hand before she could begin to spew out her venom.

"Your son assaulted a guest in my home," he said sharply. "Keep a tighter rein on the lad if you don't want to be attending his burying."

"You arrogant bastard," Gunnild spat. "Who are you, coming from Artane to take over *my* hall?"

"I am no bastard, as both my parents will attest," Montgomery said evenly, "and this is not nor was it ever your hall, as much as it pains me to remind you of that. My father was prepared to settle a very large sum upon you, but you refused. He offered you the choice between two of his own quite suitable properties, but you refused those as well. It falls to me to place you in other quarters, so I will offer you a choice of your son Arnulf's hall or the nunnery at Seakirk."

"Never," Gunnild spat.

Montgomery shrugged. "I would, of course, be willing to listen to other alternatives, should you desire them. But rest assured, lady, that neither you nor your children will be under my roof as winter sets in. Not after today."

If she'd dared, she would have plunged a knife into his chest, he was certain of that. As it was, she shot Pippa a look of pure hatred, turned, and shoved Ada toward the stairs.

Montgomery looked at Pippa and made her a small bow. "My solar, lady?"

"I'm not going to argue with you right now," she said with a shiver.

"You will not argue with me later, either."

She squeezed his hand. "You're bossy."

"You have no idea."

She smiled faintly at him, then walked with him to his solar. He sent Fitzpiers's son — a scrappy lad of ten-and-two named Maurice, who was apparently quite handy with a knife and relished the thought of taking on all sorts of dangerous tasks — to look for needle and thread, then gathered Phillip up and stood with his back to Pippa whilst she donned his other tunic. He took the first from her, saw her settled in a comfortable seat before the fire, then accepted what he'd asked for from Maurice. He didn't look at Pippa as he threaded his needle.

"Did he cut this cloth with a knife?" he asked casually.

"No."

"Then he lives another day." He held the tunic up and frowned at it, wondering where he might best begin. He was momentarily tempted to begin by carving warnings into Boydin's flesh, but he supposed that was unnecessarily vengeful.

"You know," Pippa remarked, "I could sew that. It is my business, after all."

He looked at her briefly before he bent again to his work. "I promised to keep you safe. Since I failed in that today, allow me to at least keep you from untoward drafts."

"I'd rather have you play the lute for me again tonight."

"I'll do that as well, if you like."

"I like."

He smiled to himself, then concentrated on the task at hand. He finished it as quickly as possible, then looked at Pippa. She was watching him with a bit of a smile, but her hands were trembling.

He suspected he was going to kill Boydin before the se'nnight was out.

He set the tunic aside, handed his tools to Maurice, then hooked a stool with his foot. He pulled it over in front of him, then rose and went to look for a blanket of some sort. He found one atop a trunk, then walked back over to the fire and pulled Pippa to her feet. Her hands were as cold as stone, which he supposed shouldn't have come as a surprise. She'd just had a mild taste of the dangers of his world.

She wouldn't have another, if he could prevent it.

He sat her down on the stool, wrapped the blanket around her, then sat down in the chair behind her. He pulled her hair free, then looked about him for some sort of brush. Phillip smiled a bit shyly as he held one out.

"My father does that often enough for my mother," he admitted. "I suspected you might like to do the same for our lady Pippa."

Montgomery nodded his thanks, then pointed to another stool. "You sit there. I don't want either you or Persephone out of my sight for the next few days. Understood?"

"Of course, my lord."

Montgomery set to his labors with single-minded diligence. He worked the tangles from Pippa's hair until there were none, then he merely brushed it until he thought she might have either gone to sleep or tired of his ministrations. He finally set the brush aside, then leaned forward and wrapped his arms around her. He rested his chin lightly on her shoulder.

"Better?" he asked very quietly.

She put her hand over his arms crossed at her shoulders. "You see too much. But yes, I'm better. Thank you."

"Must I still play for you?" he asked.

"And sing. Both."

"Saints, woman, you're demanding."

"Hmmm," she said, sounding as if she were smiling.

He released her, only then realizing that he'd kissed her hair before he did so. To distract the entire bloody chamber from the sight of something he shouldn't have done, he made a production of seeing Pippa seated in a proper chair and fetching his lute before he had to look at her again. He wasn't sure he wanted to know what her reaction would be, given that he was supposedly betrothed to another. The saints preserve him if he had to give a name for his betrothed.

If he managed to survive the next fortnight, he was never in his life going to tell another lie again.

"Fetch us something to eat, if you would," he said to Phillip. "Take Maurice with you. You may as well guard each other's backs in this nest of vipers."

"Of course, my lord," Phillip said, rising immediately. "Let's be away, Maurice."

"Aye, my lord Phillip," Maurice said deferentially as they left the solar.

Montgomery smiled at Pippa. "And there I was worried that Phillip would fear Maurice was usurping his place."

"Phillip loves you."

"He should," Montgomery said dryly. "I have spoiled him relentlessly from the moment of his birth."

"Tell me about the rest of your family," she said, pulling the blanket closer around her and pulling her feet up into the chair with her. "Are they as wonderful as Nicholas and his wife?"

Montgomery started to say he would tell her about his family if she would tell him more about hers, but he found he couldn't. He plucked absently at the strings of his lute to purchase a bit of time. Aye, his family was as wonderful as Nicholas and Jennifer, and he was more grateful than he thought he might manage to say that he had them within a fairly easy distance. He knew that he could have, had he been so inclined, traveled to Artane or Ravensthorpe or Wyckham without undue effort. The journey to France to see his parents would have been more difficult, but he could have managed that with a minimum of fuss as well.

But if he asked Pippa to stay with him, she would never have that choice open to her.

The thought of that was so devastating, he could hardly bear to entertain it.

He frowned fiercely, because it was either

that or weep. He didn't consider himself overly sentimental, but he would freely admit that the loss of his brother John eight years earlier had been almost enough to do him in. Perhaps it was that they were mirrors of each other, or that he had never known a moment where John hadn't been there to either provide cover or be his shadow. When John had disappeared, a hole had been left in his heart —

He cleared his throat roughly and forced his thoughts away. What was done was done and there was no remedying it. The point was, he understood perfectly what Pippa's family would go through if they lost her.

And he wasn't going to be the reason for that grief.

"Montgomery?"

"I am well," he said hoarsely. "Truly."

"You know, you don't have to sing for me," she said quietly. "I'm not my sister."

He attempted a smile. "Aye, I know." He decided on a song, then took a moment to tune his lute. He would play for her, perhaps exchange other tales of family with her, then he would see that she was kept safe —

Until the time he took her back to the faery ring and sent her home.

Because he had no choice.

Chapter 18

Pippa walked down the passageway, wondering where Montgomery had gotten himself to. She had spent all afternoon and evening with him the day before, first trying to shake off what had been a very unpleasant attack from his cousin, then allowing him to lord over her as he pleased. Since that had been limited to having her hair brushed, being entertained with stories and song, and getting to talk as much as she liked about Tess and Peaches, she'd hadn't objected. He had seemed a bit more serious than usual, but she chalked that up to medieval things on his mind. He had cause, to be sure.

She realized that morning that he'd been serious about keeping her within eyesight constantly. She had sat with him through breakfast, then on a log twenty feet from him as he worked through his garrison. It was then that she'd begun to wonder why it was his fiancée was stupid enough to let him out of arm's reach. There were obviously things about medieval England she just didn't understand, but that one she thought she could have.

His future wife was nuts.

Lunch had followed, then Montgomery had banished her to his solar so he could go off and take care of business where he might be more exposed to the slings and arrows of outraged cousins than he might otherwise be. She had put up with that for at least an hour before she'd ignored the protests and warnings of Fitzpiers, Phillip, and Maurice, and decided that her stick wasn't going to be found if she didn't do the looking. She'd promised to keep a good eye open for potential attackers, then headed out to carefully retrace Cindi's steps everywhere she could remember her sister having gone.

She had wound up, in the end, in Montgomery's bedroom. She'd bolted the door behind her, which had turned out to be a good thing, as it had saved the rest of the castle from hearing her unladylike exclamations when she'd found the note Cindi had left her under her pillow.

I've got your stupid little drive with me, so I win. Again.

Pippa could hardly read the words without shaking, so she left Montgomery's bedroom to look for him, hoping the note would remain intact long enough for her to show it to him. She wasn't sure where he was at the moment, but a bird's-eye view from the roof couldn't hurt her search.

She climbed the stairs to a guard tower, then walked out onto the parapet. She wasn't a fan of heights, and she was even less a fan of heights that weren't protected by sturdy guardrails. Montgomery's battlements were protected by nothing more useful than crumbling rock. She began to wonder if she'd made a terrible mistake.

And when Montgomery, who had been talking to a guardsman, looked over his shoulder at her, his expression confirmed her fears.

"Oh, my," said a voice from behind her with exaggerated concern. "I think, my lady, that he is highly displeased with you."

Pippa wasn't sure if the hands suddenly on her shoulders were there to keep her from falling down in fear or to keep her from escaping.

Or if they were there because their owner was about to heave her over the wall.

She had just realized that Door Number Three was the winner when she found Montgomery's sword half an inch from her ear.

"Release her," Montgomery said coldly.

Pippa was torn between bursting into tears or having a bladder malfunction, but stuck with option Number Three, which was freezing in place. She permitted herself a quick eyes-alone movement to see what Montgomery's expression might reveal, then wished she'd hadn't. She had never in her rather short acquaintance with him seen him so . . . well, he was about two seconds away from unleashing something Vesuvius-like. His face was a mask of calm, but his eyes were blazing with fury.

Martin, the dark horse she hadn't suspected of evildoings, seemed to be considering, then he flinched suddenly. "Cease," he squeaked. "I was thinking."

"You won't be alive to attempt that if you don't release her *now,*" Montgomery said. "Unless you'd rather I continue to push my sword into your chest."

Pippa felt Martin's hands remove themselves from her shoulders. Montgomery took her by the arm and pulled her carefully behind him. His sword was still tickling Martin's chest.

"I was just trying to help," Martin complained, stepping backward and rubbing a spot under his collarbone. "I was just keeping her from stumbling."

"My mistake, then," Montgomery said coldly, "for it looked to me as if you were beginning a journey down that same unpleasant path your elder brother has been traversing. I daresay you should reconsider, lest you find the path to be not at all to your liking."

"Your father won't like how you've treated me," Martin said, his tone coming very near to a whine. "I'll make certain he learns of it."

"Please give him all the details," Montgomery said. "He'll be vastly interested in them."

Pippa hardly dared peek over Montgomery's shoulder to see Martin's expression, but when she did, she was unsurprised to see the naked resentment there. Martin might not have been as vocal as the others about wishing Montgomery gone, but he obviously wanted it just as badly.

"You'll regret this," Martin blustered.

"Somehow, I imagine not."

Martin cursed him, then turned and stalked off the roof. Pippa opened her mouth to comment on his good sense only to find herself facing a no-less-furious-than-before lord of Sedgwick.

"What are you doing here?" Montgomery snarled, resheathing his sword with an angry thrust.

"Getting fresh air," she stammered. She'd never seen him angry before — no, that wasn't true. She'd never seen him angry before at *her,* but she had the feeling she was about to catch the full brunt of the storm. "You aren't going to take me out in the lists and make me miserable like you do your guardsmen, are you?"

"For future consideration," he said tightly, "there is healthful air on the ground, and nay, I don't take women out to the lists."

"Are you going to take yourself out to the lists?" she asked hopefully. "You know, to work out some of that frustration you seem to be feeling?"

He only glared at her, which helped her decide that the time for examining what he might and might not want to do had not yet come. He still looked perfectly capable of wringing someone's neck, so she supposed she would do well to make sure that neck wasn't hers. Medieval men. How was a modern girl supposed to figure them out?

Montgomery brushed past her, took her by the hand, and pulled her along after him toward the front of the castle. She put her hand on the wall to steady herself only to have that piece of wall fall over the edge. She gasped and looked over in time to see it land in the moat. She'd been there and done that before with no desire to do it again.

She stumbled along after Montgomery into one of the barbican towers, smiled sheepishly at the guardsmen he threw out, then looked around for escape routes as he unbuckled his sword belt. Good heavens, he wasn't —

No, he wasn't. He caught her by the arm before she could run, then led her over to a stone bench near the window. He sat down and pulled her down next to him. Well, he pulled her down practically on his lap, but not quite. Maybe he was afraid if he left any space at all between them, she might run. Maybe he thought if he kept her close, he'd have an easier time of shouting at her. Maybe he had absolutely no concept of personal space.

Again, a topic better left for examination at another time.

He glared at her again, his mouth working as if he simply couldn't come up with just the right thing to say to break the tension.

"What?" she asked, attempting to look clueless.

"Woman, when I tell you to stay in the solar, you *will* stay in the solar!" he exclaimed.

A dozen things were immediately on her tongue, tripping over themselves to get out, beginning with telling him he was a medieval barbarian — which he was — and ending with telling him that she was a modern woman perfectly capable of taking care of herself — which she was. In the twenty-first century. As long as she wasn't walking down a darkened alley in a crappy part of a thuggish town.

But since she wasn't in the twenty-first century, and she had almost taken a nose-dive into a sewer, she had no option but to agree she had blown it.

She took a deep breath. "You're right."

He frowned, as if he hadn't understood her. "I'm what?"

"You're right. I'm sorry. I made it difficult for you to protect me when I didn't stay where you'd put me."

He looked at her suspiciously. "I'm having difficulty believing you're in earnest."

"I'm being tractable. Isn't that what you want?"

"The saints preserve me from a Future wench with delusions of acquiescence," he grumbled. He shot her another look of disgust, but the tension began to ease out of him. "A bit of tractability might serve you quite well in the future, given how close you've come to running fully afoul of my ire today."

"I'll keep that in mind."

"You're not nearly as intimidated as you should be," he said with a frown. "Obviously I've failed at some point to instill the proper amount of deference in you."

She'd watched him instill deference in others and really had no desire to have a place in that line. She leaned back against the wall carefully, then attempted a smile. She had a scowl as her reward, then a gusty sigh.

"I would like not to repeat that," he said pointedly.

"I'm sorry," she said, meaning it fully. "I didn't really think I was in danger."

He took her hand and held it in both his own for a moment or two in silence before he looked at her with the full extent of his concern plain on his face. "Please, Pippa, don't leave my sight again." He took a deep breath. "I'm not sure I'm equal to describing my distress at seeing you there in Martin's power."

Pippa decided at that moment that every woman should have at least a week with a medieval lord who felt compelled to protect her at all costs. She did her best to remind herself that he was holding her hand in a brotherly sort of way and meant nothing by it. She also reminded herself that reminding him he was engaged would really ruin the moment. She limited her comments to a nod she was certain he understood.

"Did you find your little stick?" he asked after a bit.

She remembered suddenly why it was she'd been looking for him in the first place. She pulled away from him and fished around in her pocket. "It seems that she had the stupid thing in her pocket the whole time. Still does, I imagine. She did me the favor of being lucid enough to write this note before we left to go to your brother's."

Maybe *lucid* was pushing things a bit. Cindi had written the words *I'm not stoned,* but she'd apparently fallen in love with making swirling, curly Os because they'd gone on for the rest of the page. Turning the page to continue with her poisoned pen had apparently been the only thing to snap her out of it.

Montgomery frowned as he listened to Cindi's literary stylings. "Why would your sister do such a vile thing?"

"Because she thought it would inconvenience me, maybe," Pippa said with a shrug. "Or maybe she wanted to get to the Future ahead of me, steal my designs, and sell them as her own."

"Surely not," he said, sounding appalled.

"I wouldn't be surprised."

He took the note and set it aside, then reached for her hand again. He held it in both his own, staring down at it for quite a while before he spoke without looking at her. "You should likely hurry back home, then."

"Fashion world domination awaits," she agreed, though she suddenly found herself suffering a serious lack of enthusiasm at the prospect of it.

He met her eyes briefly. " 'Tis too late to start today." He nodded toward the window. "And it's begun to rain. Will tomorrow be soon enough, do you suppose?"

"Of course," she managed. One day wasn't going to make any difference. Well, it might to her heart, but she would pay the price for that later when she was at home busily trying to avoid dating jerks. "What do you want to do?"

He looked down again at her hand. "Pass the time with you."

She closed her eyes briefly. Maybe one more day was one day too many. If she managed to escape medieval England without leaving her heart behind her in pieces, it would be a miracle. "Shall we play chess?"

she asked, latching on to the first thing that crossed her mind. She wasn't good at it, but it was probably more reasonable than suggesting charades.

Montgomery shook his head. "That would require going and fetching a board and pieces."

She smiled. "Montgomery, it's cold up here."

"Your fault, not mine. I was happy to stay in my solar, but you had to climb the stairs to the roof." He lifted an eyebrow. "Therefore, here is where we'll remain. We'll enjoy the added benefit of my being less tempted to kill my useless guardsmen if I don't have to look at them." He stood up, took off his cloak, then wrapped it around her and sat back down. "Better?"

"I am, but I imagine you won't be."

"Trust me, I could use a bit of chill," he said, half under his breath. He shot her a look. "I suppose 'tis your chivalric duty to keep me warm."

She smiled, because she couldn't look at him and not smile, then arranged half his cloak over his shoulders. She couldn't bring herself to protest when she found herself again pulled against his shoulder and her hand taken again with both his own.

It was torture, pure and simple.

"I have provided warmth and a comfortable seat," he said. "You may determine our activities for the rest of the day."

She considered. "I could tell you a fairy tale."

"Do you think that's entirely appropriate right now?" he said dryly.

"As long as nobody's eavesdropping, we'll be fine. I could talk quietly."

He leaned his head back against the stone and smiled. "Very well, if you like."

She thought for a minute, then decided on one that just couldn't miss, given the circumstances. "I'm going to tell you the story of Cinderella."

He winced. "Please tell me this isn't about your sister."

"No, she's just named after that character. Actually, given how she's treated me for the past ten years, *I* should have been the one named Cinderella, but that's another story entirely. And yes, she was named after the story." She spared a thought — a very brief one — that she hoped would pass for concern about her sister's having made it to the right place in time instead of winding up as a servant in some Tudor household where she really would be sleeping by the kitchen hearth, then allowed herself the no-doubt unwise pleasure of making herself comfortable next to Montgomery before she started her story.

She couldn't say her parents had been particularly coherent during her childhood, but mother — stoned or not — had always known how to tell a good story. Pippa wasn't quite ready to credit her mother with instilling a love of a good fairy tale in her, but as she retold Cinderella's story, she had to admit that it was probably true.

She knew she was mixing equal parts Disney and half a dozen other remakes of the story, but part of being a good storyteller was recognizing the audience's tolerance for embellishment, sort of like knowing how many sequins she could put on a costume before the leading lady protested.

Montgomery, as it happened, was the perfect audience. He laughed in all the right places, looked indignant when called for, and wore a rather tenderhearted look on his face as the prince looked through his kingdom for that special girl with the right-sized foot. He was silent after she finished, looking off through the opposite window at the mist that hung in the trees, then he cleared his throat.

"Do you have your prince waiting for you at home?" he asked quietly.

"Me?" she asked in surprise. "Not even

close, but I've dated plenty of toads that didn't turn into princes. Not kissed them, mind you, because we never get past the first date. But I've had plenty of first dates."

"Toads?" he echoed. He looked at her with a frown. "Dates?"

"Are you sure you want to know?"

"I've no idea," he said weakly. "Do I?"

"You never know when another future girl is going to walk across your bridge. You might want to be prepared."

"Persephone, I'm not certain I would survive another future gel," he said with a faint smile. "You have finished me for this particular lifetime."

He didn't sound all that bothered by that, but maybe he was just being polite. She cleared her throat.

"I'm sorry. I'm sure we've inconvenienced you terribly."

He shot her a look that she couldn't decipher, then he brought her hand up and kissed the back of it quickly before he pulled his cloak back over it. "You have been no inconvenience," he said roughly, "but you might be considered a vexation if you don't go about bludgeoning me with these details about toads and dates I'm sure I'll never believe. Curiosity is, as you know, one of my greatest faults."

As was a gruffly tender sort of chivalry displayed in cold guardtowers. She ignored the fact that her hand would definitely never be the same, then quickly latched on to the distraction of discussing with him the niceties and rituals of modern dating. She admitted to the two guys she had actually kissed over the course of her rather eternal and unsatisfactory dating career, then she told him all the other fairy tales she could remember.

And all the while, Montgomery watched her, held her hand, kept her close to him. After she had finished her last story, then told him again the final part of Cinderella where everything worked out as it was supposed to, he simply sat with her, trailing his callused finger over the back of her hand.

"And they lived happily ever after?" he asked quietly.

"So the story goes."

He looked at her, his gray eyes very serious. "I imagine the prince's castle didn't have holes in the walls."

"I'm not sure the princess would have cared if it had," she said quietly.

He took a deep breath. "Pippa —"

Pippa waited for him to finish his thought, then realized he wasn't going to because he was suddenly no longer next to her. She looked up to find him on his feet in front of her with his sword in his hand, then found herself fumbling with the scabbard he'd tossed at her.

Obviously it would take a lot of practice to be a medieval sort of gal.

Phillip came to a skidding halt just inside the tower door. "Half the garrison is gone," he blurted out.

Pippa found herself on her feet without knowing how she'd gotten there. Montgomery swore, then held out his hand for his scabbard. He belted it around his hips, then resheathed his sword with an angry thrust.

"Damn them to hell," he growled. "Who led them off?"

"I'm not certain, my lord," Phillip said faintly. "There is too much confusion below to tell."

"Come along, Pippa," Montgomery said shortly. "I'll see you safely downstairs."

She wasn't going to argue. She simply trotted along after him and kept her mouth shut until they were standing at the top of the stairs. Even she could hear the shouting below. She felt her breath begin to come in gasps. "I'm sorry."

He looked at her in surprise. "Why?"

"I kept you from seeing to your duty —"

"You forget who was keeping whom captive, which means you've also forgotten who is in charge. And nay, you aren't responsible. This battle has been brewing since Lord Denys died."

"Battle?" she echoed weakly.

"Not to worry." He looked over her head at Phillip. "There are a handful of knives in the trunk in my solar. Teach her to use a pair of them."

"As you will, my lord!" Phillip said with all the enthusiasm of a twelve-year-old boy facing an enormous stack of video games and unlimited time to play them.

Montgomery paused, then looked at her. "We may have to fight our way to the solar, but once we're there I want you to go inside and bolt the door."

"Sure," she managed, wondering if she would even manage to get herself downstairs without her knees buckling. "No problem."

He squeezed her hand, hard. "I *will* keep you safe."

She wished she'd been a little more militarily minded when she'd designed her gowns. A corseted bodice that would have doubled as body armor would have been nice. She would have to ask Tess about that sort of thing when she got home.

If she got home.

"Pippa."

She wrenched her gaze to his. "You'll keep me safe."

"I will."

But who would keep *him* safe?

CHAPTER 19

Montgomery pulled the door of his solar shut and waited until he heard the bolt slam home before he spun around and looked over his great hall. He cursed viciously. It was empty, which wouldn't have troubled him any other time, but somehow it now seemed an ominous sight. He decided it was best to see what had actually befallen the inhabitants of the keep before he closed the gates and tried to block the holes in the walls. No sense in locking enemies inside with those who needed to be protected.

He walked across the hall and into the kitchens. François was standing there, a wicked-looking knife in his hand and his lads clustered behind him. Joan was standing by his side, clutching a spit in both hands as if it had been a sword. Montgomery paused, then leaned against the wall and smiled.

"Preparing for battle?"

François's eyes widened, then he shouted out a warning. Montgomery spun, ducking as he did so and narrowly avoiding losing his head to Boydin, who had apparently decided he'd had enough of not being lord of his own hall. Montgomery drew his sword, for he had also had enough of not being lord of his own hall.

He pushed Boydin back into the hall, giving him no choice but to retreat until he was backed up against the lord's table. Montgomery continued to fight him until he saw other lads pouring into the hall. He quickly rid his eldest cousin of his sword, caught him full in the face with his fist, and sent him slumping backward into the remains of supper.

He turned to find what was left of his garrison, all twelve of them, wearing murderous looks. Ranulf and his lads were suddenly standing beside him with swords drawn. He supposed they could have made quick work of the garrison by themselves, but he wasn't going to discourage Petter and the handful of masons who came running up the passageway from the kitchens carrying quite useful-looking swords.

A glance toward his solar revealed his squire, his steward, and his steward's son hurrying out the doorway, accompanied by their own bit of decent steel. Montgomery saw the door shut again, which eased him some. He could only hope Pippa would have the good sense to keep that door shut. He couldn't get her home if he couldn't keep her alive.

Never mind how little he wanted to think about getting her home.

He turned to sweep his garrison with a look he hoped came close to revealing his fury. He suspected part of that fury had less to do with the mutiny afoot than it had to do with the cracks the thought of Pippa leaving were causing to appear in his very hard heart, but so be it. If his pain fed the fire of his wrath, so much the better.

"Which one of you started this?" he snarled.

The men only looked back at him belligerently.

"You live an interesting life," Petter murmured from where he stood nearby. "A pitched battle in your great hall?"

"My father would be appalled," Montgomery said shortly, and that was the truth.

His sire, however, would have done just what he was about to do without hesitation, so he didn't spare any regrets for what he was certain would be unpleasant ends to miserable lives.

"Lay down your swords and honor your fealty oaths," he said, through gritted teeth, "or draw your last breaths. You will not leave the hall without having made one of those choices."

A handful of lads lowered their swords, but they were heartily jeered into renewed compliance by their less intelligent fellows. Montgomery cursed under his breath. The choice was clear: he had to have men belonging to the keep who were willing to guard him and those he loved. Anything less was simply unacceptable.

Death it would be, then.

He engaged the first man who stepped forward, then slew him without hesitation. That seemed to change a few minds, but not nearly as many as he would have liked. He drew a knife from one of his boots and fought with both blades, preferring to inflict damage where possible instead of death. Unfortunately, the lads he encountered seemed to have an especial determination to do him in. Perhaps they had been promised something particular by Gunnild if he was removed as lord of the keep. Why they hadn't bothered to think that through far enough to realize that his father would only send another of his vassals — as well as a very large contingent of angry guardsmen to repay them for their disloyalty — Montgomery didn't know. He began to wonder if he might do well to trade those knights to Gunnild's eldest for a few of *his* most disloyal lads who might find a change of masters to their liking

He watched occasionally out of the corner of his eye to see how his men were faring. They needed none of his support, which didn't surprise him. Ranulf had, as he boasted as often as possible, squired with Jackson of Raventhorpe, who was no poor swordsman himself, and he'd been hell-bent on proving his worth. Montgomery had made him captain of his own guard three years earlier, sure in not only his skill but his loyalty. Even Phillip was holding his own quite well, needing only a thrust or two from Fitzpiers to keep him from being skewered. At least Pippa was . . . safe . . .

His solar door was open.

He staggered, then caught himself heavily before he tripped over a corpse at his feet. He shoved away the man trying to engage him from the other side of the body, then strode across the great hall. Gunnild appeared suddenly in his way, a knife bare in her hand. He stopped and looked at her in disbelief.

"Surely you jest, lady."

Apparently not. She threw herself at him, but she was no match for him. Indeed, Phillip could have fought her and been forced to stifle his yawns. Montgomery rid her of her knife as gently as possible, then tossed it to Phillip before he looked at the former lady of the keep.

"I would like to believe you had nothing to do with this uprising," he said gravely.

"Would I admit it if I had?" she said, drawing herself up and looking at him haughtily. "And if I had, I would be justified in protecting *my* home from being overrun by usurpers!"

Montgomery would have taken the time to explain to her again just how it was that property was inherited in present-day England but since he knew he would only be wasting his breath, he forbore.

That and he had other business to see to at the moment. He ran into his solar to find Ada and Boydin there, hurling insults at Pippa. At least only words were being used, though Boydin had his sword drawn and looked as if he fully planned to use it for its intended purpose.

Montgomery looked Ada over for weapons, then pushed her out of the way and stepped in front of Pippa. He turned to face Boydin.

"Troubling my guests again, are you?" he said shortly.

"Killing my father's men, are you?" Boydin sneered.

"They are *my* men now," Montgomery said, "and when their honor does not extend to keeping their oaths, they won't be that any longer. And don't feign indignation, cousin. You would do the same in my place, did you find yourself master of Artane with men still loyal to my father."

"I wouldn't presume to take a keep that isn't mine," Boydin snapped. "And I'll fight to the death to keep you from taking this one."

Montgomery cursed himself silently. He had handled the entire thing badly. He had assumed Denys's children would be opposed to him, but he hadn't supposed they would prefer losing their own lives to going off, accompanied by a good deal of gold, and starting over again somewhere else. Somewhere, perhaps, where the keep wasn't sporting holes in critical bits of itself.

He paused. Nay, he wasn't being completely truthful with himself. He had considered just how terrible the situation might become; he had simply dismissed thoughts of it as a lack of faith in his own abilities to influence the outcome. There were times, even as he stood in his own great hall with a woman he thought he might love but knew he couldn't have standing behind him, that he couldn't help but wonder if his father had made a terrible mistake. John would have been more suited —

"Montgomery!"

He leapt aside, jerking Pippa out of the way as Boydin thrust with his sword. There was no proper space inside the solar to fight, but he made do because he had no choice. Ada was the unaccounted for element in a mixture he had little liking for. He fought with his back to Pippa, which he supposed was a good way to protect her, but it left him unable to watch her. He would have happily backed Boydin out of the chamber, but that would have left him guarding Pippa in the great hall, which didn't seem a particularly prudent thing to do. He was also having to make more of an effort to keep Boydin at bay than he had before. Perhaps his cousin was repaying him for the endings of any number of their earlier encounters.

Pippa screamed suddenly, then turned and fled from the solar. Montgomery saw Ada follow her with a knife in her hand. He leapt forward only to find Boydin in his way. He fought his cousin furiously, but Boydin had discovered yet another measure of courage. Montgomery knew he should have just run the bloody whoreson through, but something stopped him — his own foolish notion of honor, he supposed — so he feinted to the left, then caught his cousin in the face with his elbow and sent him sprawling. He bolted out the door, more unnerved than he'd ever been in any battle he'd ever fought. If anything happened to Pippa —

The great hall was still in an uproar. Montgomery made certain Phillip was still breathing, then looked frantically about him for Pippa. He saw the last of something escaping out the front door, though he supposed that could have been anyone. He knew he had three choices for a search: up the stairs, to the kitchens, or through the courtyard and out the gate. To judge amiss would be to sentence Pippa to things she couldn't possibly fight herself. Ada was, from what Montgomery had seen, ruthless and completely without honor. The saints only knew what other dangers Pippa would find along her way.

It was as he'd thought before: thirteenth-century England wasn't the place for her.

That realistic but unpleasant thought only added to his anger. He chose the door to the hall, prayed he had chosen well, then ran across a floor that was slippery with more than just leavings from supper. He leapt down the stairs and bolted through the muck that was less than before but still too much. He saw a lad up on the roof who looked as if he might be tempted to lower the innermost portcullis. Montgomery pointed his sword at him.

"Do and breathe not another moment."

The man held up his hands in surrender and Montgomery continued on his way, frantic at the thought of what could be happening to Pippa. He wondered how any of his brothers bore that sort of feeling about their wives.

At least they all had loyal garrisons to protect those wives, which he supposed helped a great deal.

He realized he was being trailed only because Boydin began to curse him. Montgomery ignored him. He could see Pippa and Ada fighting at the end of the bridge.

He could also see a shimmer in the air.

Pippa was holding on to Ada by the wrists, keeping her by sheer strength alone from plunging a knife into her breast. Pippa finally kicked Ada in the belly, sending her falling back with a gasp. Unfortunately, the motion overbalanced her, and she started to fall backward into the cesspit.

Montgomery never heard a splash.

He stood there, rooted to the spot, looking at the place where she had stood not a moment before.

And then he felt a blinding pain in his head the moment before his world went dark.

Chapter 20

Pippa resurfaced in Montgomery's cesspit, fully prepared to spit disgusting things out of her mouth again for the third time.

Only this time the water was clean. And deeper.

She swam to the bank, rather grateful for the light she could see in the distance. Maybe someone had run out of the keep with a torch so Montgomery would be able to see Boydin and do him in. She would also have to have a conversation with him about Ada. That girl was dangerous.

She crawled out of the water and found to her surprise that she wasn't covered in sewer leavings. It was odd enough that she stopped to consider it. The little lake had stunk to high heaven as they'd ridden across it the day before. She straightened, then felt a tingle begin at the back of her neck. It was almost dark, true, but she could have sworn that wasn't the lists she was looking at.

It was Tess's gift shop, tucked back in the forest where it wouldn't be seen immediately and ruin the appearance of Sedgwick being stuck in the Middle Ages.

She turned around slowly, then felt her mouth fall open. She looked up and saw a castle silhouetted against the sky in a lovely autumn twilight.

A castle in perfect condition.

She supposed it didn't matter this time what might drip down from her hair into her mouth given that she obviously had fallen not into Montgomery's cesspit, but her sister's moat. She shut her mouth and looked around her frantically, but there was no sign of Montgomery, or his evil cousins, or anything she had grown accustomed to over the past few weeks. All that was there in front of her was modern perfection with its floodlights and long wooden bridge and moat water that contained nothing more nefarious than fish and frogs.

She turned around and around frantically, looking for the sparkles that signaled the opening of the gate she had used twice now, the gate that had suddenly and unpredictably taken her from a place she suddenly realized she hadn't been ready to leave yet.

Arms flung themselves around her. She fought them ferociously until she realized they belonged not to one of Montgomery's evil cousins but to her sister. She was even more surprised to find that sister was Peaches, not Tess.

"Pippa, you idiot, where have you been?" Peaches demanded, blubbering copiously.

Pippa couldn't seem to catch her breath. She wasn't prone to physical weakness, her habit of going a little weak in the knees when faced with a room full of vintage buttons and trims aside, but she thought she just might pass out from shock.

She had gone through the gate she'd been waiting to go through for two solid weeks.

The unfortunate thing was, she hadn't wanted to.

"And what in the *hell* are you wearing?" Peaches demanded. "Pip, I hate to say this, but you need a shower."

Pippa might have laughed another time, but she couldn't at the moment given that she felt as if her heart had just been wrenched out of her chest. She was making some sort of sound, though, and it sounded pretty unhinged.

She had to get back. There, that was the ticket. She had to get back to the past even if it was just to tell Montgomery good-bye properly and thank him for his hospitality. Even if she could just poke her head through the gate and wave, that would be enough. But this . . . this leaving without so much as a look . . .

It was intolerable.

"Come on," Peaches said, tugging on her. "Let's go inside before you freeze to death out here."

"No," Pippa said, trying to pull away. "I have to stay —"

"Pip —"

"I have to stay out *here,*" Pippa said, fighting Peaches's hands off. "I have to stay out here and wait for the gate to open back up."

Peaches took her by both arms and held on tightly. "Look, Pippa, we've already dealt with Cindi a few days ago after she called us in hysterics from some random native's house. Stephen's still shaking from the return trip with her. Don't make me lock you up, too."

Pippa supposed she was glad Cindi had made it back to the right time. She imagined she might at some point in the future care what Cindi had had to say about their whole adventure and more particularly where on her sister's person her flash drive could be found. Now, though, she could only stand there and shake. She looked up over Peaches's head at the castle that stood there, visible now only thanks to the floodlights and not the sky behind it.

Montgomery would have been pleased with how it looked.

"Pippa?"

Pippa dragged herself back to the present — a shocking thing to contemplate, truly — and looked at her sister. "Cindi?" she echoed. "You locked her up?"

"We put her in an involuntary detox program," Peaches said briskly. "She's now peeling the wallpaper with her swearing and entertaining her keepers with all kinds of interesting stories." She squeezed the fabric of Pippa's sleeves. "You're sopping wet, sister. Did you fall into the moat?"

Yes, three times now was what she wanted to say. Instead, she simply looked around her for things that had disappeared centuries ago.

Or five minutes ago, depending on one's point of view.

She pulled away from Peaches, then walked back and forth in front of the end of the wooden bridge that spanned Tess's almost pristine moat. She stopped each time at the spot where the time gate should have been, but each time there was nothing there.

Or, at least she thought there was nothing there. It was a little difficult to decide that given that she was so cold, she could hardly think straight, much less pay attention to her surroundings. Five minutes ago, she could have reached out and touched Montgomery de Piaget, thrown herself into his arms, told him that even though there were a whole slew of reasons it was crazy, she thought she just might love him.

Now, she couldn't even write him a letter.

Things started to go a little fuzzy, but she didn't go for a swim as she might have at another time in those circumstances. She felt herself being caught suddenly and lifted up in strong arms. She managed to focus on a face she recognized.

From the future, unfortunately.

"Oh, not you," she moaned.

Stephen de Piaget looked a bit startled. "I am having terrible luck with women these days. Is it something I'm doing?"

Pippa pushed herself out of his arms. That he let her down without a peep in protest showed that he was obviously not used to the determination of a woman who'd just spent half a month going toe-to-toe with a medieval lord. He did, though, take hold of her arm. When Peaches took the other, she looked at her sister in surprise.

"You aren't going to put me in the loony bin, are you?"

"The shower," Peaches said. "I think

you'll feel better when you're warm."

"I can't go inside," Pippa protested.

"Yes," Peaches said firmly, "you most certainly can. And you will. I'll come back out here with you later, after you've warmed up."

Pippa didn't want to go, but she could tell the fight wasn't going to be worth it. Peaches was tougher than she looked, and the silent message she'd telegraphed to Stephen had resulted in his taking a firmer grip on Pippa's arm as well. Maybe if she humored them for a bit, she could escape out the front door and camp out by where the gate should be.

She honestly didn't know what else to do.

And the truth was, at the moment, a shower sounded heavenly. Hot showers had certainly been on the list she'd made of things she loved about the future and couldn't wait to get back to, hadn't they? She was five minutes from having something she had wanted very badly.

Too bad she'd had to give up something else she wanted very badly in order to have it.

She stumbled when she walked into the courtyard only because she was so used to picking up her feet to keep them from sinking into the mire. It was only then that she realized she was no longer wearing her shoes. Maybe she'd lost them in Montgomery's courtyard. She stared down at her feet and felt the world begin to spin. Only Stephen's arm around her shoulders kept her from falling on her face.

"Now, shall I carry you?" he asked kindly.

She looked up at him numbly. He looked so much like Montgomery, yet not at all. He was all polished modernness, not all rough around the edges, not at all likely to draw his sword and do serious damage with it. He was a lovely man, true, but he was not the one she wanted —

No, she didn't want Montgomery de Piaget. She latched on to that thought with all the tenacity of a woman barely holding on to her sanity. Of course she was thrilled to be back in her time with all its myriad luxuries and opportunities. She could hardly wait to pour herself a big bowl of Cheetos, plunge her face into it, and revel in all the unnatural cheesiness.

She paused. That didn't sound as good as she'd hoped it would. Maybe there was a French restaurant nearby where she could go, just for old time's sake.

She realized Stephen was still waiting for an answer. She shook her head, because that seemed a reasonable response to whatever question he'd asked her that she could no longer remember, then she accepted his arm and walked with him across the courtyard. Peaches still had a hold of her on the other side, so perhaps she looked a little more fragile than she felt.

She entered the great hall and gasped in spite of herself. She stepped away from Peaches and Stephen and stared at her surroundings. She turned around in a circle — which she couldn't seem to stop doing — and looked at the hall. The tapestries were lovely, the fireplaces perfectly capable of keeping the hall smoke free, the furnishings obviously quite new and sturdy.

It was devastating somehow.

She saw Tess come to a skidding halt in the middle of the hall, then watched her sister start to weep. It was odd, the sight of that, because Tess was not a weeper.

"I've had an adventure," Pippa croaked.

Tess almost tackled her where she stood. "I thought you were dead," she said, hugging Pippa so tightly, Pippa lost her breath. "I had divers out to comb the moat for you and Cindi both."

"I'm sorry," Pippa managed. "I . . . I got lost."

Tess pulled away and looked at her searchingly. "You aren't hurt, are you?"

Pippa shook her head. She didn't suppose a heart that felt like it was broken — especially since she was *thrilled* to be back in her proper place and time — counted as being hurt. Maybe that ache in her chest was indigestion, or contact with something in the moat she hadn't remembered.

"Pippa?"

"I'm fine," Pippa managed. "Cold, but fine."

"I'll take her upstairs," Peaches said, taking Pippa's arm in that no-nonsense grip again. "Tess, your shirt is wet. Go change and we'll meet in Pippa's bedroom later."

"I'll bring tea," Tess said weakly. "And something to eat. Stephen, are you hungry?"

"I'll forage for something for you girls," Stephen said, "then deliver it. I'm not sure you'll want me underfoot for anything else."

Pippa forced herself to focus on him. "Stephen de Piaget, you're a very nice man."

He shifted and looked almost as uncomfortable as Montgomery did when enduring the heaping of praise on his head. It must have been a family trait hardwired into generations of de Piaget men. Pippa managed a smile, then let Peaches pull her away and help her up the stairs. She squelched down the hallway next to her sister.

"When did you get here?" she asked finally.

"About thirty-six hours after you disappeared," Peaches said, sounding as if she hadn't enjoyed the process. "Tess called and I came running."

"Expensive."

"Lord Stephen paid for my ticket."

"Those de Piaget men are very chivalrous," Pippa said, before she realized what she was saying. "Or so I've heard." She shivered violently, once. It apparently didn't matter what century Sedgwick found itself in, it was still cold as hell inside the walls.

"That's an interesting observation," Peaches said carefully.

Pippa imagined Cindi had told all sorts of interesting stories — interspersed no doubt with drug-induced hallucinations. She supposed she would have to set the record straight at some point, but she wasn't sure she could manage that at the moment. It was all she could do to get herself into her bedroom.

She realized eventually that she was simply standing in one place, staring at the instant water heater attached to a showerhead. Someone somewhere along the way had obviously knocked out a wall between rooms and turned one of them into a bathroom. Handy, that.

She realized, after she heard Peaches say her name again, that she hadn't answered her sister's question. That was becoming a bad habit, that losing touch with what was in front of her.

The hazards of time travel, apparently.

Which she was never going to do again, of course. She was happy, happy, *happy* to be back in the twenty-first century with all the noise and junk food and hot water that hadn't been heated by a servant.

"Pippa," Peaches began in the same voice she used while beginning the weaning-away-from-useless-junk process with her clients, "I think you would feel more like yourself if you got in the shower, don't you?"

Pippa looked at the water that Peaches had turned on, then nodded numbly. "Can't think of anything I'd like more."

"Pippa," Peaches said slowly, "do you realize you're speaking French? Well, sort of. Your accent has really gone downhill."

Pippa laughed a little, but she stifled it very quickly. She sounded as if she was about to lose it. That was ridiculous given that she was so perfectly happy. She hadn't lost anything but cold fingers and toes. Montgomery was going to marry his docile, mousey bride, and she was going to go on to rise Godzilla-like from the sea and stomp all over competing designers in Manhattan's garment district. Being lost in the Middle Ages for even a brief time had been very good for her. She was feeling damn fierce.

"Do you want me to stay with you?"

Pippa shook her head and concentrated on using the right English words. "I'm fine, Peaches."

"You don't look fine."

"I've been camping."

"Cindi says you were stuck in Faery."

"Cindi was strung out on valium during the trip," Pippa said. "I'm fine."

Peaches sat down on the toilet lid. "I'll wait right here to make sure."

Pippa supposed there was no hope of dislodging her sister from her perch, so she stripped and got into the tub, pulling the curtain around so Peaches wouldn't watch her fall apart from the sheer joy of being where she was supposed to be. She was already getting back in the swing of things. The proof was that she was able to weep silently. She was sure that was an improvement over the sounds she'd been making earlier.

She still wasn't warm when she finally shut off the water.

Peaches waited for her to dry off, then

wrapped her in a fluffy robe that had obviously been warmed in front of the fire. Pippa followed her sister back out into a room she was very grateful to discover wasn't Montgomery's, sat while her sister combed out her hair, then happily wrapped up in a blanket that had also been warmed against the fire.

She realized quite suddenly that her hair was almost dry and her sisters were sitting in chairs nearby. She wasn't holding a cup of anything, but there was one on the table next to her chair. It was cold. She looked at Peaches and Tess.

"Did I fall asleep?"

Tess shook her head, looking more grave than Pippa had ever seen her.

"You were very far away," Tess said quietly.

"I don't remember it," Pippa said faintly. "I seem to be losing chunks of time." She almost laughed. That was an understatement, but maybe one she shouldn't elaborate on at the moment.

"Want to give us any details?" Peaches prodded gently.

Pippa shook her head. She couldn't. Not until she'd gotten back to the gate and at least said a proper good-bye. Then she would be able to give her sisters the entire story.

"It might make you feel better to know I have your flash drive in my room," Tess said suddenly. "Cindi fessed up to hiding it from you."

Pippa realized that her sister wasn't blurting out things in a random way. She had apparently been saying quite a few things that had somehow simply disappeared into a void while Pippa had been trying to simply breathe in and out. She focused with difficulty on her sister. "What did you say?"

"I pried your backup stick out of Cindi's grasping hands," Tess said carefully. "I threatened her with the revealing of all kinds of embarrassing things about plastic surgery if she didn't cough it up."

"And you still locked her up afterward?"

"I'm a terrible person," Tess said, "and she was driving us crazy."

"The truth is," Peaches said dryly, "it was either a very nice detox facility with people who were paid to care about her or Tess's attic where *I* would have left her with a jug of water and a loaf of bread. It seemed like a better alternative for her."

"Did she give you any details about her adventure?"

Peaches exchanged a look with Tess, then shook her head. "Nothing that made any sense."

Pippa supposed Peaches wasn't one to be talking about things making sense given that she was the one who bought into all that time-traveling romantic drivel. But given that she'd just lived two weeks of it quite happily, she supposed she wasn't the one to be offering any criticisms.

"You know," Tess said slowly, "I think the best thing for you would be to have a cup of tea, then get yourself to bed. Things will look better in the morning."

Pippa nodded, because she couldn't have agreed more. Things would indeed look better in the morning because she was now in a castle that was perfectly restored with all the things she knew she simply couldn't live without. She watched Tess get up, empty out her cold tea, then refill it with something that steamed. She waited for a minute or two, tried to sip what Tess had poured for her, then gave up. She sat back, pulled the blanket closer around her, then looked around for a distraction. Trying to get to sleep was definitely not going to be it. She looked at Tess.

"Tell me a story."

Tess exchanged a look of alarm with Peaches before schooling her features into something less troubled. "What kind of story?" she asked.

"*The* story," Pippa said. "You know, your fairy tale."

"You don't believe in fairy tales," Tess managed.

Pippa didn't want to tell her that she'd recently had a change of heart, because that would have led to too many questions, so she settled for a reasonable-sounding falsehood. "I've had a rough couple of weeks and I need a distraction." She paused. "I just want to hear about something that works out the way it's supposed to."

The look Tess shared with Peaches had attained an entirely new level of alarm, but Pippa closed her eyes so she wouldn't have to watch her sister try to turn it into something . . . well, less.

Tess cleared her throat. "If you want," she said slowly.

"I want," Pippa said, keeping her eyes closed and leaning her head back against the chair. "Go on and entertain me."

"All right," Tess said carefully. "Let me set the scene for you, because that's what good storytellers do."

Pippa supposed her sister was doing that less because she wanted to set the scene and more because she probably wanted time for Peaches to get the guys in white suits on the phone, but she wasn't going to protest.

Might as well enjoy the time she had where she was. Who knew when that time would be over?

"About a year ago, I was speaking at an academic conference —"

"On medieval political thought," Peaches put in.

"Well, yes, since that's what my degree is in, I thought it appropriate," Tess said. "So, I finished my presentation, then chatted with the attendees afterward, as I usually do —"

"You're so polite," Peaches said.

"Are you going to let me tell this story?" Tess demanded.

"I don't get castles dumped in my lap," Peaches said. "I'm trying to live vicariously through you."

"Live silently," Tess suggested. "So, to continue, there I was, working my way across the room, when an old man walked up to me and asked me if I wanted a private tour of a gem of a castle hidden away in a forest."

"Did you think he was hitting on you?" Pippa asked, because she supposed Montgomery would have asked the same thing. She imagined that if Montgomery had been standing next to Tess, that old man wouldn't have dared approach her without a proper,

Regency-style introduction.

"He was every day of eighty," Tess said with a snort, "so no, I didn't think he was hitting on me. But yes, I brought along a couple of friends for protection just the same because I'm suspicious by nature. I took his tour, was apparently speechless enough to suit him, then remained speechless as he just up and handed me a key to the front door."

"Just like that," Peaches said with a sigh. "Why don't these sorts of things happen to me?"

"Because you don't like to drive on the left?"

"I could get used to it."

Pippa was torn between thinking she could get used to quite a few things and suppressing her overwhelming joy that she would never have to. Really. A world without cell phones, air travel, and neighbors' stereos keeping her up all night was a terrible thing to contemplate.

"And then the guy disappeared," Peaches said with a sigh. "It really does seem like a fairy tale."

"It does," Tess agreed, "but there were no special effects sparkles involved. He just said he was tired of the medieval reenactment business and thought I would take it over quite well, given my background. He left and I haven't heard from him since except for a letter about six months after the fact from his lawyer telling me there was a safe-deposit box he'd been instructed to tell me about if I lasted in the castle that long."

"What was in the box?" Pippa asked, though she already knew the answer.

"Money," Tess said with a smile. "Money enough to see to repairs and taxes for a very long time, though the note said he thought I wouldn't have any trouble keeping the business going. People are fascinated with the Middle Ages."

"I can see why," Peaches said, stretching her feet out toward the fire. "Romantic stuff."

Pippa supposed she might have some not-so-romantic details to add to the conversation, but now was not the time. Besides, Peaches was right. Even the thought of medieval life was romantic stuff.

Especially when there was a medieval lord involved.

"I can thank a certain Lord Darling for the modern amenities," Tess continued. "The castle had fallen into a bit of disrepair by the end of the eighteenth century. He bought it in 1850 and poured all his fortune into restoring it."

"Maybe he's your mystery geezer," Peaches said with a yawn, "and he was just waiting for the right girl to come along and love the place like you do. Maybe he was a time-traveling sort of guy."

"I don't believe in paranormal incidents," Tess said firmly.

"To the endless despair of your ghosts," Peaches laughed.

Pippa listened to her sisters discuss the merits of having resident ghosts in a proper English castle, then wondered if along with stories of old guys with stuffed safe-deposit boxes and ghosts in kilts, her sisters knew anything about the former inhabitants of Sedgwick.

But if she asked, then they would want to know why she wanted to know. She wasn't quite ready to talk about that yet.

"Pippa, you should go to bed," Tess said quietly. "I think you've had a long day."

Yeah, about seven hundred fifty years' worth of long, she wanted to say, but that would invite even more questions she didn't want to answer. She nodded, let Tess and Peaches put her to bed, then didn't argue when Peaches said she thought it might be useful if Pippa had someone to watch over her. And given that Peaches didn't kick like Cindi did, Pippa wasn't unhappy to have the company.

She also wasn't unhappy to have a toothbrush, a flush toilet, and a luxurious hot water bottle to put at her feet when she finally put on a nightgown and crawled under a down comforter that was covered with exquisitely soft sheets. Yes indeedy, the future was a great place to be.

She supposed if she repeated that often enough, she might actually begin to believe it.

She wondered what Montgomery was doing, if he was even thinking about her past being relieved that she was back in her own time and he didn't have to be responsible for her any longer.

She fell asleep, ignoring the tears that leaked down the side of her temples and got her hair and her very lovely, ergonomically correct pillow wet.

Yes, the future was the place for her.

Chapter 21

Montgomery woke to crushing pain. He turned his head, then grunted as the side of his head came in contact with the floor. Obviously, his current straits could be credited to a sword hilt to his skull. He lay there, simply breathing in and out, waiting for the pain to recede enough to allow him to think. And once it did, he almost wished it hadn't.

His last memories were of seeing Pippa being chased across his drawbridge by not only Boydin but Ada as well.

Right before she ran through nothing and disappeared into the ether.

He could hardly believe he'd witnessed the like, but he couldn't deny it. He'd started after her, fully intending to follow her through that faint hint of shimmer, but apparently he'd been felled before he could do so. He wondered if he'd been rescued or if someone had captured him. He decided quickly that the latter could not possibly be the case. If he'd been in Gunnild's clutches, he never would have woken at all.

He opened his eyes and stared at the ceiling, then jumped as Phillips's face appeared suddenly hovering over him. He closed his eyes briefly, then looked up at his squire.

"How long have I been senseless?" he asked hoarsely.

"Three days."

Montgomery sat up, but that didn't last long. He didn't protest as Phillip and Maurice helped him lie back down. He supposed another few minutes of being prone wouldn't hurt him. At least his lads had dumped him in front of the fire, which he greatly appreciated.

He lay there until the chamber stopped spinning around him, then gritted his teeth and pushed himself upright again. He forced himself to remain where he was until the urge to retch left him. He gladly accepted a cup of wine when Phillip pressed it into his hands.

He drank it, only realizing then that he was starving. He wasn't, however, going to pour things down himself he would be revisiting soon thereafter, so he decided food could wait.

"My lord," Phillip said, kneeling down

next to him, "I have grave tidings about Mistress Pippa."

Montgomery focused on him with an effort. "Aye?"

"I think she drowned."

"What?" Montgomery exclaimed.

"She fell into the cesspit, or so Boydin said, but she never resurfaced." He paused. "I would have normally refused to believe him, but I've not seen her since that time. 'Tis possible she fled into the woods. Forgive me, my lord uncle, but we've not dared to search for her. The situation here in the keep is . . . dangerous."

Montgomery could only imagine. He put his hand over his eyes for another moment or two until he felt like he could manage the pain, then he reached out to take Phillip by the arm.

"You did right," he said. "I don't think she drowned, my lad. I think she is safer wherever she is than she would be here with us right now." That was perhaps an understatement, but there was no sense in saying as much. And it was likely better that the souls in his keep believed her to be either dead or escaped into the surrounding woods. If she ever returned —

He put the sword to that thought immediately. She wouldn't return and he wouldn't want her to. She was safely back in her time with complete fashion world domination to see accomplished — whatever she'd meant by that. He supposed he shouldn't have felt any sort of jealousy at all that his nephew Stephen, who likely had all the wealth in the world to offer to the right gel, would be there to ease any lingering discomfort Pippa might have felt from her sojourn in a time not her own. Perhaps she would find someone else to love who could provide for her things he couldn't possibly manage —

"My lord?"

Montgomery unclenched his jaw. "Nothing, Phillip. Pain from my head, of course."

"Of course."

Montgomery didn't dare turn his head to look around the solar, so he supposed Phillip would have to be his eyes for the moment. "How many are we?"

"Besides you and me and your guard, my lord, we have Master Fitzpiers, Maurice, Petter and the masons, and François, Joan, and the rest of the kitchen help. The stable master has barricaded himself in the stables with the horses and Master Petter has offered aid there to keep your horseflesh safe."

"And the rest?" Montgomery asked with a sigh.

"We threw the lords Boydin and Martin into the dungeon," Phillip said, sounding particularly satisfied by that, "and confined the lady Gunnild and her daughter to one of the chambers above. As for the garrison, we have eight men left, but I couldn't say where their loyalties lay."

"I'm not sure I could, either, Phillip," Montgomery said grimly. He looked at his squire. "I'm sorry to have dragged you into this."

Phillip lifted an eyebrow in a perfect imitation of his father. "Oh, no need to apologize, Uncle. One never knows how these things will be of use in the future. Perhaps I'll need to lay siege to a keep where I'm not welcome — begging your pardon, of course."

Montgomery managed a laugh. "I wouldn't wish it on you, lad, but I suppose you'll know what to do if you're faced with it." He touched the back of his head and almost fainted. "I'm not sure I'm entirely capable of a fight today, so I fear I must rely on you all a bit longer."

"Of course, my lord," Phillip said, rising easily to his feet. "We'll keep watch."

Montgomery nodded, carefully. He didn't like the display of weakness, but he knew what he needed to do was sleep a bit longer.

He didn't hold out any hope that things

would have improved the next time he awoke.

Six days after Pippa's departure, he was thoroughly recovered and profoundly furious. He paced in his great hall, grateful for the exceeding hardness of his head that had repelled what could have killed him, and took stock of just why his fury had burned so brightly for almost a se'nnight.

He was just sure it had nothing to do with the fact that he had lost the one woman he had ever loved.

His household was greatly reduced, which probably should have pleased him given that there were now fewer people who wanted him gone, but it angered him to be feeding garrison knights who couldn't be entirely counted on to fight with him instead of against him. The kitchen staff was more dependable than those lads.

Petter and his masons were easily as fierce as he would have expected them to be, indeed they had been who had saved him from being tossed into the cesspit after Pippa and left to drown. Fitzpiers had then led the charge to herd the Sedgwick cousins into a group and send them to places they hadn't been happy to go.

Those lads, added to the eight guardsmen

left who were only slightly disturbed instead of beside themselves at the thought of serving one whom they considered to be a warlock, were all that was left to him. He had, once he'd been able to see straight, freed Gunnild and Ada from their prisons because it bothered him to keep women captive, but that had resulted only in many whispered conversations with the remaining garrison knights.

Montgomery hadn't discouraged that. He had to force their hands somehow. Carrying on without a loyal garrison was simply impossible. If they were besieged, he didn't want to have to be watching both halves of the battlefield to determine which was against him.

He had begun to wonder, however, if he would manage to carry on with any success even if he managed to sort his household. He couldn't turn a corner in his keep that he didn't walk over a spot where Pippa had walked before. He'd been convinced that sending her back to her time was the only thing he could do. He'd known the pain her family would feel at her loss.

He just hadn't expected that pain to be his.

He wrenched his thoughts back to solvable things that made him angry. His problem now was twofold: convincing the villagers he was no practitioner of the dark arts and determining which of his cousins it was who had hit him over the head. He knew it wasn't Ada because he had seen her fighting with Pippa. He hadn't seen Martin on the bridge, though that certainly wasn't enough to exclude him from the list of suspects. Boydin was the most likely lad, and he certainly had reason to want Montgomery dead — above and beyond the reasons his siblings and mother shared. Humiliation was a powerful reason for revenge.

It would have been easier to have shipped them all off to France, but he supposed he would be a fool to do that until he'd convinced them it wasn't wise to cross him. He didn't want to be looking over his shoulder for the rest of his life.

And despite all signs pointing to the contrary, he couldn't shake the feeling that he shouldn't send them off quite yet. If nothing else, perhaps he could parade them about the surrounding environs and have them announce that he was indeed just a man, not a fool bewitched by the Faery Queen.

Or that queen's younger sister.

He walked out of the hall, slogged through

the courtyard he hadn't had time to empty of horse droppings, then continued on through his gates. He supposed if he'd had any sense at all, he would have kept the drawbridge raised, but in truth there was little reason for it. Petter had worked wonders already, but there were still half a dozen holes in his outer walls. At least if someone attacked, the inhabitants of the castle could flee out the front doors.

He stopped in front of the outermost barbican gate and looked across the drawbridge. There was nothing there, of course, nothing but autumn grass and leaves falling from the trees. He sighed, then began to pace. He supposed he would eventually wear grooves in the stone, but he didn't care. He had much to think on and the castle was too confining for his taste.

To ease his distress, he reminded himself of every tale Pippa had told him on that gloomy afternoon before things had gone so rapidly downhill for them both. He had enjoyed them all, but the tale of Cinderella had intrigued him the most, likely because it was so accurate a portrayal of Pippa and her older sister —

He blinked, then frowned.

Were those shoes there?

He walked over to a spot of particularly

thick muck and leaned down — carefully. He felt recovered, but dizziness still caught him up if he bent too quickly. That would pass, he was certain.

He pulled a pair of shoes out of the mire and almost had to sit down. Very well, so it was one thing to consign Pippa to events of the past that he no longer had control over; 'twas another thing entirely to hold something of hers and remember that she was a living, breathing, beautiful gel . . .

He stood there, looking at her filthy shoes, and considered things he hadn't before. It was ridiculous, of course, but he couldn't help but wonder if he shouldn't do as Cinderella's prince had done: take that glass slipper, mount his noble steed, and search the kingdom for his love.

Of course, that didn't provide him with an easy answer for how they might live, or even if she would be happy to see him. For all he knew, she was perfectly happy to be back in her world — assuming she had returned to her world — and was counting herself well rid of him.

He half wondered if he dared find out.

He walked through the barbican gate and looked across his bridge. The sun was setting, turning even the watery, disgusting contents of the cesspit to a rather lovely color. It was a magical time, twilight, a time he had been rather fond of from his youth. Of course, during that time he had also believed in all sorts of magic he couldn't see —

He froze.

Was that a shimmer?

He found himself standing suddenly upon the edge of the proverbial knife. There was, he could say with relative certainty, a time gate opening at the end of his bridge. He could, he imagined with equal certainty, walk through it and find himself in a time not his own, a time in which he might be able to at least take Pippa her shoes.

He might try offering her his heart whilst he was about that goodly work, but he supposed he would have to wait and see how the winds were blowing first.

He turned and hastened back into his courtyard, almost plowing over his squire and his garrison captain. He put out a hand to steady Phillip, then looked at Ranulf.

"I need to make a journey," he said briskly.

"We'll be ready momentarily," Ranulf said, with an equally brisk nod.

"Nay," Montgomery said quickly. "I want you to take Phillip and the rest of the household and make for Segrave. Petter and the lads can decide for themselves where they'll say whilst I'm away, but I daren't leave either François or Fitzpiers at Gunnild's mercy."

Ranulf frowned, obviously finding it difficult to reconcile the command with his oath of fealty. "But you'll need men to guard your back, my lord," he said quickly, as if he needed to spew the words out whilst he still could. "Surely you need —"

"You to guard what I cannot," Montgomery said. He attempted a smile, though he found that his haste hampered his efforts at it. "I must go *now,* Ranulf. Keep Phillip and the others safe, and remain at my grandmother's hall until I come fetch you."

Ranulf spluttered.

Montgomery put his hand on his captain's shoulder. "I will be frank with you, because of the service you have offered me and my family. I am about to engage in a . . . a paranormal oddity."

Phillip's mouth fell open.

Ranulf only looked at Montgomery with a gaze that was far too assessing for a man who knew only about steel and strategy. Montgomery patted his captain, then looked at his squire.

"Stay with Ranulf."

"But, Uncle," Phillip said, retrieving his jaw from where it had fallen to his chest, "you *cannot.*"

"I must."

"But 'tis perilous!" Phillip exclaimed. "My father has warned me countless times to avoid those sorts of things."

"Your father is a very wise man," Montgomery said shortly, glancing up at the sky. It was darkening rapidly and for some reason that made him unbearably anxious. "I will come to Segrave to fetch you when I'm finished with my business."

"Are you going to Faery?" Phillip whispered reverently.

"I'll tell you when I return." He looked at Ranulf. "Execute my commands without deviation. Take all the horses and leave Gunnild and her cohorts to their own devices. We'll resurrect our assault when I return."

"As you will," Ranulf said, with a low bow. "Good hunting to you, my lord, in whatever forest you travel to."

Montgomery could only hope he would manage to travel anywhere at all. He gave Ranulf one last look of warning, turned it on Phillip, then turned and ran from his courtyard. He could see the gate still shimmering there in the distance. He honestly wouldn't have believed — well, not entirely — that such a thing existed if he hadn't seen it with his own eyes more than once. All it would take was a quick sprint down the bridge —

And into his cousin.

He almost ran into Boydin's sword before he realized his cousin was standing there with it bared. He drew his own sword and engaged the fool furiously.

"I'm going to finish what I started the last time I saw you on the bridge," Boydin spat. "I would have managed it if your damned squire hadn't gotten in my way."

Montgomery looked past Boydin and saw the shimmering begin to fade. He glared at Boydin. "Your life is what you make it into, you fool. Take your fury over being the second son and use it to start anew *somewhere else.*"

"I want Sedgwick!" Boydin thundered.

The gate began to close.

Montgomery kicked the sword out of Boydin's hands, resheathed his own sword, then took his cousin by the front of his tunic and heaved him over the bridge. There was a splash, then the sound of hearty curses. Montgomery left him to it and bolted down the remainder of the bridge.

The gate had almost closed completely.

He flung himself at it just the same and hoped death wouldn't be the result.

CHAPTER 22

Pippa stood on the edge of Tess's great hall and watched the occupants without really seeing more than just swirls of color. The party had started an hour ago, and looked as if it might go on forever. The guests looked as if they might have constitutions equal to dancing not only the evening but the entire night away. Pippa shook her head. Those silly reenactment types with their delusions of medieval grandeur. Maybe all their excess energy came from only pretending to live in the past instead of actually having to spend the mornings in the lists training their garrisons and the rest of their days trying to figure out how to feed themselves during the winter.

She was tempted to try to make a quick exit, but Tess was watching her from the hallway that led to the kitchen, and Peaches was standing at the base of the stairs, guarding them like a rottweiler.

Pippa scowled. She didn't need babysitting. After all, it wasn't as if she'd caused *that* big a scene in the gift shop earlier. Surely she could get herself through the evening without someone following along five steps behind her. She'd managed it earlier that morning, hadn't she?

Admittedly, it had been the first time in almost a week that she managed to elude her sisters long enough to have a little time to herself. After a week's worth of hot showers — plus a few extra to make up for her earlier lack — a week's worth of decent meals, and a week to wonder why it was that Montgomery de Piaget had obviously decided she wasn't worth following, glass slipper in hand, she'd needed to get out of the castle. She'd needed the distraction from the inescapable conclusion she'd come to.

She loathed fairy tales.

She wasn't sure she didn't feel the same way about her life. Tess and Peaches had been wonderful to her, if not a little stifling. Stephen de Piaget had seemingly taken up temporary residence in the castle. She wasn't sure why, but he seemed to feel some sense of responsibility where she and her sisters were concerned. Either that, or he was just desperate to get details about medieval England he somehow thought she could provide. She wouldn't have been surprised by either, though she was a little startled every time she ran into him and he was Stephen and not a modern version of his medieval uncle.

She had given in on Day Three and told her trio of keepers of her trip to the past — not everything, but enough to satisfy the barest minimum of their slack-jawed curiosity. If she'd neglected to elaborate on her feelings for a certain medieval lord or left out a recounting of the times he'd held her hand, well, who could blame her? There had been enough detail about mayhem and attempted murder to keep her sisters and Stephen satisfied without having to divulge more personal details.

Never mind that Tess and Peaches had exchanged glances, as if they guessed quite a bit of what she'd left out. Either that, or their knowing looks had been a twin thing she just didn't understand. She hadn't had the energy to ask.

The only bright spot in the perpetual October gloom had been that Cindi was still drying out from things none of them realized she had been on — and screaming at the top of her lungs for more Botox, apparently — so Pippa found herself free from the burden of having to deal with that. Over the past week, all that had been required of her had been to get up in the morning, get through the day, then go back to bed. She'd found a sketchbook and her favorite pencils waiting for her in her room on Day Four of her return to the future, which she had shunned at first, then found herself turning to more and more often.

Too bad all she seemed capable of drawing was Montgomery, and a damned good likeness those drawings of him were, indeed.

She knew she was eventually going to have to stop thinking about him. Not only was he centuries out of her reach, he was set firmly beyond her possible matrimonial grasp. He would marry his compliant medieval gal and she would be stuck trying to find someone remotely like him in her century. She was afraid not even Stephen would fit the bill. He was utterly gorgeous, of course, and rich, and brilliant, and a decent swordsman.

But she didn't love *him.*

All of which had led her on what had turned out to be an ill-advised trip to the gift shop earlier that morning to do a little research. She'd had a distinct and unpleasant feeling that she should have just left well enough alone, but she had ignored it. There was nothing wrong with trying to find out how Montgomery's life had gone. She had hoped that seeing in print that he'd married that compliant mouse, had a dozen children, then lived to a ripe old age in a castle that had eventually stopped looking like a piece of Swiss cheese would be enough to put that particular chapter of her life to bed.

She had stood in front of the small shelf of books published just about Sedgwick castle and selected one at random. It had been full of all sorts of paranormal experiments yielding interesting things, but it had yielded nothing of interest to her so she'd put it back without even creasing the very slender spine.

It had taken her half an hour before she'd hit the mother lode. She'd begun to read, then had to sit down on the floor right in the middle of books and china and tea towels to devour everything she could about the early lords of Sedgwick.

She read about the history of Montgomery's family's link to the castle, about his father's dealings with the lords of Ayre and Segrave, then Rhys's eventual inheritance of Sedgwick itself and how it had been handed over to his brother for safekeeping until one of his sons could grow up and claim it.

The youngest son, as it happened.

Montgomery de Piaget had indeed been

given the castle, but the rumors surrounding him had begun almost immediately and had seemed to include most notably his falling in love with a fairy.

Though the writer had cast some doubt on whether or not such a thing was possible.

Pippa had found herself rudely interrupted at that point by the shopkeeper, who seemed not to care that she was the owner's sister. There had been a bit of a scuffle over the book. Pippa would admit that when she had jerked it away from the woman, she might have overturned a teapot or two. It was also possible that she might have thrown a rather substantial resin replica of the castle in the direction of the woman's terrier who had been ordered to sic. In return, she'd been clobbered over the head with a stitchery kit that had contained not only cloth and thread but wooden stretcher bars.

Things had spiraled out of control after that.

Pippa supposed the only reason she was now standing in her sister's great hall instead of languishing down at the local pokey was because Tess had come looking for her at just the right time. The shop had suffered minimal damage, but the shopkeeper's pride had been grievously wounded.

Pippa had apologized, grudgingly, but she hadn't let go of the book. Never mind that she'd almost dropped it in the moat when she'd managed to get it back open to the place where she'd been keeping her middle finger and read what was written there.

Lord Montgomery had never married.

That might have been because he'd been killed.

Tess had yanked the book away from her and instructed her sternly to stop making noises that frightened them. Pippa had agreed meekly, then followed her sister up to her room where she'd been pushed into a chair and told to sit. She had sat, because her legs hadn't been equal to the task of holding her up any longer. It was one thing to think Montgomery was miserable without her; it was quite another to think his life had been cut short, perhaps even because of her.

It had taken the rest of the morning to get her sisters to leave her alone so she could break into Tess's office, find the book, and read the rest of the story. The only comfort she'd subsequently found was that there was apparently some disagreement on the fate of that early lord of Sedgwick. Some reports said he'd been killed outright while others said he'd been maimed so badly in an attack that the rest of his life had consisted of merely being carried to a sunny spot in his courtyard and left there for the day whilst others went about their work.

For Montgomery, she wasn't sure which would have been worse.

She'd spent the afternoon getting pruny in the shower, because that had seemed the safest place to be. She'd managed to forget about Montgomery for long stretches of time — at least five minutes a shot — and concentrate on her own life.

Her life in which every moment that passed was full of the knowledge of how his would end.

Tess and Peaches had dragged her out of the shower eventually and forced her to come downstairs for the party. They'd insisted it would cheer her up. What would have cheered her up was the ability to send Montgomery a note that said that he really should keep an eye out for cousins with his death on their minds.

Then again, he probably knew that already.

She sighed and rubbed her hands over her face, struggling to bring herself back to the present. What she really wanted was for him to dump the mouse and come for her, but she was living in the Land of Reality, not some fairy tale, and in the real world, medieval lords didn't risk everything to come to the future to look for a woman they probably didn't have any feelings for.

She pushed away from the wall, then shot Peaches a dark look when she did the same thing. "I'm going to go get something to drink," she snapped.

Peaches only clasped her hands behind her back and smiled. Pippa didn't imagine Peaches's shoes were nailed to the floor, so she would probably be making her own trip to the kitchen as part of her guard-dog duties. She sighed and started trudging across the hall, dodging dancers who were like a continual stream of motion in front of her. Well, except for one of them who was simply standing in front of the fireplace. Pippa looked up, intending to toss him a compliment on his good sense.

Only she found, quite suddenly, that she couldn't.

There, standing across the way from her was a man dressed in medieval clothing, sporting a medieval sword, and looking more handsome than any reenactment knight could possibly have looked. But that might have been because he wasn't a reenactment knight.

He was the real deal.

Pippa made some sort of noise, but she didn't want to identify it. Instead, she started walking again before she realized she was moving. Well, she actually ran, but she didn't think anyone would fault her for it. Montgomery strode toward her rather quickly himself, then caught her as she threw herself into his arms. Pippa gasped as he clutched her to him, but she wasn't about to ask him to let her go.

"I say," a disgruntled male voice said from next to them, "I don't think that's part of the dance."

Pippa laughed, because she couldn't help herself, then caught the breath she'd lost as Montgomery set her back on her feet. "No, I suppose it isn't," she managed. She looked up into Montgomery's beloved face and couldn't stop smiling. "You came," she said, breathless still.

"The gate opened," he said, sounding a little breathless himself. "And it just about shut itself on my arse."

She laughed, feeling altogether giddy. "I'm relieved you're undamaged."

He reached up and brushed her hair back from her face. "I am as well," he admitted, then he smiled gravely. "You left your shoes in my courtyard. I thought I should bring them to you and see if they still fit."

"It's an awfully long way to come to bring back a pair of shoes," she said. "Wouldn't they fit your fiancée?"

The words were out of her mouth before she could stop them. She supposed if she'd had any sense at all, she would have put her arms back around him and spent her time convincing him why she was a better choice for him than some no-name girl with big ears and a petite nose, but apparently she didn't have any sense left.

And he didn't seem inclined to let her go.

"She has enormous feet," he said solemnly, "and hands like a blacksmith. Now, might we discuss other things? Perhaps we should move out of the way of the dancers to do so. I fear someone will draw a blade on us soon."

"I don't think you have much to worry about," Pippa said, finding it hard to breathe properly. She realized that her teeth were chattering as well. What next, weakness in her knees?

Or being pulled behind a medieval lord who had a bad habit of doing just that. She peeked around his shoulder to find Tess and Peaches standing there.

"Montgomery, those are just my sisters," Pippa said. She paused. "They're twins."

"So I see," he said faintly.

Pippa tried to walk around him only to walk into his arm that had extended suddenly like a railroad-crossing guard gone awry. She pushed his arm down and moved to stand next to him, then looked at her sisters with what she hoped was an appropriately disinterested expression.

They weren't buying what she was selling.

She gave in and smiled so hard it hurt her cheeks. "Tess, Peach, this is Montgomery de Piaget. Montgomery, these are my sisters, Tess and Peaches."

He took their hands one by one and bowed low over them. *"Enchanté,"* he said politely.

And then he reached for her hand and tucked it into the crook of his elbow.

Pippa thought she just might have to laugh soon. She listened to Montgomery exchange basic pleasantries with her sisters and smiled at the sound of his French with its medieval inflection. It was without a doubt the most wonderful thing she'd ever heard. She didn't even protest when she found herself suddenly with her nose pressed against his back. She only sighed and looked around his shoulder again to now find Stephen walking toward them.

"Montgomery —"

"I'm keeping you safe, woman. Stop fighting me."

"That's your nephew, my lord, not the French army."

He grunted at her, then must have gotten a good look at that nephew because he flinched. Pippa took the opportunity to pop out from behind him and attempt to get a good look at his expression. He was gaping at Stephen as if he'd just seen a ghost. She couldn't blame him. Stephen looked enough like him that they could easily have passed for brothers. Stephen came to an ungainly halt and gaped back.

"Montgomery de Piaget meet your nephew, Stephen," Pippa said, trying not to let her giddiness turn into uncontrollable shivering. "Stephen, meet Montgomery." She paused and looked at Tess's colleague. "I believe his father built your father's hall."

Stephen held out a hand that shook just the slightest bit. Pippa couldn't have said Montgomery's was any steadier when he shook his nephew's, but that moment passed too quickly for her to make much of it. They were suddenly exchanging some species of male chitchat, but she didn't pay attention to it. She was too busy trying not to read anything into the fact that Montgomery had put his arm out in front of her and had scooted her so she was standing just slightly behind him, or that he had kept his hand wrapped around her wrist, as if he wanted to make certain she didn't escape. She supposed she wouldn't have been surprised to see him draw his very sharp sword soon to mark his territory, but maybe he thought that might be going a step too far.

She looked at her sisters to find them looking between Montgomery and Stephen with expressions of astonishment. Peaches managed to tear her gaze away from the men long enough to gape at Pippa.

"Wow," she mouthed.

Pippa only smiled. Again.

"Perhaps, my lord," Stephen said, inclining his head, "you would care for something to eat?"

"Later, if you don't mind," Montgomery said with equal politeness. "I've actually come to dance with this lovely woman here. Persephone, will you favor me?"

Pippa realized Montgomery was talking to her, though it took a moment or two before what he'd asked registered. She smiled, feeling altogether breathless.

"You're sure you don't want something to eat first?" she managed.

"Later, after I've looked my fill."

She took a deep breath and tried to put

the brakes on her rampaging imagination. It was possible he was talking about the great hall. It was, after all, quite a bit more spectacular than it had been in his day. He could have been interested in Stephen, or Tess's guests, her sisters. He could have simply wanted to hand her her shoes, scope out the twenty-first century, then hightail it back home before he turned into a pumpkin.

Then again, it was her hand he was holding as he led her across the hall and it was her hand he kept hold of as they waited for the music to change. She was tempted to grill him one more time about his fiancée, but even she could see that might ruin the moment. The man had traveled over eight centuries to bring her a pair of shoes, and now he wanted to dance with her. The least she could do was humor him.

She smiled when she heard the musicians play something that sounded a bit like what she'd heard at Wyckham. "I think I know this one."

"I daresay you do, my lady."

She found that while she might have known the dance, she wasn't able to concentrate on it. That might have had something to do with the fact that she was unable to take her eyes off Montgomery. She had no idea why he'd really come. Coming all that way simply to put shoes on her feet was easily one of the lamest excuses she'd ever —

She stumbled to a halt.

That *was* a little on the Cinderella-ish side, wasn't it?

"Persephone?"

She smiled up at him and did her best to concentrate on what she was doing. That was made ever more difficult each time she touched his hand in passing or looked up at his face to find him staring at her with a level of intensity that passed even her father's ferocious attention to the Plexiglas seams of the cases that held his signed *Abbey Road* album. No, this was intensity in an entirely different league.

Fortunately for her, the music ended before she embarrassed herself too badly. She stood in front of Montgomery, forced herself to keep her arms down by her sides instead of throwing them around him again as she so desperately wanted to do, and looked for something innocuous to say.

"Let me feed you," she offered. "Though I should warn you that there might be a few new additions to your kitchen."

"I know," he said with a shiver. "I've seen them."

"Frightening?"

He chewed on his words for a moment or two. "I'm not sure I want to admit to that."

"I'll keep you safe," she promised.

He smiled ruefully, and she fell in love with him all over again.

She was in *deep* trouble.

"I'll allow it tonight," he said. "Tomorrow, however, I will be back in charge, as usual. This is an aberration."

"Whatever you say, cupcake."

He tucked her hand under his arm. "Lead on, lady, if you will. And pray find me something I might recognize."

Given the excellence of Tess's chef, she didn't doubt there would be something on the fire that would be at least edible. Perhaps Montgomery was fortunate he'd arrived on an evening where his particular time was being celebrated. She heard him catch his breath softly as they entered the kitchens, but he didn't give any other sign of being freaked out. She had a quiet word with Tess's cook, then found a stool for Montgomery and a place at a worktable. He pulled the stool out for her instead, then went to fetch another for himself. He sat, then looked at her gravely.

"I left your shoes outside in the current year's courtyard."

She had to take a bracing breath. "I can't

believe you braved the gate to bring me shoes."

"The truth is —" He looked up suddenly, then rose.

Pippa thought she might like to kill whoever had interrupted what she was sure would have been a stunning confession of his true motives. She looked up to find that her future victims were her sisters trailed by a still stunned-looking Stephen de Piaget. Tess put Stephen on a stool, then smiled at Montgomery.

"I should be out there playing host," she said in her excellent French, "but I wanted to make sure you were comfortable, um, Lord —"

" 'Tis just Montgomery," Montgomery supplied. "I am pleased to see the castle looking so well."

"I can't take credit for that," Tess said, blushing. "It was restored in 1850 —" She had to take a deep breath. "I suppose you don't want all the details now. I can give them to you later, if you like." She paused. "If you're staying —"

"I would like to, if you have room for me," Montgomery said with a grave look. "I will, of course, pay —"

"Of course you won't," Peaches interrupted with a snort. She laughed a little. "I just meant that, well, you're almost, um —"

She trailed off uncomfortably, then fell completely silent as Montgomery favored her with the same sort of charming smile she'd seen his brother Nicholas wear as well. Genetics at work again, apparently. Pippa looked between her sisters to find them both blushing furiously. She rolled her eyes. Her sisters looked as if they'd never been in the same room with a man before. Admittedly, Montgomery was luscious, but blush-worthy?

He took her hand, then favored her with a very small, private smile before he continued on a conversation with her sisters in French that seemed to bridge almost eight centuries quite easily.

She blushed as well.

At least Stephen was refraining from that kind of reaction. He simply sat on another stool and gaped.

"Stephen," she whispered, then she pantomimed closing her mouth with a finger under her chin.

He shut his mouth with a snap, but looked no less overcome.

Pippa understood completely.

"How is your sister Cinderella?" Montgomery asked politely. "Is she happily recovered from her camping experience?"

If her sisters hadn't been felled before, they were then. Pippa watched as they shared a brief look of approval, then found themselves seats where they could more easily fall all over Montgomery. She might have given them a territorial sort of shove and a warning look, but she honestly couldn't blame them because she was doing the same thing.

And, after all, hers was the hand he was holding.

He let go of her long enough to examine a very lovely meal of beef and vegetables with whole-grain rolls. He tasted everything hesitantly at first, then apparently found it all familiar enough to down with obvious pleasure. He didn't care for the glass of wine Peaches handed him, but he was quite happy to have water. Pippa hadn't eaten dinner, but she didn't manage it then either because all she could do was watch him.

The truth was, she hadn't expected to see him again. She'd spent an inordinate amount of time telling herself that she didn't *want* to see him again, that her life was back to normal and she was happy, happy, *happy* about it.

She was a dreadful liar.

And that made her very nervous. She needed the future with its marvels. She didn't want the past with its cold and crumbling walls and people who would just as soon have killed her as to look at her. She wanted murder and mayhem to be limited to the big screen —

Murder and mayhem.

All of a sudden she didn't feel very good. Everything she'd read earlier that day came back to her in a terrible rush. If the historians were to be believed, the man next to her would in the very near future either die or be wounded seriously enough that he would live out his life a shell of his former self.

"Pippa?"

She felt his arm go around her. She turned toward him and pressed her face against the rough weave of his tunic because it was easier to hide her expression that way.

"It's nothing," she managed.

"You've had a long day," he murmured. "Perhaps I should see you to your chamber."

She had to blink a time or two. She'd had her miserable future planned out, she'd already begun to grieve over what lay in store for him in *his* future, she'd been prepared to soldier on and make do —

And then she'd seen him across the great hall and everything had changed again.

She pulled back and looked into his very

lovely gray eyes. "I'm fine."

"I will be here tomorrow, Persephone." He brought her hand to his lips. "If you wouldn't mind if I stay."

She couldn't answer without falling apart, so she simply squeezed his hand, hard, and hoped he would take that as answer enough.

Stephen rose and made Montgomery a low bow.

"You will take my chamber, my lord," he said in a fairly decent imitation of Montgomery's accent. "I will find other quarters. I will also find clothing for you on the morrow, if you like."

Montgomery sized him up. "Can you wield a sword, Stephen?"

Pippa had to smile. Stephen de Piaget was obviously not one to back down from a fight, but he swallowed very carefully at present.

"I might attempt it."

"Then let me see my lady to her bedchamber and we will discuss your skills and see if they meet with my approval." He blinked, then looked at Pippa. "I'm starting to sound like Robin."

"Better go to bed until it passes, then," she advised.

He smiled, a smile that showed off his dimple to its best advantage. "I daresay you're right. Let's be off. I'm sure there will be many marvels to examine on the morrow."

She wasn't sure he had any idea what he was in for, but she wasn't going to argue. She also wasn't going to complain about the fact that he didn't seem inclined to let go of her hand. She exchanged a brief look with her sisters before she walked with Montgomery and Stephen out of the kitchen and back up to the great hall. The party was starting to break up, but she wasn't particularly interested in waiting it out. She thought it might be all she could do to get upstairs and fall into bed without falling to pieces.

Montgomery paused on their way through the great hall, looked around him, then shook his head and sighed as he walked with her up the stairs and down the hallway. Pippa stopped him in front of her door, then looked up at him.

"Thank you," she said quietly.

He tilted his head and smiled. "For what?"

The list was too long and potentially too revealing. She settled for simple. "For the dance."

"We'll have others," he said quietly, "if you're willing." He paused, then started to say something else, but stopped and glanced to his right.

Pippa looked as well to find Stephen there, looking helpful. She thought it would have been rude to punch him, so she bit her tongue and decided that maybe she would have to borrow a couple of horses from someone so she could take Montgomery out for a private ride and figure out why it was he'd come to see her.

"My lord?" Stephen said, with a small bow. "If you're ready, I'll show you to your room."

Montgomery nodded, then took Pippa's hand and bent over it. He didn't kiss it, which she supposed shouldn't have disappointed her. He was, after all, still engaged eight hundred years in the past.

"Tomorrow," he promised.

She nodded, then slipped inside her room as he held the door open for her. He smiled, bid her another soft good night, then pulled the door shut.

Pippa turned and leaned back against it. She could hardly believe what she'd just seen in her sister's great hall. It was all she could do not to wrench the door open, chase after Montgomery, then beg him to hold on to her and never let her go — his fiancée be damned.

She hadn't had the chance to even take a

decent breath before a sudden knock on her door made her jump. She put her hand over her heart, then opened her door to find Peaches standing there practically hopping from one foot to the other.

"Let me in," Peaches said, pushing past her. "I want details."

Pippa shut the door behind her sister. She imagined their duet would become a trio soon enough, but maybe she could sit down for a moment or two before Tess showed up. She walked across the room and collapsed in a chair next to the fire.

"Well?" Pippa asked.

"Well?" Peaches echoed in disbelief, coming to sit across from her. "Is that all you can say? If you ask me, there aren't words to describe how perfectly hot he is. Where in the world did you find him?"

"I told you where I found him," Pippa said with a scowl.

"You neglected to mention his absolute hotness."

"I didn't tell you everything about him because then I would have had to tell you also about his mousy, tractable, future wife!"

Peaches blinked. "He's engaged? Then why is he here with you?"

"He took a wrong turn?"

"Oh, I don't think so, and I think that's

Tess at your door. Better go open it."

Pippa did, only to have her other sister push past her into her room. Tess made herself at home in Pippa's chair and shook her head with a low whistle.

"Wow."

Peaches laughed. "Is that the best *you* can do? He's dreamy!"

"And engaged," Pippa said pointedly, "remember?"

"Engaged?" Tess asked in astonishment. "Then why is he here with you?"

Pippa couldn't bring herself to even look for an answer or point out to her sisters that they sounded like recordings of each other. She ignored the question and sat down heavily in the last chair there in front of the fire. "I tell you both, it's Karma again, coming to repay me early for as-yet-unexperienced success."

"I think I would choose Montgomery's luscious French over Stephen's deep pockets any day," Peaches said, fanning herself vigorously. "It's too bad you can't take him back to Seattle and introduce him to your gazillion first dates. I think you'd really enjoy that."

Pippa imagined she would. She looked at her rather unsteady hands for a minute or two, then at her sisters one by one. "This might count as a second date, wouldn't you say? If he weren't already hooked up with someone else? Or does this put him in total loser territory because he's here with me and not with Miss Mouse?"

"He's not married to her," Tess said reasonably. "He could change his mind, you know."

"Or he could have just come for a tour of the castle," Pippa said grimly.

"Get real," Peaches said with a laugh. She looked at Tess. "Did he look like he was here for a tour?"

"Absolutely not," Tess said, "though I will admit to being vastly relieved just the same that I hadn't trashed his hall. I have the feeling he's going to be checking the closets before it's all over." She looked at Pippa. "Go put on your jammies and go to bed. You look shell-shocked."

"A man just traveled over seven hundred fifty years to bring me a lousy pair of shoes," Pippa said shortly. "Of *course* I looked shell-shocked!"

Her sisters only exchanged a look. It was the same look they'd been exchanging for as long as Pippa could remember, a look that usually involved twinnish secrets and plots she couldn't possibly fathom. It was trouble, pure and simple.

But since she was already in deep trouble, she ignored it and headed for the bathroom before she had to either sit down or fall there. Her knees were just not equal to the events of the morning.

He had come.

She took a deep breath. She would brush her teeth, put on something borrowed from Peaches whose clothes she liked better than Tess's, then see if she couldn't just let events unfold the way they would. She didn't sense any karmic tentacles reaching for her, so maybe she could just relax and enjoy the coming days, however many they were.

And she would try not to think about the fact that a man she could no longer deny she loved had come eight hundred years to make sure she wasn't running around barefooted.

Cinderella would have approved.

CHAPTER 23

Montgomery paced uneasily before the fire in the great hall and wondered not only about what might startle him next, but if he had the stomach to find out. He had leapt through that time gate with all the confidence of a man who had decided what his heart wanted and was going to let nothing stand in his way of having it.

Unfortunately for him, the Future had turned out to be a bit more intimidating than he'd expected it to be.

The changes in how man conducted his life weren't beyond his ability to make sense of, but they had indeed been remarkable. The lights had been astonishing, and he'd found the improvements made in garderobe mechanics to be quite useful. Electricity, something he'd required Stephen to explain to him the night before at great length, had seemed a most marvelous tool he would regret not having the use of in the past, as would be the luxurious bed he'd slept on and the blade he'd used to shave with that morn. He suspected that those were only the beginning of the marvels he would be faced with.

Marvels a Future gel would have to leave behind if she consented to go live in the past.

If he had been made of lesser stuff, he might have thought twice about even speaking of his heart's desire. But he hadn't come across centuries into a world of wonders simply to remain silent.

He supposed his first task was to overcome his astonishment at everything he saw so he looked less like an unsophisticated village brat. Perhaps he would spend the day simply attempting to grow accustomed to Pippa's world and cease trying to commit it all to memory so he would know what improvements to make in his own time — which Stephen had warned him against doing. Montgomery could see the wisdom in that, though he could certainly bring to mind several odd things about Wyckham that seemed much less odd now that he'd seen their likeness several centuries in the future.

Stephen had been gracious enough to make a loan of several items of clothing that

Montgomery had happily donned. There was no sense in not fitting in whilst he could. He had promised Stephen to return the favor should his nephew ever find himself lingering in the thirteenth century, something Stephen seemed to consider with horror.

Obviously, the man needed a bit more time in the lists to stiffen his spine.

Unfortunately that happy moment was not to be that day. Stephen had acquired entrance to some sort of display of things that he was sure would interest Pippa and their travels required them to have an early start. The thought of traveling to London during the course of a single morning, much less a single day, had left Montgomery shaking his head, but what did he know of modern wagons? Perhaps the horses were fed and tended so well that they ran on wings.

He took the opportunity to look at his hall. He understood now that expression of disbelief Pippa had worn so often that first handful of days, as if she dreamed what she was seeing. He hadn't ever doubted Sedgwick's potential, should he have ever managed to rid it of its unsavory personalities, but to see it adorned with lovely tapestries and full of clean air instead of smoke from clogged flues was a marvel indeed.

He heard a heavy footstep and turned around to find Stephen walking toward him. He had decided early on the evening before that whilst Stephen seemed to be quite protective of Pippa and her sisters, he was limiting himself to brotherly feelings. He would therefore live another day.

"Good morning, my lord," Stephen said, stopping in front of him and bowing.

"You needn't do that," Montgomery said, feeling slightly amused by the deference. "You are older than I am, I daresay."

"I'm ingratiating myself in order to have a lesson or two in swordplay."

"I can't imagine why you'd need it here in the Future, but I'll humor you. Perhaps tomorrow. I wouldn't want to interrupt our journey toward London today —"

He looked up at the sound of other light footsteps running across the hall, sure it was Pippa. It was indeed, though he was shocked to find she had arrived half dressed. He clapped a hand over Stephen's eyes and gaped at his would-be love. Never mind that she was dressed as he was, in jeans and a tunic-like shirt. Those clothes left her so exposed, she might as well have been wearing nothing at all.

She stopped short. "What's wrong?"

He gestured at her clothes, then decided that perhaps he should set the example and avert his gaze as well. He looked up at the ceiling. "Saints, woman, go back up and put on something . . . well, something *more.*"

"Why?"

"Because you're wearing jeans!"

"So are you."

"I am a man."

Stephen might have laughed. Montgomery wasn't certain, but he was certain 'twas never too soon to teach the man a few manners. He lifted his hand from Stephen's eyes and glared at him.

"Look at her and you'll die by my hand."

"I've already seen —"

Montgomery reached for his sword only to realize he'd left it above in Stephen's chamber. He scowled at his nephew. "I don't need a sword to kill you."

"I imagine you don't," Stephen said faintly. He smiled briefly at Pippa, then very wisely began to study the tapestries lining the walls near the fireplace. "I'll humor you, my lord, though I will point out that this is the least of the things you'll see today." He shot Pippa a brief look. "I told you it was a mistake to take him to London."

"I don't want to leave him behind," Pippa said firmly, "and I'm not going to waste your very expensive tickets. He'll be fine."

"Pippa, my dear, it's the twenty-first century," Stephen warned. "I'm only saying he won't like what he sees."

Montgomery opened his mouth to state that he would be the judge of what he did and did not care for, but Pippa took his arm and pulled on him before he could. He shot Stephen a warning look, then allowed Pippa to lead him across the hall and out the front door. She stopped in the middle of the very clean courtyard and looked up at him.

"Things are different in my time."

"So I see!" He drew his hand over his eyes. "And I've seen too much already this day."

"Would it make you feel better if I put on a long coat to cover up what you've already seen too much of?"

She was laughing at him, he could tell that much. "I'm not sure anything would help at this point," he muttered. He considered, then looked down at her. "I don't like to admit weakness, but I might be a bit, ah —"

"Overwhelmed?" she offered.

"Overwhelmed by my ability to manage difficult things, perhaps," he said, knowing he sounded exactly like his eldest brother but somehow unable to help himself. He cleared his throat. "I fear I'm losing my wits."

"I understand, completely," she said. "You know, I don't have a sword, but I do know my century. I'll keep you safe. If you'll let me."

He took a deep breath, then reached out and pulled her carefully into his arms. He rested his cheek lightly against her hair. " 'Tis a grievous blow to my pride, but since you're the one wielding the sword, I suppose I'll endure it. Now, tell me again where specifically are we going on this journey of Stephen's?"

"To a fashion show in London. We'll watch women walk up and down a raised sort of path showing off the clothes a designer has created to sell to others."

"I would rather see yours, of course," he said, "but I'll come today because I don't want to leave you unprotected in London." He paused, then attempted to tread carefully, because he didn't want to make her look foolish. "Though I don't see how we'll manage to return home tonight. 'Tis too far."

She pulled back and looked at him seriously. "That's something we need to talk about. We're going drive in a car. It's a wagon that requires no horses. We'll be to

London very quickly — or not, depending on the traffic. It's Friday, so apparently it could be a real nightmare."

Montgomery wished heartily that he'd had a peek at that manuscript Nicholas was rumored to have in his trunk of secrets, the manuscript that detailed all manner of Future marvels. He could have at least been familiar with the sight of a few of the things he had already been subjected to, such as the shower and jeans and the Aga stove that delivered such lovely, hot repasts, though he supposed no manuscript could ever have prepared him for the reality he now faced.

"Do you want to come look at the car?" she asked.

He would have preferred to remain in his courtyard with her in his arms given that she was the reason he had leapt through that shimmer in the air, but he supposed he might do well to be prepared for the journey. He nodded slowly, for he knew he must.

She smiled, pulled away, then took his hand. "You did leave all your blades upstairs, didn't you?"

"What difference does that make?"

"You'll see."

The saints preserve him, he feared he just might.

■ ■ ■ ■

Eight hours later, he was still trying without much success to pick his jaw up off the floor. The journey to London had seemed like something from a dream. The surrounding countryside had been a blur and the number of other cars on the road had made him claustrophobic. He had sat in the front of the car with Stephen, trying not to look as unnerved as he had been.

He couldn't say he'd been any happier when they'd stopped in London. He felt as if he had truly been dropped into another world. The city had been full of souls in his day as well, but now that number seemed quite manageable compared to what he'd seen that afternoon. He hadn't minded what the men had been wearing for the most part, but the women had terrified him. He didn't consider himself particularly weak-stomached and he was certainly not unused to the mores and complexities of court life, but modern London . . .

It was enough to make a man of a medieval vintage suspect he should never have left his village green.

Now, he was sitting in an Italian restaurant hoping that the food that would soon come from the kitchens might be something he would recognize. He looked about himself and tried to make a list of things he cared for and didn't, but it was difficult. The noise in the tavern was excessive, the music unfamiliar, and someone on the other side of a low partition was smoking something that made him ill. He turned to listen to Stephen, Tess, and Peaches discussing the clothing they'd seen that afternoon, clothing that made what the sisters were wearing look fit for a nunnery. The trio had said more than once that Pippa's designs were far superior. Though he hadn't had the chance to see for himself, he imagined they had it aright.

In fact, as he had sat next to Pippa during the production, he'd come to several conclusions, the most momentous of which had been that despite her fierce declarations that she intended to conquer the world of fashion, he couldn't imagine her happy in that world. The severe women — bags of bones, really — who had been wearing the clothing, the hard-edged men and women who had designed that clothing — nay, he couldn't see Pippa associating with them for the rest of her life.

He could however see her holding court in a fashionable chamber with tapestries lining the walls and the floors so she wouldn't be chilled as highborn women came to her so she could drape them in exquisite fabrics and give them the same fairy tale she'd given to him. He supposed it was a rare thing to have an opinionated Future lass leave a medieval sort of lad feeling as if he were a noble prince, a prince who would have gone to any length to make that princess his, but she had certainly done it.

He glanced her way to find her watching him with a very small smile on her face. He smiled in return. "How are you?" he asked.

She shook her head slowly. "I was just wondering how *you* were."

He supposed no one would understand his French, so there was no reason to be discreet. "I can't say I've ever cared for London," he admitted, "though I have been here far more often and for longer periods of time than I would have liked."

"Hobnobbing with the king?" she asked politely.

"As it happens, aye."

Her mouth fell open. "I was kidding. Do you really know him?"

"My father first pressed me into the service of representing him at court," he said with a shrug. "Eventually, I made the required visits for myself."

"That must be strange," she murmured. "To be in the same place you were before but find it so different."

He smiled. "I imagine you understand."

"I suppose I can," she agreed. She leaned closer to him. "So, what do you think so far? What do you like the most?"

"You," he said without hesitation.

"Be serious."

"I was. You are by far the most entertaining thing I've seen all day. Then I find myself fond of your sisters, my nephew, and water carried conveniently in a bottle." He paused. "And chocolate."

She smiled at him. "Stephen wants to take you to Harrods after dinner. From what I understand, you could probably kill yourself by the abuse to your tender medieval tummy you'll find in their food court. There's an entire spot there just for chocolate lovers."

He wasn't sure why food should hold its own court anywhere but France, but perhaps the London of Pippa's day was more sophisticated than the one of his time. But as he listened to her describe the reputed splendors of Harrods, he began to wonder if he had underestimated modern London's appetite for luxuries. Perhaps 'twas little wonder that so many souls from so many places sought refuge there. He had heard, just whilst walking down the street, a handful of languages he recognized and another he didn't. A man might spend his lifetime roaming those streets and still not be familiar with everything there.

The truth was, he could think of many other things he would rather spend his time doing, such as haunting his lists, or sitting in his solar watching Pippa by the light of his fire, or riding for leagues with nothing to listen to but the wind in the trees.

Perhaps he had been born in the right century after all.

Supper was lovely, and the conversation pleasant, though he spent the walk back to the car dividing his time between reaching for his sword and glaring at lads he thought looked too long at Pippa and her sisters.

Some things obviously had not changed.

The journey back to the castle was less unsettling than the earlier one had been, though seeing his keep — his intact keep — flooded with lights that certainly hadn't come from torches made him gasp before he could stop himself.

Stephen walked with him across the bridge, looking faintly amused. "Surely the castle can't be that different in your day."

"It has more holes in its walls," Montgomery grumbled, "but the general shape is the same."

Stephen laughed. "I am keen to have the details," he said, "but I may be fighting Pippa for your time. Do you have any idea how long you'll stay?"

Long enough to convince Pippa she might someday learn to love me was what he thought, but he avoided saying as much. In truth, he hadn't given it much thought, mostly because there were too many things associated with it that he wasn't prepared to consider, such as if Pippa actually wanted anything to do with him and if she did, where — and when — they would live. He returned to thoughts of fairy tales and princes doing the impossible to win their ladies — even crossing centuries.

Even, he supposed, giving up his past if it meant she could be his future.

He gave Stephen a noncommittal answer, because he honestly didn't know. Though 'twas tempting to consider staying in Pippa's time, it wasn't a thought he could entertain seriously. For better or worse, he was lord of Sedgwick and he couldn't walk away from that responsibility.

He looked again at Sedgwick as he entered the courtyard. He couldn't say that there wasn't a small pang of envy that coursed through him at the sight of his keep's perfection in future years, but perhaps he should consider it a beacon of hope for what could be done. After all, his father had built his keep from absolutely nothing and Artane had turned out to be a magnificent place.

He stopped suddenly as a new thought occurred to him. What if he took Pippa to Artane and showed her what his father had built? If she could see what was possible, perhaps —

Well, perhaps she might be more amenable to his suit than she might have been otherwise.

"Pippa," he said as they made their way back to the kitchens, "would you be interested in a small journey?"

She looked up at him in surprise. "Where to?"

"Artane," he said, trying to make it sound as if it were nothing of particular interest. "I thought it might be interesting for us both to see it in its current state."

She paused. "Are you sure you want to?"

"Is it destroyed?" he asked in surprise. "I thought not, given that Stephen's father lives there still."

"Oh, it's still intact," she said. She smiled faintly. "Want to see a picture?"

He'd seen pictures before, on a little box

Stephen had called a phone. He supposed seeing his father's hall captured in the device wouldn't trouble him any more than all the other miracles he'd seen over the past day. He managed a nod, then accepted an invitation for a small bowl of ice cream before they retreated to Tess's solar to look at pictures and Pippa's designs both.

He watched her surreptitiously as they ate. She was very quiet, but perhaps she was overcome by what she'd seen at the fashion show. He couldn't blame her. He would be long in forgetting the absolutely appalling lack of cloth he'd seen covering models who had terrified him with their frowns.

A small journey was definitely the cure for what ailed them both, a journey to a place of comfort and security might soften her heart where he was concerned. And if not, he would lay siege to that heart and see if that provided him with better results.

He was, after all, a medieval knight.

There was no sense in not using his skills, even, the saints preserve him, in the twenty-first century.

Chapter 24

Pippa sat in the kitchen and tried to inconspicuously ingest a rather crunchy piece of cold toast. She would have looked around for Karma lurking in the shadows, but she knew better than to do that. There had been enough monkey wrenches thrown in her path in the past month without begging for any more. So she kept her head down, continued to pretend to make inroads into a breakfast that tasted like dust, and forced herself to face the facts, as uncomfortable as they were.

She was, she could honestly say, in the midst of a crisis.

She should have been thrilled with her life. She had toilet paper, British packaged snacks, and racks that instantly cooled her toast so she couldn't possibly burn her mouth on it. She had the possibility of endless supplies of any sort of fabric she wanted, the potential funding for her meteoric rise to fashion world superstardom, and electricity to power all sorts of machines that would save her hours of hand sewing.

But none of it set her heart aflutter as it should have.

She had realized that as she'd sat in the front row of a very exclusive design show next to a man who had gasped a little and averted his eyes every time he might possibly have had to look up a model's very short skirt. She might have found that slightly amusing, but she'd been busy with the other realization that had pounded at her mercilessly.

She didn't want Manhattan.

She wanted Sedgwick.

Or, more accurately, Sedgwick's lord.

It was all complicated by the fact that Sedgwick's lord had come across eight hundred years with apparently no other goal in sight than to improve his nephew's swordplay and sample all sorts of future cuisine, damn him anyway.

"You look like you're going to throw up."

Pippa looked up from her half-eaten toast to find Peaches standing five feet from her, assessing her. She tried to smile but failed. "I'm having a midlife crisis."

Peaches pulled up a chair and sat down next to her. "Tell me more."

"I might scare you if I did."

Peaches looked down at her hands for a minute, then lifted her head. "Would you live with him? In 1241?"

Pippa had a hard time catching her breath. She had considered it, looked hard at what it would mean giving up, but she had never discussed it with anyone. She wasn't sure she could even voice the thought aloud without feeling like she was having an out-of-body experience.

"I don't know," she said finally, because she realized Peaches was waiting for an answer. She had to take several decent breaths before she could say what else she had to. "I just wish I could have you all in the same place."

Peaches blinked a time or two, rapidly, then cleared her throat. "Does he have a brother or two available?"

"Not that I know of, but he has some cousins who could use some serious reorganizing of their personalities."

"I like to limit my projects to people's closets and filing cabinets, not their psyches," Peaches said dryly.

"What about Stephen de Piaget?" Pippa asked. "I bet his closets are a disaster. If you don't believe it, look at the mess he's made in Tess's office."

Peaches shook her head. "He's dating the daughter of a duke. Actually, I think he might be dating two or three of them. I don't think he's ready to settle down."

"Which is why he's hanging out here."

Peaches shrugged. "He's a guy. I have no insights into the way they think."

"I don't think it would help even if you did," Pippa said, pushing her toast away. "I think I'm going to become a nun. I'm sort of at the point where I have to start my life over again anyway. No money, no fabric, no ten grand worth of embroidery machine waiting for me at home to keep me warm."

Peaches choked. "How much was that again?"

"I needed it," Pippa insisted. "Fashion world domination is expensive."

Peaches reached out and helped herself to Pippa's other piece of toast. "At least you wouldn't need a serger if you lived —" She paused, and then grimaced. "I can't bring myself to say it." She took a deep breath of her own. "Honestly, Pip, I just can't imagine Montgomery came all this way just to see how the other half lives."

"Well, he's certainly not tripping over himself to profess undying love, either, is he?"

"Maybe he's comparing himself to the

glories of modern life and finding himself coming up short."

"Montgomery?" Pippa said incredulously. "Never."

"Oh, he looks tough," Peaches said, "but underneath I get the feeling he's pretty softhearted. And I think he loves you."

"He doesn't."

"You didn't watch him watch you yesterday."

Pippa got up and threw the rest of her breakfast in the trash, felt slightly guilty over it given the difficulty of even getting breakfast in Montgomery's time, then turned to face her sister. "I don't think I can think about this anymore."

"Then let's go get distracted. The boys are playing with toys over by the gift shop. Tess is already thinking about ways to use them as an advertisement for her parties, but I'm not sure either of them will go for it."

Pippa nodded, went to grab a coat, then walked with her sister across the long bridge over Tess's moat. She led Peaches over to a bench she was just certain couldn't be in the same place as the log she'd sat on in 1241, then sat down next to Tess who was already there, ogling.

"You could have brought the video camera," Peaches said to Tess.

"I was afraid I would miss something," Tess said faintly.

Pippa could understand. She sat between her sisters and watched for several minutes before she realized they had put their arms around her, as if they just weren't quite ready to let her go.

She was not a weeper, but she had to blink fairly rapidly a time or two. She loved all her sisters — even Cindi, to a lesser degree — but Peaches and Tess had been her bedrock, her endlessly comforting buffer against things she hadn't been ready to face, then two pairs of loving hands shoving her out from behind that buffer when she'd needed to get on with her life. The thought of not having them as close as a phone call was almost more terrible than she could face.

She took a deep breath. She was probably imagining things that would never happen. Montgomery had likely suffered from a brief and fleeting desire to be noble and bring her shoes he no doubt thought she really liked. He would go back to his perfectly tractable fiancée, and she would once again discover her inner diva, purchase more shears, and get cutting on new and more marvelous creations than she'd created in the past. She would still have her sisters and no hole in her heart.

Well, except the one that Montgomery would leave when he left.

She sighed, rested her elbows on her knees and her chin on her fists, and thought Gloomy Thoughts. She wasn't sure where Stephen had dug up more spare clothes, but Montgomery was dressed today in sweats with a T-shirt that should have been outlawed. He was instructing his very grateful nephew about the finer points of swordplay and not breaking a sweat. Stephen, however, couldn't quite say the same thing.

Peaches and Tess made appreciative noises.

Pippa couldn't begrudge her sisters the looking. It was a pretty impressive display for at least another hour before Stephen called it quits. He thanked Montgomery profusely for the lesson, then limped over to them.

"He's all yours, Pippa," he wheezed.

"I wish," she muttered under her breath.

Stephen only smiled and walked away, looking as if he badly needed something strong to drink. Montgomery bounded over to her with all the enthusiasm of a medieval guy let loose in a modern sporting goods store. He looked faintly startled at what

Pippa assumed was the sight of Tess and Peaches there together, then he seemed to pull himself together admirably.

"What shall we do today?" he asked cheerfully. "Make a visit to the local pub?"

How about I clunk you over the head with that sword instead, bucko was almost out of her mouth before she could stop it. More food? The man had a one-track mind and she was beginning to suspect she wasn't even on the list of attractions to visit on his way to the nearest fridge.

"I'm not hungry," she said shortly.

He looked at her with a faint frown. "I think you should eat. Your humors are unbalanced."

Peaches laughed and stood. "Let's go, Tess. I think we don't want to be in the middle of this." She patted Montgomery on the shoulder. "Good luck with her."

Pippa watched Tess do the same thing, then walk off with Peaches. She waited until she thought she could bite her tongue sufficiently before she looked back up at Montgomery. Before she could edit any other verbal offerings, he had reached down and pulled her to her feet.

"I've neglected you this morning."

"Of course you haven't," she said, trying to capture a cheerful tone. "I'm only surprised that you let Stephen off the hook so easily. Maybe he has cousins you could run through after you finish with him every day." *For as many days as you're here* she would have added if she'd had the guts, but she was a coward, so she kept her additions to herself.

He clasped his hands behind his back and seemed to be wrestling with something — no doubt how to tell her it'd been fun, but he was going to be on his way right after lunch.

"What would you say to making our journey north today?"

"I suppose there are plenty of places to eat on the way," she said grimly.

He looked at her as if he had no clue what she was talking about. "I suppose so. I'm more concerned with seeing for myself what's left of my father's keep. Your pictures were reassuring, true, and Stephen says it has been cared for well, but his standards may be different from mine. I know they are when it comes to breakfast pastries."

Pippa didn't doubt it. She also didn't doubt that an entire trip heaven knew how far away with a man who was more interested in snacks than he was in her might just do her in.

"My father started with nothing there, you

know," he added. " 'Tis possible to build a keep from the foundation up and have it be a lovely, comfortable place."

"Has your fiancée seen it?" she asked shortly, because she just couldn't help herself.

He didn't reply. She looked up at him reluctantly only to watch him purse his lips and take her hand.

"Persephone, you and I must have speech together," he said. "Now."

She supposed they must, and she was beginning to think she had a few things to say to him, beginning and ending with asking him why the hell he'd come all this way just to torment her. She also wanted a detailed description of that mousey wench he was set to marry so she could imagine him being saddled with her for the rest of his life — which wasn't going to be a very long or a very comfortable one, apparently.

"Pippa," he said in surprise, catching her by the arm.

She realized he'd had to do that because she'd almost gone down to her knees. She managed to avoid that, but somehow she didn't manage to keep from bursting into trembles like another might have burst into tears.

It was PMS. That and the stress of just

thinking about having to work under the burden of immense success for the rest of her life. It was no wonder she was beginning to crack under the pressure of just the thought of all the glory. It certainly had nothing to do with the fact that she'd just been wrapped in the arms of a rugged, chivalrous medieval lord who wasn't going to see the far side of thirty.

"Pippa, what ails you?" he asked softly.

She shook her head and shook a bit more. She didn't protest when he took her face in his hands and kissed her cheeks.

And her mouth.

That was enough to snap her smartly back to reality. "Miss Mousey would *definitely* not approve of that," she said in surprise.

He looked particularly unrepentant. In fact, he was still looking at her mouth. He bent his head and brushed her lips again with his, very softly. "We must talk."

She supposed they must, and the sooner the better. She didn't protest when he took her hand and strode back toward the keep. She trotted along with him wherever he wanted to go partly because she was still floored by that unexpected kiss and partly because it had just become a bad habit. She was really going to have to get back in touch with her inner diva or the man was going to run roughshod over her for the rest of however long she knew him.

"Might we find water first?" he asked as he burst into the great hall, towing her along after him. "I don't much care for the bubbling business for it tastes like dust, but I do like whatever tart thing that was you squeezed into my water last night at the restaurant."

"Lemon," she managed.

"Aye, lemon. Does your sister have one, do you suppose? I brought gold along —"

"Tess can spare a lemon or two to keep you happy," she said, quite happy herself that he'd finally slowed down a little bit. "I'll make you an entire pitcher of it if you like."

He apparently liked because ten minutes later, he had gulped down a pitcher of unsweetened lemonade and was looking around surreptitiously for more. Pippa allowed Peaches to make the second batch because her hands were shaking too badly to do it. If Peaches noticed — which Pippa was quite certain she had — she at least had the good sense not to say anything.

Montgomery, however, was not so discreet. Pippa found him watching her with a very grave expression on his face. She scowled at him, but his expression didn't change. He still watched her as if he had something terrible on his mind that he wasn't quite sure he should talk to her about.

She had to look away. Maybe he regretted coming to the future; maybe he regretted having kissed her. She didn't know and she wasn't sure she cared. She wasn't irritated with him; she was irritated with herself for having fallen, she realized, quite fully in love with him, she was annoyed that he'd come all the way to her time just to eat his way through Tess's pantry, and she was furious that instead of punching him, what she wanted to do was find a corner, curl up in it, and bawl her eyes out.

Montgomery turned to Peaches. "If you'll excuse us, sister, we're off for a walk. I promise to drink all you've so skillfully prepared later, however, and relish every sip."

Peaches simpered under the compliment like the bamboozled feng shui–er she was, but Pippa was unmoved. She jammed her hands in her jeans because that's where they were most comfortable, ignored the arm Montgomery offered her, then limited herself to a bit of mild stomping as he led her out of the kitchen. He walked around the courtyard for a few minutes, simply looking around himself as if he strove to memorize what he saw.

Pippa almost felt sorry for him then. His version of Sedgwick was such a wreck. It had to have been difficult to look at it in all its twenty-first-century glory, with running water and flush toilets and stables that had obviously been built by a man with lots of money and a great affection for those going on four legs. Apparently Montgomery agreed with the last because he walked with her over to those stables and down the aisle. He stopped at an empty stall and leaned his forearms against it.

"We could leave now for Artane," he said, finally. "If I could borrow Stephen's automobile."

"Over his dead body, probably."

Montgomery shot her a quick smile. "Aye, that was what he said earlier when I suggested the like."

She took a deep breath, then blurted out what she really hadn't intended to say. "I can't do this."

"Do what?"

"This," she said, waving helplessly between them.

He frowned. "This what?"

Could he really be that dense? Pippa was just sure he couldn't, but then again, she wondered about herself sometimes, too. "I can't do this thing where we pretend that we're just friends," she said, through gritted teeth. "Where we pretend that your stupid fiancée doesn't exist, and where I continue to pretend the fact that you're engaged to *someone else* doesn't bother the hell out of me."

There, she'd said it. He could do with it what he wanted, but it was out there in the air between them. Foolishly, unadvisedly, hopelessly perhaps, but out there where he could examine it for himself and hopefully fill in the blanks that it wasn't just driving her crazy, it was breaking what was left of her heart. The craziest thing of all was how hard she'd fallen for him. He was out of her league and she was out of his time. It was the worst case of star-crossed non-lovers she had ever —

"I never lie."

It took her a moment to have what he'd said register in her poor overworked brain. She blinked. "What did you say?"

"I do not lie," he said. "Ever."

"And what in the world does that have to do with any of this?" she asked incredulously.

He shrugged. "I thought you might find it interesting."

Well, why not? She had spilled her guts, and he was changing the subject. She waved him on because if she'd opened her mouth again, she would have chewed his head off.

"I have," he continued, "actually prided myself on and made my mother quite happy by never telling a falsehood. But I told one on the night your sister tried to drag me into that full-blown farce of a marriage."

She wasn't sure she wanted to know what it was —

"I am not betrothed."

That took another moment or two to sink in. When it did, she felt her mouth fall open. "What?"

He turned to lean his hip against the stall door. "I am not betrothed."

"Then why did you say you were?" she asked in surprise.

"Because, apart from the fact that I did not wish to wed your sister, the truth is I love someone else."

Pippa wasn't sure what was worse, that he had been fake engaged, or that she'd wasted days and days being jealous of a fiancée who didn't exist only to now find out that that mousey nonexistent wench didn't matter because he was in love with yet *another* girl who wasn't her.

She shouldn't have been surprised. If she

managed to survive the length of time it took to find that time gate and shove him through it so she didn't have to look at him any longer and have her heart break with every glance, she was never, ever going to read another fairy tale for as long as she lived. She looked away, because she just couldn't look at him anymore.

"Why aren't you taking *her* to Artane?" she asked, before she thought better of it.

"I'm trying to."

Pippa could hardly believe her ears. Not only could the lout stand there, bold as brass, and spend all that time with her when what he really wanted to be doing was taking the woman he loved . . .

Her silent rant slowed to an awkward halt.

Realization started to bloom, tentatively, a bit like a rose that wasn't quite sure spring had arrived. It took a minute, but what he'd said finally sank in.

He was trying to?

She looked over her shoulder just to be sure, but no, she was the only one in the stable. She looked back at Montgomery, who was watching her solemnly and a bit hesitantly. She pointed to herself and raised her eyebrows questioningly.

He nodded.

She swallowed, hard. "Why didn't you say

anything?"

"I just did."

She suppressed the renewed urge to punch him. He must have seen the thought cross her face because he laughed a little, then pulled her into his arms.

" 'Tis madness, Persephone," he said, holding her close, "and I am likely damned for having said anything at all. I just know what my life was like that se'nnight when you were gone."

"That's not encouraging, Montgomery, considering you were unconscious for most of that week."

He buried his face in her hair. "Come to Artane with me," he whispered. "I'm not asking for an answer now on anything else. I'm not sure I could bear to hear it even if you were inclined to give it, lest it be something less than I hope for." He lifted his head and looked down at her seriously. "Please come with me."

"I'm pretty sure Stephen won't let you drive," she said breathlessly.

"Then you drive. That will give me ample opportunity to lust after you."

"Stop that," she said, feeling her cheeks grow rather hot.

He smiled and took her hand. "Let us take it day by day. I may like it so much here in the future that I'll wish to remain. Surely your sister could use a good stable lad."

She shook her head. "You need your hall."

"I need you more."

She felt her mouth fall open, watched him laugh at her, then found herself trotting along obediently after him when he pulled her toward the great hall, as if she'd never had an independent thought in her head.

"We could take your sisters with us to the past," he said as he opened the door for her.

"I don't know if Peaches could give up chocolate-covered doughnuts."

"Doughnuts?" he asked, looking intensely interested.

"We'll grab some at the store on the way north."

He looked absolutely thrilled by the idea. Apparently Montgomery de Piaget was on vacation and he had no plans to stick to his diet. She could only hope he wouldn't fast food himself to death.

He asked Peaches to give him a take-away version of her lemonade, instructed Pippa to pack quickly, then headed off to make use of Stephen's en suite facilities.

She tossed a few things in her backpack, took a deep breath, then went downstairs to wait for the man she wasn't entirely sure wasn't going to poach the keys to Stephen's very expensive sports car and refuse to give them back.

Stephen was loitering near the lord's table with Tess and Peaches, looking slightly unsettled. Pippa set her backpack down on the table.

"I think we're going on a little trip."

"So I understand," Stephen said faintly.

"What's wrong, Stephen?" she asked lightly. "Too much swordplay this morning?"

"Though I have been shown the depths of my deficiencies," he said, taking a deep breath, "what worries me more is the deficiencies that will be left in the fenders of my car if I let my uncle anywhere near it."

"Pippa hasn't wrecked anything lately but her scooter," Peaches offered, "but the totaling of that wasn't her fault."

Stephen looked pained. "Couldn't you two take the train — no, don't answer that. I think you might be safer in the car." He looked at Pippa. "I phoned my father this morning and told him to expect you. He was happy to host you and who I told him was a long-lost cousin. I'm sure our good Montgomery will soften the blow when he arrives."

"You like him," Pippa said with a smile.

"Who wouldn't?" Stephen asked. "Of

course, that assumes that he doesn't distract you so thoroughly that you plow my car into a tree."

"Stephen, I can't drive your car."

"You're more qualified than he is," Stephen said with a snort, "and given that I'm quite sure my uncle will not want me along as any sort of chauffeur, despite my edifying conversation and the potential for hacking at me with his sword, I think I'll make sure —" He looked over her head, then scowled. "There he is with my keys, damn him to hell."

Pippa laughed as she turned around, then she stopped laughing abruptly when she got an eyeful of Montgomery in his preferred future uniform. The truth was, the man had been made to wear jeans. She wasn't sure where Stephen had gotten those lovingly broken-in button-fly Levi's, but it had been a great acquisition. Montgomery was wearing the hell out of them, along with a T-shirt with *medieval geopolitical warfare expert* written on it — obviously something else of Stephen's — and a jacket and backpack slung over his shoulder. If she hadn't known better, she would have sworn he had been born in her time. What she did know was that she would have turned backflips to have had him look at her twice.

As he was doing presently.

"That doesn't look like a man in love with someone else," Tess murmured.

"He just told me he was never engaged," Pippa murmured back. "It was self-defense to get out of marrying Cindi."

"I could have told you that much," Peaches said with a snort. "And don't look now, but I think he has plans for you, sis."

Pippa agreed. She blushed furiously as Montgomery walked over to her, took her hand, then bent over it and kissed it. Her sisters were making strangled noises of appreciation, which Pippa understood completely.

She was in big trouble. She was beginning to seriously consider the thought of medieval fashion world domination and, frankly, that was really rather frightening. What would she do without Peaches and Tess and big brown trucks delivering vintage goods right to her doorstep? For all she knew, *she* would be the vintage goods.

Montgomery leaned close and whispered in her ear. "One day at a time, Persephone." He pulled back far enough to look at her seriously. "Nothing is fixed."

"Are you telling me you're fickle?" she asked breathlessly.

"I wasn't talking about my affections. I

was speaking of the location of their consummation."

Stephen cleared his throat. "I hate to interrupt, but, Montgomery, old man, you're going to leave her unable to drive if you don't cease with that."

Montgomery straightened and patted his pocket. "My ultimate plan."

"You are *not* driving my Mercedes," Stephen said firmly. "You have no license, and no, you may not claim mine, no matter how much we resemble each other."

Pippa watched Montgomery consider, then sigh heavily.

"Very well," he conceded reluctantly. "The reins are hers."

Pippa looked at a suddenly much-less-stressed Stephen. "Any advice from you?"

"Be ginger on the clutch, don't speed, and call me if you need more funds. I left you a few quid under the seat."

"I have gold," Montgomery said stiffly.

Stephen shot him a look. "When I come to visit your hall, my lord, you can fête me all you like. When you're in my world, I will see to your expenses."

Montgomery looked at Pippa. "I will leave him gold."

"I imagined you would."

Montgomery walked around the table to

shake hands with his nephew, then took Pippa's gear from her. She looked over her shoulder to see Stephen, Tess, and Peaches watching her with smiles. She waved, then followed Montgomery out of the castle to where Stephen's car was parked. Montgomery opened the trunk as if he'd been doing it his entire life, then shut it and lovingly stroked the silver-gray metal.

"Ah, what a beauty," he said with a manly sigh.

"Gimme the keys," she said, holding out her hand.

He took that hand, then pulled her into his arms. "If I kissed you long enough, do you suppose you might forget my nephew's instructions?"

"I wouldn't. He'll kill us both if we wreck his car. I think he's very fond of it."

He sighed lightly, then bent his head and kissed her very chastely on the cheek. "I'll wear you down."

"Oh, please don't try," she said with an uneasy laugh. "I'm not sure I can get us out of the car park as it is now."

"You will surrender to me eventually, Persephone. Eventually."

She had to clutch his arms to stay on her feet. "Are we still talking about the car?"

He kissed the end of her nose, then put

the keys into her hand. "You'll see."

Pippa managed to get herself into the car without incident, though she was the first to admit she wasn't all that steady and took a deep breath before she attempted anything more serious. She reached for the gearshift to put the car in neutral only to find the gearshift was on the wrong side of her. The pedals were in the right place, but the rear-view mirror was angled the wrong way, the wipers and blinkers were opposite, and she dropped the keys three times before she managed to get them in the ignition. Then Montgomery slid into his seat, shut the door, and began to purr.

"The car?" she asked.

"Nay, you." He paused. "Mostly."

She laughed in spite of herself. He was honest, at least. And he wanted to take her to a place his father had built from scratch so she could see what his own keep could look like in time.

"We'll take our time, Persephone."

She assumed he was talking about more than getting to Artane, took a deep breath, then concentrated on getting out of the car park without clipping Stephen's side-view mirror on Tess's car. She did take one last look at Montgomery before she really got going. She could hardly believe he was sitting there, but there he sat, watching her with a small smile.

"Leave it, love," he said, reaching out to tuck her hair behind her ear. "Whatever it is, leave it for now. We'll go home, walk along the strand, then work out our future. Together."

Pippa nodded, because she could do nothing else. The truth was, she couldn't do anything at the moment besides get them north in one piece. The future would just have to take care of itself for a while.

Though she couldn't help but wonder how extensive the gift shop was at Artane and if they might have a big book on the history of all those born in the keep for her to peruse for pertinent facts about the man sitting next to her, a man apparently torn between touching her and fussing with the radio.

It might mean the difference between life and death.

For them both.

Chapter 25

Montgomery generally had no trouble concentrating on the thing before him to the exclusion of all else. He could ignore with ease conversations, bloodshed, and the babbling of his brothers if swordplay or life demanded his full attention. Unfortunately, that skill seemed to have deserted him over the past three days. He'd been torn between poring over the map Pippa had bought that first afternoon, watching the scenery fly by, and staring without pause at a woman he could hardly watch without feeling his heart break a little more with each moment that passed.

He closed his eyes, but that left the motion of the car making him slightly ill, so he turned his attentions to the map he held. They had taken a fairly circuitous route north, mostly because he'd been curious as to the condition in the future of places he'd known in the past. Those stops had been substantially more unsettling than he had expected, so they had quickly turned their attentions to the great houses and estates that had been built long after his time, which had suited him better. He had submitted to a brief shopping trip to purchase extra clothes, though it had galled him to use funds that were not his own.

Pubs had been pleasant diversions, though he had eschewed the ale in favor of drinks that didn't immediately make him want to retch. Their accommodations had been nothing short of kingly and he wondered how it was that his modern-day kinsmen took for granted the luxuries they enjoyed. He supposed the noises of modern life made up for that, though he would admit that the previous night had been better, with quieter chambers and a quite lovely morning repast prepared by a woman who obviously knew her way about a kitchen.

Which left him nothing, he supposed, but to give in and do what he truly wanted to do, which was stare at the part of the future that intrigued him the most.

Pippa's brow had unfurrowed in direct proportion to how far away from the south and its environs they had traveled. There were fewer cars, true, but he supposed the reason she was happier was that she'd become accustomed to Stephen's car — and she hadn't plowed it into a tree, which had also been one of her worries. His only worry was that he would soon beg her to pull over and then ravish her before he could get them both in front of a priest.

Assuming she would want to stand in front of a priest with him.

He hadn't dared ask her that specifically, lest he be forced to face things he wasn't ready to, such as what century they would live in and who would pay the price for that choice. He wished it could have been neither of them, but he knew that wasn't possible.

He turned his mind to other, more pleasant ruminations, such as contemplating the fact that while he'd known before that his heart was given, the last three days had only convinced him of it beyond all doubt. Persephone Josephine Alexander was a sparkling, intoxicating, delightful creature worthy of Faery's glittering halls, and he could hardly believe she might possibly be his.

"What are you looking at?" she asked, glancing at him with a smile.

"Your jeans."

She raised her eyebrow. "What do you think of them now?"

"They are scandalous," he said lazily, sliding his hand under her hair to trace equally lazy circles on her neck.

"Stop that."

"Nay."

She laughed and pushed his hand away. "Stop it, Montgomery. I'm trying to concentrate."

"We're in the moors. Not a tree in sight."

"Then we'll wind up sinking like the crown jewels, so *stop* it."

He considered. "What am I allowed to touch?"

"The map," she said in exasperation. "Where are we?"

He set the map in the backseat. "I don't need a map to tell me that. We're twenty leagues from home, give or take a bit. We should be able to see the castle soon in the distance. I don't suppose we can just cut across those fields, though, can we?"

"Not in this car." She drove on for a bit, then pointed ahead. "Look up there. I think it's the sign for Artane."

Montgomery shook his head. If his father had any inkling his castle would find itself written there plainly on a road sign almost eight hundred years from the time he'd built it, well, he would have shaken his head as well.

And he might have caught his breath, just

as Montgomery felt himself do once they turned off the main road and started toward the coast. Artane rose up in the distance, still enormous, still guarding the lands about it for leagues.

Pippa looked at him. "That's it?"

He could only nod.

"It's spectacular."

"Aye," he managed.

She was silent for a moment or two, then reached over and put her hand on his. "I understand there's a purveyor of particularly tasty fish and chips in the village, if you're interested in a brief distraction."

"I'm going to fat."

She laughed. "I'll chase you up and down the beach if you're that worried. And we don't have to go eat. Stephen just texted me earlier with the address. I think he wants to make sure you don't starve."

"He just intends to eat through my larder should he find himself at Sedgwick during a century not his own," Montgomery said with a snort.

We'll need to be prepared was what he intended to say next, but he forbore. He hadn't spoken to her about their immediate future past a traveler's curiosity about what he wanted to see and where she wanted to stay, though he supposed they would need to broach more serious subjects soon.

"Do you want to stop for a minute and catch your breath?" Pippa looked at him with worry plain on her face. "I would understand."

He looked at her in surprise, then shook his head. " 'Tisn't Artane," he said, then realized he should assuredly shut his mouth or he would say more than he wanted to. "I think too much."

"I understand," she said with a faint smile. "I do, too."

He covered her hand with his own until she needed it back, then he ventured the appalling familiarity of putting his hand on her knee. She didn't seem to mind it, so he took the opportunity to familiarize himself with a bit more of her leg.

"Lecher."

He laughed out loud and his gloomy thoughts were banished. "I will have you know that I am the most proper of knights, never taking liberties where they are not offered freely."

"And just how many liberties have you taken, Montgomery?" she asked tartly.

"I would tell you, but then you might tell my brothers and I would never be able to show my sweet visage at their halls again without raucous and unrelenting laughter greeting me."

"Phillip told me you have a continual stream of women throwing themselves at you, in and out of your bedchamber."

He felt his mouth fall open. "When did you speak to him about *that* sort of thing?"

"He thought I should know."

"The little wretch," Montgomery muttered. "I should say I hope he's safe, but after that I think he deserves what happens to him." He paused. "I told Ranulf to take him and the rest of the lads to Segrave."

"I never asked you the details of your abrupt departure," she said, glancing at him briefly. "Was it the usual thing?"

"Cousins wanting to kill me?" he asked. "Of course. I couldn't be so fortunate as to have them fight amongst themselves until none remains."

She watched the road for a bit, then cleared her throat. "This isn't any of my business, of course, but I wonder if your father gave you Sedgwick because he thought you had the negotiating skills to bring warring factions together?"

"I would like to believe that," he said wryly, "but I think he intended to give the keep to my twin brother, John. When John disappeared, he was left with me."

She looked at him in surprise. "You're a twin?"

"Didn't I tell you?"

"You most certainly didn't," she said. She watched the road for another moment or two, then spoke quietly. "Where did your brother go?" she asked. "If you don't mind my asking."

"I don't mind, though I will admit that I haven't spoken freely of it to anyone else." He had to take a deep breath or two before he could go on. Even though he was certain his audience would understand, actually talking about the events surrounding John's disappearance was still difficult.

"Montgomery, you don't have to tell me anything," she said quietly.

He shook his head. "You should know, I think." He shot her a quick smile, then plunged into his tale before he thought better of it. "Several years ago — eight, to be exact — John and my father argued, though I'm not sure over what. John demanded his inheritance, left the keep, then disappeared. We searched, of course, but 'twas all to no avail. My parents grieved for almost a year, then took themselves off to France for a distraction." He shrugged. "They return now and again to Artane, but my father has essentially turned over his title to Robin."

"Can he do that?" Pippa asked in surprise. "Does the king allow it?"

"When you are Rhys de Piaget, you find you can do quite a few things," Montgomery said dryly. "And my father flatters Henry by sending him lavish gifts now and again, so His Majesty is pleased to allow my father his little oddities."

"You de Piagets use that word a lot."

"I would like to say 'tis without justification, but I cannot." He leaned his head back against the seat. "So, my brother is no more, and I have been given a castle I cannot easily claim."

"But it sounds like your father has confidence in you," she said. "I also understand that you are quite a favorite of the king because he values you for the many languages you speak and your ability to sway everyone in the room to your point of view without their having realized what you were doing." She shot him a look. "Phillip says it's your delicious wit and lovely eyes that do it."

"He talks too much."

"He loves you," she said with a smile, turning back to the road. "You should know, however, that he grilled me on my accomplishments, though I can't imagine why. Does he audition all the women you date?"

Montgomery turned in his seat to look at her. "I never said I wanted to date you, Pippa."

She blinked. "You don't?"

He frowned. She looked a little taken aback and he couldn't fathom why until it occurred to him that he hadn't made himself clear. It also occurred to him that she was thinking too much about things they hadn't even begun to discuss. "Stop the car, Persephone."

"You are the bossiest man I've ever had the misfortune —"

He put his hand over hers on the gearshift. "Pull over, love."

She shot him a dark look, then found a place where she could pull the car off the road. "I need to stretch my legs," she muttered as she turned the car off and opened the door. "And get some air."

He knew what she needed, and it wasn't air. He pulled the keys out of the ignition, then crawled out of the car, pocketing the keys before he had to run rather fast to catch his escaping chauffeur. He caught her by the hand, then pulled her around and into his arms.

"You're weary," he said quietly. "You have done all the labor of getting us here and I have given you no rest from it. We should have taken more time."

"I'm fine."

He kept her close with one hand and stroked her hair with the other. "I do not want to date you, Persephone. I want far more from you than that." He paused. "I'm not unaware of the difficulties that presents for both of us."

"Montgomery," she said with a sigh.

He took her face in his hands, tipped it up, then bent his head and kissed her very gently.

She trembled. Or that might have been him. He honestly couldn't have said. He just knew they were both in trouble. He might have been something of a novice at bedding women, but he'd certainly kissed more than his share of them. He took Pippa's hands and put them up around his neck.

"Heaven help me," she breathed.

He smiled against her mouth, then made serious inroads into proving that he was most definitely not just interested in a casual alliance with her.

By the time he lifted his head and looked down at her, he wasn't sure he would be walking well — or at all — any time in the near future. He rested his forehead on her shoulder.

"Are you carrying me back to the car, or am I carrying you?" he asked weakly.

"I'm completely unaffected."

She looked a little cross-eyed, but since that was how he felt, he couldn't fault her for it. He swept her up into his arms, narrowly missing her elbow in his nose as she threw her arms around his neck.

"I'll drive," he said confidently.

"You will not."

"I believe, lady, that you forget who is lord in this relationship."

"This is the twenty-first century, bucko. I'm emancipated."

He walked back to the car, set her on her feet, backed her up against the Mercedes's lovely silver side, and kissed her again. Repeatedly. Until he felt some small bit of ground had been gained. When he lifted his head and looked down at her, she looked thoroughly kissed, not completely unhappy, and almost compliant.

"No," she said languidly.

"How hard can it be?" he asked, slipping his hand under her hair. "I have the keys."

"Yeah, but you don't know how to use the clutch —"

Several minutes later, he looked at her again. She didn't open her eyes.

"You know," she remarked, "you can't just

kiss me every time you want to get your way."

"Why not? It works for my brothers."

"No."

"Persephone, you are a stubborn case."

"Divas often are."

He marched forward into the fray, as it were, with enthusiasm and no small bit of determination. And he had to admit, as the morning began to wear on, that if he didn't regain some sort of control over himself, they were going to be finding a priest that afternoon.

He retreated and examined the battlefield. Pippa was collapsed against the car, looking as if she'd been chocolate left out in the sun too long.

"Well?" he asked pointedly.

She managed to squint at him. "You're going to get me in big trouble."

"I have a sword. Stephen will respect that."

She pursed her lips. "All right. Drive up and down this very long stretch of very straight road twenty times without creaming his car, and I'll think about letting you drive through town."

He grunted. "You forget —"

"That you don't have a license and that this thing's packing about four hundred horsepower," she said pointedly.

He considered the absolute improbability of that for a moment or two, then conceded the battle. He swept her up in his arms and carried her around to the passenger side whilst he still could. He saw her inside, leaned over to buckle her in, then found her fist curled into his shirt.

"What?" he asked.

He wasn't quite sure how it happened, but he wound up sitting on her lap long enough for her to kiss him quite thoroughly before she begged him to move.

"I'm not going to be able to drive properly if you don't stop that," he warned.

She gave him a friendly shove. "Get out of here and go cool off. I'll wait."

"It might take a while."

She laughed and shut herself inside the car. Montgomery walked around it a score of times until he thought he could think of something besides things he couldn't engage in that afternoon, then slid in under the wheel.

He was growing unfortunately fond of the twenty-first century.

"Clutch," Pippa advised.

"I know," he said. "I've been watching."

She put her hand on his leg. "Be careful."

He took her hand, kissed it, then put it back in her lap. "Stop touching me."

"You started this," she pointed out.

"Aye, and I'm paying a steep price for it, believe me." He started up the car, then had to take a deep breath. And he wasn't sure what had overwhelmed him more, kissing Pippa or putting the powerful beast in gear and actually driving down the road.

"I've been replaced," she said, sounding rather amused.

"Only until we get to the keep, then you'll need to run continually to escape me."

She laughed a little, then fell silent. Montgomery looked at her after a moment. She was simply watching him, affectionately and without worry.

"Are you frightened?"

She shook her head. "You'll keep me safe."

"There aren't any trees near the road."

"Well, I didn't want to say as much," she admitted, "but yes."

He drove, turned about, then drove a bit more until he'd completed a score of trips up and down that road that was indeed very straight. He pulled over, then looked at her.

"Now might I go very fast?"

"No," she said immediately. "Just get us through town. Stephen says there's a spot to park the car right next to the castle. We're supposed to tell the lady at the ticket booth that you're a guest of Stephen's, or she'll make us pay to get in."

"Pay?" he asked in disbelief. "To get into my own home?"

"Welcome to the Future, cupcake."

Montgomery shook his head, then looked behind him before he pulled back onto the road.

The journey through the small bit of town was substantially more difficult than the travels down the road, but he managed it, found the car park, then put Stephen's car there. He turned the car off, then looked to his left.

And he felt a shiver go down his spine.

He glanced at Pippa to find her gaping at the keep, so perhaps he wasn't the only one overwhelmed.

"You grew up here?" she squeaked.

He found it in him to smile. "Aye. 'Tis impressive, isn't it?"

"It's enormous."

He looked past her. "It doesn't seem to have changed too much." He unbuckled and removed the key. "Wait for me."

"Of course."

He looked at her quickly to find her watching him with what he supposed he might dare to call affection. He leaned over, kissed her once, firmly, then pulled away and got out of the car. He shoved the key in his pocket as if he'd had pockets and car keys the whole of his life, then went around to fetch Pippa whilst he could still think straight. He hesitated, then gladly turned when she pulled him around and put her arms about his waist.

He held her close and, to his shame, had to close his eyes for a minute to block out the sight in front of him. His father, at that moment, was eight centuries deceased, as were all his siblings, their spouses, and their children. It was, he had to admit with all candor, a terrible realization.

"Montgomery?" she said softly. "Do you want to try the beach first?"

"Nay," he managed, but he didn't open his eyes and he didn't release her, "I am well. I simply feel as if I'm walking over my parents' graves. I didn't expect this."

"You can go home again," she said quietly. "I'm positive of it."

He was, too, though that didn't make the present feel any easier. He sighed deeply, then lifted his head and looked down at her. "I believe there are several time gates in England," he said slowly. "There was one near Artane, once."

She didn't look terribly surprised. "I think I've been near it." She managed a faint smile. "I had come to England with my parents one summer and we were doing a little medieval faire near here. I was watching the sunrise over the beach, then turned around and saw a guy standing behind me in chainmail. He was, I will admit impartially, the most gorgeous young man I'd ever seen."

He tucked a strand of hair behind her ear. "And you were easily the loveliest faery *I* had ever seen."

Her mouth fell open. "Did you see me?"

"I did. Perhaps you can imagine my surprise when that same ethereal creature came walking out of my bedchamber the morning after I pulled her from my cesspit."

"You didn't pull me, buster. I crawled."

He laughed and hugged her tightly. "That I carried you upstairs should count for something. And that I didn't faint when I realized your wings were not attached should also count for something."

She began to blush. "I don't think I want to carry on any more of this conversation. I'm fairly sure I know where it's going given that I woke up that next morning missing a bit more than my wings."

"I didn't look."

"You're a terrible liar."

He laughed and pulled her close again. He could scarce believe they were standing near the place where Fate had given them a glimpse of their future all those many years ago, but it seemed somehow quite fitting.

He stood quite happily with Pippa, relishing the smell of the sea and the sound of the gulls crying from the shore, until he thought he might manage to actually go into his father's gates and not expect to find his immediate family there. He pulled back and looked at Pippa.

"I'm not sure I'll let you from my arms very often," he said. "If you don't mind."

"We don't have to go in yet, if you want to stay out here," she offered quietly.

He shook his head. "It was a momentary weakness." He put his arm around her shoulders. "I'll come back later for our gear. Let us see if we can get ourselves past the woman who wants to make me pay to enter my father's keep."

She put her arm around his waist and walked with him across the rock path and up to Artane's outer gates. He was accosted immediately by an older woman bearing pointed metal implements of torture, who took one look at him, then swayed.

"I'm a guest of Lord Stephen's," Montgomery said, trying out his best modern English on her.

"So I see, lad," the woman said. She

waved him on. "I'll be in me booth, waiting for other odd happenings. Have them often enough here, I'll tell you."

He imagined they did. He moved quickly past her glass chamber and continued on up the way to his father's courtyard. It was only as he'd walked past where the blacksmith's forge had been in times past that he realized the pain in the side of his head was coming from the glare Pippa was giving him. And then he realized what he'd said. He slowed, stopped, then looked at his love.

"Um," he began.

"Yes, um," she said crisply, in that same modern English he'd used. "I believe, my lord, that you have some explaining to do."

"Might we sit down first —" he began in French.

"Oh, don't you even think about any more of that medieval French business," she said. She pulled away and frowned again. "I'm finding myself unpleasantly surprised by your linguistic skills and wondering what other secrets you've been keeping."

"Could you say that more simply?" he asked with a wince.

"Yes," she said shortly. "You're in big trouble, buddy."

Well, that he understood. He considered, then held open his arms. She could either run him through, or walk into his embrace. She scowled, then stepped forward and put her arms around his waist. He sighed in pleasure, more content than he deserved to feel over standing on his father's cobblestone path with the woman he loved in his arms. He could only hope that, as usual, a comfortable meal and a hot fire awaited him inside. If he managed to get there without Pippa snatching the dagger out of his boot and stabbing him first, he would indeed count himself fortunate.

"Well?" she asked, her voice muffled against his shirt. "What do you have to say for yourself?"

"Would you believe me if I said there have been, over the years at Artane, a few paranormal oddities?"

"Would you believe that I fully intend to repay you for the enormous headache I had for almost two weeks trying to get your medieval Norman French right?"

He laughed a bit. "I daresay I would."

"I want answers."

"You shall have them. After lunch."

She pulled away from him. "Let's go then. Stephen says Artane has a fabulous chef. You probably should have something from him before I start repaying you for all your secret keeping." She shot him a warning look. "You're not going to get out of this conversation."

"I imagine I won't," he agreed. He paused. "At least we can rest assured that all things of a paranormal nature are behind us. I think today the only things we need to worry about are a few squeaking floorboards and explaining to Stephen's father just how we're related to each other."

She looked up at him seriously. "Do you think so?"

"I'm sure of it," he said confidently.

And he was. Fate had obviously had a hand in bringing Pippa into his life from across the centuries, but surely she was finished with her work in his family. If he could convince Pippa to wed with him, that would no doubt bring an end to inexplicable happenings on his father's soil — and his, too, apparently — leaving them to live out their lives in peace and obscurity.

He smiled, kept his arm around her shoulders, then walked with her toward his father's hall, hoping that his skill with modern English would be the last of the surprises awaiting them. He had wooing to do, and he didn't want anything untoward coming between him and the woman he loved.

Chapter 26

Pippa had to make a conscious effort to keep her mouth from hanging open as if she'd been a medieval farm girl who'd never been more than ten feet from her mother's cooking fire. To say Artane was impressive was badly understating it. The place was nothing short of magnificent. She looked at Montgomery, who was apparently spending less time watching his ancestral home than he was watching her.

"Did you bring me here to impress me?"

He lifted an eyebrow. "Is it working?"

He was back to French, so she decided she would humor him. It seemed fitting to speak his native tongue while he was on native soil, but that wasn't going to last when she got him back to Sedgwick. She fully intended to wring answers from him one way or another.

"Absolutely," she said faintly.

He looked around the bailey with a smile.

"The stables are much finer than they were in my day, and the blacksmith's hut is gone, but the chapel still stands." He frowned. "That might be some sort of shop over there where the garden once was." He considered. "I wonder what they sell?"

"Chocolate, undoubtedly."

He shook his head. "It was a very bad habit to start."

"Especially since I don't think it hits England until, well, I'm not sure exactly when. You'd have to ask Tess for the exact date."

"I'm not sure I want to," he said with an uncomfortable laugh. He eyed the shop one final time, then nodded toward the hall. "I'm not sure who's expecting us, but perhaps we should just knock and see who answers."

Pippa nodded, then let him take her hand and lead her up the stairs. She waited with him on the little landing and smiled at his long-suffering sigh, sighed, no doubt, over having to knock instead of just walking inside. They didn't wait as long as she'd expected. Within moments, the door opened and Jennifer de Piaget stood there.

Or at least Pippa thought so at first.

Montgomery covered his gasp quite quickly, though he stammered for a moment or two before he finally managed something coherent.

"I am, um, a friend of Lord Stephen's," he said in his English that was a happy cross between British and American. He paused, started to speak, then simply shut his mouth and held out his hand.

The woman, who couldn't have looked more like Nicholas's wife if she *had* been Nicholas's wife, took Montgomery's hand and shook it as if she were moving in slow motion.

"I'm Megan," she said faintly. "Stephen's sister-in-law. I mean, I'm married to his younger brother, Gideon."

"Ah, Lady Blythwood," Montgomery said, making her a low bow. "Stephen told me about you. I'm Montgomery. Actually, Stephen and I are . . . related." He paused. "In a roundabout way."

Pippa couldn't take her eyes off Megan. It would have been rude — or made her sound like a complete idiot — to have asked Megan if she had a sister who now lived in medieval England, but she almost couldn't help herself.

"Please, come in," Megan said, stepping backward and beckoning them inside.

Pippa exchanged a look with Montgomery. She was almost surprised to find she had no trouble telling what he was thinking.

Something strange was definitely going on.

She leaned close as they followed Megan across the great hall. "Is she related to Jennifer, do you think?" she murmured in French.

"If she isn't, then Fate is toying with us to make us believe so."

"Any personal insights on this, Lord Secret Keeper?"

He looked profoundly uncomfortable. "Would you believe I once believed Jennifer was a fairy?" He shot her a look. "I saw her spring up from the ground. Now, I suspect she walked through a time gate."

"You must have suspected more than that sooner than today," she said pointedly, "given that it was your brother Nicholas we went to ask about a few strange happenings on his land."

He smiled faintly. "Aye, well, we should probably have speech about that, too."

She supposed they should. She remembered quite suddenly what it was she'd heard Jennifer humming that particular morning after she'd woken from such a luxurious night's sleep.

"Here We Go 'Round the Mulberry Bush."

She supposed she was somewhat relieved she hadn't realized that at the time. It might have led to questions she wouldn't have wanted to have answers for right then. She could only assume Megan knew what had happened to her sister, which had to have been difficult.

She wondered if they had any way at all to keep in touch.

Perhaps it was better not to know that presently. She took a deep breath, then turned back to the matter at hand, which was waiting with Montgomery near the lord's table while Megan ran upstairs to get her husband. She glanced at Montgomery to find him staring at the hall with a thoughtful look on his face. He caught sight of her, smiled, then reached out to pull her close. Pippa went happily into his arms, then took the opportunity to look over the father's hall from the security of that father's son's arms.

Artane's insides were no less impressive than its outsides. The great hall was enormous with equally large hearths set into opposite walls. Tapestries lined the place, but the stone floors were free of rugs, filthy straw, and any vestiges of dirt. She wondered idly what it had looked like eight hundred years earlier, but she suspected it hadn't been much different. It was, as Stephen had promised, remarkably well preserved.

She rested her head on Montgomery's shoulder. "Well?" she asked. "What do you think?"

"I think my father and Robin both would be amazed the place is still standing," he said, sounding equally amazed. "Then again, Sedgwick seems to be as well so perhaps it isn't as rare a thing as I think."

"Oh, I don't know," she said slowly. "There are many castles that haven't been so fortunate. I'm no expert, but I think between wars and time, lots of keeps were either destroyed or left to rot." She paused. "We could see if your family has any sorts of books here that might tell about happenings in the past."

He nodded, then started to speak only to shut his mouth and stiffen. Pippa pulled away, because it seemed the thing to do, then found herself watching as a blond version of Montgomery came bounding out of the stairwell into the great hall. He stumbled briefly, collected himself, then continued over with a smile and outstretched hand.

"Gideon de Piaget," he said, looking not the least bit uncomfortable. "I wonder if you're a cousin?"

"An uncle, actually," Montgomery said gravely.

Gideon only smiled. "I suspected as much, and I must say your English is excellent. Whose son are you?"

"Rhys's," Montgomery said. "I'm his youngest."

Gideon looked him over. "You're missing your sword."

" 'Tis in the car."

"Of course it is," Gideon said with a bit of a laugh. He looked at the entrance to the stairs and held out his hand until Megan had walked over to them, carrying who Pippa supposed was their offspring. Gideon held out his hands for a little girl, who immediately squirmed to get down. Gideon smiled at his wife. "I was afraid you might drop her when you find out who's come for lunch."

"Do I dare ask?" Megan asked faintly.

Gideon nodded at Montgomery. "Nicholas's youngest brother. You know, darling, the Nicholas who is married to your sister."

"I *knew* it," Pippa said, then she clapped her hand over her mouth. She looked at Megan. "I'm so sorry."

"Have you seen Jennifer?" Megan asked in surprise.

"About a week ago," Pippa admitted. "She

looks just like you. Well, a little more harried. She had four little boys to chase after."

Megan smiled, though tears were suddenly running down her cheeks. "I'd like to hear about it." She shot Montgomery a look. "And I imagine, my lord, that you could tell me quite a few stories yourself. I understand you squired for Nicholas off and on, didn't you?"

Montgomery's mouth fell open. "How did you know that?" he asked Megan.

Megan opened her mouth only to be interrupted by a robust laugh coming from the kitchen.

"Gideon, you coward, where did you go? I thought we were meeting in the lists at noon. The lads have worn me down a bit, but I'm . . . still . . . ah . . ."

Pippa watched as Montgomery's twin walked out of some passageway or other. She realized almost immediately that he wasn't Montgomery's twin, though he could certainly have passed for it.

No, that man was older, perhaps by fifteen years or so. His English was laced with crisp, posh British consonants, but he seemed to be quite comfortable in his jeans with his sword propped up against his shoulder. Or at least his sword was there until it was dropped. The hilt clattered against the stone for a moment, then fell silent.

A string of hearty curses escaped the man, then he strode across the hall and jerked Montgomery into a manly hug complete with many slaps on the back, another look or two, then more curses and backslaps.

"Montgomery," the newcomer said finally in perfect medieval French accompanied by an incredulous laugh, "what in the *hell* are you doing here?"

"Needing to find somewhere to sit down," Montgomery said faintly. "Kendrick?"

"Who else?"

Montgomery pulled away and felt his way over to lean against the table. Pippa found herself pulled over — well, yanked over, really — apparently to be used as something to keep him from falling on his face.

"What are you doing here?" Montgomery asked hoarsely.

"Well," Kendrick said, rocking back on his heels and looking contemplative, "it's complicated."

Pippa leaned close to Montgomery. "Paranormal oddities?"

Kendrick looked at her and smiled. "You've met my father."

"I haven't," she said, shaking her head, "but I've heard quite a bit about him."

Montgomery gestured weakly in Kendrick's direction. "This is, if you can believe it, Phillip's younger brother, Kendrick. Kendrick, this is my lady, Persephone." He took a deep breath. "I brought her home to woo her."

"You couldn't impress her with the holes in your own walls?" Kendrick asked, his eyes twinkling. "You had to bring her centuries into the future and show her what a real castle looks like?"

Montgomery looked at him narrowly. "You know, there was a time when I could thrash you whilst scarce suppressing my yawns."

Pippa found herself the recipient of Kendrick's wink. "Ah, but I don't imagine you'll have that same success now. Wouldn't you agree, Mistress Persephone?"

"It's Pippa," Pippa said, "and I'm not sure I should be offering any opinions. I don't want to get between the two of you and your swords."

"A pity he doesn't have his blade," Kendrick said, looking at Montgomery with raised eyebrows, "else we might settle the question once and for all."

" 'Tis in the car," Montgomery growled.

"Then go fetch it, *lad*."

Montgomery made a noise of disgust,

then looked at Pippa. "What is that mystical force your sisters spoke of?"

"Karma?"

"Aye, that," he said, pursing his lips. "I believe Karma has come back to haunt me."

"Or bite you in the arse, rather," Kendrick said. "What horrible thing did you do to deserve it? Oh, wait, perhaps it was the abuse you heaped upon me in my youth."

"I spoiled you beyond reason," Montgomery said shortly, "to my eternal shame. 'Twas obviously poorly done, judging by the results."

Kendrick only laughed, then looked over his shoulder. "Here come my lads. Pretend you weren't born in 1214, won't you? Then let's be off to do a bit of true manly labor outside. I can see already that you've gone soft during your sojourn in a century not your own."

"I'll humor you in the lists," Montgomery said evenly, "*after* I've had something to eat and brought in my lady's gear."

Kendrick looked at him, grinned again, then walked off making chicken noises. Pippa laughed, then looked at Montgomery.

"What did you do to him?"

"Nothing, so far," Montgomery said darkly. "But I believe I'll spend my energies making up for that if I have the chance."

Pippa smiled, though she felt slightly sick to her stomach. *If he had the chance* —

And the answer to that, she realized with a start, might just come from Kendrick de Piaget. She watched him gather up five boys, including a set of triplets who looked to be about thirteen, and shepherd them over to meet their long-lost cousin. The boys looked suitably impressed, Montgomery was his usual charming self, and she had to clutch the edge of the lord's table she was leaning against to keep herself from sidling over to Kendrick to ask him a few pointed questions. The time was definitely not right.

Montgomery finally extricated himself from questions she could tell he didn't particularly want to answer, then came back to stand beside her.

"Let's go fetch our gear," he said in French. "You can hold me whilst I fall to pieces." He nodded to Megan and Gideon. "If you'll excuse us? We'll return posthaste." He looked at Megan. "I have stories for you, my lady."

"I'd love to have them."

He squeezed Pippa's hand. "Shall we?"

She nodded and walked with him thorough the hall and down the stairs to the courtyard. She waited for him to get whatever it was he had in his system out of his system before she elbowed him in the ribs. She supposed she hadn't waited as long as she could have, but she was dying of curiosity.

"Well?"

He stopped, turned, and pulled her into his arms. "I'm wondering what other surprises your Karma has for me —"

"Don't," she said quickly. "Don't even ask. The list could be endless and very painful."

He closed his eyes briefly. "I hope the revelations have ended. I'm not sure I will survive any more."

Pippa had to close her eyes and rest her head against his shoulder. She wasn't sure she could survive any more, either, but there was at least one more thing he had to know before . . . well, before he decided what path he would take through the future. What if he decided that he wanted to go back without her and he was killed because she wasn't there to help him? What if she went back with him, he died just the same, and she lived and died in some hovel because Gunnild and her evil children kicked her out of the keep?

Or worst of all, what if she went back with him, he was wounded beyond all aid, and he sent her away?

"You're trembling."

"I'm cold," she lied. "We're standing in the shade."

"Pippa, 'tis noon."

"It's cloudy then," she said, which was something that stood the best chance of being true. "And I need some chocolate. You could go get our stuff and I could hit the gift shop and get us some." *And look through a few books for details I'm dying for.*

"I think I would be better off keeping you close," he said, wrapping his arms more securely around her. He bent his head and kissed her cheek. "How else am I to woo you?"

"Oh, I don't know," she managed. "Showing off for me in the lists might be a pretty good start."

He laughed a bit, then pulled away. "And it will soothe my bruised ego as well." He shook his head. "That Kendrick. He was trouble from the moment he was born."

"I think his five sons have been payback," she said. "He seems to be pretty happy about it anyway. I can hardly wait to meet his wife."

"I can scarce wait to find out how it is he's been here in the future long enough to sire so many children," Montgomery said. "There's a tale there, and we'll have it at our earliest convenience. But our gear, first, so I'll have something to use on him in the lists."

Pippa walked alongside him down the cobblestone path to the gates and came to a quick decision. Until she could verify what she'd read in a book that had been written over seven hundred years after the fact, she wasn't going to get her knickers all in a twist. She would enjoy the fact that she had Montgomery and tasty snacks all in the same century, let him woo her all he liked, and enjoy the chance to roam over his boyhood haunts with him. She would tell Megan de Piaget everything she could remember about her very brief visit with her sister Jennifer, happily listen to Montgomery relate all the stories he could, then see if she couldn't talk Stephen into bringing her sisters up for a little visit as well.

And when the opportunity presented itself, she would sneak over to the gift shop, hope it was open for visitors more than once a month, and see what she could find out in what she was sure was a big genealogical section. If worst came to worst, she would beg Gideon for some computer time and see what a quick search produced.

And she would hope Gideon wouldn't go along behind her and look at the things she was searching for.

But until then, she would enjoy every minute she had with a man who was currently standing five feet from his nephew's car, playing with the remote locks just because he could.

He looked at her. "Marvelous."

She laughed and put her arms around his neck. "You're adorable."

He put the keys in his pocket. "My sword can wait; let's examine that sentiment a bit more closely, shall we?"

She supposed along with all those other things she would allow herself to enjoy, she might as well add Montgomery de Piaget's most excellent kisses to the list.

While she had the chance.

Chapter 27

Montgomery bounded down Artane's stairs at dawn, just as he'd done for almost a score of years, not just ready but eager to be out in the lists perfecting his swordplay. After all, his most cherished dream had been to be the same sort of honorable and skilled knight his father and brothers had been.

Only now, he realized there was so much more to it than just the ability to wield a sword.

He shook his head as he walked across the great hall and turned for the kitchens. He supposed he had realized that several years earlier; he simply hadn't had the opportunity to ply his chivalry on a woman he loved. He could scarce wait until she awoke so he could begin again for the day.

But until that happy time, he would quite happily pass an hour or two working on his swordplay. He walked down the passageway and into the kitchens to find Kendrick and his sons already there tucking into a hearty breakfast. He sat down in the proffered chair, then helped himself to what they were having. There was little talk, but that was to be expected when the lads in question were busy filling their bellies.

Some things never changed.

What had changed was the fact that he was looking at his nephew, who was no longer a babe of almost eleven summers but a man of two score and a bit with his own eleven-year-old babe, who was younger than his elder triplet brothers. Robin would have been greatly pleased to see such strapping grandsons; a pity he would never meet them. Montgomery shook his head, fully willing to admit that the thought of how the twists and turns of time had left Kendrick with such a family was enough to give him pains in the head.

As was Kendrick's tale. Kendrick had sat with him in the lord's solar, courtesy of Edward, the current Earl of Artane, into the wee hours, giving him details Montgomery hadn't had to assure his nephew he would carry to his own grave. The tale was so fantastical Montgomery could scarce believe it, but apart from the fact that Kendrick never lied, the proof had been sitting there across from him. And given his own adventures with things he'd never expected, he could see how it was all too possible.

He looked up from his quite tasty porridge to find Kendrick's three eldest watching him with identical looks of curiosity. They looked so much like their father in his youth, Montgomery almost choked.

"They're frightening me," Montgomery said to his nephew.

One of the triplets looked at his father. "His French is as good as yours."

Montgomery noted that the boy's French was quite excellent as well.

"He's a bright lad," Kendrick said dismissively, applying himself to his meal.

"He looks like you, Father," said yet another of the eldest three. "Uncannily so."

"Good genes," Kendrick agreed.

"Didn't you have an uncle named Montgomery?" the third one said, then he gulped at the look his father shot him. He glanced at Montgomery briefly again, then bent his head and concentrated on his porridge.

Montgomery looked at Kendrick, had a wink as his reward, then decided the boys had the best idea. He finished his meal, thanked the cook, who seemed unaffected by the fact that there was a small collection of swords propped up in the corner, then watched Kendrick's five sons scamper back up to the great hall, boasts of their exceptional swordplay ringing in the air. Montgomery looked at his nephew.

"They're much like you were."

Kendrick smiled smugly. "You expected something else?"

"Actually, I'm just curious to see if you did anything with your time in your youth I have yet to experience besides investigate things you should rather have left alone."

"You'll have ample time to see and admire this morning."

Montgomery snorted. "By the saints, Kendrick, you couldn't be any more like your father, something he would consider to be the highest of compliments."

Kendrick hesitated in mid-step, then stopped suddenly and turned to him. "Speaking of my father, I will confess that I didn't tell you all last night."

Montgomery shrugged. "You weren't obligated to."

"Nay, this is something you should know." He shrugged, though he looked slightly less than casual. "Jake knows everything."

Montgomery felt his mouth fall open. "Jake Kilchurn? How in the world would *he* know any of this?"

"Because he's from the Future of course," Kendrick said, his mouth twitching. "Come now, Montgomery. You don't still believe he's a faery, do you?"

Montgomery suppressed the urge to hit him. "I've outgrown that, thank you very much."

Kendrick shrugged, but his eyes were twinkling madly. "I had to ask. Anyway, so you don't worry yourself into a stupor, I asked Jake to tell Father what befell me — after the fact, of course, lest he change history. Both he and Mother will know the truth. Jake will leave the rest of you to suffer, of course, at my behest."

Montgomery shoved him before he could stop himself. "You obnoxious brat."

Kendrick only laughed and continued on his way. "I've been perfecting that character trait for years, you know."

"You had perfected it by the age of eight, believe me."

"And only added to the misery of it for you by my superior swordplay." He looked over his shoulder. "Come along, Uncle, and let me school you in a few things you didn't teach me."

Montgomery shook his head in admiration of Kendrick's cheek, something he had definitely learned at his father's knee and apparently indeed nurtured by himself into an arrogance that was truly disgusting.

He walked through the hall, loped down the steps, and headed for the lists as if nothing had changed — but it had. He was wearing sweats and trainers, he had the luxury of a very fast car awaiting him outside the gates, and he'd been offered the sight of a football match on the telly that evening if he promised to leave all sharp implements outside the door where he wouldn't destroy Lord Edward's solar in his surprise and terror.

Kendrick's words, not his.

Kendrick tossed away the sheath to his sword. "I promise to leave a bit of you left for Pippa to rub horse liniment into this afternoon."

"Good of you," Montgomery said sourly.

Kendrick only laughed and raised his sword.

The sun was at its zenith before he looked closely at his nephew to see if Kendrick was as ready as he to be finished for the day. Given that Kendrick was peering at him in like manner, there was no shame in leaving the battle for another day. Montgomery exchanged a few final insults with a man Robin would have been terribly proud of, then looked over to find Pippa sitting on a bench pushed up against the wall, gaping at him.

"Has she never seen you with a sword in your hands?" Kendrick asked with mock horror. "What, too busy plying your lute to pick up a bit of steel?"

"Shut up."

Kendrick only laughed and went to gather up his sons. Montgomery had already worked each of them for a brief time that morning, so he felt no guilt in concentrating on his most important task, which was wooing the woman who was looking at him as if she'd never seen him before. He walked over to her, then dropped down onto the bench next to her, trying not to drip sweat on her. He dragged his arm across his forehead, then looked at her.

"What is it?"

She only gestured toward the field. Her mouth worked, but no sound came out.

He frowned. "Did I fight poorly?"

"Good heavens, Montgomery," she managed. "I've never seen you fight like that at *all.*"

"I would say that I hadn't wanted to terrify my garrison," he said, "but then I would sound like my eldest brother, which I simply couldn't bear."

She leaned back against the wall and smiled faintly. "Is Kendrick like Robin?"

"Exactly like him," Montgomery said without hesitation. "I'm not sure how his wife bears him, but then again, I'm not sure how Anne tolerates Robin, so I am perhaps not the one to be offering an opinion."

And he wasn't. He had had the pleasure of meeting Kendrick's wife, Genevieve, and their daughter, Adelaide Anne, the afternoon before, offering her his condolences over being trapped with his nephew for the rest of her life, then paid for his comments in the lists just as he'd known he would.

Some things never changed.

"She seems very happy," Pippa offered. "Genevieve, I mean. And her French is very good."

"So is yours, my love," he said, reaching for her hand and kissing it. "I have to wonder, however, if the comforts of the Future soften the blow of having to live with a medieval blowhard."

Pippa laughed. "I don't think that's it."

"Then are you telling me the men in my family are tolerable?" he asked.

She squeezed his hand. "You know I am."

He looked at her hand in his for a moment or two, then met her eyes. "Let me clean up, then why don't we go for a walk along the strand?"

"Wouldn't you rather go for a drive?" she

asked with a twinkle in her eye.

"We'll do that tomorrow. Today, I want to focus all my energies on you."

"Heaven help me."

He laughed and rose, then pulled her to her feet. "Maybe a small journey in the car first," he conceded. "To that chippy in the village. I concentrate better when I'm not hungry."

"I'm afraid, my lord, that you're becoming far too accustomed to fast food."

He agreed, then walked with her back to the keep. Though it was a delicious luxury to simply be in a time that wasn't his own, without responsibilities, without impossible tangles to unravel, he knew he couldn't avoid forever the subject that stood between him and Pippa.

He waited until they were standing outside the hall doors before he stopped. "I think," he began slowly, "that we should discuss a thing or two."

She looked rather less comfortable than he would have liked. "That sounds serious."

"I think proposals often are."

Her mouth fell open. "What?"

"I'm doing this badly," he said with a wince. "Let me try again. Will you, Persephone, come to the shore with me today and allow me to kiss you as often as I wish? I could woo you with chocolate, if you'd rather."

"Well," she said thoughtfully, "that's a difficult choice."

He laughed a bit, because he could see she was teasing him. He reached out and tucked an errant curl behind her ear.

"You decide what your perfect day might contain and I'll do my best to fit it all into this afternoon. Then I think we should perhaps retreat somewhere quiet and discuss what our perfect future might contain." He hesitated, then cast caution to the wind. "And where that future might be carried out."

"Oh, Montgomery," she said quietly.

He shook his head. "Let us not speak of it yet. We'll take the afternoon for our own, then we'll speak of other things."

She looked away. "You know, I don't have anything to use for a dowry — if that's the sort of thing we're talking about."

"You are enough, Pippa."

Tears sprang to her eyes. "I'm about to throw my arms around you and not let you go."

"Let me shower first," he said, feeling as if he should have been appalled at how quickly he'd become accustomed to the simple pleasures of the Future. "Then I wish you would make good on that threat."

She nodded and walked with him inside the great hall. Genevieve and Megan were sitting in front of one of the hearths with their girls playing at their feet. Montgomery saw Pippa settled with them, hoped they would give their de Piaget husbands good marks, then ran for his borrowed bedchamber and washed up.

It was only as he was running back down the stairs that he ran fully into reality. It was one thing to imagine what he was asking her to give up for him; it was another thing to ask her to do it. The Future was so marvelous, so full of ease and delights —

He sighed. He wasn't one to envy others overmuch, but he could honestly say at the moment that he envied Kendrick. His nephew had his lady, his children, and all man's modern inventions in the same place. He didn't have to worry about the weather, or the harvest, or what sort of sauces his cook was using to cover the taste of rotting meat. Kendrick had warned him the night before that things weren't always as they seemed and that the Future held its own dangers. He'd promised Montgomery to send him home with a book or two that would make him appreciate the ease and simplicity of medieval life.

Montgomery wasn't sure that was possible.

But as he walked across the floor and caught sight of Pippa sitting with his nephews' wives, then found himself the recipient of a look that bespoke her pleasure at seeing him, well, the rest of it seemed less important than it had but a moment before.

He thought about how quiet she'd been at the fashion show, about how wistful she'd been during her recounting of the tale of Cinderella, and how many things he would break his back to provide her did she but agree to consider his suit.

Jennifer was happy. Could not Pippa be happy as well?

He made the ladies a low bow, complimented them on the perfections of their daughters, then politely excused himself and Pippa on the pretext of needing to feed her. He walked with her across the great hall, then paused at the door.

"I don't like to boast," he began slowly.

She smiled. "What in the world are you talking about?"

"I thought," he began uncomfortably, "that it might serve me to give you a list of my redeeming qualities, which will be very short, and another list of my monetary assets, which will be much longer."

"Montgomery, you don't have to sell yourself."

"I think you should know what you're purchasing, if you're interested in that sort of transaction."

"Shall I make a list, too, or are you already familiar with all my diva-like qualities?"

He decided she likely wouldn't object too strenuously if he put his arms around her, which he did without hesitation. "I am already familiar, Persephone, with your beautiful blue eyes, your sweet smile, and your ability to sit with me in a drafty tower chamber and make me feel as if I'd wandered into a marvelous fairy tale. If I knew nothing else about you, that would be enough."

She studied him for a moment or two in silence. "Montgomery de Piaget, did you come all this way to bring me my shoes?"

"It's what Cinderella's prince would have done."

She managed a little huff of a laugh. "You're a romantic."

"Only for you —"

"Oh, by the saints," a voice bellowed from the far end of the hall, "either kiss her or propose to her before we have to watch any more of these nauseating displays!"

Montgomery glared at Kendrick and had

a hearty laugh as his reward. He did, however, take the opportunity to kiss Pippa briefly before he pulled her out the door.

"Food," he said as they ran down the steps, "a long drive, then a longer walk along the beach. Without my family there to offer us any more advice."

"They love you."

"And you?"

She shook her head. "Oh, no, I'm not going first with that one."

He stopped and looked at her. "Could you love me, Persephone?"

She threw her arms around his neck and held on so tightly, he could scarce breathe. He supposed that was answer enough, however, so he didn't press her. He simply held her in his father's courtyard and vowed he would do whatever was necessary to make her happy.

He could only hope that didn't include going back to 1241 without her.

He walked along the shore with her as the afternoon waned. He couldn't remember a finer day, nor one filled with more simple pleasures.

Well, that and he'd gotten to drive Stephen's car to Edinburgh and back. It had been, as he'd heard Nicholas mutter on more than one occasion, mind-blowing. He didn't imagine it was possible to drive the bloody thing through a time gate into the past, but he'd been tempted.

"Montgomery, will Lord Edward let me into the shop, do you think?"

He pulled himself away from thoughts of speed and looked at Pippa in surprise. "I imagine so, if you wanted him to. What do you need?"

"I want to look through the books there," she said. "Before we talk."

He stopped and turned to look at her. He'd seen a hint of worry in her eyes over the past pair of days, but the worry had finally blossomed fully into distress sometime during the past hour. "Pippa, love, what is it?"

She put her arms around his neck and held him tightly. He couldn't say he'd been counting, not truly, but if asked, he would have said she'd done that at least a score of times over the course of the afternoon. There had been no rhyme or reason to it. She'd simply embraced him fiercely as the mood seemingly struck her — not that he'd been inclined to protest.

He realized now, however, that it hadn't been just affection motivating her. He put his arms around her and held her close.

"Pippa, I'm not going anywhere."

She didn't release him. "Have I told you today that I love you?"

"Nay," he said quietly, "and I've been trying to pry the words from you since before lunch."

Her laugh was unsteady. "You have not."

He smiled against her hair, then pulled back and kissed her soundly. "I have. And I love you. I would have said it before, but I didn't want to terrify you."

"Why would it terrify me?" she asked.

"Because it means that I must either stay in the Future with you and somehow find a way to buy you a Mercedes like Stephen's, or it means you must come back to the past with me and have patience whilst I turn Sedgwick into a place of comfort and beauty for you."

She hesitated, then pulled away from him suddenly. "Books, first."

He wasn't going to argue with her, though he did find her insistence to be a little strange. He walked with her over the dunes, a slightly more arduous trek than it had been in his time, then looked at her in surprise when she dropped his hand.

"Let's run," she said.

He shrugged. "As you will, love."

She was fast, he would give her credit for

that, but since he was accustomed to running in boots, running in trainers made him feel like he was flying.

Which, he realized suddenly, he was, down into some unearthly sort of whirlpool that opened up in front of him before he could stop himself from running right into it. He felt himself falling endlessly.

And then he knew no more.

Chapter 28

Pippa tripped and went sprawling. She might have been profoundly embarrassed, but Montgomery had done the same thing, so she didn't feel all that bad about it. She crawled to her knees to tell him at least they were equally yoked when it came to baseline dorkiness —

Only he wasn't there.

She gaped. He had vanished.

She pushed herself to her feet and turned around in circles, looking for Montgomery, only to see nothing at all except that faint shimmer right there in the middle of the field. She started toward it only to have someone catch hold of her. She sighed in relief. Obviously she'd been so fixated on getting back to the keep that she'd simply misplaced him. She turned around, vastly relieved.

"Oh, Mont —"

It wasn't Montgomery standing there.

The man holding her by the arm was tall, dark-haired, and fantastically handsome. She tried to pull her arm away, but he wouldn't let her go. She was tempted to try to elbow him in the nose, but he honestly didn't look dangerous. He just looked very concerned.

"Don't," he said quietly.

"Don't what?" she asked him in surprise.

"Don't step on that patch of grass behind you," he said. "It isn't safe."

Pippa jerked her arm away from him, but he shook his head sharply.

"I'm not kidding."

The tone of his voice was enough to have her rethinking her plans. She stepped away from him far enough to look at what was behind her yet still keep him in her sights. She glanced at the spot where she'd last seen Montgomery, then realized exactly what she was looking at.

A time gate.

She started to shake. In fact, she began to shake so terribly that she almost frightened herself. A hand again took her by the arm.

"Let's go back up to the keep."

She turned to the man. "Who are you?"

"Zachary Smith," he said with a smile. "Who are you?"

"Pippa Alexander."

Zachary Smith looked at her for a moment or two, then stared at the gate that was now nothing more than dead air. "Who were you running with?"

She could hardly breathe. "You wouldn't know him," she managed.

"Maybe not," Zachary agreed, "but why don't you try me?"

"Montgomery de Piaget," Pippa said, taking hold of a sudden feeling of defiance. "Now, are you going to tell me why I can't back up five feet and try to go find him, or am I going to punch you really hard in the face and leave you on your knees wishing you'd let go sooner?"

He smiled, but it wasn't a condescending smile. It was a smile that somehow said that he might understand a bit what she was feeling.

"I'm properly cowed," Zachary said gravely, "but I hope you're properly warned." He paused. "I couldn't decide if it was Montgomery or John. They're twins, you know. And they look so much like their eldest brother that I think if we were to see them all at the same age, it would be difficult to tell them apart."

Pippa retrieved her jaw from where it had fallen to her chest. "What in the world are you talking about?"

"Their older brother," Zachary said patiently. "Robin de Piaget."

"And how the hell do you know *him?*" she demanded.

"He's my father-in-law."

Pippa found herself flat on her backside before Zachary even reached for her. He squatted down in front of her and put his hand under her chin, lifting her face up.

"I think you're going to faint," he remarked.

"I'm not."

"Hmmm," was the last thing she heard.

She woke in a bed. She wouldn't have called it her bed because her bed was now ashes in a landfill, but it was definitely the bed she'd woken up in that morning. She opened her eyes and looked at the ceiling for a bit, then turned her head.

Peaches and Tess were sitting there in two chairs by her bed, looking like identical statues carved from marble. They were very pale and very still.

"When did you two get here?" she croaked.

"About an hour ago," Peaches said seriously.

"Stephen had the feeling we should come," Tess added. "I had no idea my car would go that fast."

"We're lucky he didn't get a ticket," Peaches said with a shiver.

Tess shook her head. "He drives a lot between the university and a flat he keeps in York. I think he knows where all the speed cameras are." She looked at Pippa. "We heard about Montgomery."

Pippa sat up, but her head began to spin so badly that she found herself lying back down again without really knowing how she'd gotten there. "I think he was going to ask me to marry him."

"I expect so," Peaches agreed.

Pippa allowed herself approximately thirty seconds of dizziness before she sat back up. She gritted her teeth and swung her legs to the floor. "I need to get to a library, or a bookstore, or something. Now."

Peaches exchanged a look with Tess, then reached behind her and pulled something out of her bag. "This what you're looking for?"

Pippa looked at the book that had started all her stress, then met her sister's gaze. "I've already read that one. I want more information."

Peaches set the book on the floor, then stood. "All right. We'll go with you. Where to?"

"I want to look in the castle's gift shop. If that doesn't tell me what I want to know, I might have to break into the public library." She looked at Tess. "Do they have libraries here?"

"Probably not in the village, but up the coast surely," Tess said, standing up. "Why don't we try the shop first? If that doesn't work, we'll go up the coast tomorrow."

Pippa had no intention of waiting until tomorrow, but she supposed she didn't need to say as much. If the gift shop didn't cut it, she would beg Stephen to rifle through his father's books. One way or another, she had to have details that night.

She had to stand still for a moment or two until she felt more herself, then she walked over to the door and opened it.

Stephen was standing against the wall under a fake torch, looking so much like Montgomery that she almost wept. Instead, she put her shoulders back and lifted her chin.

"I need books."

He inclined his head. "Of course, my lady."

The thought of the very rich and powerful son of the Earl of Artane giving her such deference was ridiculous, but she wasn't about to argue with him. She took the arm he offered and walked down the passageway, then down the stairs to the great hall. Stephen stopped so suddenly, he almost ripped her arm out of its socket. She looked up at him in surprise.

"What is it?"

He could only nod in the direction of the lord's table. Pippa looked, but only saw Kendrick and Gideon laughing over something. Gideon looked over, then smiled.

"Stephen, get over here, old man. I don't think you've met the Earl of Seakirk."

Pippa understood suddenly why Stephen looked so shocked. "Haven't you ever met him?" she asked.

"Heard a bit about him," Stephen said faintly, "but no, I've never met him. I'm not home all that much."

"He's Montgomery's nephew, you know," she said. "I think that makes him your uncle."

Stephen took a deep breath. "He couldn't look any more like Montgomery."

"Or like you, actually." She smiled up at him. "You should get to know him. I can guarantee there will be swordplay involved."

"Heaven help me," Stephen said with feeling.

Pippa laughed a bit, feeling a very brief respite from the grief that felt like a fist clutching her heart. She walked Stephen over to the table, then stood back as Gideon, with irrepressible glee, introduced Kendrick and Stephen to each other. He seemed to find his older brother's consternation to be endlessly amusing. Pippa supposed there was good reason for it, but she didn't have the time to figure out what it was.

She stood back and watched something of a little family reunion. Stephen pulled Tess and Peaches into the fray, as it were, introducing them to his parents and his newfound relations. Pippa went to stand against one of the walls, because she had to have something to lean against. She wasn't going to be rude, but she really needed a little foray into history before it completely got away from her. Either that, or she wanted a brief trip to the time gate.

Unfortunately, Zachary Smith was watching her, so she supposed the latter wouldn't be happening anytime soon.

She jumped when she realized Kendrick was no longer over with his family but had come to stand next to her instead.

"It was like this then," he remarked.

She looked up at him. "What do you mean?"

"My father's hall, during his time. Artane

was always full of cousins and aunts and uncles."

She turned to face him. "Do you remember me?"

He looked more serious than she had ever seen him. Admittedly, she hadn't spent all that much time with him, but there was no trace of anything remotely resembling teasing in his face.

"Please don't ask me that," he said very quietly.

She caught her breath. "Why not?"

"Because to change your future is to change your past, my past, and Montgomery's past." He took a careful breath. "Do what you have to, Persephone, and let Fate play her hand as she will."

"Do you believe in Fate?"

"Absolutely."

She looked back over the hall. "If Genevieve were in the past, would you leave all this and go back to live with her there?"

"Do you have to ask?"

She supposed she didn't. She looked up at him. "I love him."

"I know."

"Aren't you going to tell me how he feels about me?" she demanded.

He lifted one eyebrow. "Do I need to?"

She looked at him narrowly. "I just want

you to know that if I get back there and we both survive it, I will make your young life a living hell."

He scratched his head. "You know, I get that a lot. Can't think of what I do to deserve it."

"I'm starting a list. I'll let you know when I've finished it."

He laughed and put his hand on her shoulder. "One of your sisters — and damn me if I'm not surrounded by copies of either my sons, my uncles, or your sisters everywhere I go — one of them told me you were looking for a little history."

"Have any locked away?"

"I can get you a key to the shop," he offered. "I don't let my wee ones in there, but I have been known to snoop now and again myself." He winked at her. "I have a fondness for history."

"I imagine you do." She paused, then looked up at him searchingly. "Montgomery didn't tell me anything about why you're here in this time instead of your own. In case you're curious."

"Did you ask?"

"Nope."

He smiled. "You are a discreet woman, Persephone Alexander."

"Go get the key, my lord."

He pulled a silver key out of his pocket. "We'll take Stephen with us, just so the bobbies don't come and handcuff us. Besides, that'll give me a chance to watch him gape at me a bit longer. 'Tis vastly entertaining, truly."

She imagined it was and she imagined she wished he would just shut up and start walking. She did manage to get him and his nephew out the door in a reasonable amount of time, with Peaches and Tess coming along for the short walk across the courtyard. Within minutes, she was standing in front of a rather long shelf of things that pertained either to the castle or its inhabitants. Kendrick took one end, Tess took the other, and she began in the middle.

It took almost an hour, but she finally found what she was looking for.

And when she did, she avoided hyperventilating only because she was afraid she would pass out right into a rack of very pricey-looking china. She shoved the book at Tess.

"Read it."

Kendrick and Stephen stood there, still as stone, watching gravely as Tess read the paragraph to herself, then read it aloud.

Montgomery had died. Twenty-four hours before a woman who announced herself as his fiancée had arrived to save him.

Pippa turned and walked out of the shop. She continued on back into the great hall and then upstairs, ignoring questions, comments, and concerns that were gently floated her way. She was going to stop in her room, but she found herself carrying on down the passageway and up other stairs that seemed to wind forever.

It was probably already too late to even attempt a rescue.

She pushed open the door to what she assumed was a circular tower room, then flicked on the lights, intending to just have a bit of peace from prying eyes. She was surprised enough to see it occupied that she could only stare stupidly at the four men clustered there. One of them was in a chair, bound with ropes, and the other three were standing around him, dressed, respectively, in a kilt, another kilt, and Renaissance England duds.

She knew that because she was a costume designer.

She wondered if she might be heading down the road that led to Cindi's room in the local crazy hotel, but got hold of herself before true hysteria set in. She started to back out the door, an apology on her lips, then realized she recognized the red-haired

Scot. She'd seen him loitering in Tess's castle.

Well, before he'd vanished, of course.

He made her a low bow. "Mistress Pippy," he said with a gap-toothed smile.

"Ach, Hugh, you'll terrify the lass unless you make a proper introduction for us," said the other Scot, walking over and making a low bow. "I am Ambrose MacLeod, Miss Alexander. These are my partners in crime, as it were, Hugh McKinnon and Fulbert de Piaget."

Pippa nodded to herself. She'd known it would all come down to crime. Trespassing in castles not their own, tying up innocent guys, also in castles not their own —

She realized, with a start, that she wasn't looking at D-list actors in the midst of rehearsing a scene from a lousy cop movie; she was looking at ghosts. Somehow, given the month she'd had, she knew she shouldn't have been surprised.

Ambrose MacLeod smiled kindly. "We've tidings for you, my dear. Tidings from that miscreant there which will help you in your quest."

Pippa spared a brief and futile wish for something out of her mother's stash to help her deal with what she was seeing, then decided that since it might be classified as the least of the weird things that had happened to her over the past month, she could probably deal with it by normal means. She took a deep breath, nodded to her hosts, then pointed at the man sitting in the chair with the hood of his cloak pulled over his face.

"Who's the miscreant?"

Hugh pulled the hood back with a flourish. Pippa gasped at the sight of Martin of Sedgwick sitting there, looking particularly belligerent.

"What are *you* doing here?" she asked in surprise.

"Spilling his cowardly guts," Fulbert said, plucking a mug of something out of thin air and having a swig. "Of course, he wouldn't need to if Hugh hadn't put his oar in where it wasn't wanted."

"I was well within me rights to do so," Hugh said, glaring at Fulbert. "She's *me* kin, ye unimaginative Brit."

"She is *not* your kin," Fulbert said. "By the saints, man, can ye not read a pedigree chart?"

"She's kin of someone I didn't want to kill," Hugh said, through gritted teeth, "a someone who just happens to be a cousin several spots removed, which *makes her family*." He shot Fulbert a look of promise, then turned a smile on Pippa. "I didn't mean to push ye into the moat, missy." He doffed his cap and bobbed a quick bow. "I meant to acquaint you with young Stephen de Piaget, but me pushing went awry."

Pippa blinked. He had pushed her? Somehow, she just wasn't surprised. She would have thanked him, but he seemed suddenly quite occupied by exchanging insults with Fulbert de Piaget. She wished desperately for somewhere to sit, but since there didn't seem to be anything handy, she leaned against the wall and watched as Ambrose MacLeod walked over to a glowering Martin and put his hand on his shoulder.

"Now, friend," Ambrose said mildly, "give her the tidings I've told you to reveal."

"Or you'll do what?" Martin spat.

"Make the rest of your unlife hell is my guess," Fulbert offered. "Don't think ye'd care for it, but that's just my opinion."

Martin turned his glare on her. "I didn't kill him and that's all I'll say. You divine the rest, since you're so clever."

"Does he die?" Pippa whispered.

Martin clamped his lips shut and only glared at her. Pippa looked at him for a long minute, then at the three ghosts.

"Will any of you tell me about the past?" she asked.

Ambrose shot Hugh a look, then turned to her with a gentle smile. "We can only give you a push in the right direction, lass. The rest is up to you." He paused. "I think you know more about young Montgomery's situation at Sedgwick than we ever could, especially considering the trustworthiness of this lad here."

Pippa considered Martin for a moment or two, then thought about his siblings and his mother. She supposed she should put Lord Everard of Chevington into the mix as well given his blatant insults sent Montgomery's way. The unfortunate truth was, the murderer could have been anyone.

Assuming the history books were right.

She looked at Hugh and managed a smile. "Thank you for the push."

He twisted his cap in his hands. "Then ye don't mind the past —"

"*I* certainly would," Fulbert said, draining his cup. "Bedbugs, winter, the French. Or, worse still, the Scots —"

Hugh spun around to glare at him. "Apologize."

Fulbert looked at Hugh in silence for a moment or two, then flicked his mug into oblivion. "Nay."

Swords were drawn. Pippa decided it was past time to leave ghostly antics up in towers where they belonged. She thanked Ambrose quietly, ignored Martin, then left the room with the sound of metal ringing in her ears. She paused on the landing, then decided she wasn't quite ready to face either questions or decisions quite yet. A few minutes on the roof to simply let the sea breeze blow through her overworked brain was probably what she needed the most.

She walked out onto the roof, then along the parapet until she found a likely spot to look out over the ocean. The endless roar was mesmerizing, which was handy given that she needed to be mesmerized. She wished she'd had more ghostly assistance, but when it came right down to it, no one could really help her but herself.

If she had the courage to do so.

She listened to the waves for a bit, wondering if Montgomery had ever stood in the place where she was, or if he was standing there now —

Before he rode off to Sedgwick to meet a death he likely expected, but might not see coming.

She was preparing herself to jump right into that thought when she realized she wasn't alone on the roof. She realized with equal certainty but even more terror that she was all on her own without Montgomery's very sharp sword to protect her. She carefully turned her head, then almost fell off the roof when she realized who had come to join her.

"Come to organize me?" Pippa asked her sister faintly.

Peaches walked over to her, then leaned against a wall that looked sturdy enough to hold up to that kind of thing. "I think you're conflicted."

Pippa shook her head sharply. "No, I'm terrified."

"That you'll lose him, or that you'll manage to get back to save him?"

"Peaches, that's too blunt."

"You need blunt," Peaches said in a normal voice. It wasn't even her soothing organizer voice. It was just her everyday voice, as if she just had something to get off her chest and didn't really care how it was received. "Sometimes, sister dear, you just can't have it all."

"Can't I?" Pippa asked, stalling.

"No," Peaches said, "you can't. No one can. You can't have a full-time life as a clothing designer in New York and a happy marriage back in the Middle Ages. I can't spend all my time traveling the world while at the same time organizing peoples' sock drawers. Tess can't be a full-time academic, and a full-time party planner, and a full-time mystery writer with a dozen kids running around the castle poking each other with fake swords."

Pippa managed a smile. "Does she want all that?"

"I don't thinks she knows what she wants," Peaches said frankly, "but I think *you* know what *you* want."

"I don't —"

"Pip, why do you design things with a medieval flavor to them?"

"Because I love medieval things."

"Why?"

Pippa shrugged helplessly. "Because I like dropped waists and sheer fabric draping from conical headgear. I like the romance — the very unrealistic romance, I might add — of men and women dancing by candlelight in a stone-walled great hall."

"That isn't it," Peaches said relentlessly. "When women put on your dropped-waisted, open-chain-belted, silk-and-velvet gowns, how do you want them to feel? Itchy? Uncomfortable?"

Pippa laughed a bit, then suddenly found it not quite so funny. She clutched the rock under her fingers. "I want them to feel like princesses."

"Why?" Peaches asked gently.

Pippa felt tears spring to her eyes. "Because that will mean they've found their handsome princes and they'll go off to live in their castles full of music and love and the laughter of children."

Peaches stepped forward and hugged Pippa tightly. "I suspected as much."

"You didn't."

"I did. Let's go. I think you have your answer and I think you need to pack. The earl's invited us to stay as long as we like and he is seemingly resigned to all sorts of very strange goings-on in his castle. We'll all fit right in."

Pippa stopped her before she walked away. "I'll miss you."

Peaches blinked rapidly. "I didn't come up here to talk about that. We'll deal with that later. You have a few phone calls to make to sisters and sundry. Lord Edward's giving you free rein in the gift shop so you can take a few things back for your future husband, and Mary's offered to give you a riding lesson in the morning."

"Who's Mary?"

"Zachary Smith's wife." Peaches looked at her. "She's Robin de Piaget's daughter. You know, Kendrick's younger sister." She paused. "That would make her, I believe, Montgomery's niece."

"I have a headache."

Peaches laughed and linked arms with her. "You need dinner."

Pippa suspected she might need something a little more bracing than dinner, but maybe that wasn't such a good idea considering she needed a clear head.

She walked with Peaches along corridors and down stairs, considering what they'd discussed earlier. The truth was, it wasn't so much that she loved the fabric she sewed with, or the designs, or all the vintage trim, it was that she loved what it represented: a connection with the past, beautiful women standing on battlements waiting for their knights to come riding home, ladies who had their lords watch them from across a noble-filled court with love in their eyes. Her clothes represented the fairy tale and the fairy tale boiled down to a man and a woman falling in love, having children, and living happily ever after.

She wasn't as dewy-eyed as she'd been in her youth. She knew that didn't work out for everyone.

But she wanted it to work out for *her.*

And she could either keep on with fabric and sequins and dreaming of her knight in shining armor, or she could turn the fairy tale on its head, take a chance, and go off to rescue him before one of his bloody cousins managed to kill him.

No matter what the history books had said about her timing.

She looked at her sister. "Thank you."

Peaches only hugged her briefly. "Not yet, Pippa. I'm not ready to talk about that yet." She dragged her sleeve across her eyes and cleared her throat. "But you're welcome."

Pippa smiled in spite of herself and continued on down the hallway.

Chapter 29

Montgomery woke, realizing only then that he'd been unconscious. He sat up and looked around him, then leapt to his feet. Artane was there behind him.

Only it was missing several modern additions he'd noticed over the past pair of days.

He spun around and froze. There in front of him was the time gate. He knew it, because it was the same gate he'd ventured near scores of times in his youth. He leapt forward only to find himself jerked backward. He whirled around, his hand on his sword, only to realize he didn't have his sword. It was inside Artane, true, but that Artane found itself several centuries in the future.

And that Artane was, he knew with a sinking heart, several centuries from where he now stood.

He shook off the hand of his brother-in-law Jackson, who stood in front of him, watching him gravely.

"Don't," Jake said calmly.

"Are you mad?" Montgomery demanded. "I must —"

Jake took hold of him again in a grip that wasn't so easily brushed off that time. "Listen to me, Montgomery. Look at what you're stepping into before you do something stupid that I can't fix."

Montgomery cursed, but the tone of his brother-in-law's voice checked his impulse to rush ahead and consider the advisability of it later. He supposed it wouldn't cost him too much to at least look. He wasn't sure what he expected to see, but he knew what he didn't see and that was any sign of Pippa.

Instead, he saw warriors of different vintages, scenes of bloodshed, the ghosts of women and children fleeing. Or at least he did for a moment or two. The scene then changed to men and women in other dress, men with weapons he didn't recognize, ground that didn't look as it should have. The scene shifted again and again, more times than he could count. Unfortunately, none of the scenes was the one he wanted to see. He took a deep breath and looked at his brother-in-law.

"What are you telling me?" he asked, weary beyond belief.

"I'm telling you that if you step into that spot, you won't wind up where you want to be."

Montgomery considered. "How did you know to be here at this particular time?"

"I felt a great disturbance in the Force," Jake said dryly. "No, I'm kidding. I just had a hunch I might see something interesting this morning."

Montgomery rubbed his hands over his face. "I have to get back."

"Not today, you don't." Jake looked him over from head to toe. "And just so we're clear, if you do go back to the future, I want those jeans before you leave."

Montgomery pulled out Stephen's keys. "Want the Mercedes, too?"

"Damn you," Jake said with a laugh. "Don't tell me someone let you drive."

"Not as much as I would have liked."

"No doubt," Jake said. "Whose car was it?"

"Stephen, son of the current — or future — lord of Artane, Edward." He slid Jake a sideways glance. "Know either of them?"

"Our twenty-first-century lord Edward? Aye. Stephen? Never met him. I'm surprised, though, that he let you drive his very expensive beast."

"He let my future wife drive. I only convinced her to give me a turn."

Jake looked at him with a smile. "Your future wife? That sounds promising."

"It would be, if I could get myself back to her. And to answer what you haven't managed to ask yet, I followed her to the Future so I could ask her to wed me." He shoved the keys back into his pocket. "And now I need to follow her again because I got separated from her before I could spew the question out." He looked up at the sky. "It was evening when I felt myself falling, but it's now morning here." He dragged his hands through his hair and cursed. "She must think I'm dead."

"Which you very well may be if you try the gate right now." Jake's expression was very grave. "Please, Montgomery, trust me on this."

"How do you know so much about this?" Montgomery asked, pained.

"I'll tell you later," Jake said, then he nodded toward the keep. "Let's go inside and regroup. I'm sure we'll find answers in a bottle of your father's finest."

Montgomery blinked. "Did you know you're speaking modern English?"

"So, brother, are you."

"Which I can thank *you* for," Montgomery said with a scowl, "given all the times I eavesdropped on you."

"Real knights don't eavesdrop," Jake said airily.

"They do when they can't escape the incessant chattering in a tongue not their own," Montgomery grumbled. "I will admit it was rather involuntary, at first, but my curiosity did get the better of me. After all, I thought you and Jennifer were faeries. Well, and Abigail, too, I suppose. Imagine my surprise to recently find out the truth."

"I can only imagine," Jake murmured.

Montgomery shot him a dark look, but couldn't find it in him to say anything else. He simply turned and looked at the gate. He could still see echoes of things swirling in it, things he didn't particularly care for. He studied it for several moments in silence, then looked at his brother-in-law.

"It won't work now, will it?"

Jake considered the spot before them, then shook his head slowly. "I'm no expert, of course, but I don't like the feel of it. You might try to force the gate to your will, but I'm fairly sure you wouldn't manage it now. A different time, perhaps, but not now. Then again, there's no guarantee it would work even under the best of circumstances."

"But I have to reach her."

"I understand," Jake said quietly. "Believe

me, I understand." He paused and considered for a moment or two. "I suppose you could wait here for her to come to you, if you think she will. It might take hours, or it might take months."

Montgomery sighed deeply. He looked down at himself, spared a brief flash of regret for pleasures and comforts left behind — and grief he couldn't face at having lost Pippa, even briefly — then looked at his brother-in-law.

"I don't suppose I should go back to the keep in these clothes."

"You could just strip," Jake said with a smile. "No one would think anything of it."

" 'Tis a different world," Montgomery said, shaking his head.

"That's the truth," Jake agreed. "I wouldn't worry about it. Head for Robin's solar and I'll go fetch you something else to wear. We'll talk once you've changed."

"Nay, we'll go to the lists."

Jake rolled his eyes. "Very well. I'll meet you in the stables with clothes, we'll march out to the lists, *then* we'll talk. Fortunately, I can safely say that after ten years in this family, I have become accustomed to discussions over swords."

"Is there any other way?" Montgomery asked.

Jake laughed. “Of course not. Let’s go.”

Three hours later, drenched with sweat and shaking with weariness, Montgomery held up his hand.

“I’m finished.”

“You’re soft,” Jake said with a snort. “What have you been doing lately?”

“First, recovering from having my skull crushed,” Montgomery said, “then trying to woo my lady, then suffering a colossal headache from too much candy.”

“I should have warned you about that last stuff,” Jake said, “but that would have necessitated telling you things I didn’t think you needed to know.”

Montgomery leaned on his sword. “Are you going to tell me now?”

Jake paused, seemed to consider deeply his response, then resheathed his sword and started off the field. “Nah,” he threw over his shoulder, “you’d just be sad you didn’t try more junk food.”

“Junk food?” Montgomery echoed, striding off after him. “What sort of junk food?”

Jake grinned at him, then continued on back to the keep. Montgomery fetched his Future gear — which he was *not* giving up — then caught up with his brother-in-law. He walked with him through the courtyard and up the steps to the great hall. The tables were being set up for supper, but Montgomery didn't think he could ingest anything at the moment, so he shepherded Jake straight to Robin's solar. Jake paused in front of the door.

"Will you tell me the whole tale?"

"Will you answer every question I have for you?" Montgomery countered. "I don't imagine Robin will mind if we use his solar for that purpose given that I'm quite sure he knows everything."

Jake smiled ruefully. "Your brother hurts me in the lists when I don't tell him what he wants to know, so I have, as you might imagine, spilled my guts without hesitation over the years. You, however, only make me flinch so I've managed to keep a few secrets from you." He shrugged. "I suppose you could work a bit harder tomorrow and see what that earned you."

"I don't have time to wait for tomorrow."

Jake studied him for a moment in silence, then turned and knocked on the door. Montgomery wasn't surprised to find his brother inside poring over some bit of business or another with his steward. He looked up, seemed unsurprised to have visitors, then nodded toward the chairs sitting in front of the hearth.

Montgomery made himself at home, accepted wine from one of Robin's pages, then waited whilst the steward and the lads were ejected from the solar. Robin poured himself a glass of wine, then walked over without haste to cast himself down in an empty chair.

"Well?"

Montgomery pushed himself to his feet and began to pace. All of a sudden, he wasn't sure he could bear to talk to either his brother or his brother-in-law. Jake was perfectly content with the life he'd made for himself, and Robin was his usual impossible self, lording over everyone in sight as if he deserved to. Their troubles with inheritances and time gates and future brides were long in the past.

"Do you think you could stop that?" Robin complained. "You're making me dizzy."

Montgomery stopped and glared at his eldest brother. "I'm not sure you want to provoke me right now."

"Oh, I don't know," Robin said calmly, "I'm always game for another hour or two in the lists."

" 'Tis dark outside."

"Then we'll use the great hall, if you'll promise not to put your feet on my furnishings as you escape my magnificently flashing sword."

"Robin," Jake said with a half laugh, "stop tormenting him. He's had a long pair of days."

"Travel does that to a body," Robin said with a yawn. "I know every time I must go anywhere, I can scarce wait to be home to sleep in my own bed again. Then again, I have my lady with me —"

Montgomery was grateful Robin had stopped speaking. Then again, that might have been because the tip of the sword he'd borrowed from the armory was resting against Robin's throat.

Robin pinched the blade and very carefully moved it away from his flesh. "I may have crossed the line into poor taste there."

Montgomery resheathed his sword, then sat. "Forgiven."

Robin studied him for a moment or two in silence. "May I speak freely in front of Jake?"

"Of course."

"Then I'll be blunt and tell you you're a fool."

Montgomery blinked. "Excuse me?"

Robin leaned forward. "I've been watching you all day. You've obviously been thinking too much because that little pucker on your brow has become a trench deep enough for me to walk in. You are here and your lady is there. Accept it and move on."

"Accept it?" Montgomery echoed incredulously. "Are you daft?"

"Then *do* something about it," Robin insisted. "There's obviously a reason your lady did not come with you —"

"I took a wrong turn and she didn't!"

"Or perhaps you have things to do to prepare for your bride," Robin said sharply. "By the saints, lad, that hall of yours is a wreck. I wouldn't take my lamest nag and leave it there. I can scarce believe I left my son there. What wench in her right mind would want to live there with you? Go home, fix your keep, then wait. Your Pippa will find a way to come back to you, if she cares to. Can I assume you told her of your affection for her?"

"Aye," Montgomery said with a deep sigh, "though I hadn't quite gotten to asking for her hand."

"Did you talk to her father?"

"I was going to do that, too." He dragged his hand through his hair and sighed deeply. He had to chew on what else he intended to say for quite some time before he could manage to spit it out. "There may be a reason she wasn't fated to come back with me." He paused. "Perhaps someone else is destined to repair Sedgwick."

Robin's mouth fell open. "Who else would be daft enough to attempt it?"

Montgomery looked at his brother. "I'm certain Father would have preferred it go to John."

Robin looked at Jake. "Is it possible that he could be this stupid?"

"Robin, my friend, I'm not sure you should be the one to be asking that," Jake said seriously. "I wasn't here to enjoy it, but I've heard you spent your own share of time wondering if you were worthy of Artane."

"Ridiculous," Robin said with a snort.

Montgomery met Jake's gaze. Jake only held up his hands in surrender.

"He's your kin."

"I'm unpleasantly aware of that," Montgomery said heavily.

Robin refilled Montgomery's cup. "Drink this, my lad, and let me tell you the truth of it. If you're interested."

Montgomery drank, then shrugged. Aye, he was interested enough, he supposed, though he couldn't imagine —

"Father had always intended — and believe me when I tell you he *still* intends — that Sedgwick be yours. I was fairly certain either Gunnild or Boydin, or both, would chew you up inside a fortnight and spit you over the walls — and I said as much, repeatedly — but Father believed otherwise."

Montgomery had to wait for a moment or two before he thought he could speak without revealing too much emotion. He cleared his throat. "Is that so?" he managed.

" 'Tis so," Robin said cheerfully. "You see, if Father had listened to me, I could have saved you all this grief. *I* certainly wouldn't have sent you south, but Father has more faith in your abilities to charm and delight than I do." He reached out and kicked Montgomery's boot with surprising gentleness. "If it eases your tender heart any, Father never would have given the keep to John, even were he here to ask for it and you to refuse it."

"Why, do you think?" Montgomery asked roughly, because he had to say something. "Was he afeared Gunnild would have vanquished John more quickly?"

Robin shook his head. "I suspect John would have run Gunnild through, then found himself strung up outside the king's gates as a reward. You, at least, are skilled in all that courtly nonsense that makes me daft." Robin smiled wickedly. "Then again, perhaps Father simply thought you had an affinity for stacking rocks."

"I believe Montgomery's paying someone to do that," Jake said dryly. He looked at Montgomery. "If you want my opinion, I think your father wanted you to have Sedgwick because he thought you could take things that were not quite so desirable and create something very lovely from them. Actually, if you want the truth, that is what he said, on more than one occasion." He shot Robin a look. "I believe you were there for several of those occasions, Rob."

"I'd fallen asleep due to the tediousness of the subject," Robin said promptly. "Don't remember any of it."

Montgomery blew out his breath. "How is it I endured you for so long?"

"You love my sunny smiles and sweet humors," Robin said, leaning back in his chair and smiling smugly. "And I set a tremendously fine table. Don't plan on having your wedding feast here, though. I'm not going to be responsible for feeding all that bloody royalty who would come along and linger like vermin in my larder."

Montgomery sighed and finished his wine. "I'll leave on the morrow." He looked at Jake. "Will the gate open in the south, do you think?"

Jake shrugged helpessly. "I wish I had a good answer for you, brother. I think if she's meant to come back, she will. But I'm fairly sure she won't if you haven't done what you can to assure your side of the bargain is seen to."

"Meaning I must fix the walls?" Montgomery asked.

"That, and perhaps accept that you were your father's choice and as such, you have a purpose and destiny at Sedgwick," Jake said.

"The poor lad," Robin said, rising with a yawn. "The thought of it is absolutely exhausting. I'm for bed in my lovely, luxurious, goose-feather mattress alongside my lovely, delightful bride." He ruffled Montgomery's hair on his way by. "Best catch some geese, little brother, and begin plucking."

Montgomery watched his brother leave, then looked at Jake. "There are times I want to kill him."

Jake laughed, then rose as well. "You know he feels it's his duty to annoy you. If it makes you feel any better, he'll probably bring you a few geese as a wedding present. How can you fault him for that?"

Montgomery didn't want to list the ways, so he sighed, banked his brother's fire, then followed his brother-in-law from the solar.

He suspected that both Jake and Robin had been right about various things, loath as he was to admit it. Hadn't he thought as much himself? No lady would have graced the end of his drawbridge with his castle in its current state. He could hardly ask a woman who came from the innumerable luxuries and conveniences of the Future to do the same.

Nay, he would see to clearing out his cousins from his hall so Pippa might actually be able to walk from the bedchamber to the kitchens in safety, then he would see to restoring his keep as quickly as possible. And then he would hope she would take another chance, step through the gate at the end of his drawbridge, and into his arms.

But as he walked across his father's hall dressed in its medieval finery, he prayed Pippa wouldn't take any foolish chances.

And, most of all, he hoped she knew how much he loved her.

Chapter 30

It was high noon two days later — or as high noon as it could have been under foggy English autumn skies — when Pippa stood on the edge of the time gate, ready to go in a dress she'd whipped up herself. She hadn't wanted to wait as long as she had, but Zachary had insisted she not go off half-cocked, reminding her there were many perils for a woman alone, even if she managed to go straight from Stephen's Artane to Montgomery's.

Well, he'd also said that he hadn't liked the condition of the gate, and advised her to wait things out for a day or two until it calmed down from whatever turmoil it seemed to be suffering from. And given that he seemed to know what he was talking about, she had trusted him.

Impatiently, but she'd trusted him just the same.

She'd used the time to its best advantage.

She'd had horseback riding lessons from Mary, who apparently could outride even her own father back in the day but hadn't seemed inclined to actually demonstrate anything herself. Pippa had her suspicions that something was up with her, but she hadn't asked any personal questions about reasons why a gifted horsewoman wouldn't particularly want to be up on a horse.

Zachary had given her a crash course in self-defense, as well as teaching her a bit about basic medicinal herbs. Kendrick had given her family details he'd thought she might find useful, but no hints as to whether or not he thought she might accomplish what she set out to.

She had attempted to call her parents, but found them checked out. She'd left a message telling them she was taking off on a magical mystery tour in a big yellow submarine, which she assumed would make perfect sense to them. To her surprise, she'd found herself picking up the phone to call her aunt Edna, then listened in continued surprise to words of gratitude and affection coming out of her mouth. Edna had been speechless, another first, then unbent enough to express equal felicitations and other words appropriate to the Victorian moment of too-much-uncomfortable-sentiment.

She'd had a brief conversation with Cindi as well. She wouldn't go so far as to say Cindi had apologized for anything, but she had been speechless when Pippa had promised her the infamous flash drive. Of course, she hadn't told Cindi that the files were locked, but she hoped to be very far away when her sister realized that. After long conversations with her other sisters, she had spent the rest of her time soaking up every last possible minute with Peaches and Tess.

It had almost killed her, that soaking.

But she was resolved, so she had continued on doggedly with her preparations. She was actually quite grateful for the fire that had destroyed her entire inventory of possessions. That made it somewhat easier to choose what to take, which was basically the clothes on her back and a handful of gold coins Mary had insisted she sew into the hem of her gown. She had been slightly stressed over her lack of dowry, but Kendrick had assured her that Montgomery had buckets of gold and could easily manage to feed her for a couple of years before she was forced to take on sewing to keep them afloat. Genevieve had elbowed him firmly in the ribs at that comment, so Pippa assumed Kendrick was teasing her.

She had filled a rustic sort of rucksack with things she'd thought Montgomery might appreciate, then set it aside to have a final hot shower and a decent breakfast. The very last thing she'd done was share two last eternal hugs with Peaches and Tess.

That had been half an hour ago. Now her sisters, along with Zachary, Kendrick, and Stephen, had come to see her off. She could hardly believe what she was doing, but if she thought about the finality of it all, she would never do what she knew she had to do.

What she wanted to do.

She looked at her sisters one last time, then turned away and walked forward into the midst of the gate before she thought better of it.

And nothing changed. The sea still roared in the background, the day was still overcast, the gulls still cried in the distance. In fact, she was pretty sure she could still hear construction going on near the keep.

Or maybe that was the ring of swords inside the castle walls.

She closed her eyes, wished her most fervent wish for her fairy tale to come true, then turned around.

And she gasped.

Her family was gone. She felt tears spring

to her eyes at their lack, but she forced herself to put away her grief for a less perilous time. She blinked, then realized she was now facing a little girl of about seven who was staring at her with wide eyes.

Maryanne de Piaget, as it happened.

"You're Mary," Pippa said, stepping away from that big red X so she didn't, as Zachary had warned, find herself carried off to somewhere she might not like.

Mary's eyes were huge. "How do you know who I am?"

"I know your uncle, Montgomery," Pippa said with a smile. That wasn't how she knew Mary, of course, but there was absolutely no point in saying as much. If she managed to catch up with Montgomery and keep him alive, she was obviously going to be joining him in his secret-keeping activities.

"Who are you?"

"Persephone."

"Uncle Montgomery's lady?" Mary asked in surprise and no small bit of apparent delight. "He'll be so relieved! He said he lost you."

Pippa closed her eyes briefly, then smiled at Mary. "Your uncle did, for a bit, but I found myself for him."

Mary looked at her with eyes that saw far too much. "He said his villagers think you're a faery."

"I'm not," Pippa said, suppressing the urge to gulp. That was the sticking point in all of it, something she knew she was going to have to address right off the bat. Zachary and Kendrick had suggested she call herself the princess of Alki, but she wasn't sure that would go over with any credibility. She decided she would settle for simple. "You can call me Pippa, if you like."

Mary nodded slowly.

"Why are you out here all by yourself?" Pippa asked.

"The lads were vexing me," Mary said. "I never have a moment to myself without a brother or a cousin telling me what to do." She lifted her chin. "I like a bit of independence."

Having gotten to know Mary for a few hours in the future, Pippa wasn't at all surprised by that statement. She held out her hand. "You and I, Mary, are going to get along famously. Why don't we go back to the keep and you can tell me about your horses?"

"How do you know I like horses?"

"Someone, once upon a time, told me that you did."

That seemed to satisfy Mary. She slipped her hand into Pippa's and led her back toward the keep. Pippa went with her and found herself rather more impressed with Artane in the past than she had been in the future, in spite of what she assumed was its lack of running water and wireless Internet connections. It was one thing to see an enormous castle sitting on a bluff when it was surrounded by a modern village; it was another thing entirely to see the same place when it was the only civilization for miles.

She tried to look as noble as possible as she walked under the barbican gate. No one seemed to take much notice of her. Well, except the boys that ran down the front steps followed by who could only have been their father, Robin de Piaget. He looked enough like Montgomery that she had no doubt as to his identity. She would have hesitated, but Mary kept hold of her hand and pulled her forward to meet them.

"Pappa, this is Pippa," Mary said brightly. "Kendrick, Jason, look what I found! She walked out of the sunlight and almost into me." Mary paused, then leaned close to her brothers. "She says she isn't a faery, but I'm not sure."

"Oh, no," Pippa said quickly. "I was wandering away from my, um, company full of very fierce guardsmen, and they seem to have been left behind in a sudden panic."

Kendrick, Zachary, and Stephen were very fierce and they had been her guardsmen, so that wasn't entirely untrue. She had also been in a sudden panic, so that hadn't been a lie either.

Robin was only watching her without any expression of disbelief or irritation, so she took a moment to look at his kids. She realized, with a start, that she was looking at a very young incarnation of the grown man with six children she'd met in the future. She looked at Kendrick, blinked, then looked at his father, Robin.

Weird.

She took a deep breath, then made Robin a deep curtsey. "My lord Robin."

Robin stroked his chin. "Persephone Josephine Alexander, I presume?"

Pippa smiled in relief. "The very same."

Robin tilted his head. "Are you not a noblewoman of some sort?" he asked. "I've heard tell that your bloodlines are enough to leave those in England who know of you quite desperate to make your acquaintance."

She couldn't imagine Montgomery had come up with that whopper, so someone else had obviously been doing some thinking at the keep.

"Good thing Uncle Montgomery found her first," Kendrick interrupted. "Don't you think, Father?"

"Aye, son, I think it is a good thing." Robin sent his sons off to think about other things, hugged his daughter and sent her back into the hall, then remained where he was and folded his arms over his chest. "It isn't too late to avoid a life of misery with my youngest brother, you know," he said with a straight face.

Pippa had been warned about Robin's rather warped sense of humor, so she answered him with an equally straight face. "I am afraid, my lord," she said, "that it is too late for me." She paused. "Unless your brother has changed his mind."

"Oh, don't worry about him," Robin said dismissively. "He's completely besotted. In fact, he's gone back to Sedgwick to try to put his keep back together so you'll have somewhere safe to lay your head. Why you'd want to lay your head there with him, I can't imagine, but I suppose if you're determined —"

"Rob, leave off," said another male voice as its owner approached from the stables. A tall, handsome man made her a bow. "Jackson Kilchurn," he said, holding out his hand to shake hers. "I married Robin's sister, Amanda."

Pippa shook his hand automatically, then

realized something that seemed completely out of place. Her mouth fell open. Jackson Kilchurn was speaking in English.

Then again, so was Robin.

Robin sighed deeply. "Another council of war, I can see. In my solar, friends."

Pippa looked around her, just to make sure she was in the right century. "I'm confused," she said.

"Join the club," Jackson said with a smile. "It's chilly out, so why don't we go sit by Robin's fire and chat? Amanda and Anne have been hoping you would come through Artane. I think they're eager to meet the woman who captured Montgomery's heart."

"Or offer her their sympathy," Robin said with a snort. "Then again, I suppose that task falls to me. Whatever the case, we should sit and have speech together. There are plans to be made."

"I don't mean to rush either of you," Pippa put in hesitantly, "but I really have to get going." She took a deep breath. "If I don't get to Sedgwick soon, Montgomery's going to die."

"Will he?" Robin asked, looking very interested. "Cousins do him in, is that it?"

"I'm not sure," she admitted. "I just know someone does and I have to get there in time to stop it."

"A mystery," Robin said, rubbing his hands together. "One of my favorite things and, I suppose, reason enough to hurry. But let's have supper first. I always plot and scheme with more success when I'm not hungry."

That sounded familiar so she didn't protest. She did, however, venture one last question. "You believe me?"

He winked at her. "I've been to Sedgwick, you know, and I know my reprehensible cousins there. Do you know which cousin it is that does Montgomery in, or should I guess?"

"Rob, leave off with that," Jake said seriously. He gave Robin a shove for good measure, then took Pippa by the arm. "Come inside, Persephone, and we'll make plans. Ignore Robin. Sometimes he just doesn't know when to quit."

" 'Tisn't that," Robin said, striding along on her other side. "I'm just so tenderhearted that I'm always afraid that if I show too much emotion, I might unman myself in front of my men. It wouldn't do to have them see me weeping over my youngest brother who is perfectly capable of slaying anyone who vexes him. I will ride to his rescue, however, only because I feel honor bound to deliver you there safely." He lifted an eyebrow. "Unless you've come to your senses during that complete baring of my soul. You're not wed to him yet, you know."

Pippa only smiled.

"And if I'm allowed to ask, how is it you know our wee Montgomery's life is in danger?"

"A ghost told me."

Jake laughed out loud.

Robin looked at his brother-in-law, then shook his head. "My life," he said with a long, drawn-out sigh, "is very strange."

Pippa had to agree. She had, in the past hour, been in two different time periods that spanned almost eight centuries, spoken with ghosts, and taken a leap of faith into a life where her only anchor was a man hours away by horse who might not live long enough for her to rescue him.

She suppressed the urge to wring her hands. She would trust Montgomery's family because they had just as much reason to want him alive as she did. She watched Robin excuse himself to take care of some brief business, then took the opportunity for a little look around inside the gates. She tried without much success not to gape at the fully functioning medieval stables, blacksmith's forge, and garden where the gift shop had once been.

Jake elbowed her very gently. "I have a few current-event questions to ask you."

She looked up at him. "I'll just bet you do."

"I'll even tell you stories about your beloved if you want — after you tell me who won the World Series this year."

She frowned. "I have no idea. I just know it wasn't Seattle."

"You don't know," he mouthed in shock. "Woman, you don't follow baseball?"

"No. It's appalling, isn't it?"

"Absolutely. I suppose that leaves me no choice but to pepper you with questions about other important statistics before we round up men and take off." He smiled briefly. "Don't worry. Montgomery's a pretty clever guy all on his own."

"I know," she said. "I'm just afraid he won't be looking where he needs to."

He smiled wryly. "Riding to the rescue, are you?"

"He brought me shoes I'd left in the past. I thought I would return the favor."

"Very romantic."

"It was," she agreed. She hesitated, then cast caution to the wind. "There's one more thing." She paused. "Montgomery's garrison knights think I'm a fairy. Well, so do his cousins." She paused. "And most of the villagers in the surrounding environs."

"At least they don't think you're a witch," Jake said ruefully. "Don't give it another thought. We've been talking about that very thing. We'll think of some way to introduce you as a girl with a medieval pedigree, perhaps from obscure but very desirable locale in southern France. No one will dare argue, especially if Robin is your escort."

"That would be very nice of him."

"He loves his brother and his brother loves you. Besides, the paranormal overtones to the adventure will give him something to complain about for months. Everyone wins."

She sincerely hoped so. She followed Jake into the hall and across it, then looked at him as he stopped in front of a particular doorway. "We can hurry, can't we?"

"I imagine we'll leave before dawn," he said, smiling reassuringly. "Montgomery left yesterday, but even though he'll no doubt ride hard, he still has to stop at Segrave and gather up his men. We'll ride just as hard and be at Sedgwick well before too much mischief can be afoot."

Pippa closed her eyes briefly, unable to even express gratitude. She didn't want to sound melodramatic — Peaches would have enjoyed that far too much — but every moment that passed was another moment where Montgomery's life hung in the balance.

She couldn't bear the thought of getting there twenty-four hours too late.

She would just trust that Montgomery's family would know what to do and pray they would get there in time.

She couldn't do anything else.

Chapter 31

Montgomery stood in the middle of his great hall, waiting. He had thought about his plans on his way south, during a brief pause for a decent meal and to collect his household at his grandmother's, and as he continued along the well-made road to Sedgwick. Phillip had seemed eager to help as much as he could, though Montgomery still worried about the advisability of what he had decided to do. Unfortunately, he couldn't see any other alternative. He had to find out which of his cousins hated him enough to actually slip a blade through his ribs.

Or Pippa's.

Unless it wasn't one of his cousins. He had considered that as well, but he couldn't, in all honesty, say which of his personal household he would have suspected of wishing him harm. His own men he had trusted repeatedly with his life and would continue to do so. Petter and his lads were equally trustworthy. He supposed Fitzpiers might have been one to watch, but betrayal seemed out of character for that man.

He drew his hand over his eyes. The one person he did trust without reservation was hundreds of years away from him with no fail-safe way to come back to him — even if she had wanted to. He had discussed the gates with Jake for several hours, and though the conversation had been interesting, it had yielded nothing particularly useful.

Jake suspected that if the gate near Robin's house was to ever work again, it would work in a capricious, faerylike fashion. Robin had, during that conversation, remained blessedly silent. Montgomery had accepted Jake's assessment of the gate near Artane, taken his brother-in-law out to the lists to discuss the locations of other gates, then decided that it was as Jake had said at first: he would do well to attend to the problems in his own hall before inviting a bride there.

He could only hope she would want to be invited once he had solved those problems.

He jumped a little when he saw Fitzpiers come striding across the hall. He waited until his steward was standing close enough for a quiet conversation before he spoke.

"I can't imagine the tidings are good," he said grimly.

Fitzpiers shook his head. "Your cousins have accepted your challenge for a battle to determine control of the hall and gone to the garrison hall to gather their wee army," he said in disgust. "I imagine they'll be here soon."

Montgomery looked at his steward. "I'm pleased to see you didn't join them."

Fitzpiers only returned Montgomery's look steadily. "I cannot blame you in the slightest, my lord Montgomery, for questioning the loyalty of the souls about you. I certainly would in your place. You should know, however, that I take my oaths of fealty quite seriously and relish the opportunity to use my sword in my lord's defense whenever possible."

"Did you make me an oath of fealty?" Montgomery asked, just as mildly.

"Not to you in particular, but I gave my word to your father when you were a boy that I would serve him. When Lord Denys took the keep, I continued to honor that oath, despite the difficulties." He looked at Montgomery seriously. "I will honor that oath still, until I can offer you one personally."

Montgomery let out his breath slowly. "I

will accept it, gladly."

"I will also offer my sword," Fitzpiers said, looking as if the thought didn't displease him in the least. "And if you'll know one last thing, I should tell you that there are peasants standing in the courtyard, looking terrified."

Montgomery looked at him in surprise. "Are they here to aid us?"

"I daresay not, my lord. They seem to have taken Lord Everard of Chevington as their leader. As you know, he went about the countryside spreading rumors about the lady Persephone." He paused. "I suppose you can imagine what those rumors might be."

"Ridiculous," Montgomery scoffed. "I can personally guarantee she is not from Faery, should such a place actually exist."

"I agree, of course, my lord," Fitzpiers said with not a trace of inflection in his voice. "I was grieved to hear she had become lost in the forest. Did you find her?"

"I did," Montgomery said, "but she is now attending to business of her own. I hope she will join us soon enough."

Fitzpiers inclined his head. "I hope so as well, my lord. And I will be happy to aid you in correcting any of these terrible lies that have been circulated." He paused again.

"I understand our young lord Phillip will be impersonating her this night that you might discover who bore her ill will?"

"I hope it isn't a mistake," Montgomery said with a sigh.

"I'll keep an especially close eye on him," Fitzpiers promised. "And for Lord Everard. I don't trust him, my lord. He seems to stir up mischief and superstitions both wherever he goes."

Montgomery agreed, but he supposed there was no point in saying as much. He nodded to his steward, agreed with him that perhaps a last check of the men was in order, then looked back at the front door. Unfortunately, Fitzpiers would be using that sword sooner than he hoped, apparently.

Gunnild stood at the head of her little army, as Fitzpiers had called it, fighting for that place with Boydin, who seemed determined to have his mother out of the way. They were followed by eight of Montgomery's twelve remaining guardsmen. Montgomery glanced over to the passageway that led down to the kitchens to find the remaining four being prodded into the hall by Petter and his masons with François and the rest of the kitchen staff bringing up the rear. He looked to his left to find his captain and personal guardsmen standing there, their swords bare in their hands. Ranulf glanced at him, smiled briefly, then turned back to the spectacle.

Montgomery would have joined him in that interesting activity, but he was distracted by a noise behind him. From down the stairs came flying suddenly a figure dressed in a gown and swathed in a wimple that covered all but the lass's eyes. Montgomery supposed he was going to need to dig very deep indeed into his purse to recompense his squire properly for his willingness to portray himself as any sort of woman.

"Oh, my lord Montgomery," Phillip said in a high, squeaky voice, coming to stand very close to him, "what will befall us here? I see many very frightening lads with very sharp swords!"

"Aye," Montgomery said shortly.

"I am not accustomed to this sort of thing in Faery!"

He elbowed Phillip in the ribs, but agreed loudly with the terrible danger they both seemed to face.

"This is *my* hall," Gunnild said loudly. "Rid me of that usurper and his demon lover!"

Montgomery drew his sword, then rested it against his shoulder as he watched Boydin and Martin begin to argue with Gunnild about just who was in charge. Montgomery looked at Ranulf, who only shook his head. If he hadn't still had quite a battle in front of him, he might have smiled. It was no wonder the keep was in the sorry state it was. Denys had likely spent all his time trying to keep his children — or his wife — from killing him so they might have what they seemed to want so much.

"Glory and riches," Gunnild said, raising a sword that was obviously too heavy for her. "To me, men!"

"Food and wine," bellowed Martin. "And wenches! Many wenches!"

The men looked torn. Montgomery would have gone to sit down and wait out the arguing that now ensued as Gunnild and her second son attempted to out-do each other's promises, but out of the corner of his eye he'd caught Boydin slithering along the back wall as if he wanted to attempt an attack from where it wouldn't be expected.

"Stay near me," Montgomery said quietly to Phillip.

"Oh, my lord, I'm so frightened!" Phillip screeched.

Montgomery looked at him only to find the hafts of two wicked-looking knives poking out from his belt and the hilt of a sword gleaming in the depths of his cloak.

"You are your father's son," Montgomery murmured.

"Aye — my lord, to your left," Phillip said sharply.

Montgomery turned and found himself engaging Boydin thanks to a rush against his men by lads who had obviously been unimpressed with Gunnild and Martin's offerings. He fought off a very poor attack, then slapped his cousin's sword out of his hands and glared at him. "I don't particularly want to kill you," he said shortly, "but I will."

"You will not, you woman," Boydin spat, diving for his sword. He staggered back to his feet with a curse. "All that talk of fierceness is nothing but talk. You haven't the spine to run me through —"

He gasped.

Montgomery saw the bloody point of a sword protruding from Boydin's chest, then watched him fall. Fitzpiers cleaned his sword on the back of Boydin's tunic, then looked at Montgomery.

"One sent to Hell. Who next?"

"I don't think you need to be choosey," Montgomery said grimly. "Behind you!"

Fitzpiers spun around and engaged a garrison knight who apparently was interested in glory and wenches both. Montgomery shook his head. He didn't want to, particularly, but he suspected he was going to need to start afresh with an entirely new set of guardsmen.

He took a deep breath, then threw himself into something that had evolved into a fierce fray. He wondered if the current pattern of absurdity was going to color the rest of his life. Gunnild and Martin were standing on the edge of the hall shouting at each other, his squire was making an enormous production of preparing to swoon from fear, and his steward was in danger of being relieved of his tasks as steward and taking on the one of garrison captain. François was guarding the four previously captured guardsmen and Petter and his lads were gingerly herding peasants bearing makeshift weapons into a group as well.

That left him and his trio of personal guardsmen to see to the rest of the garrison, a task he didn't relish but could easily see the necessity of. He went about his work with his own lads for perhaps a quarter hour before he took a moment to reassess the situation. Peasants were standing in a large group in a corner, Phillip had pinned Martin in a corner with his sword, and someone else had taken over the swooning in the middle of the hall — Fitzpiers's son Maurice, no doubt, who would also need a hefty infusion of gold in his purse to repay him for the humiliation —

He frowned.

That wasn't Maurice in the midst of the hall, weeping loudly, that was Phillip. Maurice was taking on Gunnild under the watchful eye of his father, who stood there with his sword resting on his shoulder and a forbidding scowl on his face.

Then who was now fighting off Martin?

Montgomery finished the lad he'd been fighting, then ran over to the corner of the hall and jerked Phillip away.

Only it wasn't Phillip.

By the very saints in heaven, 'twas Pippa.

Pippa gasped, then shoved him aside just before Martin's blade would have gone through his belly. Martin pulled back for another thrust, then there was the sound of a slap. Montgomery looked and saw the haft of a knife sticking out of Martin's chest. 'Twas a very nice knife, golden handled and adorned with all manner of important-looking engravings. Montgomery looked over his shoulder in surprise. His brother was leaning back against the lord's table looking utterly bored. Robin de Piaget, at his most dangerous.

Robin waggled his fingers negligently.

Montgomery vowed to thank Robin and Pippa later but he had too much to do at present to attempt it. He looked back at Pippa, then felt terror slam into him. Pippa had stepped away from the wall — only to have someone creep up behind her.

He reached out and pulled her behind him, then raised his sword against her attacker only to find that soul suddenly impaled on his sword. The lad's hood fell back from his face to reveal not a lad, but Ada herself. Montgomery pulled his sword free of her body, feeling slightly ill at the sight, only to find Everard of Chevington standing there with a smirk on his face.

"I didn't think you slew women," he drawled.

Montgomery pushed Pippa behind him, then looked quickly for aid. Phillip was standing at his elbow with his sword in one hand and a knife in the other. Robin was, as it happened, now standing but a handful of paces away from his son. Montgomery exchanged a look with his brother, then turned to his own business. He threw himself at Everard furiously, forcing him back to the hall door where he rid him of his sword. He put the tip of his sword against Everard's throat.

"Go in peace," he said in a low voice, "or stay and meet your end in my hall."

Everard jerked his head back, then stepped away from death. "You'll regret this."

Montgomery suspected he might, but he said nothing; he only watched as Everard backed away, then picked up his sword and ran across the courtyard. Montgomery supposed he might regret not having killed him, but something had stopped him.

He supposed that sort of mercy might catch him up one day.

He watched two other lads slip through the shadows as if they had something particular to accomplish. They weren't his men, but he couldn't have said whose they were. He turned back to the hall only to run bodily into his brother who was also watching those lads.

"Yours?" Montgomery asked.

Robin only lifted an eyebrow briefly. "You'd best go protect your lady, considering she kept that bloody Martin from sticking a sword into your back. You can thank me for her exceptional swordplay, you know."

"Indeed?" Montgomery asked in surprise.

"Indeed. She wanted a special little something for Martin. I do believe she suspected he meant you harm."

"How did she know that?"

Robin leaned close. "A ghost told her."

Montgomery felt his mouth fall open.

Robin laughed and walked back into the hall. "Who's left for me?" he bellowed. "By the saints, this has been a tedious battle with a depressing lack of skill shown!"

Montgomery smiled to himself, then strode back along the wall to stop near Pippa, then pull her behind him whilst the last pair of traitors were collected and added to the group standing in front of the hearth.

"You're crushing me," she squeaked.

He gave her a bit more room, but put his arm behind him and pulled her against his back. "I'm allowing you to hold me up," he said weakly. "By the saints, Persephone, I didn't expect to see you here in the midst of this madness." He shivered. "Martin would have killed me if you hadn't been here."

"He would have, the liar," she said with a snort. "No, don't turn around." She patted his back, then slipped out from behind him. "Gotta go. I'll tell you everything later."

He would have stopped her, but he was suddenly in the midst of backslapping from his men and howls of outrage from Gunnild. He ordered his men to escort Gunnild out to the lone intact guard chamber in the outer gates, then turned toward the midst of the hall in time to see Pippa running past Robin toward the kitchens. Robin looked at him, shrugged, then exchanged a laugh with Petter over something before he too left through the kitchens.

Montgomery took stock. There were three guardsmen left, huddled uselessly in a corner. Petter and his lads were enjoying something François's lads had brought them to drink, and Fitzpiers, Maurice, and Phillip were standing in a cluster, looking terribly fierce. He made certain Ranulf could manage the inside of the hall, then took himself out down the passageway and through the kitchens.

He caught someone slipping out a hole in his foundation just before he — or she, rather — managed it.

"Let me go," Pippa said breathlessly. "I'm arriving tomorrow with a contingent of nobility."

Montgomery felt a little breathless himself. "You came."

She looked over her shoulder at him. "I'm assuming you wanted me to."

He leaned forward and kissed her almost as thoroughly as he dared. "I believe the fact that we're betrothed sheds light on that."

"I don't think you got quite around to that betrothing part, buster."

He smiled. "I'll remedy that as soon as possible." He kept hold of her by means of an arm around her waist, then sat on the edge of the rock. "Whom shall I expect on the morrow?"

"Persephone, the lady of Alki," she said, making herself at home on the rock with him. "Your brother was good enough to provide an escort for me."

"I imagine he was."

"He also brought a collection of unencumbered garrison knights who were tired of the damp, a few more horses, and some things to unpack in your kitchen."

He kissed her again, because he couldn't help himself. "And what did you bring besides your own sweet self?"

"Why would you think I'd brought you anything?" she asked archly.

He pursed his lips. "You've obviously spent too much time with my brother because you're beginning to sound like him. And the reason I imagined you brought something with you is because you're intimately acquainted with my sad addiction to all things twenty-first century."

She kissed him quickly then pulled away and stood on the opposite side of his wall.

"Hope the trunk in your solar has a good lock."

"Pippa," he said, reaching for her hand before she could escape entirely.

"Aye, my lord?"

He smiled. "I love you."

"I love you, too," she said.

"Oh, nay, not any more of this," said a voice from the other side of the wall. Robin's face appeared in the torchlight. "I had a delicious meal at Grandmere's this morn and I don't want to lose it. Come along, Persephone, before I'm too nauseated to stagger away from this rat-infested hole."

"Robin?" Montgomery said.

"Aye?"

"Shut up."

Pippa laughed, slipped her arm through Robin's, then waved at Montgomery before she walked off with his brother to what Montgomery could see was a very luxurious, well-guarded, and quite enormous camp.

"Still time to bolt," Robin said loudly.

"Not a chance," she said, just as loudly.

Montgomery was going to kill his brother. After he thanked him for several things, namely his very useful and quite critical aid not an hour ago.

"He is besotted beyond all reason," Robin

bellowed. "If you didn't agree to wed him, he would spend his days pacing a trench in front of his hall, waiting for you to change your mind."

Pippa looked over her shoulder. Even in the faint moonlight he could see the expression of affection on her face. Aye, he would have. If he'd been alive to do so.

He waited for them to disappear into the darkness, then sighed and sat on the edge of the hole. He looked out over his keep and found that it was suddenly quite a bit more full of light than it had been but an hour ago.

It was all because of Pippa.

He smiled to himself, then heaved himself to his feet and walked across his courtyard. The princess had come to rescue the prince. Preparing the hall for her reception on the morrow was the very least he could do in return.

He was very grateful to be alive to do so.

Chapter 32

Pippa sat on the horse Robin had loaned her, took a deep breath, then looked around her and was overcome yet again by the generosity of her future in-laws.

Anne and Amanda had taken her under their wings that first afternoon at Artane and pressed on her every conceivable medieval frill. She might have been lacking hot showers and bagels, but she had enjoyed luxury camping, perfectly delicious meals, and the company of souls who loved Montgomery very much and were full of stories about him they thought she should know. Robin's were told, she had been convinced during a lesson or two in swordplay, to help her see the error of her ways. Jake, Amanda, and Anne told her only what they thought would convince her she was doing the right thing — not that she'd needed any convincing.

She supposed she would have time enough

in the future to talk to Jake about his adventures, find out how Jennifer had survived without chocolate, and meet Abigail, who was apparently married to Montgomery's brother Miles.

"Paranormal oddities," Robin had said, more than once, with a knowing nod, also more than once.

Pippa wasn't going to wish those oddities to be anything but what her mother would have said they were: the long, long reach of Karma finally delivering on what had been paid for in advance.

Then again, perhaps that was giving credit where it wasn't due. She wasn't sure even Karma could manage to deliver something as wonderful as a man who paced in front of his barbican as he waited for his future bride to arrive.

Montgomery strode down his bridge, then hopped off the end and walked over to take the bridle of her horse. He smiled up at her. "Good morrow to you, my lady."

Pippa almost fell off her horse into his arms, but Robin cleared his throat so loudly that she didn't dare. She contented herself with looking at the man she loved and being grateful that she was two feet from him instead of eight centuries. She held her hand down and had a lingering kiss on the palm for her trouble.

"Oh, by the saints, none of this," Robin said, urging his horse forward and almost sending Montgomery into the moat. "This is the lady of Alki, and she isn't accustomed to such familiarities. I can see I'll need to sit between the two of you constantly until the wedding. And as you can see by my company, Montgomery my lad, we've come for a long engagement."

"Not unless you've brought food, you haven't," Montgomery said pointedly.

Robin pointed over his shoulder at a wagon behind him. "Compliments of Grandmère, who would like to come but is feeling poorly. She sends her good wishes, things for your lady's pleasure, and a demand that you both present yourselves at her hall as soon after the wedding as possible. Nicholas, Jennifer, and the lads are a day behind me, as well as Miles, Abigail, and their terrifying brood. Nick sent a message to Mother and Father, who have invited you to come eat through their larder after you've made the required visit to Segrave. I believe they have extended their hospitality to last through the restoration of your hovel here. I understand Isabelle has also issued an invitation for a lengthy stay where you might sun yourself amongst her grapes."

"Very generous of them all," Montgomery said.

Robin pursed his lips. "Aye, think of me fondly whilst you're in lovely France and I'm freezing my sorry arse off in the north."

"I will," Montgomery promised, then he promptly ignored his brother in favor of Pippa.

Pippa tried not to blush profusely as Montgomery led her horse across the bridge as if she had indeed been a very fine lady. It was difficult to access her inner diva while on horseback where she wasn't entirely sure she wouldn't land facedown in courtyard muck, but she did the best she could. She couldn't say that she wasn't profoundly relieved to put her hands on Montgomery's shoulders and let him help her off her horse.

"No kissing," Robin bellowed from behind them.

Montgomery bent and whispered in her ear. "Do you know who he reminds me of?"

"Kendrick?"

"Exactly, the poor lad."

She laughed and pulled away from him before she was the one who would be creating rumors about her entirely inappropriate pre-wedding behavior.

"I suppose you could wed her here in the stables," Robin said distinctly. "Don't see any holes in these walls."

Montgomery took a deep breath, no doubt counting to ten at the same time. "I'm going to kill him."

"He got me here without trouble," Pippa said. "That might earn him a reprieve."

"A temporary one," Montgomery agreed. He looked at the wagons behind her. "What, love, did you bring in those other wagons?"

"All kinds of stuff," Pippa said, "including Robin's bed. He wasn't going to sleep in one of yours —"

She would have finished her sentence, but Montgomery had pulled her behind him and drawn his sword. She put her hands on his back, then peeked around him in time to see a rider come thundering into the courtyard. It wasn't one of Robin's men because he was wearing the wrong colors.

"Who is that?" she asked uneasily.

"Bloody hell," Robin wheezed. " 'Tis Henry's messenger." He leapt down off his horse. "Where can I hide?"

"Behind your elegant, courteous wife," Montgomery said with a grunt. "And don't you dare slither out any of the holes in my foundation until you've introduced Pippa properly to the king. You'd damned well better have a decent history for her."

Robin sighed. "Always the man's work for

me. Never a day of leisure, I'll tell you that."

"Rob?" Montgomery said.

"Aye?"

"No one's listening to you."

Pippa laughed at the dark look Robin shot his youngest brother.

"I won't make it so you can't kiss your bride, but I'm tempted." He went to help Anne down from her horse, still muttering not quite under his breath.

Pippa felt Montgomery resheath his sword, then looked up at him as he turned toward her. She felt slightly more faint than usual, and unfortunately it had nothing to do with Montgomery. "The king?"

He felt for her hand and linked his fingers with hers briefly. "Why don't you take Anne and Amanda into the hall and make yourself comfortable? I'll see to this lad, then come find you and see you settled." He paused. "I imagine Henry will be here within the hour. His outriders don't proceed him by much."

She wished quite suddenly for a place to sit down. "King Henry?"

Montgomery lifted an eyebrow briefly. "Welcome to 1241, my love."

"I appreciate the extra-fancy shindig you're throwing for me," she said, not really caring if that translated well or not, "but shouldn't I be fixing supper or something else useful?" she asked, feeling unaccountably breathless.

He looked at her, then pulled her into his arms and hugged her tightly. "Nay, love, you should simply go take a moment or two to rest yourself from your journey, then send one of Robin's pages for wine for your pleasure. In a half hour, if it pleases you, you could certainly descend and confer with François about the menu."

"Menu," she managed. She cleared her throat. "Tell me he'll know what to do."

"He will," Montgomery said confidently. "And Mandy and Anne will help you. I don't even think you'll have to ask."

She shivered, once, then stepped away. She had to take a couple of deep breaths before she thought she could not hyperventilate. "Will he believe it?" she asked. "You know what I'm talking about."

"Trust Robin," Montgomery said quietly.

"Do you?"

"With my life. Without question." He smiled, then raised her hand to his mouth and kissed it. "His faults are legion, but when it comes to family, he is absolutely ruthless in his quest to keep those he loves safe. If it eases you any, that is one of my brother's traits I have vowed my whole life to emulate."

She smiled. "I love you."

"I love you," he said, sounding as if he truly meant it. "Now, love, come you here —"

"No kissing!" Robin bellowed from across the courtyard.

A muscle in Montgomery's jaw tightened briefly, then he blew out his breath. "He lives another day, but only because of his care for you. And because he will soon be out of the reach of my sword."

Pippa smiled and pulled out of his arms. "I'll see to chatelaine duties, then meet you later, on the roof."

"You will not," he said without hesitation. "I don't trust those walls — though I fear after our king descends, the only privacy we'll have is in the stables."

She shrugged. "I like hay."

"Let's just hope we're not using it for our wedding bed," he muttered. He looked at the messenger dismounting in front of the hall door, then back at her. "I might need help tending horses later."

"I'll be there."

He hesitated, then turned and pulled her into his arms so quickly, she gasped. "I'm not sure how to tell you how grateful I am you're here."

"The feeling, my lord, is mutual."

He kissed her quickly, then released her. "Go be warm by the fire with my sisters. I'll come as I may."

She nodded and watched him walk off. She soon found herself flanked by his sister and sister-in-law. They linked arms with her and simply stood and watched with her for a moment or two before Anne squeezed her arm.

"I think you'll be happy," Anne said gently.

"He's desperately in love with you," Amanda added. "He'll see that you're comfortable."

Pippa looked at them in turn. "Thank you both," she said hesitantly. "You've made me feel very at home."

"We can imagine, Pippa," Anne said slowly, "what you gave up in the persons of your sisters." She glanced briefly at Amanda. "We can't replace them, we know, but we'll do our best to be poor substitutes."

Pippa had to blink very rapidly a time or two. "Don't make me cry yet. I've got to get through a month or so of being engaged."

"A month?" Amanda echoed with a laugh. "Pippa, love, once Henry learns Robin has arranged this betrothal for Montgomery without his royal knowledge, you'll be wed by the end of the day."

Pippa found her mouth was suddenly

quite dry. "Do you think so?"

Anne and Amanda exchanged another glance.

"We'd best claim the second-best chamber," Anne said briskly. "You'll want a bath, then we'll do your hair and dress you."

"Nay, Anne, there will be no wedding today. His Majesty will have to wait for Nicky and Jenner." Amanda smiled placidly. "I'll have Jake distract him with the thought of another portrait whilst I shape up his courtiers and you see to making Pippa comfortable. We'll all pass the time most pleasantly."

Pippa didn't dare hope she would manage it as easily as Montgomery's sister and sister-in-law. She also didn't protest when Anne and Amanda led her off toward the kitchens, more than happy to get out of the hot seat. She managed a look over her shoulder to see how Montgomery liked the temperature only to find him watching her.

He smiled, then turned back to the king's messenger.

Pippa took a deep breath and continued on. The king of England? In her living room? It wasn't exactly how she'd imagined her first legitimate week in medieval England would go.

Heaven help her.

■ ■ ■ ■

It took over twenty-four hours for Henry to arrange Montgomery's wedding to his satisfaction, and by then Pippa thought her nerves would simply shatter. She had cast herself into the entertaining-of-royalty fray, thankfully with copious amounts of help from Anne and Amanda, and had had not a single moment's privacy with the man she was about to marry. Even the stables had been occupied by various children belonging to Montgomery's older sister and brothers.

She supposed that, looking back on it from her current vantage point on her husband's topmost step, it had been a blessing that Sedgwick had needed the repairs it had. The king had taken over the castle long enough to have a meal or two and see them properly married before he'd had enough of camping and packed up just after lunch to go delight another of his subjects with his royal presence. Pippa thought it might take her a while to digest the fact that she had just met a figure from history — and a famous one at that.

Then again, considering how nervous she'd been for that past twenty-four hours, digesting anything was going to be a trick.

"Are you unwell?"

Pippa looked up at Montgomery. "I think I'm going to throw up."

He took her by the hand and pulled her back through the hall, through the crowd of well-wishers, and basically right over his brothers who were standing in his way.

"She's going to be ill," he said shortly.

Robin laughed. "The poor gel has finally realized —"

Pippa gaped at the sight of her husband's fist quite suddenly in the middle of his brother's mouth. Montgomery looked at his brother Miles.

"Finish that for me, would you?"

"Well," Miles drawled, "I didn't bring you a present, so —"

Pippa managed a look over her shoulder to find brothers Number One and Three launching into what she suspected would turn out to be a glorious brawl.

She wasn't sure how she made it up the stairs, or down the hall, but she did manage to make the garderobe before she lost it. She wasn't sure how having her husband hold her hair while she threw up was a very dignified start to her marriage, but there'd been nothing to do about it. She couldn't even blame jet lag, though she thought some of her nerves could definitely be laid at Henry's feet.

She let Montgomery lead her into his bedroom, then accepted a cup of water to rinse her mouth out with. She soon found herself sitting in a chair in front of a roaring fire, smiling at the man who sat down across from her.

"Hey, stranger," she said.

He laughed. "Feel better?"

"I think I was nervous."

"I can see why," he agreed. "I am intimidating."

"Please, Montgomery," she groaned, "don't channel your brother."

He reached over and pulled her out of her chair to come sit on his lap. He put his arms around her and smiled at her. "That was a jest, Persephone." He took a deep breath, then let it out. "Privacy, at last."

"Did you bolt the door?"

A look of panic descended on his face.

"I'll do it," she said, pushing herself up to her feet. "I'd put a trunk against it, too, if I could move it."

"Robin knows where to stop," Montgomery said with a smile. "And if he doesn't, Nick does. We're safe."

Pippa realized as she walked back to the fire that there was a small feast sitting on a table pushed up against the wall, her backpack was in the locked trunk underneath it, and there were bedclothes she certainly didn't recognize on the bed. She stopped in the middle of the room, turned around, then looked at him.

"Someone was thinking of us."

"Anne," Montgomery said with a smile. "And Amanda. Abigail ran after the entire brood of offspring whilst they came up and tried to make things lovely for you."

She walked over to him, then sank down onto his lap. "I didn't need anything but you, but yes, the rest is lovely."

He reached up and tucked a loose strand of hair behind her ear. "I have scores of things to ask you."

"And yet you haven't asked me the one question I expected," she said pointedly.

He laughed. "Did I not ask you to wed with me?"

"I don't think you had a chance."

He slipped his hand under her hair, then leaned forward and kissed her softly. "Wed me," he said with a grave smile.

"Oh, all right," she said with a fake shrug. "Since you went to all the trouble of bringing the king of England here to have his bishop marry us."

"I wanted to make certain you didn't

regret your choice."

She shook her head slowly. "Montgomery, I will never, ever, regret my choice."

"Are you keeping a list?"

She smiled. "Of all the lovely things you do for me? Of course."

"Perhaps I might try to add a thing or two to it this afternoon."

She brushed the bangs out of his eyes, then trailed her finger down his cheek. "Are you going to tell me a fairy tale this time?"

"Nay," he said seriously, "I'm going to make one, just for you."

She put her arms around his neck and held him tightly. Yes, she had given up things that she was sure would break her heart, but she had gained in return a man who she was certain would heal that heart in a thousand ways.

He set her on her feet, tossed another log onto the fire, then held out his hand for hers.

And then the reputedly quite noble lady of Alki bestowed her best smile on her handsome lord, put her hand into his in the best bedchamber of his fairy-tale castle, and prepared herself to live happily ever after.

Even the Brothers Grimm would have approved.

Chapter 33

Peaches Alexander walked along the edge of the water near a beautiful keep on the edge of the sea and thought deep thoughts. It had been two weeks since her sister had departed for points unreachable by either cell phone or Her Majesty's postal service. She supposed she should have gone home already, but she hadn't been able to bring herself to. She wanted to say she was happy, but she had to admit to herself that she had been happier. She was positive Pippa had to be content given how much she loved Montgomery, but still, it would have been nice to know for sure. She'd been tempted to go riffle through Lord Edward's private library and see if there might be a few details available there, though she knew how that had worked out for Pippa so she hadn't dared.

She looked up to see Tess and Stephen walking down the beach toward her. She was momentarily tempted to panic, but Tess didn't look stressed so she supposed there was no reason to feel that way herself. She met them halfway, then frowned.

"What?"

Stephen smiled. "I wore Kendrick down in the lists this morning," he said, sounding rather proud of himself.

"Don't let him kid you," Tess said with a smile. "He knocked Kendrick's sword out of his hand. Apparently that's a pretty big deal here at Artane."

"Did you win anything for it?" Peaches asked with as much of a smile as she could muster.

"A peep into his wee brain," Stephen said, straight-faced. "He has details —"

"Why didn't you say so?" Peaches said, taking them both by the arm and pulling them back up the beach. "Let's go."

Half an hour later, she was sitting in Lord Edward's solar with potential sources of information who hadn't been willing to divulge details before. Peaches wasn't sure what had convinced them to cough up those details at present, but she wasn't going to investigate. The prize was too close to risk it by asking pesky questions.

Stephen held out the chair of honor for her by the fire, then sat down next to her with Tess. Peaches was happy to see Gideon and Megan, but she dismissed them right along with Genevieve and Zachary. But Kendrick, yes, there was someone who had been annoyingly closemouthed about a few things he was probably the authority on. Mary had been equally mum, though Peaches wasn't sure she could count on any answers yet from that one. When she hadn't been bolting for the nearest bathroom to throw up, she'd been looking as if she were about to bolt for the nearest bathroom.

Apparently, morning sickness was taking its toll.

Peaches waited for Mary to leave and return again before she turned to Kendrick.

"All right," she said faintly, "I want details."

"Oh, I'm not sure," Kendrick said with a thoughtful frown. "Wouldn't want to upset any karmic balance —"

"Be silent, you horse's arse," Mary groaned, throwing a pillow at her brother. She managed to focus on Peaches. "I will tell you what I know — quickly, before I need to go lie down. Zachary and Stephen can beat the rest of the details out of my brother later, if you want them."

Peaches wished she could have relaxed

and anticipated merely the retelling of an interesting story, but she had too much invested in a happily ever after for that.

Mary smiled, as if she understood. "Of course by the time I truly knew Pippa, she had been in the past for several years, but I can tell you that she and my uncle had eight children, four sons and four daughters, all of whom survived and most of whom had very interesting names."

Peaches took a deep breath. "I can only imagine."

"Peaches, Tess, and Gwen were delightful gels," Mary said with a smile, "as was their wee gel, Valerie. I spent many a fortnight enjoying their company — as well as that of your sister. She never said aught to me about having known me in a different time, nor did my uncle. They were discreet, lovely souls who adored each other and their children."

"Did Montgomery finish Sedgwick?" Tess asked.

Mary nodded. "Very quickly, actually, though Kendrick would know more about that than I. He went along with them to France whilst the keep was being repaired."

Peaches shot him a look. "And you didn't say anything."

"I am a vault," he said solemnly.

"I imagined Pippa was really irritated with you."

"Fortunately for me, your sister was too kind to hold a grudge," Kendrick said with a smile, "though she would have had good reason to. Now, my uncle Montgomery was a different tale entirely. I think he was altogether too harsh on me in the lists during my tender, formative years."

Peaches didn't doubt that Kendrick had deserved every bit of what he'd gotten, but she wasn't going to say as much on the off chance he might have goods for her later. She turned back to riper pickings.

"Tell me more, Mary. What was Pippa's life like? Did she sew?"

"Oh, aye," Mary said with a smile. "She was extremely choosey about who wore her gowns, which made them, as you might imagine, all the more desirable. She sewed fashions for ladies at court when she could be prevailed upon to do so. I suppose 'tis fortunate she knew so much about the history of it all otherwise she might have changed things past what history could bear. I didn't care overmuch for gowns, as you might imagine, but I wore your sister's with pleasure."

"Was she happy being a mother?"

"Almost as happy as she was being a

wife," Mary said, smiling briefly at her husband. "My uncle pampered her relentlessly and was forever trying to invent new and modern ways to make her life more pleasant." She shrugged. "I think, as strange as it may sound, that she was born for that period in time. It was simple, elegant, and peaceful. She and my uncle moved in that world with a grace that was admired by all. Of course," she added, "that isn't to say that Uncle Montgomery wasn't acknowledged for his superior swordplay and his ability to negotiate the complexities of court life without misstep. He preferred, however, to be at home with his love and his wee ones."

"Most of the time," Kendrick added, then he shut his mouth, as if he'd said too much.

Peaches shot him a look, but he only returned that look with wide-eyed innocence. Peaches scowled at him, then sat back and let Tess take over the questioning. It was enough at the moment to simply watch the souls there who were connected over centuries. In spite of the fact that she had cut her teeth on some fairly far-out ideas, the thought of time traveling and ghosts and all other things paranormal was almost too far-fetched for her.

She looked at her sister Tess and pursed her lips. Now, there was one who'd been made for traipsing around in the Middle Ages. She was half surprised her twin hadn't learned to use a sword, but maybe that was next on her list of things to do, now that she'd gotten used to hanging out in Sedgwick, pretending to live in another century.

"Who?" Genevieve asked incredulously.

Peaches snapped back to the conversation, feeling like she'd missed something she shouldn't have.

"William of Sedgwick," Kendrick was saying with a shrug. "He was our cousin Arnulf's eldest. Montgomery took him in trade for Gunnild, which I suppose wasn't a good trade, but better than the alternative." He was holding the book Pippa had found in Artane's gift shop. "And this obscure little tome was written by a certain William Sedgwick Maledica." Kendrick shot his wife a look. "I imagine that name is familiar."

Peaches watched the blood drain from Genevieve's face. There was a story there, but she had the feeling it wasn't going to be a good one.

"Why is the name familiar?" Tess asked, holding out her hand for the book. "Do you know him?"

"Knew him," Kendrick said. "It's a very long tale, one far too tedious to tell today. Suffice it to say, he had reason for not wanting your sister to travel back and save my uncle."

"Kendrick," Genevieve said in a low voice, "why didn't you say anything to Pippa? She could have told Montgomery —"

"And changed history," Kendrick said, reaching for her hand. "My history in particular, which would have left me without you." He kissed her hand. "You wouldn't want to sentence me to a life of hell, now, would you?"

"Even I couldn't wish that on you," Mary said with a sigh.

Kendrick shot his sister a wry look. "Thank you so much, love."

Mary started to speak, then clapped her hand over her mouth. She leaped to her feet, then bolted from Lord Edward's solar. Zachary stood, wished everyone a good afternoon, then hurried off to follow his wife.

Peaches watched them go, then looked up as Kendrick and Genevieve excused themselves as well. Megan shifted her sleeping daughter in her arms and exchanged a look with her husband. Gideon helped her to her feet, then clapped Stephen on the shoulder on his way across the room.

"Come home more often."

"I'm not sure I can stomach the odd happenings here," Stephen said faintly.

Gideon only laughed and put his arm around his wife as he walked with her from the room.

Peaches continued to sit in front of the fire until the silence became a warm, comforting thing. She finally came to the point where she thought she could look at Tess and not weep.

"I think she's happy."

"How could she not be?" Tess said quietly. "He was crazy about her."

"Hot showers," Stephen said distinctly. "Hot tea, fast cars, and scones with clotted cream."

Peaches smiled at him. "Are fast cars still on your list considering your uncle has your keys?"

He pulled another set from his pocket.

Peaches laughed. "Come on, Tess. Let's go home. I'll help you organize your prop room and get Pippa's hope chest organized. She's going to wonder what that key I stuck in her backpack is to."

"How will she take possession of it?" Stephen asked with a frown.

"Zach said to just shove it through the time gate and hope for the best," Peaches said. "I get the feeling he knows what he's talking about."

Tess shivered. “Please don’t give me any details. I don’t know about you two, but I’m done with paranormal happenings for a while, thank you very much.”

“You shouldn’t have accepted a castle,” Stephen said wisely. “They’re generally layered with history and other unusual things.” He rose with a sigh. “I daresay I need an extended spell in a very pedestrian, unmagical library. I think tomorrow I’ll see you ladies back to Sedgwick, then embark on a research project to soothe my frazzled nerves.”

Peaches looked at Tess and knew they were thinking the same thing: Stephen had seen too much to go back to what he’d been before.

Then again, so had they all. It had been a month full of things she’d never expected, things that had changed the way she would look at life forever. Pippa was living the fairy tale in the past, Tess was wallowing in a fairy-tale present, and she was happy for the moment to let her fairy tale linger in the future. It was nothing any of them had expected, but she had the feeling in the end it would be, one way or another, what they each had dreamed of.

All because of one enchanted evening at Sedgwick when Pippa had walked through magic shimmering in the air.

She rose and left the solar with her sister and Artane's heir. She silently wished Pippa and Montgomery every happiness, closed the solar door behind her, and followed her sister and her cousin-in-law down the reputedly ghost-free, unenchanted hallway.

family lineage in the books of LYNN KURLAND

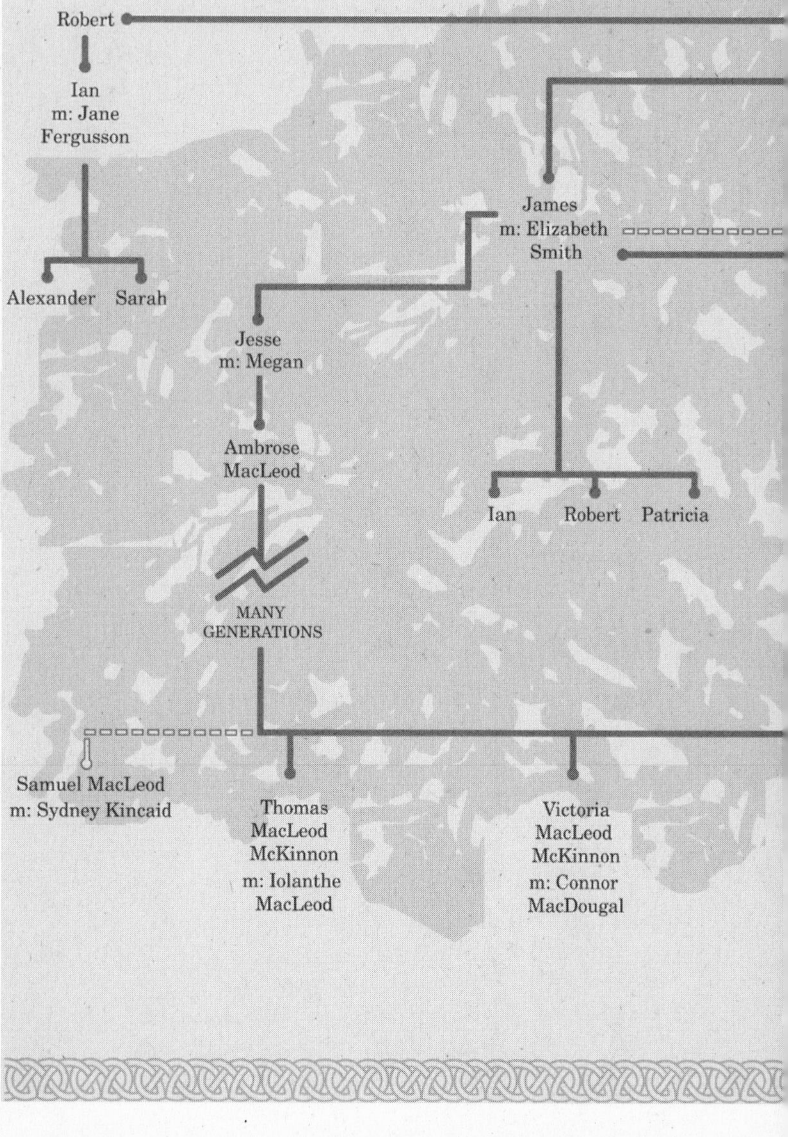

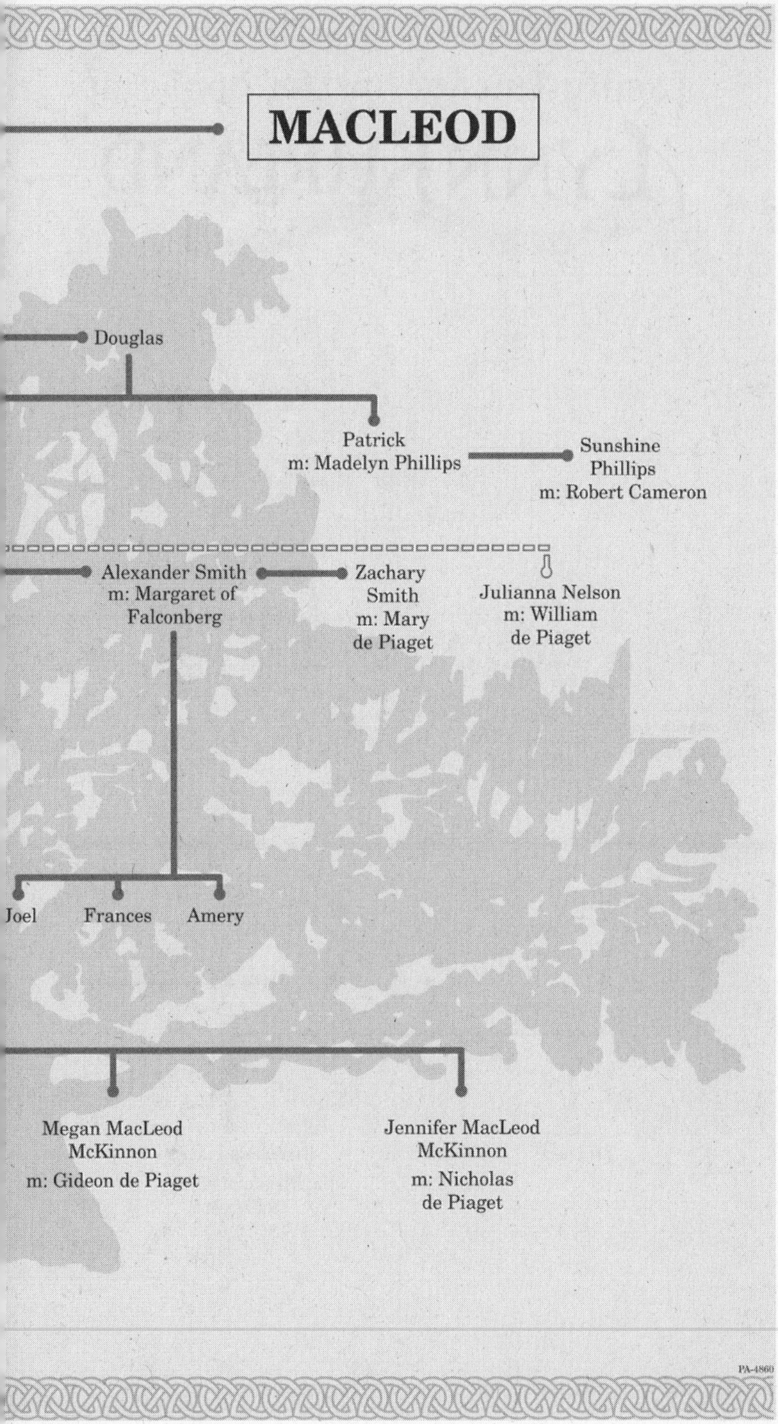
MACLEOD
Douglas
Patrick
m: Madelyn Phillips
Sunshine
Phillips
m: Robert Cameron
Alexander Smith
m: Margaret of
Falconberg
Zachary
Smith
m: Mary
de Piaget
Julianna Nelson
m: William
de Piaget
Joel
Frances
Amery
Megan MacLeod
McKinnon
m: Gideon de Piaget
Jennifer MacLeod
McKinnon
m: Nicholas
de Piaget
PA-4860

family lineage in the books of
LYNN KURLAND

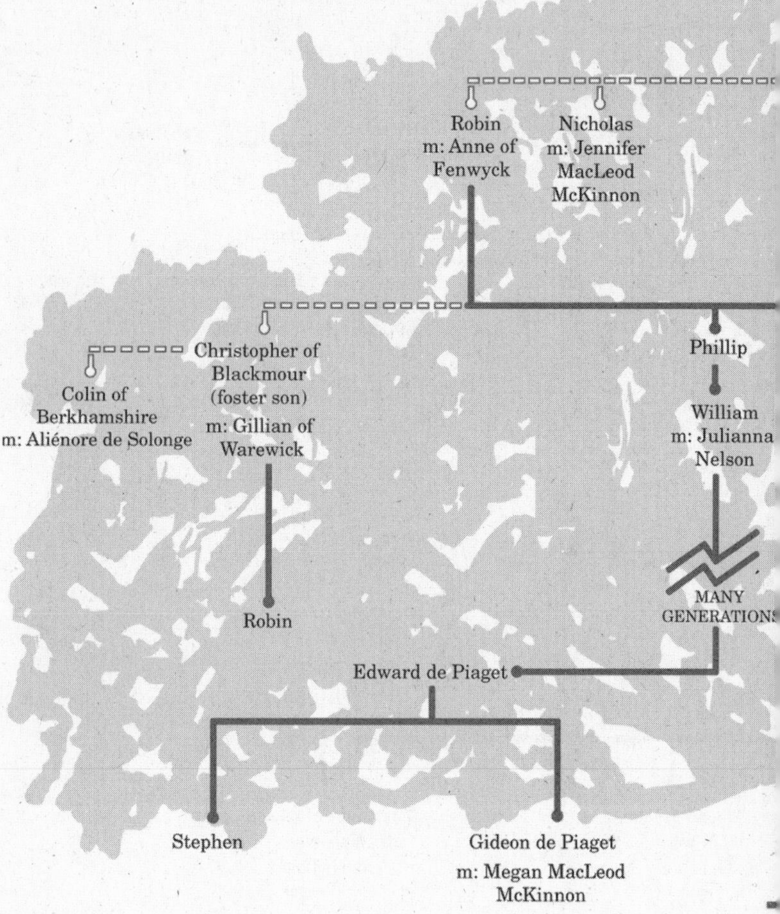

DE PIAGET

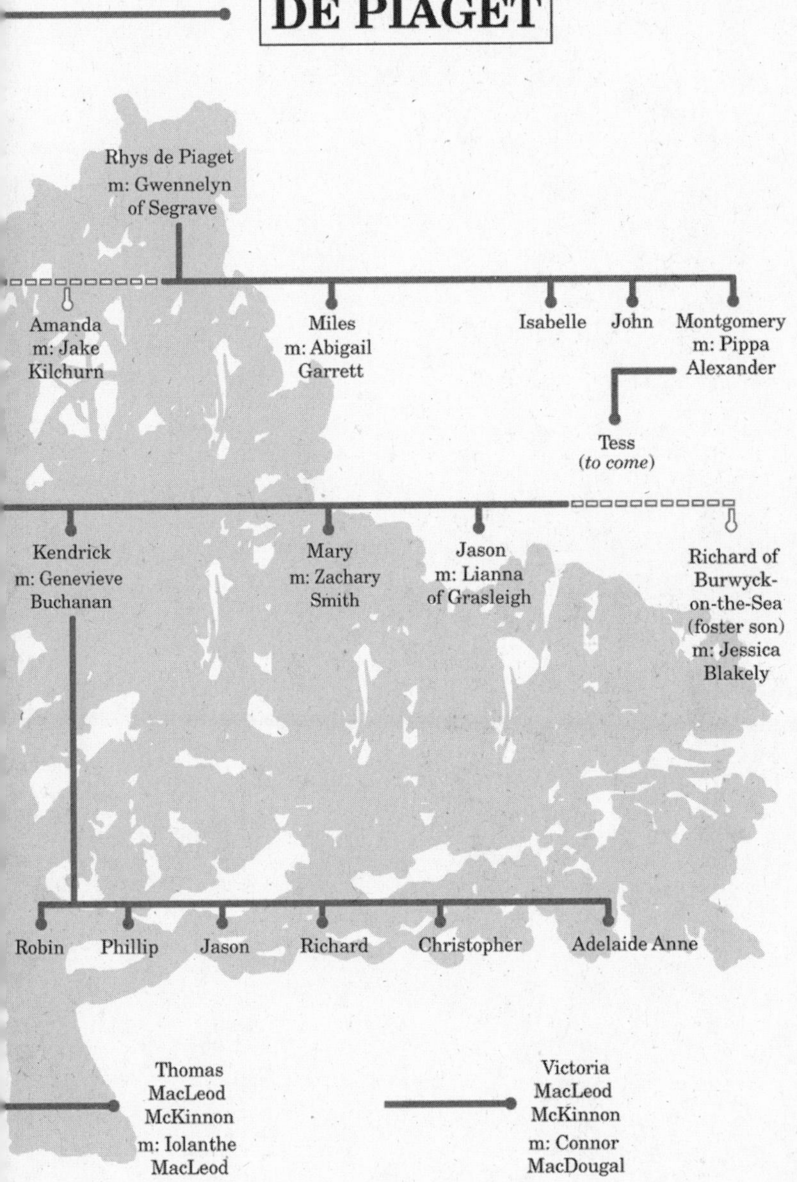
Rhys de Piaget
m: Gwennelyn of Segrave
Amanda
m: Jake Kilchurn
Miles
m: Abigail Garrett
Isabelle
John
Montgomery
m: Pippa Alexander
Tess
(to come)
Kendrick
m: Genevieve Buchanan
Mary
m: Zachary Smith
Jason
m: Lianna of Grasleigh
Richard of Burwyck-on-the-Sea
(foster son)
m: Jessica Blakely
Robin
Phillip
Jason
Richard
Christopher
Adelaide Anne
Thomas MacLeod McKinnon
m: Iolanthe MacLeod
Victoria MacLeod McKinnon
m: Connor MacDougal

PA-5913

ABOUT THE AUTHOR

Lynn Kurland is the *New York Times* bestselling author of numerous novels and novellas. Her website is www.lynnkurland.com.